PROGRAMMED FOR DEATH

Navtov? Director Robinson queried through the system.

Yes?

The data have begun to come in on the radio signals beyond Far Side. The anthropologists have just arrived aboard the Patrol ship, Bullet. It appears we do have a planet of humans outside our sphere of control. Robinson waited, allowing fellow Director Navtov time to study the information he'd sent through the computer net.

And you recommend? Navtov's inquiry returned.

I think it appropriate that all parties familiar with this particular case be removed or "adjusted."

Navtov considered. *It would create difficulties for us if this knowledge got out. I see social unrest as a result of such information. I am determining which individuals are familiar with the discovery now. Orders are issued. Those individuals will be erased. . . .*

THE WARRIORS OF SPIDER

Book One of the *Spider* Trilogy

W. Michael Gear

DAW BOOKS, INC.

DONALD A. WOLLHEIM, FOUNDER

375 Hudson Street, New York, NY 10014

ELIZABETH R. WOLLHEIM
SHEILA E. GILBERT
PUBLISHERS

DEDICATION
THROUGH TIMES OF HEAT AND THIRST
COLD AND HUNGER, TRIAL AND SORROW.
PAIN AND LONELINESS
YOU MADE IT BEARABLE.
PITY THOSE WHO ORDERED YOU
OUT OF THEIR LIVES
THEY KNOW NOT THEIR LOSS.
THEY KNOW NOT OF NOBILITY
THEY KNOW NOT OF HUMILITY

THIS BOOK IS GRATEFULLY DEDICATED
TO MY BEST FRIEND
J. B. SARATOGA TEDI BEAR
SHETLAND SHEEPDOG

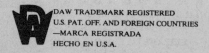

CHAPTER I

It began with an accident.

A billion-year-old stringer of gas, molecules, and dust twisted its way across the path of the fully-automated GCI cargo ship. The dust didn't mass much—just enough to trip the warning sequences. The ship's brain initiated a drop from the nothingness above lightspeed; the giant cargo-hauler warped into the universe humans think real.

The ship's brain took an instant to scan the cloud ahead, noted its composition, and calculated it posed no threat for hyperlight travel. Mass was present—just not enough to cause concern for the ship's safety.

As the drives sent a brilliant streak of light across the black of space, the brain caught a faint transmission, hesitated, and damped the hellfire raging in the antimatter reactors. Brain trained sensitive antennae on a faint red-shifted radio source in the curling mist of stars and listened. The cyber-human elements registered surprise; the computers scrambled to record all they could of the poor signal.

Deciding it had enough, the ship's brain activated the drive again and powered the shields as the CGI slipped beyond into the insanity of hyperlight.

A dim room, shimmering with cerulean blue light, surrounded Director Skor Robinson as he floated easily over a large rainbow-hued instrument panel that hovered in mid air. The Director was a tall man, thin, with the facile bone structure indicative of the station born. Even with his height, his huge bulbous head was one of grotesque proportion—that of a mega-cephalic embryo's on an underdeveloped stick-caricature body.

Though encapsulated by a metal-dull, helmetlike,

computer link headset, the calotte did nothing to hide the Director's bossed cranium; it emphasized his morphological difference—a man who was half machine—transmitted his mental patterns to the Gi-net, and physically cooled his mighty brain, a brain five times that of a normal human's. Only the weightless environment of the control room allowed his fragile neck to support such a head.

Tubes formed an umbilical which fed his body, removed his wastes, and monitored his metabolic rate, blood composition, and health. That information looped in a constant feedback to his mighty brain and the Gi-net, ensuring his physical self performed at optimum.

The headset no burden in the zero g, Robinson sorted and analyzed the information streaming from the UBM Gi-net. Trained from before birth, Robinson was one of a handful of genetically engineered people who could interface with the giant computer . . . and supposedly humanity as well.

Each second, thousands of pieces of data required his attention. Increase production of coffee on Zyman's World? Yes, while cutting back on crystal manufacturing in Hebron Station. With the population growth trends, it would be a necessary precaution in the next five years. At the same time, another portion of his faculties balanced toron production against potential use if the Far Side Sector was opened up for commerce. Decisions flowed like thought.

As he canceled the price stimulation that would open Far Side, his tranced face barely twitched. Too much chance for instability to develop if he allowed human expansion so far beyond the borders of the Directorate. Peace was so very, very fragile. His reins on humanity stretched so incredibly thin. Just a slight imbalance in the system and . . . disaster.

A job of gossamer webs, humanity hung precariously above chaos. Robinson's control would have been impossible without the huge UBM computers that filled the station around him. They processed the mass of information constantly flooding their banks. They implemented the policies decided upon by Skor Robinson and the few other Directors like him. Control, like a dust mote in the wind, could disappear at any second.

A little slip of data suddenly caught reflexively in one of Robinson's thoughts. Not much, just faint radio transmissions accidentally picked up by a cargo ship beyond Far Side. Important? Skor hesitated. An inner sense was triggered and he routed a request through the phenomenal memory of the UBM.

No colonies in that direction. No exploration out there either. Nothing. Blackness and stars. Still? Curiously uneasy, Robinson didn't have time to ponder. He routed the report to Semri Navtov in Population Control before he delved into the wheat crisis on the Station at Anten IV.

And what was happening on Sirius? Why was the social pattern there changing? He considered alerting the Patrol for a second and dismissed it. Radio out beyond the Frontier? Couldn't be important!

Dr. Leeta Dobra bit her lip, stared at the monitor, and frowned in anticipation. The analysis was coming through. She'd finished running the latest bone specimens from one of the stations in sealed containers. To get any kind of human remains away from a station took a virtual act of God.

Most stations treated their dead with religious fervor. The behavior dated back to the days when any organic material was prized. Dirt could be manufactured from asteroids or lifted from the moon; organics, at first, had only come from Earth. In time, they'd found such molecules floating free in space. More time passed before a way was found to harvest them economically. By that time station folk were appalled at the thought of bones, flesh, or excrement getting away from their steamy hydroponics tanks.

Six hundred years—Earth time—had passed since the first orbiting space station had been populated. The Julian calendar continued to give peoples far from their world of origin a point of reference, but beyond that, time was a function of mass and velocity.

She paused in thought, looking at the figures on the monitor. *Homo sapiens* had come so far—to be so different.

7

Humankind fascinated Leeta. The species was making itself into something else. People lived in far-flung stations scattered about new suns, planets, and asteroids. They were adapting, subject to new environments and radiation, changing more with every generation. Only the planet-bound bore much resemblance to the Earth-normal humans, and even there, statistical differences could be plotted.

She nodded as the results were displayed. Through her headset, Leeta made notations and sent the information into the Gi-net where it would be distributed—subject to Directorate approval—to interested parties. She leaned back and stretched, muscles rippling alongfjher planet-born arms and legs.

Dobra took a deep breath and yawned, shaking her thick blonde hair over her shoulders. Carefully she got up and replaced her headset in its holder. Checking the chronometer, she growled uneasily, "I'm coming, Jeffray. I'm coming."

Jeffray Astor would already be waiting, that look of irritation and insecurity grooving his brow. As usual, he would be fuming over her tardiness. So much had changed since that day he'd received a Directorate Health Department summons. Gone was his sensitivity, the dreams, the desire to split the galaxy with innovations in subspace communications. That dashing, smiling man who had been *her* Jeffray had come back so . . . different.

He was handsome, pale, almost albino blond, with a thin build for a planet-born man. Acidly, she wondered if birth in a gravity well was the only thing they now truly shared in common. His light blue eyes hinted at dependence, and though he pouted, a hard look from her would generally melt him into meekness. Yet he was sensitive and often kind. Brilliant when it came to transduction communication, he was self-alienated from the rest of university society. He didn't mix well, keeping to himself. He was shy, retiring, and so often depressed. Only . . . he hadn't always been that way . . . not before the Health Department.

She gave the neat white room a quick check to make sure everything was in its place. The equipment racks

8

were in order. The counters sparkled. She resealed the bone specimens in their vacuum tubes and filed them. God forbid that Dr. Chem, the department head, should find something amiss! She'd already gotten enough grief from him. Though an anthropologist, he was narrow-minded in some respects, never letting her forget she was planet-born—and, hence, by ship standards, slovenly.

Station folk were meticulous about keeping everything in order—another quirk in Leeta's eyes. They hadn't the room in the early days. Stuffed into cramped shared quarters, they'd made every spare inch count, another part of their cultural dogmatic baggage.

She shut and sealed the door, posting her handprints as the last occupant. The hallway under her feet had that constant upward bend which one grew accustomed to on stations.

Hurrying more than she'd intended, watching the lighted doors slip past, she pushed her springy, muscular stride into a distance-eating lope. She almost tumbled trying to slow for the transporter. Inertia remained—no matter what the gravity.

To Leeta's understanding of reality, the thing should be called a lift instead of a transporter. It took a person up or down, or maybe in or out, depending on how you looked at it. She requested the level she wanted and waited for one of the cars. When the door opened, she almost ran over the man before she saw him. Catching herself, she swallowed, laughed, and stepped back.

"In a hurry?" Dr. Emmanuel Chem asked, eyebrow cocked.

"I'm late for an appointment. Jeffray is already waiting in the—"

"I'm afraid you'll be a little later," Chem said absently.

Leeta stopped short, giving him a closer inspection. His bush-bearded face was intent, preoccupied. She saw something important hidden behind those dark brown eyes. The thick eyebrows were pulled down, crowding the long fleshy nose. She could see the tiny blood vessels under his aged skin.

"Something wrong with the specimens I ran?" Lee-

9

ta's guts twisted. She'd done everything right! The analysis had been perfect—even down to the subatomic level. "I can't imagine—"

"Come. It's more important than a couple of bones, dear girl." Chem was already headed down the hall, rolling back and forth in the springy walk station people seemed to share.

"My God!" Leeta exploded. "We've worked for . . . for *years* to get those specimens! Chung Station is an incredibly long way away. You know what those specimens cost the Directorate?"

"Trivial," he muttered over his shoulder. "Please, I'll explain in my office."

"Coffee!" Chem ordered, clearing his throat and growling. The machine in the corner slid out two cups as they passed it on their way into Chem's huge office.

"Doctor Chem, I don't—"

He waved her down absently.

Frustrated, Leeta let her attention wander. Chem's office was packed with tapes, files, spindles, and pictures. He also harbored a penchant for antique books. The real kind, made of paper. On one wall hung a set of ten articulated skeletons, one from prehistoric Earth, the rest detailing the various osteologies of modern humanity.

Chem fumbled over the coffee while Leeta fumed at the delay, looking up at the skeletons. On the shelves above rested a collection of some three hundred human skulls as well as another two hundred casts of prehistoric specimens not allowed off Earth: protohominids, the ancestors of mankind.

The sight of those articulated bones—men and women so long dead—had snagged Leeta in the beginning. Now they soothed her. As a curious undergraduate she'd been flabbergasted by this room. The lure of the bones had drawn her into anthropology. Working with skeletal material was magical. When her fingers met bone, it touched something deep inside her—linked past to present, and gave hope for the future in light of the span of change and time mankind had already managed to survive.

The magic had never gone away. Throughout the undergraduate years, the hard, vicious environment of graduate school, and finally, her postdoctoral work, awe of the bones carried her. Unlike the dry words in the professional journals, she could stare into the empty sockets of a skull and wonder what that individual had seen, felt, loved, and feared. What wonders had composed his world? What would he think of hers? Cold, pain, sorrows, and joys were real threads that bound them over centuries and space.

Chem startled her from her thoughts as he handed her a cup of coffee and settled himself onto one of the study couches. He indicated the headsets and put his on. Leeta settled another on her brow and accessed the system. A scratchy radio transmission seemed to echo hollow human voices.

"From beyond Far Side—beyond any known human settlement." Chem's voice was dry.

When it was over, she pulled the headset off and looked at Chem, shocked, excited, feeling her pulse race.

"My God! What . . . I mean who are they?" she whispered, awed. Her eyes strayed to the skeletons on the wall.

By means of a raised eyebrow, Chem gave her the fiery look he always did when she wasn't acting like a professional. He coupled it with an intent "I don't believe you said that" stare and added, "You tell me."

Leeta dropped her gaze, acutely aware Chem wanted cold scientific acumen. He was, after all, department head.

"That is exactly the job Associate Director Navtov has given us." Chem continued dryly. "I would suggest you dig your way through the historical files. See what you can find regarding early exploration. The Associate Director informs us that Records, Archives, and Historical have been advised. Neither Astrogation nor Commerce has any record of anything being sent in that direction."

"You realize," she kept her voice cool, "this might run back to ancient Earth." Her pulse raced. Perhaps these unknown people had the same brave stalwart qualities as the men of old Earth. She let her eyes play over the rugged features of the male Pueblo Indian skull.

11

Chem nodded. "Exactly. We just don't know, do we? I don't think we'll find out though unless you get to work. You check the historical background. I'll pull the literature on primitive societies."

Leeta chewed her thumb, eyes on the skulls above. "You think they're that primitive? They have radio."

Dr. Chem shrugged. "We know that. We also know that no one else has ever heard them. They are in a portion of space that was never settled—or at least is not recorded as having been settled." Chem stared into his coffee, lips pursed beneath his beard. "Patrol thinks it's solar background . . . a radio star."

Leeta nodded, took a sip of her coffee, and pitched into the historical literature search.

The beep was persistent. Leeta's breath caught in her throat. "Jeffray!" she moaned, misery dousing her excitement. Willing her features to neutrality, she took his call.

"Missed lunch," he said flatly as he looked at her out of the monitor. His chin bobbed uncertainly. She noted the tall, bony, planet look he had. It was one of the things that had brought them together. Station men had an aversion to women who could snap their spines without breaking into a sweat.

She nodded, uneasy at the fishlike quality of his light blue eyes. The whole image was incongruous; a pale man against a white background. Perhaps their whole relationship was as washed out as the colorless room they shared.

She took the offensive. "Look, Jeffray, something important has come up. I'm not sure when I'll be back. I may even spend the night up here. I'll tell you about it when we get some of the details put together. You'll be fascinated to hear—"

"Sure." He nodded as if he understood but she could see the emptiness behind his eyes. "You always do this to me, Leeta. You always manage to make me feel . . . I . . . See you when you get here," he stumbled, dropping his eyes.

"Talk about it later," she promised, suddenly burdened by guilt. She almost added, "I love you," but bit it off.

Sterile. Everything they did was sterile.

Her eyes wandered as the monitor blinked back to the catalog lists. The skulls gleamed in the caressing light, leering at her. "If only there were still men like you," she whispered hollowly under her breath.

And Jeffray? What of him? Boring but bright, Jeffray had a good future in subspace transduction. Why was he so damn condescending—grudgingly putting up with her eccentricities? Not once had he tried to understand her work and—if the truth be known—he could care less.

"Lord!" Leeta sighed, stretching her arms, pushing against the console. "Oh, for the good old days when Mead, Underhill, and the rest could see and talk to their subjects. Where is my blackberry winter?" There had been rumors about the early dames of anthropology. History, long past, the tales remained. Stories of liaisons among tribesmen, of strong bodies glistening in the moonlight, of love, of primitive marriages, of broken hearts when the field season was over.

The stories of Margaret Mead and all her husbands brought a smile to Leeta's face. Reo Fortune, dumped for Gregory Bateson, and Mead and Bateson had ended up great friends as well as lovers—a story to rival Heloise and Abelard, Simone de Beauvoir and Sartre.

"So go back to Jeffray," she muttered, feeling her face tighten. "Go back . . . when you're too tired to focus your eyes on the monitor." A thought tasteless as the coffee.

How many hours passed as she sent the computer searching through almost six hundred years of records? Leeta stared at the glowing words on the monitor. "Chem?"

"Yes?" Lying on his study couch, he looked up from the stimulant he was drinking. She waited while he broke free of the computer.

"I'm patching," she told him, sending him the image of the records she was reading. "Soviet prison ship, *Nicholai Romanan*, spaced 2095, reported lost in Gulag Sector."

Chem was nodding as if to himself. "I see, full complement of prisoners, American and Mexican liberals, all counter revolutionaries. Not only that, but they had a large number of Native Americans. Hmm. Arapaho and Sioux. Some Cheyenne.''

''I remember,'' Leeta added with satisfaction. ''Groshin's study! He noted that the Native Americans were neutral after the Soviet takeover. When things didn't change on the reservations, they fought back—successfully, too. Groshin documented the dissent too well for the party. They threw him in jail for it before they sent him into exile in Moscow Sector.''

''Deviants,'' Chem muttered. ''Excellent. For the purposes of survival there could have been none better. Deviants are innovators. Think of the—''

''I wonder what went wrong?'' Leeta scowled. ''They were targeted for Sirius. How did they get so far out there? I don't—''

''Long time ago! They lost a lot of ships in the early days.'' Chem paused. ''What makes you sure this is the group from the *Nicholai Romanan?*''

''Best guess.'' She shrugged. ''Figure the maximum reproductive capability of the people. There were five thousand transportees on the manifest. Assume the tapes and records of the ship survived. Assume five to six children per woman. Assume unlimited resources, and you should have a population ready to expand into space within five hundred years.''

She paused. ''Emmanuel, these were people from technologically advanced countries, not exiles from India and Africa who were transported. They would have a heritage of technology.''

''If your . . . *assumptions* are correct,'' he countered. ''Any other possibilities?''

''One.'' Her voice came stiffly as she sent him the data.

''Hum!'' Chem grunted. *''Potemkin IX.* Assumed destroyed in the Confederate revolution. Last seen headed Far Side after being badly damaged. My God!'' Chem hesitated, his voice a whisper. ''Look at the holograph! She was hurt badly, I should think.''

Already familiar with the blasted hulk, Leeta pulled the headset off and rubbed her eyes. So tired. It had been almost twelve hours since Chem had caught her at the lift and she'd gone to the lab early that day to run the bone samples.

Leeta yawned. "I think the *Nicholai Romanan* makes the most sense, assuming it wasn't one of the independent stations that got lost out there. That's always a possibility. If only . . . There are no records tracking all the fissions back that far. Half futile . . ."

"Enough for now," Chem yawned in response. "Perhaps we want it to be a lost colony too badly. Patrol thinks it's a radio star. A lost station . . . who knows?"

"Probably so," Leeta agreed. She stood up and stretched, knowing Chem's eyes were on her trim body. Her muscles always elicited that amazed response from him. Poor man, he'd spent all his life in a station. His bones were thin, delicately muscled from the light gravity of angular acceleration. She told him good-bye and palmed the door.

She walked slowly down the hall, lost in thought. Chem was probably right. Another lost station. She'd send two or three of the graduate students out to do the preliminary field work. They'd learn the language, break into the culture, and establish a communications net with the UBM Gi-net. Routine. It had happened four or five times before while she had been at the university.

Even so, it was unusual for a station to have made it that far out. They didn't move past light speed. *A lost star ship!* She ground her teeth. "Make it be true!"

As she opened the door to her room, she was thankful that Jeffray was asleep. She scooted onto the far side of the bed, avoiding his warm body. As she drifted off to sleep, the image of a man filled her mind. Barbaric, strong, hair blowing free in the wind, he stood before her and smiled, offering her a callused hand.

John Smith Iron Eyes leaned over the saddle to stare at the scuffed gray dirt. His throat went dry. The horse, his favorite black mare, side stepped nervously under him. "Hosha, we are safe," he whispered, seeing the size of the tracks impressed into the soil make a lie of his words.

The hairs on the back of his head rising, Iron

Eyes climbed down quietly, feeling the dust under his thin-soled boots.

His face was flat-boned, wide, with black, knowing eyes set widely to either side of a thin, hooked nose. His jaw was firm, beardless, supporting a wide broad-lipped mouth. He moved with almost feline grace, powerful muscles undulating underneath soft, smoke-stained leather.

He stood defiantly in the trail, two black braids hanging down his back. Dressed in tan leather, a black, eight-legged spider was drawn on the hunting shirt belted tightly at his thin waist. The sleeve undersides were fringed while a long strip of brightly colored geometric and zoomorphic designs ran down the tops to delineate his clan and Spirit Power. His leather pants were like-wise fringed and decorated. In one hand, he held a long single-shot rifle, brass cartridges sticking up along the stock where they could easily be grasped for reloading.

His belt supported a pouch, a long fighting knife, and black, gleaming *coups*—the scalps of Iron Eyes' human enemies, enemies slain by him in war. Coups—the sign of a true Spider warrior—were the pride of John Smith Iron Eyes. Coups from the heads of Santos heretics. No other warrior on World—Spider or Santos—had as many tied to his belt or hunting shirt. The grisly trophies marked John Smith Iron Eyes—marked him as the most deadly of the Spider People.

Iron Eyes looked carefully up the slopes on both sides of the dusty track. In the dim light, nothing moved. The feel of the rifle butt was reassuring under his thick fingers.

Few men had ever gone so far from the settlements of World. He had to make himself powerful again. There was no other choice. It was the way of the People to explore. It was the way of men to test themselves. He wanted more . . . needed more. Four times now, he had gone to the mountain to pray for Spirit Power. Each time he'd received the vision he sought. This time, he would go beyond where most men went. He would cure himself of the poison in his heart. He would go beyond even *her* memory.

His father's great-great-great-grandfather, Luis Smith Andojar, had seen the huge eastern sea. He'd brought back a multi-colored shell from that sea to place in the Hall of the Ancestors. It was honored as was the name of the clan—and Luis Smith Andojar. So, too, would be John Smith Iron Eyes!

Behind lay nothing but Jenny and pain. Here, deep in the Bear Mountains, was death. The tracks in the trail proved that. Bear was here. The mare behind him quivered.

The bear wasn't a creature like those in the old Earth pictures. An animal native to World, it hunted men. Big, scaled, with suction discs on two long tentacles arising from each of its two backbones to feed an acidlike, saliva-dripping mouth that could engulf a grown horse, the creature was a fierce, two-tailed beast. Bears raided the horse and cattle herds. Many men watched with radios to keep them away. The big guns could kill them at a long distance. In the time of the grandfathers the bears were truly dangerous . . . back, back before the People made the big gun. Then men had to fight only with rifles and courage . . . and the Prophets. Many men died. Only the radio and the Prophets gave them any advantage.

Now, the bears stayed away from the horses and the cattle. They were intelligent killers and quickly learned to be wary of the big guns. They stayed out here in the Bear Mountains, far beyond the settlements, preying on the green harvesters, the three-horned toads, and the lesser creatures.

Iron Eyes led the mare to the relative safety of the rocky crest of the ridge. The bear whose tracks he'd seen in the valley wouldn't come here. It was farther ahead—or at least so Iron Eyes hoped.

Tying the horse's reins to his belt, he pulled down his blanket and rolled up in it, his rifle and knife at hand. The third moon had barely crossed the black ridges marking the horizon of World. Eyes on the rising orb, Iron Eyes struggled to drown his memories.

Jenny Garcia Smith was back in the settlement. To-night she slept soundly in her father's house. Iron Eyes pressed his eyes shut, welling emotion burning in his chest. He would have to go far, so far, to make enough medicine to cure this malignancy of forbidden love.

She was Smith clan. His nominal sister. His father's

sister's daughter, she was taboo: incestuous. A Smith could not marry another Smith. The ancestors had said it was so. Clan law made it so. Most of all, Spider had proclaimed it to the people through a vision.

Spider's law! The law of *God!* God had taken the form of Spider and died on the cross so that men would be free. Spider had given them rules to live by so that men would stay free. Each year Garcia clan took a young man who had prepared himself. Dressed as Spider, he was nailed to a cross on a hill while the Spider clans danced to the sun, renewing World, for four days in the sacred lodge.

Spider's way, God's way . . . and John Smith Iron Eyes had almost committed the worst of offenses. He had fallen in love with a woman who was his sister. Had he taken Jenny . . . No, don't think it! Ultimate Shame. *Spider had decreed!*

Misery soured his belly. She was not to be his—no matter what. He'd thought of eloping. They could have done that—as long as they never wanted to see another human face. The penalty, if they were caught, would have been death.

And out beyond the settlements were only bears . . . and the Santos raiders.

Memories flooded his mind. Biting back tears, he studied his past, the viciousness with which he'd turned his wrath on the Santos bands, the fervor with which he'd sought Spider and Spirit Power. Where had he failed that he must love Jenny so? He'd done something wrong to make an angry spirit helper strike him with so unholy a love. What? As so many times before, Iron Eyes thought about all the precautions he'd taken. Yet his heart had failed him for all his valor in war.

Idly he fingered the human hair coups that hung from his belt.

He looked up to see the third moon rising higher in the sky. It was a reddish color. The first moon was yellowish, the second almost white. Together, they made the night sky so bright a man could see almost as well as in daylight.

That was an advantage of World. The old world, Earth, had only had one moon. Here, the spirits were closer because of the three. It was told by the Ancient Ones—the ones who came from the sky, fleeing the Sobyets who had taken the old world and were cutting it apart a bite at a time to feed their Red Star—that Spider came closer to men here.

It had been a terrible time for the Ancient Ones. There had been starvation and death. Clan Garcia bore the dishonor of having eaten human flesh to survive. That was why they nailed Spider to the cross—to atone for that terrible sin.

Then there were the raiders: the Santos. They lived to the north and inland. The Santos were growing more numerous, more powerful than the Spiders. They had several villages. Other scattered raiders lived in small bands which were not powerful and hung at the edges of Spider or Santos territory. All young men dreamed of riding off to steal from Santos herds or to take one of their women. And the Santos retaliated in kind.

In the beginning, the Santos had been cast out from the People for their heretical belief that God was called Haysoos and was nailed to the cross as a man. Santos were no good. They were less than men. They had a false God, no courage, and no honor. It was men like them who had sold out the Ancient Ones when the Sobyets owned the sky and gave it to the Red Star.

Even so, each of the clans had some sort of sin to atone for. The Smiths had destroyed the computer-controlled communicators so that there would be no talk from any men who might have survived the Sobyet space devils. The first Smith had feared the Sobyets would track them to this new World.

All clans were the same. All hid something and wished other people would not remember. It was a good thing, this guilt. This way, men could be men. They could have a weakness and not have to hide their heads in constant shame. When Spider was nailed to the cross and became God, he forgave men for their faults. God would forgive John Smith Iron Eyes, too, if he prayed, sweated, and sacrificed enough to make Spider or his spirit helpers see him and his plight.

If only he had taken the time to ask the help of a Prophet! Jaw muscles tensed. A potentially lethal mistake, he had ridden off without seeking aid from a

Prophet. John Smith Iron Eyes shivered. Even the thought of the Prophets sent ice daggers of fear along his bones. There was no comfort in talking to a man who looked into the future and saw your failures . . . and the time and manner of your death.

Sleep came haunted.

Day after day, he pushed eastward. As he went, the climb got steeper and rougher. He threaded his way through mountain passes where the wind threatened to rip the blanket from his body, battering the long black hair of his coups like tufts of down in a gale. Howling air screeched and roared as it blasted down the pink granite passes, rushing to the torn up flats below.

Food was becoming scarce for Iron Eyes and the patient black mare. Still he pushed on, telling himself that the one saving grace was that bears didn't roam this high. Mostly, he led the horse now. It was easier on the gaunt animal, especially as the rocks were starting to bruise and chip her hoofs.

One cold morning he finally reached the summit, winded, gasping in the thin air. He stopped to let the mare graze on the sparse grass while he looked out over a new world. The land spread before him in a level, grassy plain dotted by occasional pole plants and thorny bushes.

It was a stunning sight, the flats sloped off to the southeast, unmarred to the horizon. To the north, the plain was cut here and there by brush-filled drainages and blue-gray patches of bayonet grass spread before him like pincushions. John Smith Iron Eyes looked out to the west again, seeing the broken land dropping off below him as it led to the sea and the Settlement. It was a twisted, jagged land he'd traversed to reach the mountain crest.

Stories taught that his illustrious ancestor had crossed rough, rocky country clear to the eastern sea. There was no broad plain described in that legend. John looked back over the broken canyon-cut land that separated him from Jenny and sighed. He could just see the broad grasslands he'd passed through in the far distance, well beyond the twisted rock ridges that thrust up splintered granite. She was back there, out of sight, over the horizon.

He looked back along the faint harvester trail he'd taken to climb the pass and froze. There, below him, perhaps five miles back, three riders rode horses on the same trail.

Santos? John smiled at the thought. What did a man who had nothing to live for care about raiders? Then again, it might be some of the People, but if so, which ones? Who would come this far beyond the settlements? A curious relief filled him as he prepared for war and death and blood.

In the chill air, Iron Eyes watched. All day they climbed the rugged trail to the crest of the hill. John lay patiently in a little hollow behind the rocks. The heavy rifle rested easily on his pack. He saw the first rider pull up at the crest, his blanket wrapped tightly around him to soften the brunt of the icy, biting wind.

Carefully, John lined the front sight on the man's chest, settling the blade into the buckhorn of the rear sight. A finger's twitch from death, the man turned to look into Iron Eye's hot gaze.

"Chester!" Iron Eyes breathed a sigh of relief. Slowly he sat up and cupped his hands to shout, "Chester Armijo Garcia! What are *you* doing here?" Laughing, Iron Eyes got to his feet. Philip Smith Iron Eyes and an old man followed Chester out of the defile and onto the plain.

Still the question remained, what were his serious-minded introverted cousins doing here? They had always been such strange boys, always seeing into their heads instead of the world around them.

At his call, the old man had turned to look in his direction. Iron Eyes' heart thudded in his chest. No! It couldn't. . . .

The old man, a seer of the future, nodded, knowing Iron Eyes' unspoken words. Iron Eyes tried to swallow, feeling the blood in his veins freeze with fear. His lungs were paralyzed inside his ribs. Cold sweat covered his forehead. *Why had a Prophet followed him here?*

CHAPTER II

Lieutenant Rita Sarsa maintained her professional smile while ignoring the babble of voices around her. It was a struggle to keep her mind on these boring academicians instead of reliving her trip from the Patrol battleship, *Bullet,* to Arcturus and the university. The memory of piloting the fast transport caressed her soul like the touch of a lover. Never had she experienced the thrill of such power. To feel her body sinking in the command chair when the ship was under thrust had been ecstasy. Freedom and control had been hers. For that brief period, she had been completely her own person; in charge of her destiny.

Only, the feeling had ebbed and vanished as she nosed into the university dock and turned control back to the craft's regular captain.

Would that sense of self-controlled destiny ever be hers again?

Hollowness, aching pain, stirred the ashes of memory, reminding her of the death of her husband. The . . . *No! Don't think it!*

Emmanuel Chem was muttering something at her shoulder as he introduced yet another of a long line of scholars, administrators, students and colleagues. In God's name, why had her commander, Colonel Damen Ree, chosen her for this mad mission?

"Looks like we might send an expedition," he'd said through his clipped voice, nodding his bullet of a head slightly. The grim humor on his lips hadn't touched the hardness of those piercing eyes.

"For a radio star?" Rita had protested. Ree always left her feeling uncomfortable. That compact, muscular body of his reminded her of a tightly wound spring—always ready to explode, controlled only by his iron will and temper.

"Yeah," he had snorted. "Damn fool's errand! Orders, Lieutenant, are orders. The Directorate speaks . . . we obey. Get your ass to Arcturus." Then the twinkle formed in his raptorial eyes. "Enjoy yourself. Get drunk. Get laid. Eat good. Party like mad before we call you back to this . . . this *routine.*"

A man without a war, the drive for conflict had been born in him as surely as his facial features and blood type. Rita had often wondered how he managed from day to day . . . a gladiator in an age of peace whose only function was to shuttle his huge, potentially deadly ship back and forth along an unchallenged, no longer expanding border.

Wryly, she'd responded, "Yes, sir!" and snapped him a crisp salute.

A whiny voice rudely jarred and broke Sarsa's chain of thought. She looked over her shoulder to see a tall, bony man tugging at Doctor Dobra's arm.

"Jeffray," the blonde anthropologist was protesting. "This is important! How many times do I have to tell you—"

"Tell me?" he hissed in return. "Who's the subspace transduction expert? You're going to find nothing out there! This is just a Patrol boondoggle to get better funding for their . . ." He glanced up in time to see Rita's hot stare.

She turned to face him, feeling muscles springy in the light gravity suddenly going tense as she dropped unconsciously into a combat stance. There had been talk within the Directorate that the Patrol was no longer necessary. "Go on. You were saying. . . ?"

Lieutenant Sarsa barely caught Doctor Dobra's agonized embarrassment as the anthropologist's features reddened.

The man called Jeffray ducked his head slightly, swallowing. "I . . . I meant, well . . . you know . . . it's so sketchy at this point. There's just nothing—"

"Maybe not," Rita heard herself snap. "Then again, you would want the Patrol prepared, wouldn't you?"

He didn't meet her eyes. When he finally spoke, it

was a humbled, "Yes." He turned, tearing loose from Dobra's grip, face ashen as he scurried away.

"Forgive me, Doctor." Rita bit the words off coldly.

Leeta Dobra looked at her, mouth quivering as she fought to control mixed anger and shame. "N-no," she answered unsteadily. "My fault. He's . . . we are . . . I knew better than to bring him." A weak, weary smile formed as Dobra seemed to reach some internal decision. "He didn't used to be this way. You . . . you were just unlucky enough to see the last straw."

"Your problem, Doctor," she said in clipped tones, uneasy at the woman's discomfort. What did Dobra see in that man?

As if reading Rita's mind, the anthropologist added a cool, "If you will excuse me, Lieutenant."

Rita nodded, thinking, remembering, seeing her husband's facial features twist before he . . . She fought the memory, driving it back into the pits of her mind, walling it off.

At that moment, Chem caught her elbow and steered her across the room, all the while chattering about budgets and Gi-net time shared with other departments. Absently Rita Sarsa wondered at Leeta Dobra's expression. But what *did* she see in that . . . that *creature?*

"It doesn't make any sense, you know." Slouching on a weight bench, Jeffray dropped his head in his hands. "You're taking a long shot—and for what? A garbled radio transmission? Hell, it's probably from a star somewhere; there have been other instances where funny noises sounded human. Why are you—"

Because it might be a lost colony!" Leeta turned and shook her head, trying to clear the sweat from her eyes. Her skin glistened in the harsh light of the gymnasium, her heaving lungs gasped for air. The image of Rita Sarsa's eyes burned in her memory. The lieutenant's expression had reeked of distaste and contempt. No matter how she tried, Leeta could't shake the power and judgment in those cool green orbs.

Jeffray continued to protest, "Radio is so . . . so *primitive!* People just wouldn't use it."

Hotly, she countered, "Once there was a time when

24

men didn't know about unified fields, trans-sonance, tachyons, or iota-rega particles! Subspace transduction is only six hundred years old!''

His eyes darted nervously about the room, never stopping on Leeta's face. After a long pause he added, ''Who would use radio when transduction is so simple a child could—''

''Damn you!'' Leeta thundered, anger charging her with adrenaline. ''You never listen to me! Sure, I studied transduction! I did it for *you* . . . for us! I know transduction in and out! But did you . . . I mean . . . what did you ever learn from me? You never even bothered to—''

''I don't need this from you, Leeta,'' he interrupted. ''Who's going to make us a living?'' He crossed his arms, head cocked. ''You? Going into athletics? There's money in chasing around looking for radio signals? And you think the Directorate will approve an expedition that . . .'' He stopped at the look she gave him.

Leeta turned from where she struggled with the exercise machine. ''What the hell, at least I'll be in shape,'' she grunted. Was that a slight tremor of defeat in her words? The thought of Lieutenant Sarsa's knowing green eyes stung her again. Leeta fought the resistance of the machine harder, feeling her belly muscles rolling.

She'd allowed herself to grow soft. For the last three weeks, she'd been undergoing sleep stim. The tangle of electronic wires that stimulated her muscles through the night did nothing for Jeffray's mood. To be honest, it didn't do much for hers either. Still, when she flexed she could feel hard steel where there had been flab only weeks ago.

''I ran through the records.'' Jeffray gave her a deadpan look, trying to be conciliatory. ''If the linguistic translation is close, the signal means, 'Santos in the settlement. All spiders, return to your families for coo. Report the something'—they couldn't figure that one out—'location of the radar.' ''

''That's what it sounded like to us, too,'' Leeta agreed.

He didn't even meet her eyes. She watched him get slowly to his feet, conscious of the 1.5 gravity.

"Radar and spiders and what—for God's sake—is coo? Maybe your computers can make nonsense words out of any random static?''

After a long silence, he shook his head. "You are being a fool, Leeta. No, I don't want you to go. I won't let you. This is it. I've . . . I've had it. I'm tired of you walking all over me. From now on, the decisions are mine. Hear me? Mine. Stay with me . . . or . . . or get out!'' His pale eyes gleamed as he got to his feet, jaw thrust forward, teeth clenched.

"Whatever happened to you, Jeffray?'' she moaned, eyes searching his face for some kind of understanding. "What did the Health Department do that day? Where did the old dreamer I loved go to?''

His face was tight, angry. The muscles at the corner of his thin mouth trembled. His voice was cold and passionless. "I don't know what you're talking about.''

She said nothing, remembering her boast to Lieutenant Sarsa.

"I'm late for a meeting at the Silent Slipper. Tell me your decision there.'' He turned to give her a speculative glance.

Leeta stared at him; a curiously empty feeling yawned through her gut. He dropped his eyes, straightened, and walked stiffly through the doorway. People did that in heavy gravity. No one moved without deliberation. A simple fall invited a broken bone.

He was right, it *was* a hell of a long shot. Even Chem thought so. Was she being a fool? With a trembling hand, Leeta wiped at a bead of sweat trickling down her forehead. It didn't take much for sweat to run at 1.5 g. Conversely, with no gravity, the stuff just stuck to you and built up, not going anywhere: stagnant—like her life.

And if it were a human signal? Chem, aging, bound by his station birth, would never set foot on a planet. She was the *only* faculty member who'd been planet-born. She'd lived for most of her life on Frontier with its heavy 1.25 gravity.

She was capable. All she needed to do was get her body back in shape. Muscle tone alone wasn't enough.

There was always micro-damage to the cortical bone that couldn't be countered with anything except gravity training. As muscles grew stronger, bone had to grow with it. Systems, she thought. The human body was nothing more than systems. Blood, bone, muscles, organs, nerves, brain, integument, all worked together. It was a lesson they'd never seemed to learn in the early days of space travel.

Feeling her stomach muscles quivering, she got slowly to her feet and made herself move around the room at a fast walk, enjoying the warmth of muscles pushed just far enough.

If only . . . she pleaded to the sterile white walls with a sour grin, hoping, praying, feeling the ache grow. The stars? Or Jeffray? Adventure or stagnation? Her choice. Sarsa's face floated up in her mind. Calm, deliberate, the lieutenant had been so . . . so damn capable.

Oddly, the gleaming image of a skull from Chem's office haunted her, laughing at her dreams. Dreams? Her heart hardened. Give up dreams—for Jeffray?

It sobered her. Once, he wouldn't have asked that of her.

She tried to picture the man who might have surrounded the gleaming skull. Proud, independent, she could see him shake his head at her, judgment—like Sarsa's—burning bright in his eyes.

She took the transport up to the showers, slipped out of the class II exercise suit and undid the high-g bra. Water sliced coolly across her hot skin, tingling, bracing her for the meeting with Jeffray.

What would she say? Confusion flooded her, frightened her, took her careful mental balance and sent it reeling. Do I deserve such misery? she wondered. Cold water streamed down her face mixing with the hot rush of tears.

"I want the old Jeffray back," she pleaded into the cascading streams of water. And he won't be back. That knowledge pervaded her mind. So, it's fact, she decided, he's gone, different now: unknown. The hollow feeling spread under her heart with the certainty of death.

Tired, yet refreshed, Leeta dressed in a casual suit

and looked at herself in the mirror, fighting for self-possession.

"Your problem, Doctor." She recalled Rita Sarsa's hard voice. "Fix it yourself," she would have said.

Blue eyes stared out of a classic caucasoid face. Her brow was high, cheekbones angled, jaw firm, nose straight. She had overheard people calling her pretty, and once, even, beautiful. Her body was firmed up now, breasts high and full. Not half bad, she had to admit, not bad at all. Feeling a little better, she threw her cloak over her shoulder and headed for the Slipper.

"Fix it myself," she muttered miserably.

The place was packed. The faculty had kept the little club mostly to themselves, sending the students to the more raucous joints. This was the engineering and mathematical hangout.

Coree Mancamp and Veld Arstong were sitting in a corner with Jeffray. She made her way through the crowd, feeling light on her feet and dead in her soul. At the table, Jeffray made room for her.

"Hear you're convinced you have a bunch of lost humans out past Far Side." Coree grinned, his fleshy, red face flushed.

"She has a garbled radio signal. Nonsense the linguistic computers constructed from random stellar emissions. That's all," Jeffray added with a snide smirk, arrogance in his eyes.

Leeta started, nervous at this new defiant manner of his. Defensive, fighting to keep a smile, Leeta nodded at Coree. That critical power that had filled Rita Sarsa's eyes spurred her, heartened her. If Sarsa could be so self-possessed, so could she.

Forgetting Jeffray, she plunged in. "Nothing for certain yet. We know of two ships that went that direction. It's a bit far-fetched for an independent station to have made it that far. Even so, there's been six hundred years of exploration. We don't know the half of it. How easy is it for a star ship to have gotten lost somewhere out there during the last six centuries?"

Arstong had a knowing look on his wide face. "I'd say it was pretty easy. Back when there were pirates and wars and traders going everywhere it would have been expected. Remember? They had slavery back in the old Confederacy. That's unthinkable now.''

Good for Arstong. Leeta gave him a thank-you smile, aware of Jeffray's angry eyes. But Arstong had broken the conversation open. Jeffray's look was stricken, poisoned, as the others caught her excitement.

"Listen, sorry I can't stay. I'm wrung out," Leeta admitted. "I'm headed for home and a few hours of sleep." She stood slowly, feeling her bunched muscles, eyes going to Jeffray. Now, or never?

"I'll wander along," Jeffray muttered. "Got an early day tomorrow."

She offered her arm. They walked in silence for most of the way.

"Well," he asked finally, turning her to face him. "I want you to marry me and stop this nonsense. You've been so wrapped up in your *lost* human phantoms, I haven't had a chance to tell you. I have applied for a position in the Directorate communications center on Range. They want me. There's only the interview and we'll go."

Leeta closed her eyes. "I can't, Jeffray." She tried to swallow in a mouth gone suddenly dry. "Range? You know how provincial they are there. It would detract from your career unless we were married." She opened her eyes in time to watch his expression glaze.

"You . . . you won't marry me? Won't come with . . . with me?" His voice stretched, broke, and his fingers dug into her arms.

"When we met, I was starving my way through graduate school," she told him softly, "and you were dreaming of remaking transduction—changing the way stations and planets communicated—possibly even allowing mankind to bypass the Gi-net!" She worked her lips, looking at him. Sad. "Where . . . where did the dreams go, Jeffray?"

"I fed you!" he shouted. "Gave you a place to stay! Loved you!"

Guilt surged, only to be flushed away by anger. She jerked free of his hands. "Damn it, yes! You did!" She took a step away and whirled. "And I took care of you! Kept you company! I listened to you. Fought your damn battles and made sure you kept your life in order!

"But we had more! Can't you remember? Remember the night before my exams? Remember how you held me? Told me I'd do fine? Remember the Founding Day party at Veld's? Why can't you be like that anymore? What's happened to you?"

His mouth worked as he tried to speak, eyes wavering. "I . . . I *need* you, Leeta! I . . ."

She took a deep breath and blew it out through her nose. "I know, Jeffray." She ran a hand down the side of her face, fighting to find the words she needed in the sudden silence. "I needed you then . . . but not now." She looked at him, pleading. "I'm just a mother to you now! I tried, and I needed the opportunity to see for myself that I wasn't cut out for that. We don't talk, don't share. Now I need to be free—or everything I've worked for is gone. I can't sell my dreams like you sold yours."

His fists knotted and he shifted on his feet. "Like your dream savages?" His head shook in negation, jaw muscles tensed. "You're living in a dream, Leeta. You're a romantic fool. There is no hero out there." His voice softened. "Come, let me take you to Range. Be my wife, have my children. There's open space, clear air—"

"No!" She turned on her heel, striding down the hall.

"Leeta!" his voice thundered. "Come back to me! If you don't, I swear, *I'll make it so you never forget!*"

Colonel Damen Ree of the Directorate Patrol watched the signal come in and squinted. The probe was into regular space again. As its programming directed, the thing jumped in and out every second. Actually, it was every microsecond, but it took a while to sort out the signal and transmit. Time did funny things when something jumped back and forth between hyperlight and what men believed to be reality.

"Got it, Colonel!" Signalman Anthony called. "Nothing on that shot. It's out again."

The screen went blank then relit. This time the signalman kept his mouth shut. Ree thought the boy only talked to stay awake and to kill the boredom.

"Here it comes again," the man's voice droned on.

He turned and took a cup of coffee from the dispenser. Thank God for coffee on these late hour shifts. He sipped slowly while the signalman chattered. It wasn't that bad, this service of his. If only there were something to *do*. Take the subconscious training once every two months. Keep tabs on the mostly static sector his ship, *Bullet*, had to patrol. Periodically handle an emergency run to a station in trouble. Not much to do at all.

It drove him as stir crazy as it did the kid talking to the probe monitor.

Ree paced the deck, casually noting that the graph-steel plating should have been rutted by now. It had been a grueling battle to rise to command of *Bullet*. Yet none of his competitors had ever seriously challenged his drive or ability.

He wore the tight-fitting dress uniform of the Patrol. Space whites with the broad, flared gorget that accented his broad shoulders and narrowed to a point above his equipment belt. He padded on vacuum shoes soled with soft clingon.

His face was angular, perhaps not handsome, but craggy with wide cheekbones, stubby nose, and heavy jaw. The mouth was mobile, set and wide while the corners were hard-lined. A thick brow rose to a receding hairline of medium-brown, close-cropped hair. His dark eyes would draw anyone's attention. Darting, ever alert, they betrayed the keen intelligence, the drive, the power of Colonel Damen Ree, commander of the *Bullet*. Ree was a leader who brooked no interference, a man challenging, unyielding, competitive.

And now where? Ree wondered, smacking a bony fist into a callused palm. What do I do now? Where do I find another antagonist worthy of my efforts? He laughed to himself. A sword untried is a weapon unhoned.

Colonel was the highest field position in the Patrol. Oh, sure, there was Admiral—as if he wanted to bump old Kimianjui out. To do nothing but pace, review

31

budgets, procure equipment, and watch the whole damn thing rot from behind an Arcturian desk!

His eyes drifted to the bridge monitors. Out there, somewhere, there had to be a threat, something to keep the Patrol active—to give them all purpose. Aliens? Where?

Watching the probe was driving them all nuts. It was probably just freak emission from a star doing fusion whirligigs somewhere out there. The radio signatures of all the local stars had been plotted, of course; still, they did some strange things depending on what got fed into their atomic fires.

Wouldn't it be a godsend if there was something sinister out there? Something that actually threatened those scrawny balloon-headed Directors?

"Dream on," Ree muttered under his breath, chafing at the flickering lights on the instruments Anthony watched.

Besides, who could be sure whether or not the half-human, half-computer brain of a GCI cargo ship was doing some whirligigging of its own? Ree shivered.

The screen blipped on and off; each blip was two days "outside" for the probe. Two days that passed as a second in the real universe. Well, another day or two of this and the probe would be turned around and brought back. Then another week would pass and that would be the sum of it. Another waste of time and personnel.

"Here it comes," Anthony's bored voice chimed. "And there it . . ." He jerked up straight, voice tense. "Wait! It's still in, sir!"

Colonel Ree sipped his coffee as he peered over the signalman's shoulder. "What's it look like? Background garbage?"

"Course change to .788694, sir." The signalman checked the input. The screen blinked again. "Shorter jump. Course change to .632399. That's triangulation!" The young man was grinning now. He looked up, "The probe may have garbage out there, but it has it pinpointed and. . . .

"Just a minute, sir," the signalman outguessed the order as he mentally contacted comm to form a holographic star chart. "There it is." He pointed to a small yellow star and magnified it.

"Hell!" Ree spat. "The miserable thing hasn't even been catalogued!" He was vaguely aware of Major Antonia Reary passing through the bridge hatch to relieve him of his watch.

"In all the years we've been in space, we have less than five percent of the known stars catalogued." The signalman shrugged.

"What's that?" Ree demanded, seeing the probe's screen flickering. Major Reary walked up, her tall frame allowing her to see without restriction.

"Radio transmission, sir." The signalman bent down over the board again. "Something odd about that." His lips moved silently as he thought commands to the comm. "Non-random sequence. The probe's roughly the same distance as the GCI was when it picked up the signals. Given red shift, interference, and distance, we're lucky we got anything."

The probe was in real space, "inside" as it was called by the spacers. It was decelerating now, homing in on the source of the radio waves. Ree drank more coffee, aware his shift was over, unwilling to let command go to another until they had an answer.

"So," Reary noted emotionlessly, "the probe found something?"

Ree straightened, nodding. As usual, she was reserved. She was the only threat to his continued control of *Bullet*. As he had constantly challenged his predecessor, so she constantly challenged him. A vicious system, perhaps, yet it kept them all on their toes. But it bred a group of predators, warriors, competitors with nowhere to turn their aggression and skills but against each other.

The signalman looked up, breaking the impasse, triumph on his face. "Care to listen, sirs?"

Ree nodded and the speaker chimed in. The babble of words didn't make any sense, but one thing was obvious to all on *Bullet's* bridge. It was no star noise—human voices made those sounds.

"Translating, sir," the signalman anticipated. "Comm is running the linguistic tapes received from the Gi-net."

The speaker crackled, just like in the ancient movies and holos. " . . . four ***** on the north ridge. ***** look hurt. Santos are **** back. ***** are dead."

Another voice. "Get ***** down here. ***** fire in the fields. Tomas Ruis Carmela will sing *****pray. He has made good medicine in the past."

The first voice. "****** sending the boys in with them. There is bear sign out ***** spring camp. ***** time for coup. *Eskizin ananhe hopo hookayea.*"

The speaker went silent. "What was that last?" Ree asked, rubbing a hand over his thin, bristly hair. He could see the signalman's pinched expression. Reary was thoughtful, eyes locked on the monitor where the probe's position was marked by a flashing light.

"Got me, sir. It sure isn't in any of the translation tapes we carry. I'm sending it all to university and the Gi-net now, sir."

"Alert Lieutenant Sarsa." Ree let himself smile as he gulped down the last of the coffee. Yes, indeed, perhaps they would break the boredom. Humans? Out there? And what sort of wild men were they? Pirates?

Perhaps the Patrol was ready to resume its position of power once again. He decided not to stifle his grin. When he looked over, Major Reary was regarding him with half-closed eyes as she fingered her long chin.

Chester Armijo Garcia's life hadn't been the same since the night his dreams had begun to haunt him. For the first time since he was a child, he was having trouble telling dream from reality. Once, he had dreamed of Old Man Wattie writhing on the ground, blood gushing from his leg as Tedor Garcia Yellow Legs led his wife away, grasping her hand in one of his, and holding a smoking rifle in the other.

The next day, Chester had witnessed that same scene. Wattie lost his leg from the bullet and Tedor hadn't looked back. His action was justifiable punishment for attempted rape.

Frigthened, Chester had turned to his best friend, Philip Smith Iron Eyes . . . to find he, too, suffered from the dreams.

They had been friends for so long, sharing their ideas, thinking so much alike, wishing to be warriors and bring coup and honor to Spider. They were as alike as arrowweed seeds, enjoying the same games, knowing each other's thoughts before they could speak.

And now it was so different, so frightening. Chester swallowed, remembering the Old One. Again, the dreams had warned them both. They had known that the grizzled, old man would lift the door flap of the lodge and stare at them, black eyes gleaming in the firelight.

"Come," his cracked voice had commanded. "The time is now."

Hearts locked with fear, they had risen and followed the Prophet from the lodge, saddled their horses and ridden east into the mountains, taking the directions he pointed out.

Chester shivered. A man reviewed each moment of his life while in the company of a Prophet.

"Old One?" John Smith Iron Eyes' voice trembled, breaking Chester's line of thought.

"Come," the Prophet whispered and led them to a shelter in the rocks at the edge of the plain.

The shine of fear in John's eyes made Chester stifle a cry. Yes, even John Smith Iron Eyes feared a Prophet. Iron Eyes settled near the old man, staring dutifully at the ground, his warrior's face tense.

"You followed me?" Iron Eyes finally asked, his voice a husky whisper.

The old man twisted a sharp spear of bayonet grass absently. "I followed you." The voice was like winter grass in the wind. "Or . . . perhaps you followed me, warrior?"

Iron Eyes couldn't hide the shock. Chester began wishing for a drink to soothe his parched throat.

"I . . . I came for a vision, Grandfather," Iron Eyes used the respectful form of address. "I came to cure myself. I did not follow—"

"*Incest!*" the old man cried, pointing a crooked finger.

"*No!*" Iron Eyes pleaded, his desperate gaze shooting first to Chester and then to Philip, who bit his lip and looked miserably at the ground. Of course, they knew about Iron Eyes and Jenny and their forbidden love. And when Iron Eyes had turned to war and rov-

35

ing, the People had nodded their respect for his decision. Did the Prophet know more? Chester bit his fear back, empathically suffering for his friend—as if he could ease Iron Eyes' misery.

"No?" the old man chided softly. He lifted his age-shrunken face, eyes glittering. His voice, like a splinter, visibly stung Iron Eyes' soul. "I see inside your mind, warrior. The circle is complete between us."

Iron Eyes struggled to keep from quivering like a harvester gripped by a bear. "I . . . I came to save myself," Iron Eyes whispered. "I came to seek a vision, to—"

"Save the People," the Prophet finished, his voice like an ice fog. The wrinkled face screwed up with terror and passion. In a sibilant hiss, he added, "Save the People—*or destroy them, Iron Eyes?*"

"Save them," John protested, voice breaking, eyes squeezed shut in misery.

Chester fought to keep from reaching out, wishing he could ease his friend's wretchedness. His heart wailed sympathy for Iron Eyes. He controlled his trembling hand, keeping back.

"Tomorrow, we will see." The old man nodded to himself and stood. "Prepare yourself, Iron Eyes. Tomorrow, you will make a decision. You will prove yourself to Spider . . . or find death. This is a good place. The bear will not come until morning."

"Bear?" Iron Eyes looked up. "I don't understand, Grandfather."

"Oh, you will, nameless child. Tomorrow, you will kill the bear . . . or the bear will kill you. I cannot see the outcome. It is your cusp—your decision—and the People's. Prepare yourself, Iron Eyes. Choose. Your life? Or the People?" And the old man walked into the wind, leaving Chester staring numbly at his cousin.

The silence lasted through dragging minutes as Iron Eyes fought for control. Face contorted, he gasped, *"What is this?"*

Philip answered with a hollow, "I don't know. It is tied with dreams. I . . . I see you, John Smith. I see the bear . . . and blankness." Philip closed his eyes and took a deep breath.

Chester nodded, half to himself. From his pouch he took flint and steel—primers were too precious to waste on fire starting—and began building a small blaze.

"I share Philip's dream," he added, his voice soft. "I don't see the end of the fight either, my friend. I am sorry." Sorry that all this is happening, cousin! *Would that I could help you!*

"It is all a test," Philip was saying. "I can see it. The dreams . . ."

"Dreams?" Iron Eyes asked and Chester couldn't help but look up to study Philip, seeing the look of power in his eyes so similar to that of the Old One. A new fear shifted in his chest. Who was this old friend of his becoming?

"You," Philip was continuing, "must be the People's warrior, Iron Eyes." Philip closed his eyes in resignation. "One of us—Chester or I—will be called to the stars by Spider."

"What is this?" Iron Eyes repeated. He looked pale, as if a horse had kicked him in the stomach.

"I can smell your fear, cousin," Chester said as he placed a reassuring hand on Iron Eyes' shoulder. Flames crackled through the dry grass. "It will be all right. Spider will—"

"It is only drowned by your own," Philip answered, his eyes still haunted with the look of a condemned Raider.

"This is true," Chester replied reasonably. Fidgety, he pulled his rifle out and began taking the action apart to clean it. He worked a small cloth over the block and firing pin, casting a quick glance at the numb form of John Smith. "You must kill a bear tomorrow, perhaps you should check your own rifle."

Iron Eyes nodded numbly and took up his gun, frightened eyes darting to the shadows where the Old One had gone.

"Clean your gun, Iron Eyes," Philip whispered in half-trance, "We have seen the old man. He has a way with bears. Prepare your soul for Spider. Prove you have learned; your fate is in His hands."

Chester rose and checked the horses, feeling Iron Eyes' desire to be alone. As he saw to the pickets and

37

hobbles, Philip's words echoed through his mind. A test? Why me? He could see the dim form of the Prophet watching from the growing dark.

Shaking his head, Chester talked to the horses, happy in their company, feeling his kinship with the animals, with World and the People of Spider. So let Philip become Prophet. He had always been a man of passion and spirit.

No, for Chester Armijo Garcia, life was fine as it was. He sniffed the cool night air, feeling his soul dance at the joy of life. Indeed, let others fill their minds with the future. Here, in the night air, his soul roaming and twining with those of the horses, he could feel the subtle presence of Spider. Life was good. Existence was good. An understanding began to seep from the very soil under his feet, expanding within him. His eyes lifted to the heavens above and he catlogued the familiar stars.

"Spider," he whispered, "I am blessed as part of your creation. I am content with the simple things. Give Iron Eyes strength. Philip will make a wonderful Prophet. He is of fire and stone whereas I am of air and spirit—a player with horses and a lover of peace. Take him . . . but bless this moment for me, for truly, I am unworthy."

Yet the dreams came that night. In his intermixed reality, Chester rose from World and walked among the stars, feeling the peaceful reality of Spider. He found men there, odd men, different men in steel boxes floating in darkness and cold and void.

He peered into one, seeing himself, naked, lying on a table while men with bits of metal sliced his shaved scalp and cut his very skull open. In mounting horror, Chester watched them begin doing things to his brain, charging it here and there with electricity. Others watched boxes in which lines of light played.

"Spider, save me!" He heard himself scream into the blackness and void. On the table, his limbs jerked and bucked while hideous screams tore from his throat.

Clutching his stomach, ill to fainting, paralyzed by fear, he suffered with his jerking body until the limbs stilled. The men and women with probes shrugged, noted the failing dance of the light lines in the boxes, and shut them off. Moaning disbelief, Chester continued to watch, unable to tear his eyes away as they cut piece by piece out of his brain until an empty skull remained.

"Your death," a cracked voice told him. Chester, face soaked with sweat, sat up in the familiar darkness of World.

"Death?" he rasped, trembling with the cold-sweat of fear.

"Can you live with that?" the Prophet asked. "What if that is the price Spider demands?"

Chester turned away from the ancient face, haunted by the certainty in those gleaming eyes. Violent shivering tore through his claylike flesh. No! It was too terrible! If only he could touch that warm presence of Spider again, feel life . . . but there was only dark and cold and horror. Once again, he had seen the future. *His future*.

CHAPTER III

Hours after leaving Jeffray, Leeta unexpectedly found herself near the docks. She'd wandered aimlessly through the endless white corridors, fighting roiled emotions. Feet aching, feeling miserable, she wandered at last into one of the less savory dives.

Dimly lit in hellish red, visi-mist portrayed shadowy, nude figures in licentious holographic dance. Chrome and brass fixtures in erotic shapes surrounded the autobars and the clients slumped over them. Muffled sounds came from the muted sonic cones that projected over various tables and booths, blasting the occupants with their favorite brand of music. In the back, two men were embracing, kissing passionately. Curious eyes sought hers, evaluating, beckoning, cataloguing. She avoided all of them, seeking an unoccupied table, hurrying across the room, keeping her attention away from the others.

The grav seat provided a welcome relief to her tired legs. An order of local single-malt whiskey and red ale for a chaser rose from the autobar at her command. Leeta huddled over the drinks, thinking, seeking sense in it all. What more was there to do? He'd changed so.

"You alone, sweetmeat?" a deep tenor asked and she was vaguely aware of a thick body sliding onto the anti grav beside her.

Leeta looked up to see a blunt face, eyes lined with crow's feet. His body had a slight odor and a leer tried to pass for a smile on his thick lips.

"Yes," she answered coldly, "and I prefer to remain that way."

He nodded, a daunting smile extending to his eyes. "Well, now, sweetmeat, I'll just have to see if I can't change your mind. What's a night worth to you? Ten credits? Fifteen? Name your price and make it worth my while and I'll pay good. Maybe a bonus, eh?"

He reached for her as she started to stand. Leeta twisted away from his groping fingers, but his hand shot like a bullet to circle her waist and draw her against him. "Drink with me," he commanded gruffly and she could smell alcohol on his breath.

"No, don—"

"Oh, you'll drink!" he commanded, delight in his eyes. "I call it bad manners when I invite a girl to drink and she tries to walk off." His grin went oily as his free hand moved up the fabric of her thigh.

"No, I—"

"Drink, girl!" His eyes mocked her as his hand became bolder.

Leeta's voice wouldn't come. Meekly she lifted the ale to her lips as he laughed victoriously. Her muscles quivered under his rough hand and fear loosened her intestines. Physically ill, she set the cup down.

"There, now let me go. Please?" She heard the pleading—and hated herself for it.

"Oh, yes!" he cried. "We'll have us a time tonight! Ah, for a man who's been in deep space as long as me, I caught a good one!" His fingers traced across the tight abdomen of her suit.

Leeta, heart battering fearfully against her chest, didn't see him lean to kiss her neck. She cried out, struggling, seeing amused faces from other tables leering in her direction. His warm mouth on her neck, she almost gagged. She kicked, fighting against his strength, trying to beat her way free.

"Let her go, *now!*" The new voice caught them both off balance. A quiet contralto, it cut with the calm security of command.

Leeta shot a quick look over her shoulder. Lieutenant Rita Sarsa, still in uniform, stood with fists on her hips.

"Now, I got no quarrel with Patrol," the spacer growled uncertainly. "Me and the little lady, here, we be doing business. That's all, business."

"Let her go." Rita Sarsa slowly lifted her chin.

"I don't want no trouble with you," the spacer mumbled sullenly. "Just . . ."

Sarsa crouched, balanced in a curious stance, hands moving in slow intricate patterns. "Rigger, you want to see your guts all over the floor?" Rita's delicate lips curled maliciously. "A med unit just *might* be able to put you back together."

The spacer began shaking his head. "Hey, I mean . . ."

Leeta was free so suddenly she staggered and almost fell from the grav seat. When she looked back to her tormentor, it was to see his back headed for the door—and wasting no time. Clutching the autobar rail, she closed her eyes, breathing a sigh of relief. It was a battle to still her chattering heart.

Sarsa slid onto the antigrav and cocked her head, a tumble of red curls falling over a broad, muscular shoulder. "You always look for trouble like that, Doc? This isn't your . . . uh . . . kind of place."

Leeta's laugh was half hysterical. "No . . . no, I just . . . just needed to get away. Just had it out with Jeffray and. . . . Oh, hell, what a mess my life's in." She shook her head and reached for the single-malt, downing it in a gulp.

Sarsa's laughter was dry, half-hostile. "Doc, there's only one person in the world can control your life—no matter what the balloon-headed Directors want you to believe—and, sweetheart, that's you!"

41

Leeta bit off an angry retort. "How do you know?" It didn't come out mad—but it came out sullen.

Sarsa's mocking eyes measured her. The words were simple, laced with truth. " 'Cause, Doc. I've been there."

Leeta looked her up and down, noting the hard glint in Rita Sarsa's eyes, cataloguing her insolent posture, the calluses on her freckled hands, and the calm, assured way in which she moved. Curiously reassured, Leeta bootstrapped her own courage up again.

"Well, Lieutenant, maybe you have," Leeta agreed with a challenging, insolent smile.

"Uh-huh," Sarsa grunted, face pensive. "You might just be all right, after all."

Leeta took another drink. "There's no one to look after me but me, huh?"

"That's right." Sarsa's drink slid out of the dispenser. Star Mist on the rocks. The sign of lots of credit.

Leeta ran her fingers through her tumbled curls, drained of all emotion, aching with physical and mental fatigue. "You know, I don't know what it was about Jeffray. He changed. His dreams about improving transduction just vanished. One day he was fine. The next he was different, someone I didn't know."

Sarsa cocked her head. "Transduction?" Her eyes narrowed. "Different how?"

Leeta took a breath, feeling the pain, looking at where she rolled her ale back and forth. "As if he'd just lost that spark of brilliance. I don't know. He went for a Health Department check up. Something about statistics. He just wasn't Jeffray after that."

"Huh." Sarsa's grunt was forced. Leeta caught the strained look on her face as she said bitterly, "People do that in this society. Dance to the tune. Don't make waves. Don't question or one day you change." She sipped the Star Mist and Leeta noted the flush on the lieutenant's face, how glassy her eyes had become.

"You're half-smashed, Lieutenant!" Leeta exclaimed, brushing Sarsa's odd words aside.

"Damn right, Doc!" Sarsa grinned, elflike. "And

enjoying the hell out of it! Haven't been on a good binge since I made lewy.''

''Lewy?'' Leeta hitched a leg up and leaned back into the grav seat.

''Lieutenant, Doc.'' Sarsa shrugged. ''Yeah, this looks like a real milk run. Wonder how long I can get away with this liaison duty? I'll stuff all the good times I can under my belt before they drag me back to the *Bullet.*'' Sarsa slapped her belly in emphasis, grinned again, and belched loudly.

''What's it like out there?'' Leeta wondered, propping her chin on her knee, letting her eyes trace the jumping holos of nude men and women gyrating over the autobar.

Sarsa laughed at the awed tone of her question. ''Boring as hell, Doc.'' The lieutenant made a throwing away motion. ''The Patrol is a sewer.''

''Huh?'' Leeta exploded, jerking upright. ''Lieutenant, you can't mean—''

''Hell, yes!'' Sarsa's mouth twisted in a grimace. ''You think we do anything out there? By the Director's blasted balls! We run from one edge of Far Side Sector to the other—and then back again. We take the training psych, polish the machinery, run the simulations,'' Sarsa's voice dropped off to a whisper, ''and do it all again . . . and again . . . and again.''

''But a sewer?'' Leeta cocked her head, seeing the disgust in Rita's face.

Sarsa snorted rudely. ''You're an anthropologist?'' Rita shook her head irritably. ''You tell me. What is there about a civilization that controls all information? Hasn't established a new colony in eighty years? Hasn't had a single social innovation? Hasn't had a border dispute or trade dispute in how long? You know, in the last thirty years, *Bullet* has reduced its patrol area by ten percent? Ten percent! That's because the borders are shrinking! You hear? *Shrinking, gawddamn it!*'' She pounded a fist on the autobar and grunted.

Leeta swallowed, looking around to see if anyone could hear, nervous at the Patrolwoman's tone. ''That's the cost of social stability—but a sewer?''

''*Social stability?*'' Sarsa roared her sarcasm. ''That's a great one, Doc. Social stability?'' She lifted

43

a red eyebrow, her pale skin drawing tightly over the delicate bones of her skull. "Rat shit! I call it Directorate propaganda." A pause. "So, tell me, in all this 'stability' where do you send the folks who are a little weird, a little violent, a bit rough on the outside? We're not talking folks that need psych, mind you, just the ones a little out of phase with 'stability.' "

Leeta found it was her turn to lift a shoulder. The lieutenant's irony smacked of treason, or of moral corruption at the very least. Leeta stifled her urge to leave, overcome by curiosity.

"Where, Lieutenant?"

Sarsa leaned forward to breath expensive whiskey fumes into Leeta's face. "The Patrol, Doc. Thass where." Sarsa nodded, her face centimeters from Leeta's. "Flush 'em down the sewer. Put 'em out where they can't cause trouble. Stick 'em in a ship and let 'em go 'way, 'way where they can't hurt anything." She leaned back and stared glumly at her drink before hiccuping.

In the silence, Leeta began to think about it. They didn't speak. Sarsa finished the last of the whiskey.

"It'sh all gone rotten," Sarsa added. "Like your Jeffray, humans are all gone to mealy mush. No guts left. Everything controlled. No fire left in the species . . . no challenge." Sarsa punched for another drink before adding, "You know?"

An image of a thousand-year-old Pueblo Indian skull grinned in Leeta's mind. "Yeah," she muttered, sipping more of the ale. "I think . . . I think I've known all along." Leeta rubbed her hands nervously. "I . . . I've had a dream. You see, one of the reasons I'm an anthropologist is because I always wondered about the people. You know, the ones who lived before . . . whose skeletons we study. Think of the strength of character! They didn't have all these computers, all these civilized safeguards. Don't you see, they were free! Real people existing on their own strength. Where is that today? We're all sterile, domesticated. God, what I'd give to know what those people were really like." She filled her lungs and blew it out.

Rita Sarsa nodded thoughtfully. She sipped her

drink, eyes slitting as the alcohol worked on her. "Domestic. Like sheep!" she spit.

As she talked, Leeta studied the woman's features. Her face was well-formed; a straight nose and firm chin accented the sparkling green eyes. A high forehead gave an impression of intelligence and her mouth was thin-lipped with a hint of humor at the corners. Blaze-red hair hung in loose waves to her shoulders. Sarsa's waist was narrow above a flat belly, rounded hips and muscular legs. Her breasts were firm, balanced and high. Some might have said her shoulders were slightly too wide, but those muscular arms hid the fact. When Sarsa moved, it was with pumalike grace. Any man would have looked twice at the lieutenant.

When Leeta finished, Sarsa frowned into the amber liquid of her glass. "Too bad there ain't some way to turn the whole gawddamn mess upside-down on the pun'kin heads."

Leeta wondered about that, her keen mind beginning to draw comparisons between the past and present. No new colonies in eighty years? The borders were shrinking? In an open economic system like space, why? Not since the closed resource bases of Earth had societies failed . . . and then it was from overutilization of resources or lack of redistribution of goods.

"And you think it's the Directorate?" Leeta fingered her chin, frown deepening.

Sarsa nodded, lost in thought.

But with the Gi-net, how could redistribution fail? How could a station not find resources for any need with atomic wealth virtually floating into the fusion reactors? Asteroids, suns, and every physical element humanity needed was free for the taking.

"I'm not convinced," Leeta added.

Rita Sarsa leaned on one elbow, the cool green eyes struggling to focus. "You read stuff from the past, right?"

"Of course, that's part of what anthro—"

"And how does that compare with the stuff written today? Huh?" Sarsa wobbled unsteadily. "You tell me.

45

You see any spark in humanity today? Or are they all like your Jeffray?''

Leeta bit back an angry retort. The woman was drunk—and she was right about a lot of things now that Leeta began to thing about them. In her mind, a skull shimmered in a rictus of affirmation.

''Two women in a bar do not a social revolution make,'' Leeta reminded.

''Maybe, Doc,'' Rita grinned sourly, trying to focus her eyes. ''But then, you never know where God's gonna lead you. Bastard took me to the ends of space. Always wondered if he didn't shit on me for a reason.'' Her face puckered. ''Been a long time since I let myself think about . . .'' She pinched her eyes shut and shook her head violently. ''No . . . don't think about it. Don't . . . Rita, old girl.'' She swallowed dryly.

''You all right?'' Leeta asked. ''You want a sober pill?''

''Wow,'' Sarsa managed, shaking her head. ''Didn't know I was so far gone.''

Leeta ordered the pill, watched Sarsa swallow it, took her by the arm, and led her to a transport that would take them to executive housing.

''Two women do not a social revolution make?'' Sarsa mumbled under her breath as they entered the plush room. ''Screw 'em all if I'll believe that!''

John Smith Iron Eyes tossed in his blanket; his gut churned and roiled. All this because he had lusted after Jenny? Was this a proper thing? Had he done anything to merit such treatment? He had always taken a sweat bath, always prayed and offered his medicine to the Spider God. Why had his path gone so sour?

Could he refuse to fight the bear?

No sane man *ever* refused a Prophet!

After troubled dreams, the old man's voice pulled John Smith Iron Eyes from tortured sleep. ''The bear comes,'' the thin voice whispered.

John Smith Iron Eyes whipped his blanket off and struggled to his feet. He blinked at the lumbering form. The horses were gone. His cousins were sitting on the top of the rocks, well out of reach. How had they gotten up without his knowing? Chester looked like a corpse.

The bear waddled forward unevenly, seeking with the suction cups. John pulled up his rifle out of instinct.

"Your rifle will be of no help, warrior," the dry voice grated in the frosty morning air.

Carefully Iron Eyes settled the sights on the spot marking the bear's brain. Hidden deep in the animal's chest, it lay between the two thick backbones, encased in hard cartilage.

"Your gun will not fire," the old man said softly.

Iron Eyes ignored him. He took up the slack on the trigger and jumped when the hammer clicked. Frantically, he pulled open the breech and saw the empty chamber.

"You must kill the bear with your knife, John Smith Iron Eyes!" The old man cackled gleefully, the long cartridges held up between his fingers. "If you don't, I will die with you. The life of a Prophet is in your hands, Iron Eyes. See that you use it well.

"Believe! John Smith, Spider will give you strength!"

The bear was getting bigger now, waddling ever closer. "Get back!" Iron Eyes turned, shoving the old man behind him. Frantic, he pulled his long fighting knife and crouched, ready. A quick glance told him Philip and Chester had no intention of interfering. He cursed them vilely.

Crazy damn old fool! Why had he done all this? The bear was huge now. There was no way the Prophet could escape. Desperate, John Smith ran forward, seeking to draw the monster away from that fragile, aged body.

The huge suction disk shot down with amazing speed. John threw himself to the ground, rolling, narrowly avoiding the purple-skinned disk. The bear roared with a sputtering of foul breath. The little droplets of spittle sizzled as they spattered his flesh.

"Believe!" came the Prophet's sing-song voice. "Believe and you shall triumph! *Give your heart and soul to Spider!*"

The words burned in Iron Eyes' brain as he dove

47

under the huge body and rolled onto his back, punching up with the long blade. He was painfully aware of the pillarlike legs that thrashed to either side of his body.

The Bear roared again as the knife found its way past the small scales on the creature's stomach. Hot fluid gushed down as the big animal spun above him. Fighting to keep his grip on the knife, he flinched as one of the two tails flayed the air over his head. The beast was turning, poking its stalklike eyes under its wounded belly to seek its prey.

John scrambled to his feet, sliding on foamlike, black blood. He was behind it now. The bear straightened and, to John's horror, headed right for the Prophet.

To the People, the four old men were the Power, the law, the truthful ones. They could see the future, heal the sick, or take a man's life with a word. They were blessed by God for Spider spoke to them. If the old man died now, it would be on John's head. Worse, he would be banned, shunned, his name never to be mentioned. His clan would suffer so great a disgrace that they might be exiled from the People. No one had ever let one of the four old men die before.

If he died in defense of the old man, his clan would be cleared of shame. If he died first, he would have acted in honor. There was no other way. It would be done. His cousins could ride back and tell the People of the glory—of the sacrifice. Jenny Garcia Smith would be proud!

Desperation left him an impossible choice. Screaming a war cry, John Smith Iron Eyes threw himself forward and caught the plated skin of the bear's tail. Feverishly, he hauled himself up onto the animal's back.

The bear stopped, snorting, and turned quickly in a circle, staring stupidly as it sought the thing on its back. Iron Eyes scrambled forward.

One of the little telescope eyes came threading its way over the creature's back as it finally figured out where he was. Holding to one of the bony plates sticking out of the animal's two spines, John thrust forward with his knife, trusting to Spider, singing his war song.

Luck or fate? The eye flopped loose and hung by a

thin strand of tissue where he'd cut the stalk almost in two. The second eye came up, not so far this time, and the suckers snaked in his direction. Riding between the bony plates, John swung viciously at the eye. Again and again the long knife missed as the suckers came closer.

The left one darted in his direction. The angle was wrong. The animal was moving. Only the one eye remained to provide depth of field. John lifted his leg at the last minute and the creature's suction disk dug into the hard scales on the animal's back.

John swung all of his weight behind the knife and sawed at the tentacle. Too late, the second one homed in on his other leg. Pain flared whitely through his brain. He was gasping ragged breaths as the bear tore him off its back. John's knife disappeared. Helpless, he heard himself scream as the raging bear began to draw him toward the poisoned mouth.

Closing his eyes to avoid the horrid sight, John Smith Iron Eyes prepared to die. Carefully he sang his medicine song.

> *Death is coming*
> *Death will take me to where God is*
> *The name of God is Spider*
> *The People know God*
> *Death is coming*
> *See it comes softly over the hills*
> *It comes to take this man*
> *Death is coming*
> *Death is coming.*

He sang in the old language the way the Prophets taught. A curious tranquillity filled him, damping the blasting pain. Death was not so bad. Spider waited to reclaim his soul, to learn what he had learned.

Caught unaware, he slammed into the hard ground, the breath pounded brutally from his body. Stunned, he quivered at the shock, feeling rough gravel beneath his scored cheek. A humming roared hotly in his ears.

Through pain-glazed eyes, he looked up at the bulk of the creature, swaying now on unsteady, pillarlike legs. From his ground view, John could see the well-

49

ing mass of guts that had fallen from the knife wound in the creature's belly. The rolling intestines had caught in the legs and more had been ripped out.

The animal suddenly collapsed on one side. Awkward on three good legs, the others crumpled into the gut pile.

The pain in his leg lessened as the suction disk eased up and trembled, shaking him like a blade of grass, raking him across the bloody bayonet grass and rocks.

"The name of God is Spider." John's voice was hoarse as he sang the prayer.

The old man walked slowly forward, motioning for Chester Armijo Garcia and Philip Smith Iron Eyes to climb down from the rock.

"The bear is dying," the old man said. "You are the one we seek." The ancient voice was softer now. "You, warrior, are the one to save the People. The vision of the future is not all clear, but your choice is made. There are many cusps yet to be passed.

"Hear me, John Smith Iron Eyes, I will tell you the story of our People. Three times before we have faced the end of the People. This is the fourth. They come. They come from the stars this time.

"The first time it was the white men who came. They brought us the horses which we now ride. They killed the People and poisoned them. The Prophets all died . . . and no longer did anyone see the future.

"The People almost lost themselves. They took to many of the white ways and forgot the song of the pipe. It was a bad time.

"The Prophets had foretold of a time when machines would fly through the air. They had seen the machines that would carry men on the ground. They had seen the People growing strong together.

"We have no record of the old Prophets seeing the coming of the Sobyets. That was the second time. They came and took our land once more, forcing the People to work like slaves. This is not the way that Spider wanted. We fought again as we had done in the past. They fought better than we did.

"They took us to ships and carried us to the stars. There, the Sobyets tried to kill us. The people fought in the star ship; the very star ship that now lies near

50

the settlement. That was the third time. That time we won, but the star ship was badly damaged.

"We made the ship land us here, on this world. We did not know where we were. The communications device was smashed by your ancestors so that the So-byets would not find us again.

"Others come now. The fourth time. The Spider Holy number. They will want to come here and take our land. They are weak. We are strong. We see ahead. They do not.

"We see what might happen. It can go well . . . or it can go badly. The People need you. They need you to intercede. You must believe. You must follow the path. This is the fourth time. The number four is sacred. This is the last time. You are a warrior. One of these two is a Prophet." He indicated Philip and Chester. "We will live now—or we will die. I have spoken." The old man turned without concern, seeing something in his mind, and walked away.

John Smith Iron Eyes blinked, trying to clear his foggy vision, trying to remember the Prophet's words. Could this be true? His fingers tore on the gravel as he clutched the soil in his tired hands and struggled to pull free of the bear's suction disk.

Philip Iron Eyes set himself and ripped the suction disk loose from John's leg. Pain seared his mind; it couldn't be a dream.

CHAPTER IV

Dr. Leeta Dobra raised her disheveled head. Digging fingers into her eyes, she tried to pry herself awake. A miserable week had passed since the split with Jeffray. The little apartment she'd moved into was cramped. Anthropology didn't command the salary engineering did. She hadn't realized how much she'd taken all that space for granted.

Standing numbly in the shower, she wondered if her blood really was circulating when the room-comm announced a call. She turned to the bathroom terminal and ordered it on. Chem's grizzled, old face peered out at her.

"You're wet!" he muttered absently. "Oh, of course. Shower. Sorry to bother you. I think you should come up here. It's important." Chem was already turning away as the screen went dead.

"What?" she shouted frantically, knowing how Chem's mind—when preoccupied—worked. Having told her all he felt was necessary for the moment, he had no time for anything else.

"Damn him!" she hissed under her breath as she dried off and pulled on a white, form-fitting, duralon suit. She gave a half hearted look at her reflection and smiled. Now that Jeffray was out of her life, she paid more attention to herself. Invitations to dinner, dream sets, and other activities were flattering.

She grabbed up her cloak and rushed out the door, barely hearing it slip shut behind her. She almost sprinted down the hall. Improper to say the least! Hell! Something was wrong. Chem had that look on his face.

The transport seemed to take forever. Fragile station types couldn't take acceleration of any sort. To Leeta's trained muscles, the start and stop was almost imperceptible.

She burst through Chem's door and stared at the old professor. He lay on his couch, eyes closed, concentrating on the information from the headset. Leeta rolled her eyes in frustration and pulled a headset off the wall. She entered the system and sought Chem. He shunted her a file. Curious, she accessed it and sat back—flushed, fascinated.

Barely into the data, she perceived Chem's insistent demand for attention. Instead of meeting him in the system, she pulled the headset off and waited.

He lifted his unit to massage his brows. "What do you think?" A slight smile crooked his lips; tumbled, steel-wool gray hair thrust up in disarray.

"That's all *Bullet* got? Too bad. I sent a copy of

what Colonel Ree thought was garbled to Linguistics. I'll bet it's an old Native American language.'' She gave him a saucy grin. ''I think I have just been vindicated.''

Chem nodded, thoughts on the data. ''You saw the assignment. The Director wants us in charge of the contact. Routine so far. What we don't know is if they are planet-bound or station folk. The interference noted by the probe would seem to indicate the signal is . . .''

''. . . passing through an atmosphere.'' She nodded; that had been perfectly clear. Maybe all that time with Jeffray hadn't been a total waste. Why, he'd even taught her to build a transducer once.

''What next?'' she asked.

Chem, still thinking, rubbed his age-freckled hands together. ''Do you think you can cover my classes while I'm not there?''

''While *you're* out . . .'' A knot of disbelief choked her.

Chem threw her a slightly irritated look. ''Of course! You don't think I'd just send graduate students do you? This may be too important for that!''

Leeta struggled to keep her voice level, professional. ''And if they're planet-bound? You'd allow graduate students to make the first contact?'' *You do this to me, Chem, and I swear, I'll rip your heart right out of your body!*

Chem's brow furrowed deeper. Leeta allowed herself a breath. The old boy hadn't thought about that. He'd been too absorbed with the data. So, was he getting absentminded, possibly bordering on senility? Her eyes narrowed at the implications.

''Indeed,'' he added softly. ''I'd forgotten that, Dr. Dobra.'' He smiled warmly. ''You've been training for gravity, haven't you?''

''I had a hunch, sir.'' She met his smile, forgiving him. ''Just thought it might be necessary this time. They might have a station; if so, I can handle that too. I may be a junior professor, but you've taught me just about everything you know.''

He nodded. ''Flattery suits you well, dear Leeta. In that case, I'll find someone to cover *your* classes.

53

Maybe Rodney Woo. He's a bright lad—should have his dissertation done one of these days. He can do fine with the students.''

Chem cleared his throat loudly. ''I suppose you'd better go about putting your team together. Get to it. I didn't send you the file, but Lieutenant Sarsa's fast transport is leaving to meet *Bullet* in two days. Doesn't give you much time. Draw equipment and whatever you need. Charge it to the Directorate.''

On impulse, Leeta bent down and kissed the old man's head affectionately. She straightened, placed the headset on her brow, and started tracking down her graduate students.

The following day, hurrying down the corridor, she met Veld Arstong. ''Veld!'' she called, matching his long steps.

''I heard the news!'' He grinned. ''So, you've got your lost colony?''

''Looks that way. We're having a party in my office tonight. Wanna come? It's just me and the department. You'd be more than welcome. You could meet some of the kids going out with us.'' She threw him a warm smile.

''Love to!'' Veld nodded happily, then hesitated. ''Um, maybe I shouldn't. I work with Jeffray, you know. I'd hate . . .''

Leeta patted his shoulder. ''Oh, come on, you were the only one who backed me up. Share a little of the glory. Jeffray and I are finished. It's over, Veld. There won't be any hard feelings on Jeffray's part.'' She hoped she sounded authoritative.

''So . . . OK! I'll be there,'' Veld agreed. ''Bring anything with me?''

''Bottle of your favorite!'' Leeta laughed.

The project had become the talk of the department. She'd finally chosen three of her best students: Marty Bruk, physical anthropologist; Netta Solare, cultural specialist; and Bella Vola, linguist with some familiarity with ancient Native American languages.

Other parts of the team were being picked by Dr. Chem in consultation with Planetology, Botany, Zoology, and the others. The most important aspect of the expedition was all Leeta's.

The students—always anxious for a party—arrived early. Rita Sarsa grinned as she came through the door. Her crooked smile gave way to seriousness as she studied faces, noted the handsome Rodney Woo, and somehow immediately claimed his complete attention.

Veld came in, looking slightly out of place among the howling anthropologists. Engineers were generally more refined—less compelled to social maleficence.

"Gang!" Leeta called. "I want you to meet my one ally on the *other* side. This is Veld Arstong. He thought there would be a lost colony somewhere. Give him a hand!"

There were cheers, hoots and hollers as the milling crowd roared. Veld lifted his bottle in tribute and smiled; he had no graceful alternative.

"Some greeting," he muttered out of the side of his mouth. "You work with these . . . barbarians?"

A war dance had broken out among the undergraduates in the center of the reading room. They were chanting and jumping with abandon, trying to keep from spilling bulbs of beer, wine or whiskey.

"Didn't Jeffray ever tell you?" She laughed, taking his arm and introducing him to the anthropology faculty.

"Just said all you birds were a little weird," Veld muttered between distinguished colleagues.

"Are you part of Leeta's team?" Netta Solare asked as she pumped Veld's hand.

"I'm just an engineer." He smiled, studying the paint on her face. "That's a new fashion?" he asked.

"This?" She started, surprised. "God, no! This is an ancient Maori design. Comes from the Pacific Ocean on Earth . . . uh, perhaps eight centuries ago. I just put it on to honor the occasion." She gyrated away to join the war dance.

"Who did she say?" Veld asked, totally lost.

"Never mind." Leeta took his hand. "We don't have an engineer yet. Interested? I could get you a spot."

Veld shook his head. "I'm a station person . . . a home type. Besides, I'm not into being eaten by savages. I've seen the holos. Even the ancient ones with

55

the big pot and a dance like the one going on over there." He pointed to the mob of students.

"Ah, engineers!" Leeta sighed. "No sense of adventure."

Veld proved her wrong. He actually fit into the crowd fairly well after he'd imbibed some of the scotch he'd brought. Most of Leeta's friends took to him and by the time the night was wearing down, he, too, danced in the war dance.

"I had fun," Veld grinned, panting as he came back from the staggering circle of students and faculty. Even Chem was shuffling in the mill of singing, mumbling figures.

"I'm about done in for tonight," Leeta admitted. "I've got an early one tomorrow. Then, the next day, I leave for Atlantis." Leeta noted Lieutenant Sarsa leaving the party, an arm around Rodney Woo's waist. From the body language, they were in for a long night. The thought left Leeta suddenly empty.

"Atlantis?" Veld asked. "Wasn't that on Earth?"

Leeta shrugged, trying to stifle her yearnings. "That's right . . . lost civilization that sank into the sea. Got to call the place we're going something. We call it the need for humans to symbolize."

"Right," Veld nodded seriously, showing he didn't understand at all. "Mind if I, uh, walk you?"

The hall engulfed them in quiet as the door slipped shut on the raucous howling behind them. Two undergraduates lay passed out, sleeping intertwined in each other's arms.

"Makes me sad," Leeta whispered.

"They seem happy." Veld bent and squinted at the expressions on their faces.

"That's what makes me sad," Leeta agreed, holding to Veld's arm. She hadn't thought to drink so much. "I haven't been sleeping well since Jeffray and I . . . Well, you know."

"He's not doing well either. You miss him?" Veld asked, studying her face.

"No!" Leeta admitted with an explosion of breath. "I don't, and that's sad, too. Jeffray is just a . . ."

Veld chided, "He's still a nice guy."

"He became a cold fish," she explained. "I just

don't know what went wrong." As they walked, she tried to outline the changes, seeking in dialogue to make sense of the past.

"This your place?" he asked as Leeta finally stopped in front of her door.

"Come on in. One more drink won't hurt or help tomorrow's hangover," she muttered dryly, pulling him in behind her.

"You sure are a lot more fun now," Veld grinned as she handed him the bulb of almost straight whiskey.

"Maybe," she said thoughtfully. "Comes of freedom."

"You're not quite right either." Veld frowned, his head cocked. "You're . . ."

"Scared about what might happen out there." She gestured.

"You! Scared?" he asked, coming close. "I don't—"

"Me. Scared," she whispered. "I'd never tell Jeff that. He'd have fallen apart. He'd have . . ."

Veld nodded as he reached down to kiss her. "You won't break me in half? I'm a station type!"

She met his curious gaze. Did she need this? Did she need to have someone warm next to her on this night of triumph? Would just any warm body make her sleep? The loneliness yawned wide inside her.

"I promise," she whispered, her voice husky. "I'll be gentle."

The ride had been long and hard. The scabs had hardened and peeled, leaving his body crisscrossed with pink weals that would become scars on his sunblackened skin. They remained to remind him of the days of pain and healing after killing the bear.

John Smith Iron Eyes looked out over the rolling pasture at the spotted cattle and horse herds. Where were the guards?

Philip and Chester rode to either flank, guarding the Old One who sat his saddle stiffly. His cousins had changed as a result of what the old man taught them.

Through the long days they had journeyed, thirsting sometimes, periodically blasted by hot wind and made gaunt by hunger. Stalked by bears, suffering from cold, half-dazed, the Prophet—alone untouched by suffering—had pointed their way. And in the end, they had stumbled to the shores of a different sea—an ocean that lay far to the south instead of the eastern one found by his ancestor.

Changed now, they returned, men molded by the wilderness, haunting memories in each of their travel-weary faces. John Smith Iron Eyes rode to the home of his People in triumph. Philip, with somber, knowing eyes, seemed a pillar of power. Chester, his mild face thin from the wind and sun, kept his eyes downcast, refusing to look about as he sorted the uncertainties wheeling within. Only the Prophet—eternal as the rocks—remained unchanged.

"Smoke there?" Chester called, pointing, eyes haunted.

Iron Eyes looked, straining to see into the distance.

"There has been war and death," the thin voice of the Old One hung in the still air. "A cusp. The Santos have chosen."

"How bad, Prophet?" John Smith asked. "Why did you not warn us?"

"It was meant to be. You were not to have been here." The Prophet replied with finality.

Further questions would have done little more than exercise John's jaws. He felt a quickening of his pulse. Strange things had happened—were happening.

Heading ever south, they had crossed open grasslands, as each night the Old One told them the stories of the People. Of a time in the old world of Earth. Of the way the People lived, hunting and fighting. Of wars with the white men who became part of the People. Of how the Sobyets conquered the whites and the Mayheecans, ancestors of the Santos. He told of the fate of the People when they went to the stars. Of how the Sobyets had sent them in the ship and how the crew decided to throw the People out in space to die. The People had risen and killed the Sobyet crew, cutting them apart and taking their hair as the ancients had done.

Then the People had suffered through days and days as the Ship jumped in and out of space as they tried to learn to fly it. There was more death; the People fought each other. They hungered, thirsted, ate of each other's flesh, and finally, Spider brought them here, to World.

They didn't know where World was; but somehow they had managed to land the Ship next to an ocean. From there, the People who lived went forth, seeking new homes. One of the original Prophets had found the frozen cattle and horses deep in the Ship. Some had lived when they thawed; the herds of the People were born.

Their ears had drunk of the Old One's words. They had nodded and listened, becoming one with the People, hearing the stories that were only told to the Medicine Men in the ancient societies.

"Why do you tell us this, Grandfather?" Chester Armijo Garcia had asked.

"It must be passed on," the Old One whispered, eyes on the stars. "If the Visions are right . . . one of you will be called Prophet. Not John Smith Iron Eyes. It will be you, Chester Armijo Garcia . . . or you, Phillip Smith Iron Eyes. I do not choose you. Look inside, see what Spider has given you. Look inside your souls. What do you see?"

Neither had been the same since—they wondered, feared, and waited.

They rode past a broken-down fence. "Raid!" John Smith spat, reading the tracks. "Raiders passed here and took the horses of this man."

"They know something important is about to happen." The Old One's voice rang out hollowly. "They hear from their Prophet."

John Smith Iron Eyes looked up, wondering, no longer shocked as he would once have been. "The Santos have Prophets?" His voice carried a note of disbelief.

"They are men like us." The old one smiled a toothless grin. "They have only one man they call Prophet. He left the Four Old Men generations ago. He said God was called Haysoos."

John Smith mounted up, resting the rifle lightly in the scabbard. A good rifle, he'd killed many Raiders with it. God's name was Spider. Deep in thought, he rode on.

Smoke hung thick and miasmic around the settle-

59

ment. A dead man lay just off the road. John Smith could see his blood-streaked skull where coup had been taken. It was the way of men—of honor. Spider had given them coup. The dead man was not of the People, his clothing being decorated with Santos crosses.

"Why did they raid here?" Chester asked woodenly.

"Horses. Cattle. Women," John grunted. "Why else would men raid?"

"They wanted the radio," the Old One said softly. "This we have seen. They want the radio so they can call to the Others from the Sky."

"Sobyets!" John Smith hissed. "They come again?"

"Not Sobyets." Philip Smith Iron Eyes shook his head. "Others. Did you not hear the Old One's words?"

"Do you see?" the Prophet asked, turning to Philip, black eyes glittering with interest.

"I don't know," Philip's voice wavered. He squinted, as if there was something he didn't understand in his head. "The dreams . . ."

It only took another half mile before they found the fort. A small, barricaded construction, it lay across the road. "Who comes here?" called a voice.

"A Prophet!" John Smith Iron Eyes growled back. "I am Iron Eyes. These are my cousins! The Old One you can see for yourself."

A warrior jumped up and walked forward cautiously, rifle easy in his hands. His blanket design marked him as Andojar. He peered up at the Old One and lowered his gaze. "I am sorry, Grandfather. We trust no one."

"You are blessed. Sing your praises," the Prophet told him, motioning John to ride on. The horses picked their way through the tangle of the barricade and two more men looked up at them from fortified ditches.

The houses were low, domed affairs with entrances facing east. Behind them, in the center of the circle of dwellings, lay the gray bulk of the Ship. Sunk into the ground now, everyone knew that once it had flown among the stars. A gray-backed turtle, it crouched in the green of the fields.

"The Old One comes!" Chester Armijo shouted. "The Old One comes!" The cry was taken up and passed through the settlement. John Smith Iron Eyes watched men and women duck through doorways, watching, lifting their hands in welcome. Faces were lighting with joy.

They looked wary, too. Even as he rode, John Smith Iron Eyes catalogued signs of war. Had they made it this far into the settlement? That was unheard of! No raiders had ever dared. . . .

"Did they get the radio?" Philip asked suddenly of a man.

"No, but they almost made it to the Ship," he was told. "We beat them back—but the Old Ones tell us they may come again."

John felt himself sag in the saddle. He hadn't expected this welcome. He'd thought to be received as a returning hero. Anger growled in his gut. The Raiders had done this to him—taken his victory from him. He clenched his fists, noting that no one even asked where they had been. The Spiders' eyes were for the Old One only. John Smith looked back, the Prophet's burning gaze rested on him, a slight smile on the withered lips.

The old man kicked his horse forward. "How do you feel? Do you still believe? Do you need to sweat? Do you need to think of the name of God?"

John Smith Iron Eyes took a deep breath. "I thought they would see me come in glory. I have been where no other man has gone—and they do not see me now." His voice was sullen.

"You feel anger?" The Old One nodded, eyes bird-bright. "You act like a nameless child. Pride, Iron Eyes? You are not fit to serve the People—not fit for Spider!"

The vehemence in the Prophet's words burned in John's brain. He winced as if physically struck.

"Search your mind," the hoarse voice spoke in Power. "See the anger. Take it apart and look at it. Know it for what it is, warrior. How can you fight if you do not use your anger like a knife? But would you cut yourself with it? Would you turn it on your own People?''

John Smith swallowed hard and hunched in the saddle. *What was this old man's purpose?*

Walking the horses, they entered the dusty open space between the half moon of houses and the Ship. The Old One rode out and lifted a hand. Obediently, John, Chester, and Philip pulled up.

''Where are the dead?'' the Prophet's voice creaked.

''They are there.'' One of the Andojar women pointed. The People parted to reveal a raised wooden platform littered with corpses twisted in death. Many had been mutilated.

The Old One motioned John forward, dark eyes glinting in the graying light. The black mare shifted and sidestepped as she neared the heaped, decomposing flesh. John's nose tightened at the subtle odor of death. It wasn't bad . . . yet. Within a day, it would be overpowering.

Flies, hovering in a humming, shimmering mist, stirred at his approach. The stiff, contorted limbs didn't look real. The bellies on some were starting to bloat. He could see many whose hair had been taken by the Raiders. There was his father's brother's son, a bullet hole in his breast, dried blood black on his blanket.

Here was Raven O'Neal Andojar. There was Reuben Iron Eyes Garcia. They'd ridden their first raid together. Good fighters. Brave. One by one, John saw each of the corpses, noting the identity as he passed.

. . . And his heart stopped. His tongue stuck against the back of his mouth. He sat woodenly, seeing the blood-matted hair where the skull had been crushed. Angular chips of bone stuck out from blackened flesh. The throat had been cut, the entrails brutally torn out. Her breasts had been sliced from the body. From the ruined pubic area, he guessed a gun had been thrust into her vagina and fired. She was the last one in line.

Love? He winced. Real, sweet love? Pure love, that did not demand any giving or taking? Love that could never be fulfilled? Indeed, the same love had driven him to the far sea.

Carefully, he reached out a hand, forcing the horse

62

next to the raised platform. The mare started to balk—but obeyed—eyes wide, nostrils flared, head jerking.

Iron Eyes ran fingers down her tortured face, lightly brushing the already hardened lips. They'd gouged her eyes out of the skull, leaving gruesome pits now crawling with tiny white maggots.

From the stains on her thighs, he could see that they'd had her for a long time before they had killed her. He closed his eyes, gagging on the taint of corruption.

A deep emptiness opened under his heart. His stomach knotted and the sudden need to vomit caught him by surprise. Unable to stop—shamed before all the People—his guts lurched and his throat pumped the contents onto the ground beneath her.

Numbly, he dragged a sleeve over his wet mouth and bit his lip to still the trembling of his jaw. He looked one last time and turned the horse. Jenny Garcia Smith was dead. Her soul belonged to Spider. Her body had been ripped, torn, and violated by the Raiders—the Santos.

He didn't see any faces in his daze of horror. The mare walked slowly. His brain had gone blank, numbed by the horror and the pain. The crowd, formless in his detached mind, passed. He almost didn't stop as he neared the Old One; only the thin, reedy voice penetrated his consciousness.

"Go back to the mountain. Think of the words we have had today. Prepare yourself. Take these men. One will follow you. One will return to me. Now they lead you to the place where you need to find yourself. Spider will take you then. The People are in your hands.

"Go! Learn your anger. Learn your pain. I have spoken!" The Old One lifted his hand in salute and motioned John Smith Iron Eyes away.

He never knew whether it was he who kicked the mare into motion or if instinct led her to follow her mates. He felt himself moving, vaguely remembering the flashing images of houses, fields, warriors with rifles, grim faces, and the pain of the People.

The fast transport wasn't built for comfort—just for speed. Accommodations were cramped. The gravity

63

plates could compensate for as much as forty gs of acceleration, protecting the fragile human passengers. When the ship went autopilot, it could push more than one hundred gravities.

Leeta Dobra lay in the narrow, foldout cot and thought back over her farewells. The biggest surprise came when Chem was ordered along on the mission by Assistant Director Semri Navtov himself.

The first pictures had come in the day they left. Leeta had looked them over rapidly and patched a duplicate program to the ship's computers. It was apparent the signals came from a planet. It wasn't a station out there—as she'd known all along.

The only really difficult part had been when Jeffray had seen Veld Arstong walking out of her little apartment. Veld had hesitated, smiled, muttered some inanity—and left.

She'd leaned against the wall, crossed her arms, and given Jeffray one of those challenging looks. He had been carrying a small package; she'd known it was a gift.

"Just wanted to wish you well," he finally said, hacking slightly, as if his throat were dry, pain in his weak, bright eyes.

"Thank you, Jeffray." How hard to say that to him. Beaten, he looked away and walked off. She shouldn't have spied on him, but she saw him throw the little gift into the garbage converter at the end of the hall.

Veld. Another engineer? What did that tell her about her personality?

Grimacing distastefully, Leeta pulled herself up from the bunk. "No more men," she promised herself. Not that there had been many—only Jeffray and Veld. As a youngster, she'd been too busy with studies for sex.

"I'm sworn off!" she muttered under her breath. A faint smile bent her lips. She remembered a classmate who'd tried so hard. He'd ended up calling her the "Iron Maiden." She turned to the comm, resting a headset on her brow to review the information.

The data on Mexico, America, and the Native American groups suspected of being on the *Nicholai Romanan* were surprising. There had been an excellent clue in the phrases that kept coming in from the probe. Bella Vola had tied the language down to Arapaho/Sioux. At least, that was where the words had their origins. The rest of the language was a rich mixture of Spanish and English. No longer did anyone even question that she'd made a positive ID of the Soviet ship.

"Dr. Chem would like to speak with you," the ship said through its speaker.

"Put him on." Leeta rolled over on her bunk to look at the monitor.

Chem's florid face appeared. "Got time for a staff meeting?" he wondered. "I think we should begin to discuss a plan of action. We have at least a month yet before we can reach Atlantis. There's more than enough time for all of us to think up every alternative action."

"Sure," she agreed. "Why don't we meet in the galley? I'd rather do it face to face than over the comm."

He nodded slightly and the monitor flicked off in typical Chem fashion.

She sighed. Chem was under a lot of stress. The project was on a planet. The first investigation of its kind in more than two hundred years. And Chem was stuck in an orbiting ship. He was to be nothing more than a figurehead, an adviser. It *had* to hurt.

The galley was crowded. Mostly, the others were observers. Planetology would do their work from orbit. Zoo and Botany would go to the surface, randomly seeking specimens. The important part would be up to Anthropology and that meant Leeta's team.

"First off," Chem introduced, "let's go over the potentials. I know all of you have been considering such things for days now, but let's bring it out in the open and kick it around."

Leeta nodded. "We'll use established methods of contact. Try a similar methodology to that employed by Parker on Aristan."

"That was almost three centuries ago," Marty Bruk said, frowning, his thick dark features pinched.

Leeta shrugged. "Why shouldn't it work here? It's

a tried methodology. It's been a form of barter for years. There's—"

" 'Scuse me," the planetologist interrupted. Szchinzki Montaldo was called S for short. "What are you talking about?"

Leeta laughed. "Sorry. The Parker method involves placing goods where the subjects—in this case Atlanteans—will find them. The gifts establish that something is leaving strange goodies around their haunts. As they get used to the gifts, we allow limited sightings, always being friendly and leaving something. It trains the people not to fear us. It builds a bridge of friendship that will—"

"You ever done this?" Montaldo asked flatly.

"Uh, no. No need for the last several centuries." Chem looked smug.

"We're not very worried," Netta said with an almost patronizing tone in her voice. "This is what we've been *trained for*. We're the experts here."

Chem was nodding and Leeta gave the planetologist a warm smile. He raised his shoulders and shrugged—unconvinced.

Marty Bruk looked up in the ensuing silence. "Will we have some sort of ground transport? I'd like to set up a lab. Maybe from high altitude surveillance we can locate a burial ground and snatch a couple of bodies. The sooner we establish some physical baseline data, the better off we'll be."

"Patrol will supply that," Chem said, clearing his throat.

Subject after subject came up and was dealt with. It was going so smoothly. Leeta felt a glow on the inside. Indeed, as Netta said, they were the professionals. Even though no one had called on them for so long, it was good to see the planning was running textbook perfect.

"I'm hungry," she heard Bruk say.

"Meeting called for dinner!" Chem agreed. He had a headset on, no doubt to add some notes to his file.

Feet shuffled as people stood. Some cleared their throats, others coughed. Some stretched.

"I guess it's all right," she overheard Montaldo

66

mumbling, "but nobody said what they'd do if these guys shot first and questioned later."

Leeta stifled a laugh. God, how naive could you get? These are humans . . . just like us. How strange to think they'd be violent. Humans hadn't engaged in killing each other for over three centuries now. The species had grown beyond that.

CHAPTER V

Time ceased. John Smith Iron Eyes clung to his rugged black mare and swayed with the rhythm of her steps. The mare's head was down; she stumbled from fatigue. Chester and Philip were throwing him curious looks as they led his animal toward the heights.

Jenny Garcia Smith was dead. No, couldn't be . . . too hard to believe. But he'd seen and felt the grisly body. So defenseless, so delicate, full of love and life, she had, in the end, broken so easily. Her vanished smile twisted in his soul.

The laws of the People forbade his love for her. She must marry another man. It was the way of the People, the law, as Spider had decreed—*and Spider was God.*

From the time they had been little, John had flushed warmly inside when Jenny had been near. He remembered the way she walked, gracefully, never missing a step. The skin on her arms had been firm and smooth, the muscles dancing underneath.

The way her smile raised her cheeks brought happiness to his heart in those bygone days. Her straight white teeth flashed in warm smiles when she saw him come near. He had seen her desire—read it in her eyes, in the way she held her body. She would blush, knowing they shared a secret that was forbidden.

He saw her strong arms as she came in from the pastures with a load of hides or meat on her back.

Enticing legs swished under the alluring sway of her hips. She'd turn her head slightly, throwing him a hidden smile.

Rotting meat! She was no more. The Prophet had wanted him to see her that way. There had been flies swirling over the bodies. Of all the creatures carried to World from Earth, they were the worst.

John Smith Iron Eyes raised his fingers and rubbed the tips together, feeling again how cold her face had been. Rough, jagged splinters of bone had rasped on his skin. The lips had been so hard, gaping eye sockets allowing him to see the ripped tissue—newborn maggots feeding greedily as they wiggled.

Grief built; he felt his chest heaving with the need to cry. A warrior of the People did not weep like a woman or a child. Not even for so wonderful a love as Jenny. She was taboo: a relative.

Alive, they might have gone all their lives without marrying another—a knowledge they shared. He had passed almost thirty summers now while she'd lived twenty-five before the Santos had come to torture, rape, and kill her.

An honored warrior of the People? His clan had chided him that he hadn't taken several women. She had joked in the easy manner they'd shared that he was not providing the People with children.

For all the times he'd fought Raiders, all the times he'd hunted the bears with his rifle, waiting for the right moment to drop the huge beasts, it had been from desperation that he'd risked his neck. The times he'd gone seeking Medicine had been as a result of his fobidden love. Taunting death had made him strong.

The People whispered behind his back and wondered why he was not like other men. They would not look him in the eyes and tell him. Knife Feuds came of that. They'd seen him in a Knife Feud. He'd killed Patan Reesh Yellow Legs violently, viciously, and without remorse. Then he'd ridden from camp to pray for the spirit of the dead as was required. When his Medicine came, it was the soul of Patan Yellow Legs who had forgiven him.

"We will sleep here," Chester Armijo Garcia decided. "I will watch for the first part of the night. There may be Santos near."

Philip shook his head. "I do not think so. I think they are gone. I . . . I cannot tell. It seems . . . seems that way." He was frowning again, listening inside his head.

John Smith Iron Eyes absently dropped to the ground and mechanically picketed the horse where she could get grass. Rolling into his blanket he sought relief in sleep. Her image filled his dreams, haunting him, causing his soul to wail through the long, frosty night.

Four days they traveled toward the high, distant mountains. Chester located a small camp in the lee of the cliffs, hidden from the evening breezes blowing in from the sea behind them.

"You loved her a lot," Philip finally said, his voice soft, caring.

"It is not to be spoken," John added, wondering why his stomach hadn't desired food for so long.

"I know your pain." Philip frowned, cocking his head. "I feel it—here." He touched his fingers to his forehead.

"You must be the one the Prophet spoke of," Chester said with his calm smile. "You will be an Old One. My cousin is leaving me." There was an uncertain twist in Chester's words, his eyes hollow with the thoughts and sights in his own head.

"I'm scared," Philip said softly. "A man of the People, *fearing?* Think of that! I have fought and had courage in the face of the Raiders. I watched the bear fight my cousin and traveled to the far southern sea across strange lands, yet now I fear for my sanity!" His voice was growing strained, his eyes glittering with panic.

Chester nodded. His voice rasped, barely audible. "I know."

"We have all lost our sanity, cousin," John Smith added, reaching a scarred hand to touch his relative's shoulder.

They sat, watching the flames that licked the corkwood bush Chester had placed in the fire. Yellow-gold light flickered across expressionless faces and empty eyes. Each lost himself in his thoughts. Each voiced a silent question to Spider.

John Smith Iron Eyes left first. He climbed carefully to the highest point he could see. He folded his blanket on the rock and stared up at the two moons. Trembling with fatigue, he prayed and sang. Dawn was coming.

As the sun rose hot in the sky, he continued, praying until he was hoarse, singing the song he'd used when he killed the bear. That first night his Medicine came to him. A young man approached, walking through the air, singing as he came near. The young man gave him a smile and made the design of a green harvester over his head but said no words before fading into a cloud.

At night, he prayed again, seeing Jenny in his dreams, feeling pain in his waking hours. And the next day, through the shimmering that became World, Yellow Legs came to him once more and told him of wars, battles, and fights to come.

"Be strong, Iron Eyes." Yellow Legs laughed. "When you fought me, you had an easy mark. The men from the sky will be tricky."

"I must fight the men from the sky?" He stared at the apparition in confusion. "Then they are the Sobyets?"

"No, but they would destroy the People again. You are warned." Yellow Legs laughed and flew up in the sky toward the stars that were beginning to speckle the eastern horizon.

John Smith Iron Eyes wondered as he looked out over the green, brown, and yellow-patched plains his People called home. Clouds built far out over the sliver of ocean that was visible. The billowing white contrasted with the deep purple-blue of the clear sky. He could see the second moon up above.

The red-pink granite was rough under his buttocks and he suffered in the burning heat of the sun. Thirst tormented him, testing him, causing his body to cry. Spider was there, somewhere, watching as he watched all the universe. Defiantly, Iron Eyes looked up at the fiercely burning orb.

Bear came the following day, shimmering out of the heat waves rising from the land. Iron Eyes looked at the animal, seeing from the coloring that it was the one he'd killed to save the Prophet.

The huge creature spoke to him in thunder. "My blood washed your arms, man from another planet. My life was taken that yours be strong. Use it well. My blood will ever give you strength. One day—if you live wrongly and prove unworthy—I will have you back, man. For now, I am yours. Until that day, go in strength."

Bear was gone. Emptiness filled the void where the creature had stood. John Smith Iron Eyes frowned. Was that a drop of bear blood on the rock? He touched the black, sticky stuff, rubbing it over his fevered body, feeling strength seep into him. He tried to concentrate; his mind wandered.

Delirious, he watched shadows crawling, alive, across the land as the sun crossed the sky for the fourth time since he'd climbed to the heights. Vision wavering, he looked out over the flats, seeing the thin line of ocean beyond the settlements.

"Take your anger apart," the Prophet's words haunted him. *"Would you turn it against yourself? Would you use it against the People?"*

Puzzled, John Smith blinked, thinking of the hatred he'd felt. His soul lifted out of his body and looked down, seeing the physical being he was. He blinked at anger, awed at the Power in hatred. It drove. It killed. It destroyed. He turned it in his body and rearranged it into a weapon, feeling a rightness.

He tried to do the same with pain. It would not come free from his clinging soul. His racked cry of fear paralyzed his tormented soul.

"You have not purified yourself, brother."

He squinted into the sun to see the slim form of Jenny Garcia standing above him on the rock.

"I . . ." His voice cracked from thirst. "You are dead!" came his rasp from a dry throat.

"Only my body, brother," she laughed at him and her voice was smooth.

"They hurt you," he cried, feeling tears come.

"They hurt me." Her soft voice agreed. Tears, like acid, burned his glazed eyes. She was soothing his brow now, her cool hand wiping his pain away. Cool-

71

ness from the stroking fingers ran down his body, tingling, bringing him awake with pleasure and sensation.

"I love you," he whispered, eyes closed, feeling pain and suffering washed from his being. She had her hands lower now, working along his loins. His maleness hardened under her soft touch.

She whispered lightly in his ear, "As I love you, forbidden one. I have come to purify your body. I will make clean what is bursting inside you. A poison of the soul has built under your heart. When I am done, pain will be yours to do with as you wish."

He felt her lowering herself onto him. Swirling cool flames of ecstacy surrounded him, prickling his body with electric fire as she took his hurt from him. The pressure of her breasts on his chest was soothing. His maleness was in her now, throbbing, burning, until it flamed in a warm, tingling rush that carried his soul upward in a fantastic dance of fulfillment.

He heard himself crying out in frantic, joyous abandon as his body jerked in uncontrolled spasms. *"I love you, Jenny!"* he shrieked to the empty skies.

"Find the Santos. You must push them back. You must keep them from the People, my brother." Her voice calmed him and he felt her fingers caressing his fevered brow. "Your destiny is in the stars."

"Cut a joint from your little finger. Pain will be lost into the sacrificed part. It will give you strength. It will make you well again and strong enough to kill the Santos and drive them from our land.

"A woman will come for you from far away; take her as yours if you can. The Others can kill us—so you must be very careful. You must believe; the People depend on you. The way ahead is tricky and difficult. Even the spirits see it poorly. We have strength in wisdom and in war. One way must win." Then she was gone.

John Smith Iron Eyes pulled himself upright on the gritty rock, feeling chilled where his semen dried in the light breeze. Stars twinkled to the north, unhidden by a bank of low wispy clouds that moved in. The rains were coming.

Jenny's words echoed in his mind. First, he pulled his knife from his belt and laid his left hand on the

72

rock. "Take a joint," he muttered around his swollen tongue. "The pain will be sacrificed."

The razor edge of the long knife stung his soft brown skin as he centered the knife over the last knuckle of the little finger. Sawing quickly, he felt the tendons and ligaments parting. Blood spurted around the blade. There was resistance as the knife bit into bone. Wiggling the blade, he found the joint and neatly severed the fingertip from his hand.

The sting grew into fiery pain as the insulted flesh bled and severed nerves shrieked their message into his mind. Absently, he bound the stub tightly in the cloth of his shirt. A corner of his mind felt the pain and realized it was part of body, not soul. So much better. Jenny's ghost could go now. His love would not die—but he could live with her loss.

Suddenly, reality wavered. He clutched at the hard, unforgiving rock, teetering. His stomach lurched, heaving emptiness as he tried to vomit.

Thick tears came in his misery as another part of his mind saw through the weaving haze and darkness to a hundred fires that rippled in the night. The Santos sat there, huddled under their blankets. A tall warrior stood up and stretched, looking nervously around the camp. Finally, the black eyes stopped and looked at John Smith Iron Eyes.

"I killed your woman, Spider man." The warrior grinned. "She did not have much strength, she wasn't enough for me—Big Man of the Santos!" He thumped his chest, eyes glittering with triumph and dare.

"I'll kill you," John Smith Iron Eyes growled as he studied the bearded face, memorizing the strapping shoulders and the carefully decorated warshirt. Horse tails swung from his shoulders and a fresh human scalp John knew to be Jenny's hung at the man's throat.

"Your hair will lie next to hers." The big warrior laughed out loud, fingering the hilt of the knife that hung at his belt.

John Smith staggered to his feet. *"I'll kill you!"* he roared into the blackening skies.

The warrior laughed his disgust at Iron Eyes' words and spit casually into the fire, insolently placing fists on his hips.

"You will die!" Iron Eyes shouted, glaring into the man's mocking stare.

"I see you are having a vison. This is good," a twisted smiled crossed the warrior's bearded lips. "Make your Medicine well, Spider warrior. The ways of the Prophets and warriors differ. I care not for the radio—but for you I shall bring death!" He ended with a whooped war call that brought the men around him to their feet in surprise.

John Smith Iron Eyes cursed as his soul burst into a burning rage. At the top of his lungs he bellowed, *"Death! Death to you, Santos!"* A crack of lightning banged, hitting the rocks to the east as thunder boomed and roared against the aged granite of the peaks.

The Santos warrior laughed yet again. As with a snap of fingers, the vision was gone, snuffed like a candle. A large raindrop, cold with premonition, splatted onto the rock. Lightning ripped the sky, exposing torn, twisted clouds.

"Death," John Smith whispered into the oncoming storm. "I have seen him. It is as a vision. As the Prophets see. I will kill this man." Carefully, he picked up his things and made a small cairn of rock. Under it, he placed the fingertip from his left little finger. Then, rifle in hand, he began the dangerous descent to the camp so far below.

When he arrived hours later, it was not Chester who waited for him, but Philip. His younger cousin squatted under the soot-blackened shelter, feeding brush into the fire. The camp lay back behind the drip line of the rocks. Philip's face was tight, eyes empty, tired, as if he hadn't been sleeping. His blanket was pulled tight around him as he stared, heedlessly, into the flames.

Wicked rain pelted John's head and back as he looked around. The horses were picketed and resting. The mare hadn't spotted him yet since the wind was wrong.

"You could die that way, cousin," John Smith whispered softly. The mare raised her head and whickered suddenly, glad to see him.

Philip didn't raise his head. "I know where my death lies," Philip answered in an exhausted voice.

John Smith Iron Eyes walked into the shelter and dug around in a saddlebag for a dried steak. Careful of his smarting blood-soaked finger, he cut strips of meat to chew. Desperate hunger seized him.

John looked up. "Where is Chester?" He felt his mouth watering at the taste. He'd drunk all he could hold in the rivulets that cascaded down the drainages, the muddy, gritty water soaking into desiccated tissues.

Philip didn't raise his eyes, but his lips curved slightly at the edges. "He has gone to become an Old One." He made the gesture for "no more," indicating Chester was no longer a cousin. He had become a man without relatives, a man of the tribe, of all the clans.

"I thought it was you." John Smith Iron Eyes heard the question in his own voice.

Philip shook his head. "I wasn't . . . wasn't strong enough. The visions would have des . . . destroyed me. To be a Prophet is not meant but for a very few. There is madness there, brother. To see the future is a terrible thing. Spider has given me this way instead. It is . . . better."

"What way?" John Smith scowled, looking nervously at his cousin.

Philip said, "You decide my fate, brother." He poked another stick into the fire before he got to his feet and walked out into the rain.

"Me? Decide *your* fate?" John Smith ate yet another of the dried steaks and tended to his finger, binding it tightly and soaking it with distilled alcohol. He gritted his teeth and winced as the liquid fire burned into his veins. Nevertheless, it was sterile. Then he slept.

"The Raiders are there." John Smith pointed to the northeast as he mounted up the following morning and slipped the rifle into the scabbard. His uncle had built that gun. It was a finely crafted piece, shooting a 9.5mm 270 grain bullet at almost a kilometer per second.

Philip nodded, peering through the rain. "We will catch them. It will take four days' travel. We must hurry though. There is a dying calf ahead that would make us a better meal than it will the scavengers."

"How do you know that?" Iron Eyes asked, scowling, searching Philip's haunted face.

"I know," his cousin whispered. "Do not ask of things which would damn you to hear." Philip's voice was hollow with terror, threat, and warning.

Iron Eyes nodded, a tingle of fear in his guts. The way of the Prophets was not for all men. A knot blocked his throat when he swallowed. There was reason to fear. Perhaps he kicked the black mare too hard as he drove her onto the trail—headed toward the warrior he knew waited in the Santos camp.

Excitement built as the fat shape of *Bullet* loomed white, ever larger, in the view screens. Ships were no big thing to anyone who'd lived for more than a couple of months on a major station. But the thought of actually boarding a warship tickled a deep thrill of anticipation in Leeta.

She realized it was atavistic. Who had a use for warships anymore? Humanity kept them for policing purposes, but who was there to fight? It was said that maybe, someday, there would be a serious alien threat from outside known space. To date though, all the intelligent life forms mankind had found had no interest in human doings—a fact that had rather appalled those involved with first contacts.

A primitive element of the human psyche, she thought. I am still no more than a highly sophisticated primate. It's impossible to breed out billions of years of physical and social evolution in just a couple of centuries.

Bullet was growing larger now, filling the entire screen until there was nothing left to see but white. A few faintly discernible lines indicated ports, weapons blisters, and docking facilities.

With a hearty sigh, Leeta gathered up her scattered articles and prepared for the move to the big ship. Gravitics had made major advances since the early days. She hardly felt the docking—more imagined it really.

"You may proceed to the other ship now, Dr. Dobra," the ship's voice said softly.

The time had come. Leaving her cabin, Leeta almost skipped down the corridors to the hatch. They waited there, genuine military guards, all decked out in Patrol uniforms just like in the movies, holos, and stories. Even better, they checked her ID with skin and eye prints and actually saluted as she stepped aboard.

Instead of a computer drone, Rita Sarsa stood there, an impudent grin on her lips. "Have a good trip, Doc? I fought the urge to do rolls and inverse acceleration tactical maneuvers."

Leeta laughed, handing her belongings to an ensign. "Never knew the difference."

"I'll show you to your quarters. There will be a fifteen minute orientation and then the colonel will want to see you in conference."

As they walked down the proverbial white corridors, Sarsa added, "Uh, when this is all over, I need to talk to you."

Leeta studied the lieutenant's neutral face. She could barely see the tension in those cool green eyes.

The quarters were nice, roomy, clean, and like everything in space, white! They'd done that in the old days. White made rooms look bigger. Not only that, things were easier to keep clean. Leaks, fractures, damage of any kind showed up better, too.

The whirlwind orientation over, she found herself seated next to Chem along with the rest of her team. Rita sat at the head of the table, eyes on a comm monitor only she could see, headset on her brow. Here, for the first time, she looked the part of an officer of the Patrol. The room was large with a centrally located table at which they sat. Piped classical music turned out to be stuff from Zion. Quite pleasant.

"Colonel Damen Ree!" an orderly announced suddenly and a door opened, admitting a muscular, uniformed man. Leeta nodded; he looked the part of an officer. She noticed that the military people had all stood. For her part, she did, too, the rest of the team following uncomfortably.

"At ease." The command was crisp. Ree smiled. "It must be awkward for the civilians."

He read my mind, Leeta thought as introductions were made. Well built, maybe forty or possibly a well preserved fifty, Ree's short beard was neat, unbraided, and unadorned with jewelry. The way his dark eyes moved betrayed a keen mind.

"Ladies and gentlemen," Ree spoke formally. "We seem to be on somewhat shaky ground as far as protocol. My instructions from the Director are to furnish you with every assistance during our investigation of what seems to be a lost colony.

"I must add that I am somewhat dismayed that the Patrol was not allowed to handle the current situation in its own way. I trust, however, that your expertise is better than ours in the given situation."

Leeta noted that Colonel Ree had that sort of authoritative personality that demanded and received instant respect.

He continued. "As to your professional conclusions," he nodded to Dr. Chem and Leeta, "I am astonished at the amount of work you have been able to accomplish given such limited data."

It wasn't a criticism, Leeta realized. He appeared very professional about the whole situation.

Ree smiled mechanically. "I do have one question. In all of the planning sessions forwarded for my appraisal, I haven't noticed anything which would give me an idea as to your personal security needs on the planet you call Atlantis. Can you brief me on that?" His inquisitive eyes prowled from face to face.

Dr. Emmanuel Chem stood and made his usual throat-clearing growl. "Colonel Ree," he nodded, "anthropology has a long, distinguished history of sending unarmed, poorly equipped investigators into the field, often weeks or months away from potential help.

"Oh, to be sure," he motioned with one large hand, "in the early days of the nineteenth and twentieth centuries there were fellows who got into trouble. I might add that from the time men first ventured into space, we haven't lost a single colleague during an investigation.

"In closing, I assure you, it is quite safe. The methodology was worked out many years ago." Chem smiled and cocked his head a little as if inviting an undergraduate to question his authority.

Ree's smile was unaffected. "Very good, professor. I bow to your expertise for I am far from my own specialty here. In that case, I look forward to working with all of you. It will be an education.

"Now, to specifics. You will be furnished with ground transportation and any guards you require while on the planet's surface. We can set up a remote camp with communication and laboratory facilities. Further, the engineers are already working on the equipment Mr. Bruk thought necessary, in addition to the material you brought from university. A communications tie-in will, of course, be provided to all of your ground personnel with a transduction tie to the Gi-net at the university.

"Lieutenant Sarsa, whom you all know by now, will continue as the official Patrol liaison. Take any requests, complaints, or problems directly to her. I have every confidence in her ability to solve them. Anything else?"

Leeta raised a hand. "Yes, sir. Since you have read our proposed procedure, is there anything we have specified which you cannot provide or which would cause you excessive logistical problems? I, uh, guess what I want to know is . . . are we causing you any undue anxiety in regard to our requirements?"

The Colonel nodded slightly as she talked, listening intently. The automatic smile only bothered her a little. "Dr. Dobra, we are at your service. I mean that. For example, this ship is designed to potentially cut a planet or station in half. If necessary, we can mount an armed invasion which could overrun any planet in the Directorate within a half hour.

"Please." He held up a hand at the startled faces and murmuring voices. "I am only using that as an analogy. The point is, *Bullet* has incredible resources that you will barely dent, let alone strain." His smile was genuinely warm this time. His face gleamed with pride in the power of his vessel.

"He's really stuck on this bucket." She heard Marty Bruk whisper to Bella Vola. She'd watched the affair between them growing during the flight out.

"How soon will we arrive over the planet?" Leeta asked.

Ree didn't even hesitate. "Five days, fourteen hours, and roughly twenty minutes."

"Very good," Chem said, heartily. "Then everything should go exceedingly well."

Ree took a deep breath. "There is one slight problem." He had everyone's attention immediately. "The radio transmissions have ceased."

A babble of voices broke loose before Leeta said loudly, "You're sure of this? It couldn't be that they have taken the day off for a holiday?" It grew silent again.

"You heard the last transmission," Ree shrugged. "They said something about the radar coming in. After that . . . silence. The interesting thing, from my perspective, is that the drone probe—now in orbit—doesn't pick up any electromagnetic patterns from the type of radar we would suspect them of being able to build."

Leeta nodded. Of course, she remembered the principles of antique radar as described by Jeffray.

"Are there any video or holo transmissions from the probe yet?" Montaldo asked.

Ree slipped his thumbs into the belt on his uniform and nodded. "Yes, Doctor, we've only received them today. Projection!" Ree ordered. The planet they called Atlantis spun over the table like a solid sphere.

Leeta caught her breath. The sphere reminded her of Earth—a cloudy blue ball with mottled green-brown irregular patches of continents. The holo enhanced one pentagonal-shaped land mass.

"This appears to be the center of the human activity." Ree explained. "From the preliminary data obtained by the probe, the human population is mostly restricted to the western half of that continent. The other land masses do not contain any sign of human activity."

The holo enhanced again as if the table were falling from a great height. "This is the best view we have of a human village." Ree sounded smug, Leeta thought. "This we received only hours ago. Note the brown specks. They are evidently huts. Further, the animals around them are Earth-type cattle and horses."

There were sputters of delight. Leeta found herself smiling happily. She could see the fields scattered out around the village. "No crops," she realized. "That's odd."

"Indeed," Chem was half out of his seat, peering as if to see better.

"Masai!" Netta Solare breathed.

"Pardon?" Ree asked, clearly lost.

Solare threw him a smile. "The Masai, Colonel, were an African group before space exploration began. They lived strictly off cattle. They didn't farm in the traditional society although after acculturation they were forced into it. We call them pastoralists. They migrate where their animals must go."

"Yet they have radio," Ree said as a reminder.

"Yes," Leeta nodded, meeting the Colonel's eyes. "I've been building a model for all this. These aren't strictly primitive people. They must have had access to the *Nicholai Romanan's* tapes all these years. We should have an excellent opportunity to study a people who have adapted to a mélange of technology and pastoralism. Fascinating! No sign of factories or mining?"

Ree waved a hand apologetically. "We only have that one picture so far. It is a large planet. It will take a while for the probe to sort it all out."

"African middle level social structure?" Solare wondered aloud. "How did they get that from American, Mexican and Arapaho-Sioux cultural backgrounds? There's a lot—"

Ree laughed. "I think this will be most interesting."

It brought a round of chuckles from everyone. They were all beaming, Leeta realized. Not for six hundred years had there been anything as exciting as this for anthropologists to study.

It was a problem for theory. Pastoralists, following their animals. At the same time, these tribesmen—for that was what they should have become—were using radio. There were no examples of that in Earth's cultural records. A puzzle, indeed, and she had it all!

The ship caused the next interruption. "Personal

message for Dr. Dobra. It is recommended that you take this in your quarters.''

Leeta looked curiously at each of the suddenly interested faces, noting the tense reservation that leaped into Rita's eyes. She shrugged in resignation and excused herself.

"Colonel," Rita offered. "Perhaps I should escort the doctor so she doesn't lose her way?"

Ree agreed and within moments they were twisting down narrow corridors. Leeta entered the cabin she now called home and nodded as a tense Sarsa left. "I'm here, ship. What is it?"

"Subspatial transduction message waiting," *Bullet* intoned.

"Go ahead," Leeta looked expectantly at the monitor. To her infinite surprise, Veld Arstong's face formed.

"Veld!" she cried. "I'm flattered. This is an expensive call!" Why was she suddenly worried? She hadn't thought he'd miss her that much.

He hesitated, dropped his eyes, and wet his lips with his tongue. "I don't know how to tell you this, Leeta." His stumbling irritated her, that wasn't his style, it reminded her of Jeffray.

"Try saying it," her voice cracked sharply. "You pulled me out of an important meeting."

"Look," he raised his eyes, his face flushing. "Don't make this more difficult!"

"I . . ." she started, but he waved her down.

Impassioned eyes met hers. "I just came from Jeffray's. I went down to try and talk to him. He bombed the interview with the Directorate people from Range. He didn't have any confidence. I . . . Well . . ." Veld shook his head. "Leeta, they sent his body down to the hydroponics. He committed suicide this morning."

The retort on her lips died suddenly as her breathing constricted. "Why?" she asked, soundlessly.

"He left a message in his personal computer." Veld swallowed hard. "Said he couldn't live without you."

Leeta closed her eyes and sucked air into her lungs.

What had his words been? *I'll make it so you never forget?*

"Oh, God," she whispered.

CHAPTER VI

Skor Robinson stopped to study a stream of information dumped into the system by the Patrol and university.

So they'd found the origin of the strange radio signals. He assimilated the data, running programs to determine the potential social effects throughout the Directorate. The results were frightening.

Navtov? he queried through the system.

Yes?

The data have begun to come in on the radio signals beyond Far Side. They have called the planet from which they originate Atlantis. The anthropologists have just arrived aboard the Patrol ship, Bullet. *It appears we do have a planet of humans outside our sphere of control.* Robinson waited, allowing Director Navtov time to study the data he'd sent through the huge computer.

. . . And you recommend? Navtov's inquiry returned.

Robinson, portions of his mind never having left the problem, responded, *I think it appropriate that all parties familiar with this particular case be removed or "adjusted."*

Navtov considered. *It would create difficulties for us if this knowledge got out. I see social unrest as a result of such information. The people do not need fascinations with un-Directed humans. For their own good, I agree. I am determining which individuals are familiar with the discovery now. Orders are issued. Depart-*

ment of Health is notified. Those individuals will be erased or "adjusted."

Robinson took a quick glance at the measures taken by Navtov. *Satisfactory, Director. Anthropology, however, cannot be simply erased. We will leave an insulated core there with Gi-net monitoring of communications so there are no leaks. At the same time, they may be of service in analyzing the potentials and threats of these wild humans.*

A nanosecond later, Navtov asked, *Are you sure that study is an appropriate response? Given the potential risks, would it not be better simply to sterilize the planet?*

And eliminate what? Robinson countered. *Do we institute programs when we have no idea of the data to be run? We do act on decisions based on partially assumed data—but to act on totally assumed data seems fraught with danger.*

Navtov signaled agreement. *We must, however, be careful. Population indexes show increased social turbulence. Sirius, in particular, reflects a seven point one percent increase in Health Department "adjustments." This is not the time for "risks."*

Robinson accessed the data. *I see. Higher than the general trends. I recommend you put pressure on the authorities to run down the ringleaders of the Sirian turbulence. This Ngen Van Chow's personality seems particularly deviant. Statistically, he lies at the edge of the behavioral curve. How have we missed him for so long?*

Navtov, having finally run all the permutations, added, *From your projections, I see a pronounced danger to society should the wild humans become common knowledge. Have you investigated the probability of their susceptibility to Directorate control?*

Robinson shunted the material to Navtov. *As you see, I believe the Patrol can successfully integrate them into the family of humanity. Given our economic superiority, we should be able to establish sufficient control of their resource procurement—primitive at the very best—and with our technology, Health Departments will be high on the acculturation list within the populace.*

Navtov did not respond immediately. Robinson queried with a *Yes?*

The question was so outlandish that Robinson's heartbeat changed for a second. *Suppose they have violent tendencies?*

Robinson sent a scathing reply. *Impossible! We are talking about* humans *here!* He broke the connection and returned to his data manipulation. Yet somehow, Navtov's nagging suggestion stuck in the back of his mind.

Violent? Humans? But that was past! Besides, what weapon could they possibly have that the Patrol didn't? Surely *Bullet,* with its ability to devastate entire planets, was more than a match for a few lost, barbaric humans . . . no matter how uncivilized they might be.

And Sirius? Skor Robinson studied the situation. They had a high potential for food riots. At the same time, Navtov was asking too many questions. Perhaps the time had come to reassert control over the Directorate. Let Sirius simmer for a while. Without leaving a trace in the system, Skor retracted the arrest warrant for Ngen Van Chow.

And, as to the wild humans, sterilization was always available as a last resort.

Leeta barely heard the door chime. "Doc?" Rita Sarsa's voice came through the comm. "Uh, look, I need to see you. It's urgent."

Leeta said dully, "Enter."

Sarsa, eyes sharp, took in every detail. "Come on, we're going for a walk."

Leeta shook her head, devastated by the news about Jeffray. "I don't feel like going for a walk, Lieutenant." Jeffray, dead? Just like that? Why? What could she have done differently? Guilt built, creeping through her like a frigid wind.

A firm hand clasped her shoulder, then Sarsa yanked Leeta up from the cot. Anger flared and she turned and snapped, *"I don't want to go for any walk, Lieutenant! Leave me alone!"*

Rita's face had gone stiff. Green eyes narrowed to slits. "Oh, it's just what you need, Doc. Remember the jerk in the bar back at university? You owe me one—and I'm collecting, *now!*"

The violence in Sarsa's voice pierced Leeta's stunned mind. She nodded mechanically, suddenly aware of the actinic glint in the lieutenant's eyes. "Sure, sure, Rita. It's only . . ."

"Shut up," Rita hissed and bent close, adding in a whisper, "Just keep chattering. Tell me how horrible it is that Jeffray killed himself. Act bereaved."

Leeta shut her mouth and regained some control of her composure, mind racing, stumbling, and racing again. She acquiesced to the grip on her arm and followed the Lieutenant through the hatch and out into what seemed a maze of random corridors.

"I don't understand," Leeta began, realizing she didn't need to fake shock. "Why Jeffray? It doesn't make sense. I didn't know! What could I have said? Done?" Her thoughts wheeled.

Rita was mumbling inane things like "that's life" and "it just happens."

With sudden clarity, Leeta asked, "Wait a minute!" She stopped dead in the hallway. "How did you know? That was a personal—"

Rita's hard face didn't thaw. "Trust me, Doc! *Just keep playing the game.*" she ordered through clenched teeth.

Leeta shook her head, following the lieutenant's firm lead down a narrow companionway. Rita palmed a thick lock plate and heavy metal doors slid back. Leeta bit her lip and glanced nervously into the dark. She was about to protest when an iron hand caught her arm and propelled her into the darkness.

Sudden fear shot through the guilt and pain. "Rita! I don't know what you're . . ." White light illuminated the irregular-shaped room, revealing gleaming equipment around a large, jutting projection device.

Sarsa stepped across and settled herself on the huge piece of machinery. One wall was rounded beyond the radius of the wire and cable wrapped length of the heavy device.

"Rita?" Leeta's heart beat staccato against her ribs. Her breath was short, fear beginning to tingle in her gut. "What is all this—"

The grim smile stopped her. Rita patted a shelf on the side of the machine. "Sorry about the cloak and dagger. Didn't mean to scare you, Doc. Come on and sit. This thing is a heavy blaster—capable of ripping university right in half.

"Remember? I told you we need to talk. Now is the time. Jeffray just forced it a little sooner than I expected."

Leeta settled herself unsteadily, wary at this change in the lieutenant. "I'm still lost. I can't understand . . ."

Rita nodded, pulling a muscular leg up to cradle a knee in laced fingers and leaning back. "This here," she waved around, "is called the gun deck. Right now all the monitors are off because I turned them off. We're here so we can talk in private."

Leeta frowned. "My room is monitored?"

"Hell, yes! *This is a warship for God's sake!*" Rita shook her head in tumbling red waves.

"And that's how you knew about Jeffray's call," Leeta supplied.

"Partially," Rita agreed with a quick nod. "In fact, I've been expecting something like it. That's why I jumped to get out of the meeting. Besides, Anthony up in comm cued me that you had an important message."

"But why?" Leeta was totally lost. "How could you—"

Sarsa put a hand on Leeta's shoulder. "Let me go back and give you some background. First, you say Jeffray changed after he went to the Health Department. Then you told me he was thinking about revolutionizing transduction—maybe even cutting the Gi-net out of the system. Next, we have a group of humans appearing out of nowhere. Humans outside Directorate control. Pretty heavy stuff, huh?"

Leeta lifted a shoulder, trying to fit the pieces together. Her brow tightened in a deep frown. "But how does that relate to Jeffray killing himself? What's that got to do with your suspicions? It just doesn't make—"

Rita chewed her lip. "Listen, you've lived within the system for a long time, Doc. What I'm about to tell you will sound farfetched—but I'm hardly a crack-pot. Believe me so far?"

Leeta considered what little she knew of Rita Sarsa. "All right."

"Good, 'cause what the Health Department did to Jeffray was to psych him. You know about that?"

Leeta's heart skipped a beat. "Psych? Like for criminals . . . for insane people?" No, not Jeffray! "Why? I don't—"

"He was *dangerous,* Leeta," Sarsa said in firm, well-modulated tones. "Oh, not violent or crazy—but dangerous because of his brilliance. The Directorate doesn't like people to threaten the Gi-net. They—"

"Threaten the Gi-Net?" Leeta exploded, jumping to her feet. "How could an innovation in transduction threaten the Gi-net?" She searched Rita's face.

The lieutenant crossed her arms resolutely. "By by-passing it. How the hell do you think those balloon-headed bastards keep the lid on all those trillions and trillions of people?" She cocked her head defiantly. "Look, you're the one with the brains, Doctor Dobra. *Think!* Put the data together. Jeffray, the Gi-net, all of it! Just take a moment and think about it."

Leeta opened her mouth to protest, then shut it as Sarsa raised an eyebrow in challenge. Academically, there was a certain logic to it. "But how do you know all this?" Leeta demanded, eyes narrowing as she tilted her chin back.

Rita's smile was sour. "I'm not a nice person, Doc." She raised a hand apologetically. "How do you think I got to be lieutenant so quickly? By intrigue, sabotage, cutting corners, rigging security systems, and beating the system at its own game. That's how!"

She leaned forward. "I got here because I was a rebel. They let people like me into the Patrol. Keeps us off the streets and away from "normal" people. Lets us fulfill our desires to roam and channels our deviance for the exclusive use of the Directorate."

"That doesn't tell me how you know all this . . . if you know it," Leeta added sullenly.

Rita turned, jaw thrust forward. "Oh, yes it does, Doc. I just gave you the whys and wherefores. You see, I broke into the security files when I was still a corporal. I know exactly what the Health Department does . . . and why. I know too much of the Director-ate's dirt.''

Leeta blinked incredulously. ''You . . . broke into . . . *the security files?*'' Stunned, she shook her head. ''That's . . . that's. . . .''

Sarsa's impish grin returned. ''Yeah, they'd psych me until every synapse in my head was fried.'' A shoulder lifted. ''Can't help it, Doc. That's just in my personality. In the Patrol, I'm partly safe.''

Rita gripped Dobra's shoulder. ''But you're not, Leeta.'' The eyes had frosted hard and green again. ''I got into the files at university, too.'' She pulled a flimsy from her pouch. ''There was a reason Emmanuel Chem was assigned at the last instant.''

Leeta, her senses stumbling, took the thin sheet and studied the instructions. The words blurred before her reeling vision. ''They . . . wanted me? Wanted me to come in to the Health Department for a statistical check? But . . . Jeffray . . .'' The implications over-whelmed her.

Rita took the flimsy from her numb fingers, care-fully ripping the fragile tissue into tiny strips. ''I'll dump that into the converter. I think Jeffray turned you in. That's part of psych. They leave that suggestion hidden in the subconscious. Jeffray must have thought you were a risk. Might be part of his suicide, too. Even if he didn't consciously know he'd condemned you, his subconscious did.''

''I . . .'' Leeta shivered uncontrollably. ''Lieuten-ant, this is too much. I mean, you expect me to think they let me walk out of university without checking out through the Health Department?''

''Not at all, Doc. More background here. I have a Patrol officer's security clearance. With that, I can do a lot of things . . . get access to a lot of places. Ac-cording to the record, Health psyched you and 'ad-justed' your behavior.'' She waved a freckled hand. ''Oh, there's a discrepancy in the system if anyone ever checks. When they do, I built a loop into the program that will take them a while to figure out.''

Rita pulled her around, face to face. ''Now comes

the hard part, Doc. I'm not sure you can ever go back.''

"What do you mean? *Can't go back?*" Leeta's thoughts clouded in confusion.

Rita sighed, slapping her thigh. "I don't know. Maybe you can. On one hand, it's obvious your records have been tampered with. I may not have done you any favors."

"Then why?" Leeta cried, on the verge of tears. *"Why are you messing with my life?"* She stared into Sarsa's eyes.

The answer came back, balanced, self-possessed. "Doctor Dobra, if you wish, you can always return, report to psych, and tell them who interfered and why. That's fine with me. I knew the risks when I took them. Only, let me know if those are your intentions because I'll need time to steal a ship and get the hell out of the Directorate."

Leeta realized that her throat was dry.

Sarsa continued, "On the other hand, this is a lot to dump on you cold like this. I can damn well believe you're upset—ready to deny it could ever happen—and turn me over to the nearest Directorate authority. Right?"

"Well . . ." Leeta floundered, thrown by the logic of it, unable to hate Rita Sarsa.

Rita's grin began to spread, "But I gambled anyway 'cause I liked you, Doc. Yeah, I thought you'd find your lost colony out here. I wanted to be part of it and I thought you were the best bet to get me into the middle of it. And I thought you'd want to tackle it with a free, sharp mind. Chem was sent in case psych destroyed your ability to serve the Directorate. Besides, if I'm wrong, you're still free to let the balloon-heads turn you into a vegetable."

"Thanks," Leeta rasped.

"Don't mention it." Sarsa's smile was back. "Uh, listen, I dropped a lot on you. Some of those claims are pretty outlandish—but take a while. Think about it. The final decision as to whether I'm right or wrong is up to you. I just need to know if I have to grab a fast ship out-bound when this Atlantis thing is over."

Leeta raised her hands helplessly. "I'll let you

know." She swallowed, fighting the dryness in her mouth. "Only, you know, I hate it, but I think I'm inclined to believe you."

Sarsa let a deep breath out, leaning her head back. "Yeah, I figured you could see past the indoctrination they beat into your mind through the years. I guess I decided I'd look after you that night in the bar."

"Why?" Leeta cocked her head, her brow creasing. "Why me?"

Sarsa's cheeks crinkled as her lips curled wistfully. "Because you dream, Leeta. Humanity needs that now. And . . . and my . . . husband taught me there is no greater gift in human existence than to dream."

Iron Eyes picked up horse tracks in the soft soil. Another and yet another set of tracks joined the first. He pulled up, wondering why Philip wasn't scanning the broken, rocky terrain around them for an ambush.

"Three here," Iron Eyes grunted, aware of the throbbing in his little finger. It had started to heal and itched as a consequence.

"Ours?" Philip wondered, voice neutral.

"Don't know," Iron Eyes answered. "Come, they will camp some place."

Philip studied his companion intently.

"What does it all mean?" Iron Eyes finally voiced the question that had been on his tongue for so long.

Philip drew a deep breath. "Our world is at an end, brother."

"You keep calling me brother." Iron Eyes let the mare—ears pricked at the smell of horses—take the trail again.

Philip, eyes on the rocks above, shrugged. "From the moment we met at the top of the Bear Mountains, John, we were tied more firmly than brothers. What we share now is deeper, closer, more important than any woman's womb, stronger than the blood that binds any father to his child."

"And what is that?" Iron Eyes scoffed, angry at the delay in finding the Santos, the power of his hatred fueling his driving pace.

Philip's voice touched a fiber in Iron Eyes' soul

when he said in an eerie whisper, "Destiny . . .
brother."

Iron Eyes bit his lip, his hard face turned to the
walls rising around them. Millennia of weather had
scoured the rock, rounding the jagged edges, smooth-
ing the cracks and faults. Corkbush, bayonet grass,
thornbush, and pole trees hung by tenuous roots over
the steep trail, drawing a precarious subsistence from
the dissected land.

Overhead, the sky shaded to a subtle green-blue
where patches of cloud didn't obscure it. The glint of
the second moon lay bright in the east.

"These others," Iron Eyes pursued. "They come
from Earth—where the Sobyets are?"

Philip motioned a negative. "Once. Now they are
from the stars." His voice lowered as he spoke hesitantly. "I . . . didn't see much in my vision, John
Smith. Only, I know they are like the People. They,
too, fled the Sobyets, you know, into space to avoid
the Red Star. Now, they have heard us . . . heard the
radio. So they come. . . ."

"But what will happen?" Iron Eyes cried. "Do we
fight them? Are they friends? What do we do?" He
raised balled fists to show his frustration.

Philip squeezed his eyes shut, wincing as if in pain.
"I saw . . . saw war. I saw flashes of purple light.
There were things whistling in the air. I saw horror
. . . flying . . . burning. There were . . . *things* I
couldn't understand. Odd things I cannot explain in
words . . . only in visions that—"

"But do we WIN?" Iron Eyes thundered in irritation.

Philip knotted his hands into bony fists, muscles
writhing up and down his arms. His jaw muscles quivered and jumped with emotion. *"You ask what not
even a Prophet would tell you!"* Philip raised his
hands, open now in supplication. "Do you never hear,
Iron Eyes? The ways of Prophets and warriors are different! Leave things alone until you decide your cusp!
Do not drive me to madness!"

Iron Eyes nodded, barely able to control his own
powerful emotions. "Very well, *brother,* I will hold
my tongue on this. Just make sure we reach the San-

tos. Once I kill Big Man, the Star Men can take care of themselves."

Philip's color drained as if a plug had been pulled. "That will be *your* decision, Iron Eyes. Unless I would will my soul to eternal madness, I can tell you no more—only I fear this obsession of yours. In your hands lie the People . . . and me. Spider alone knows if you are worthy."

Iron Eyes cocked his head, tendrils of worry beginning to work in his gut. "What do these odd words of yours mean, cousin?"

Philip closed his eyes the way a man in pain did. Lines had begun to form around his mouth and eyes, as if Philip Smith Iron Eyes had suddenly aged beyond his years. His jaw worked again, as he shook his head in firm negation.

Uneasily, Iron Eyes pushed his mare forward, seeing his relation's refusal to talk. "What madness is this?" he gritted through clenched teeth. "World is no longer sane!"

Eyes darting to the rocks, leery of ambush, they continued tracking.

A hoarse scream, a human scream, echoed faintly from the canyon walls, carrying a message of pain and terror. Iron Eyes pulled his horse up, the rifle sliding like magic into his hand.

"Walking into a Santos trap is the sign of a foolish man," Iron Eyes muttered warily. "Spider guard us!"

"They are Spider warriors," Philip said in a toneless voice.

"So?" Iron Eyes questioned, lifting an eyebrow as he studied the rocks ahead.

"I have seen my near future, Iron Eyes. It is not here where you will choose that I die or live. No, these men are Spiders." Philip slumped in depression.

"Another of your visions?" Iron Eyes glared angrily at the towering rocks.

Philip's muffled voice answered, "Yes. Within minutes, Friday Garcia Yellow Legs will peek over that boulder to see who we are."

"Then what was the scream?" Iron Eyes tightened his fingers on the carved wood of the rifle, happy to have some provable truth.

"A Santos scout the warriors have caught." Philip's expression was listless, as if he'd truly determined his death lay nearby and inescapable.

Iron Eyes caught the movement. He leveled the rifle on the boulder, seeing a head rise slowly above the edge of the rock. Behind the thin blade of the front sight, Friday Garcia Yellow Legs' face emerged—only to disappear a split second later as he caught sight of the rifle.

Iron Eyes lowered the heavy gun. "Friday! Come out! I know you."

There was a scuffling from behind the rock. This time the face appeared briefly to one side before jerking back.

"In Spider's holy name, John Smith Iron Eyes, you do not know *this* person," Friday's voice yipped.

Iron Eyes cocked his head, looking skeptically at Philip. "And how is that, Friday?"

"Because the Friday Yellow Legs you knew was a brave man!" came the cry. "This Friday Garcia Yellow Legs looked over a rock to see who came. Not much for a brave man . . . until he looked down the muzzle of such a huge rifle."

Iron Eyes chuckled. "And that makes you a different person?"

"Yes, warrior! The brave Friday Garcia Yellow Legs who you know would never have blown so much brown stinky stuff into his pants at the sight of that rifle like this coward, this Friday Garcia Yellow Legs, did!"

Iron Eyes laughed aloud in spite of himself. A glance at Philip showed his flaccid face unchanged, the eyes empty—as if this, too, were already known. A shiver of premonition touched Iron Eyes' spine.

One final proof. "And who was that who screamed, Friday?"

Friday Garcia Yellow Legs peered out from behind the rock again before scrambling out, satisfied that Iron Eyes' rifle was up. He was a short man, a huge spider effigy drawn on his war shirt. A single coup hung from his belt. Yellow Legs' chest seemed as wide as he was tall. On bowed legs, he trotted forward, shiny black braids flapping behind.

"After the Santos attacked so fiercely, we gathered

together to follow them. For many days we pushed into the mountains, following their tracks. Then, yesterday, we found a scout. Fool that he was, he tried to steal a horse from us. Men who would steal horses should know just how fast they can run first.'' Friday cocked his head. ''For a Santos, he is most strong. By rights, he should have died last night.''

A cold tightness gripped Iron Eyes, making it hard to breathe. He barely shot a look at Philip, knowing the truth would be reflected in his eyes. It had all been as his cousin had said.

Drawing on his anger to keep his courage from flagging, Iron Eyes nodded. ''Then we will catch the Santos. When we do, I will find the one who led them and kill this Big Man. Only when his blood runs on my blade will Jenny's ghost be freed!'' Anger flushed him with warmth and righteousness, driving the fear of Philip's words away like dust in the fall winds.

''No!'' Philip's whispered in agony. Iron Eyes turned to see his cousin blanch before being physically sick off the side of his horse.

Friday Garcia Yellow Legs, his normal sense of humor damped, stepped back and swallowed.

''What is it?'' Iron Eyes demanded hotly.

Philip straightened, wiping his mouth with a stained leather sleeve. His voice barely carried in the still air. ''You have just condemned me . . . and the People. *Condemned us to death!*''

CHAPTER VII

Leeta Dobra stopped Lieutenant Sarsa after a meeting held as *Bullet* moved into orbit over Atlantis. ''Listen. About our talk. I've given it considerable thought.'' She felt her frown deepening. Have to quit that, it would line her forehead. ''It's just that, well, what do

I do? If I can't go back, where do I go? I mean, well, I've worked all my life to become an anthropologist. A lifetime just can't be *thrown away!*"

Rita cocked her head, her eyes thoughtful. "No, Doc. It can't. But there's a whole world full of Romanans down there needing an anthropologist."

A rushing surge of enlightenment sent new life coursing through Leeta's veins. "Of course! So, I can live the dream after all."

Sarsa burst out laughing. "Now, you're cooking with antimatter, Doc!"

Atlantis filled the bridge screens. Ree decided it was a pretty place—and not all planets were pretty. This one called to him, as all Earthlike planets called to humankind. Something in the blood stirred the subconscious like a call from home. After all, a planet had been the original birthright of humanity.

"Sensor scans coming in, sir," a lieutenant called. Grudgingly, Ree turned from the screens to review the incoming data. At last, they had pictures of some of the larger animals. Only the horses and cattle were familiar, the rest were a completely alien assortment—odd things with two spines which made them look like they'd been glued together to form Siamese twins.

Data regarding the humans was coming in, too. All over the continent Montaldo had jokingly called Star, people moved. Small bands seemed to be migrating, some toward the wrecked remains of *Nicholai Romanan,* others seemingly threading their way to the east, toward the mountains and what lay beyond.

For days, the anthropologists had prattled on about the demographics of the Romanans—as they'd come to be called. Theories of migrations, livestock rotation, and a host of other concepts dredged from ancient studies flooded the conference room.

Ree watched, listened, and learned. At the same time, he'd managed to assemble a collection of early anthropological literature himself. He was lost when Leeta and the others talked about shamanism, rites of passage, kinship types, exogamy, social structure, and resource procurement. Damen Ree hadn't made Colonel by being lost. Now, if he could just find time to read the damn stuff!

For three days, the radio had sputtered off and on. There was more talk of horses, cattle health, and a cryptic reference to how many needed to be replaced. Replaced?

Ree frowned. Leeta Dobra—who had increasingly been on his mind—had seriously assured him "replacement" explained the radio snafu.

"Obviously!" she'd cried, animated for the first time in days. "That explains so much. We arrived on the tail end of a major ceremony! That's why they didn't use the radio. They were all congregated around the ship for the dancing and feasting. Now, all those people on the move are heading home!"

Sounded plausible. They'd checked and found an inordinate amount of smoke around the wreck of the *Nicholai Romanan*. It fit her theory. Besides, Ree caught himself grinning, he was drawn to Dr. Dobra. There was something about the way she moved that, well, tempted even an old warhorse like him. He chuckled to himself, intrigued at the thought that a woman could still attract his interest. Only she had been so withdrawn lately. Good to see her spirits rising.

He looked at the screen again and gave an order through his headset. The picture of horsemen appeared. It was one of the best shots they'd taken so far. Riding up a rocky, narrow defile in a mountain pass came ten, dark-skinned riders, eyes warily scanning the country they rode through.

Lithe men, some lightly bearded, others with literal bushes springing from their chins, they wore animal hides for clothing. Each face gazed hawklike at the world from under a fur hat. They were decorated with gaudy designs. Some had bits of hair hanging from their jackets or belts.

The long tube which he could see resting over one rider's saddle had been identified as a rifle. Ree ran his tongue around the inside of his mouth as he studied the gun. It was necessary, of course. They'd seen the huge predators. Big things with two tails and suction cups that shot out to grab their prey. By now, *Bullet's*

97

sophisticated cameras had picked up the scene of one of the dragon things eating a calf. Of course, they'd be armed. It was a hostile world. So what was bothering him about it?

There had been amazement when they found the two cannons that covered the Romanan main village. First there had been worried suggestions of warfare. Then they'd watched the big guns demolish one of the dragon things when it got too close. Solved *that* in a big hurry! No wonder they used cannons. Who'd want to get close to one of those things?

Ree squinted as he looked at the lead rider. What went on in that man's head? What did he think? How was he going to react when the first team of anthropologists showed up on his doorstep?

He snapped the picture off and checked the status displays, which showed *Bullet* running at top efficiency. Whatever the natives did wouldn't matter in the end. A group of dirty, hideously-dressed equestrians with rifles weren't about to cause more than a minor irritation to a fortress like *Bullet*. Hell, they didn't even fly—let alone have rocketry!

Even as he smirked to himself—callous in his superior strength—Ree remembered that lean-faced rider and felt a growing uneasiness in the back of his mind. The man wasn't the sort Ree would like to see Leeta Dobra around without an armed guard. He nodded to Antonia Reary as she relieved his watch.

Dinner—as a result of the anthropologists—had become somewhat ritualized for Ree. He genuinely enjoyed the company of these academicians. For the first time in years, talk centered on something besides the ship and patrol parameters.

Doctor Dobra had been different since that message had come in from Arcturus. The haggard look in her eyes touched him. She'd been wounded in a way Ree couldn't guess. The spark he'd recognized before that meeting had dimmed. Only during the last few days had Leeta appeared to be on the mend—spending much time in Sarsa's company.

No matter; she'd pitched into her work twice as hard. She was on top of everything—a good supervisor, very good indeed! Brains as well as looks—all the more reason to admire her.

Under pretext of protocol, he wangled the seating to sit next to her. As he lifted a glass of wine, his eyes lingered on the line of her jaw. "I would like you to know I have obtained a new series of books on your Indians."

She threw him an absent look and smiled. "Good reading?"

Ree allowed himself his most jovial laugh. "To tell you the truth, Doctor, I haven't had the time yet. I must admit, however, when we have finished here and get back to patrol, there will be enough time to earn a doctorate for myself."

"It's *that* boring?" she asked, thinking hard, as if correlating data.

Her mind wasn't on the conversation. "It is," he confirmed. "Your work seems so much more exciting. Tell me, what was your life like in university? Did you always have such fascinating data presented to you?" He cocked his head, keeping his features relaxed.

Leeta shrugged. "Not at all. I'm afraid there wasn't anything to compare with this project. We're making history here, Colonel."

"I was looking at the horsemen again." Ree paused. "What will you do if they are hostile?" Piercing, dark eyes burned in his memory.

Leeta laughed. "They won't be hostile to *us*. I imagine they will have lost the history of the Soviets, resistance, and being transported to the stars. If they do have a cultural memory, it's probably told in tales or myths. They'll perceive us as sky gods, no doubt."

Ree nodded thoughtfully. "Yes, I suppose, should it become necessary, we could throw lightning bolts on your command." His eyes met hers, seeing her amusement momentarily overcoming the hurt. "Will you instruct them to build you a palace?"

"Let them build a palace for Bella Vola." Her eyes hardened again. "I'm tired of being enshrined."

He could see the pain come flooding back. The tone in her voice told him all he needed to know. A man had caused her the pain. Ree made a note to his personal command computer through the tiny portable headset he wore. Inquiries would be discreetly made. There were advantages to commanding a ship of the line.

"Nevertheless, you are the one in charge. If these herders have gods, they are no doubt cows or horses," Ree joked. "I'm sure you'd make a more fetching addition to their temples. They might even shower you with gifts of gold and rare fruits." He could see she liked that. She laughed distractedly.

Ree changed his tone of voice. "Seriously, how do you propose to handle these people? Obviously, they can't be picked up from their rustic little planet and shot into the mainstream of galactic life."

Her gaze sharpened. Success! He had her attention.

"We'll have to establish a baseline cultural profile first, of course; but I'd like to see the planet quarantined somehow."

She looked up, suddenly nervous. "Don't get me wrong, I don't mean for our protection—but theirs! Think of it! They'd be such easy marks for everything. Why, before they'd got over the shock of seeing our people dropping from the sky, there would be a half million tourists trying to have their holos taken with a genuine savage!

"That's what I mean by quarantine." She frowned. "The other thing I would like to establish is a long-term research station. We have the opportunity to set up the first real anthropological observation center in five hundred years." Her voice grew husky. "Think of the work we can do . . . theories we can test."

Ree bit back his next words. Rather naive of such a brilliant scholar. Did she really think that university could lay claim to such a world as this? Only the Director had the ability to set aside an entire world.

"Are you going to cease sending information to the Gi-net?" Ree asked softly.

She gave him an irritated look. "Of course not! What sort of question is that?"

"S. Montaldo has found a toron deposit of remarkable purity on the northern continent. The information has already been sent out. Besides, you will change these people just by appearing among them. They will see results of the mining activity even though it is on a different continent. Also, there will be other things found here. Toron is enough of a justification to exploit the planet. There will be more." Ree met her startled gaze with his calm one.

"Of course, I'd forgotten that. Still, you're right. I wonder if we could explain what will happen to them—lessen the effects somehow."

"What if they don't want to be studied, to boot?" Ree was beginning to enjoy baiting her.

Leeta studied him, askance. "Why would they refuse when we tell them how important it is?"

"Would they refuse mining when the companies tell them how rich it will make them?" Ree countered.

"There is more to life than riches," Leeta retaliated. "I'm sure that people as uncorrupted as these will realize that. They haven't been bought or sold by anything yet." She raised her eyes to Ree's. "Are you always so cynical?"

He lifted his shoulders in a shrug. "I'm simply a military man. You're the expert on human societies. I was just wondering about the ramifications of these Romanans of yours. A much wider galaxy lies out here beyond university." He gave her his most innocent expression.

She paused, thinking hard, chin propped on her palm. "I guess as soon as we can establish an idea of who they are, we should make some plans to protect them. Keep them . . . well, they'd be fair game for any exploitation. The old literature is full of horror stories about negative acculturation. The things that were done were horrible. Plagues, warfare, genocide, exploitation, theft, rape, torture." She shuddered. "We'd—"

"I'm sure that is precisely the reason the Director assigned us to the project, Doctor." He patted her shoulder reassuringly. "We are here to make sure that the Romanans—and you—are not bothered until wiser heads can come to some conclusion as to the disposition of these people."

"If you will excuse me." She was glaring at him now.

"My pleasure, Doctor." Why the acid look? Unsettled, Ree sat back in his chair, sipping at the last of his wine. The image came to his mind of that warrior, his harsh face whipped by the wind. Hard to believe such a man would need protection. The final word was up to the experts—and, of course, whatever the Director decided.

Marty Bruk ran his fingers down Bella Vola's back as he stared up at the holograph dominating his wall. Bella's light breath on his arm, he watched the Romanan riders climbing the pass. To his skilled eye, they looked perfectly normal for planet-bound humans.

The affair with Bella had just happened. They'd barely known each other at university. He'd thought she was attractive, but he'd been involved with another woman: a drama student. Now he was here and so was Bella. It had turned out well.

In his mind, Marty pictured the outlines of the skull behind that grim face. The way the man rode his horse showed nothing of his stature, stride, or the relative length of arms in proportion to legs. The gravity of Atlantis was 1.15 Earth normal. Bruk didn't expect to find much difference from standard Terran phenotypes—except that these men would be heavier with slightly denser bones.

To hell with gross anatomy and stuffy indexes, Bruk thought. There were finer markers that called to him. What about the variations in DNA? What amino acids had been supplanted or changed? What microevolution keyed this population to a unique adaptation to Atlantis? Did they have resistance to certain diseases? In how many ways had the human body changed to meet this new world?

They would be different. He knew that deep inside. They would be far different from any other planet-bound human race. The station folk had become something new. There were as many variations in humanity as there were stations. Genetic drift, increased exposure to ionizing radiation, increased ligase releases in the DNA replication processes, all led to increased diversity—some of it manipulated by the people themselves.

Atlantis was different. It was pure—uncorrupted by

humans living in an artificial environment. Here nature changed humanity in the same ways as on prehistoric Earth. Here humans had been isolated whereas men on Earth, Zion, Sirius, Arpeggio, or any other place had been exposed to gene flow.

Constant genetic exchange throughout known human space invariably imported new traits and exported others, blending and mixing human biological heredity. Only on Atlantis where humans had been isolated for so long, could they find the perfect natural laboratory. Lost in his thoughts, Bruk had fogotten the woman who slept so easily on his arm. The holo continued to tantalize him as he sought to imagine the very structure of the riders' DNA.

Leeta struggled to keep her eyes open and her mind sharp. She'd couldn't even remember when she'd last slept. "How does it look?" She asked the bio-tech.

"Can't find a thing," the young man said. "As far as this department is concerned, you're free to go. You might get a bit of a congestion problem from that mycobacteria we isolated from the soil samples—but nothing that won't respond to a simple antibiotic."

"Excellent!" Leeta felt a flush of excitement vying with her fatigue. "That's the last hurdle; we'll go tomorrow."

She extended her thanks to the bio-techs and wound through the stark corridors to her room. From sheer exhaustion, she ripped her clothes off and scattered them around the room. A harmless form of rebellion—to hell with station manners!

"Sleep synch," she ordered the computer. The light touch of the headset caressed her brows. "Oh, Jeffray!" she moaned softly. "Why did you do this to me?"

She thought of Colonel Ree. The man's aim was obvious—and flattering. Still he was much too old. He definitely wasn't her type—and what if he found out the Health Department wanted to toast her brain? And who the hell was he trying to kid, anyway?

Only Sarsa and the demands of her own work lessened the burden Jeffray had dumped on her. No matter how she tried to justify it rationally, she couldn't help feeling guilty. Damn it, what was she supposed to have done? She couldn't just give up her life's work to care for him. Life was tough; she couldn't be responsible for those too weak to meet its needs.

But couldn't she have done something? The thought stung as she tossed and turned, conscious that she was fighting the sleep synch.

What could she have done? Half-frantic, she tried one more time to cope with the problem. "Damn you, Jeffray!" she hissed under her breath.

He had no right to make her feel this way. No right whatsoever—*and he'd turned her in to be psyched!* Maybe if she hadn't taken to sleeping with Veld for those few days? *No!* her mind shouted back angrily. What she did was her business!

Maybe if she'd just sat down with him and talked? Was there anything she could have said? Was there any way she could have bolstered his ego to keep him going?

"I didn't know you were so desperate," she whispered, feeling a growing sense of sorrow. "Damn you, Jeffray, I hate you now," she muttered under her breath. The realization startled her. The ultimate irony. The poor sap had wanted to hurt her, but in his usual bumbling way it was backfiring in his face! He'd forced her to hate him. Driven by guilt, she hated him. Hated the fact that he was robbing her of time she needed to concentrate on the Romanans. Hated the sentence he'd passed on her very mind. Even his last spiteful attempt to gain her sympathy was a failure. Pathetic jerk! God, how had she stayed with him so long? Frustrated, she yielded to the sleep synch.

Lieutenant Rita Sarsa blocked a deadly kick. Utilizing the energy imparted, she spun to hammer the robot hard in the neck. A man's cervical vertebrae would have been crushed instantly. The machine flopped to the floor in a gratifying heap. "Match point," the robot intoned.

Gasping for breath, Rita stretched her shoulders, grabbed a towel off the rack, and viciously scrubbed the perspiration from her face and neck. Workouts left her feeling totally alive. Rita held *Bullet's* female championship—a fact she took inordinate pride in.

She stripped and stepped into the showers, cool water cutting the stench of exertion from her body. At the same time, the lifting, euphoric feeling derived from a hard workout relaxed her.

Anthony, who worked in comm, was showering next to her. "You win?" he called.

"Barely, Tony." She grinned back at him. They'd had a brief affair once. While she liked the guy, he just didn't have the drive or strength she needed. As always, she'd ended up trying him, constantly competing. The relationship had gone sour real fast. Tony just nodded and walked out to pull on his uniform.

"Hey, Tony," she called softly. He turned. "Maybe dinner sometime after I'm finished with this assignment?" She cocked her head. "Nothing serious, you understand. Just a chance to talk, relax and set things straight."

He picked up her underlying desire for a truce. "Yeah, Lieutenant, sounds real good. I'd like that. We might be as compatible as snakes and birds, but I miss your spunk."

"Friends, huh?" Rita called.

He winked, nodded, waved and was gone.

She growled to herself and stepped out to dry. Since her husband's breakdown, her life had rocked from one tumultuous upheaval to another. Scared now, she tested the men she was attracted to to see if they, too, had some fatal flaw. To date, each had lacked some inner resource of spirit. Like Tony, they could be whipped and cowed too easily.

Maybe *she* needed psych. The thought sent a chill into her bones. The need for competition—as much as her disgust with the Directorate—had driven her to the Patrol. In three short years, she'd made lieutenant through her wits, craft, and cunning, despite the fact she was pitted against university graduates who'd taken Patrol training for years. But then they played by the rules—she didn't!

"Bitch, you're a sucker for challenge!" she snapped angrily, flipping wet red hair over her shoulder as her wry sense of humor took over. Checking herself in the mirror, she grinned. "And the tougher the better. Now, sweetheart, you're off to shepherd a bunch of lily-livered anthropologists! Jesus! Thanks, Colonel!"

Rita dressed and checked to see that all her equipment was ready to be sent planetside. She hurried to meet the scientists. So what was she going to do about Leeta? The woman was under her wing now. And did she have a fatal flaw that would break her? The specter of court-martial, psych—or a death sentence—loomed in Rita's fertile imagination.

"Gotta catch me first," she mumbled out the side of her mouth. "Damn Directorate, anyway."

"Good day, Lieutenant," Leeta greeted—and winked! There was excitement in those blue eyes, real animation. So maybe Doc had passed the hump?

"Your things have been placed in the shuttle as you requested." Rita smiled, hating herself for it. "We're ready as soon as you can assemble your personnel."

"Excellent," Leeta triggered the headset and requested the landing party to meet on the shuttle deck.

"Come on, Doc, I'll give you the guided tour."

Impressed by the shuttle, Leeta smiled eagerly. Cradled in the huge gantry hooks, the craft waited, needlelike at the nose, tapering back to four stubby wings, terminating in nasty-looking fusion rockets. Dobra's interest was obvious.

"Like it, huh?" Rita propped fists on her hips.

"Why fusion?" Leeta asked, turning.

"Simple. Hydrogen can be found anywhere. Fusion doesn't require the heavy stasis fields used for anti-matter reactors. Further, it doesn't take such careful monitoring or as much computer support. Even with as high as a 90% computer and electrical failure, a person can fly this baby. Doc, you yourself could pilot it back to *Bullet*," Rita explained as she pulled a suit from a locker and began to press it onto her body. It fit like a second skin.

"What's that?" Leeta asked. "Do I need to put one on, too?"

Rita shook her head and grinned. "I don't think so, Doctor. You wouldn't have the first idea of how to use this stuff. This is combat armor."

"Rita, I really don't think it's necessary," Leeta

said uncomfortably. "These are primitives; they have rifles and two awkward cannons."

"Trust me. Don't worry. This is routine for any preliminary reconnaissance. The only nonroutine thing is that you aren't required to wear a suit, too."

Leeta's mouth screwed up and she shrugged.

"Ready?"

Rita swung up to the lock. Dobra hesitated, surprised to find Professor Chem. "You can't go, Emmanuel!" Leeta exclaimed. "It would kill you!"

His face broke into a warm smile at her words. "No, Leeta." His voice was soft, husky. "I just came to wish you well. You're headed for grand things. I only wish I were a little younger." There was pain in his voice.

The old man nodded faintly. The soft brown eyes were misty as he straightened himself and moved out of the lock. He was slow, precise, his body all angles with a stooped, deliberate ungainliness.

Leeta muttered under her breath, "Hope he doesn't turn into another basket case like Jeffray."

"Worry about it later—if it happens," Rita grunted for Dobra's ears only. She checked the crash harness worn by each scientist. Wonder of wonders, they seemed to have gotten it right.

The headset chimed in as the communications links were checked. Rita listened to the routine clearances from pilot and bridge. The hatch dogged shut and she barely sensed movement as the shuttle was thrust from the ship and sent spiraling toward the planet.

She studied Doc Dobra where she lay in the crash webbing, eyes glued to the monitor that showed Atlantis spinning beneath, cut through one quarter by the terminator. Yeah, she was coming out of it, accepting reality, ready to go. Good choice back at university! Score one for the red rebel!

The descent took less than twenty minutes. Atmosphere was felt as a ragged vibration; then the rush of air could be heard. In spite of herself, Rita felt a tingle of excitement. If only she didn't have to hang around!

They had decided to land on the open plain east of the mountain range and to the southeast of the *Nicholai Romanan*. The village would be less than an hour's ride in aircars and their position gave equal access to what appeared to be the two biggest outlying tribes.

As the shuttle touched down, the pilot's voice rang out. "No sign of humans or any of the larger native life. Disembark at your discretion."

"Let's go!" Leeta ordered as the hatch opened and the antigrav lift deployed itself.

Rita slung her blaster over her shoulder and beat Leeta Dobra to the door. She could see the excitement on the woman's face. "Excuse me, Doctor," she said easily. "I don't want to steal your thunder, but me first."

Leeta swallowed, annoyed, then nodded reluctantly. "After you, Lieutenant."

Rita stepped into the drop and led her fifteen marines to the ground. She snapped out orders and watched with approval as they secured a perimeter.

Leeta stepped into the lift and dropped lightly to the ground. She stumbled and almost fell as she stepped out of the antigrav tube and real gravity caught her off guard.

Rita motioned the privates to break out the equipment where the shuttle bay doors were opening. She took sensual pleasure in the fresh, sweet air. A wild, free scent permeated the breeze. It reeked of life, of grass, dirt, dust, and the musky odor of decay, hinting of moisture, warmth, and vigor.

"Wonderful," she heard Vola breathe behind her. "Marty, it's too bad we have to work." She gasped a romantic sigh that irritated something deep inside Rita Sarsa.

Rita hollered to her marines. "I want the camp established. Hop to it, we're not here to lollygag. Let's go, people!" Under Sarsa's supervision, they were more adept than the scientists. Models of efficiency, Rita's marines built the base in minutes. It was as if they had done this a thousand times before.

The shadows and the changing position of the sun were spooky phenomena. How long had it been since she'd seen an open sky? Not only that, there was sound here. To be sure, there was always sound in a station or on ship. But this was different. Instead of the hum of machinery, she heard a constant rustle of wind, grass, and small creatures. Wild, untamed vitality surrounded her! It called to some unsettled element of Rita's troubled mind.

"Maybe we've missed something in the stations," Leeta said absently as she paused to stand beside Rita and stare at the rolling grasslands.

Rita shrugged, though the doctor's words seemed to parallel her own thoughts. "There aren't that many habitable planets. The station-bred are happy. They wonder how the rest of humanity can stand to live without their sense of community. Humans judge reality by what they know of it."

She hesitated, then added in a cynical tone, "I knew a boy who'd lived all his life in stations. He'd worked in the lowest levels of Arcturus as a diplomatic envoy like his father. As a result, he was more than used to the gravity, being familiar with everything from zero g to 1.6. He was a very agile and graceful man. He also had an insatiable desire to set foot on a planet." Sarsa smiled softly to herself, remembering.

"What happened to him?" Leeta asked curiously.

Rita allowed herself a wry smile. "Oh, he got his chance. He wanted to go out and sleep under the stars on Earth. He'd arrived at night and of course his wish was granted. The only problem was when he awoke the next morning and looked around, he went quite mad."

She looked at Leeta as if to impart the seriousness of the story. "You see, Doc, he'd never seen an open sky before. He was suddenly unprotected. The psychs were very good, but he was never really the same."

"You seem to have known him well," Leeta said as she took another breath of the warm, humid air and enjoyed the spectacle of sunshine.

"I did," Sarsa replied carefully. "He was my husband, Doc." At that, she walked off to the perimeter of the camp, looking out over the empty plain, carefully cradling the long shoulder blaster in her arms. After so many years, none of the pain had eroded.

Leeta bit her lip, seeing the hurt in Sarsa's eyes. So that was the secret? Rita's husband had dreamed—and it destroyed him. And that memory, or some perceived guilt, drove Sarsa's rebellion?

Her heart went out to the solitary figure at the edge of the perimeter. Biting her lip, she turned back to the laboratory dome, attending to the installation of equipment, comm relays, and the crates of supplies they would live off of.

On the wall, Bruk had already projected that well known portrait of the horsemen and the mountains. Leeta let her thoughts stray to it, seeing the vitality behind those dark eyes. They betrayed passionate strength. They seemed strong men, men who wouldn't break. Men like those who had always filled her dreams.

Staring at the lead rider, she imagined her fingers tracing the line of his hard jaw. A man like that wouldn't leave her to feel guilt and misery. He wouldn't leave her to remember his weakness or defeat. His memory wouldn't hound her.

She shot another quick look at the holo and went to check the living quarters. All the time, she was aware of the planet beyond the dome, beckoning, singing in a subtle siren's song. Chiming over and over again, "Here I am, come and let me take your measure, star woman."

"And here I am," Leeta whispered back. "I have my dream, and nothing left to lose by living it. Take your best shot!"

CHAPTER VIII

Chester Armijo Garcia pushed his pony up the last ridge and looked out over the brown, grassy flat toward the star camp. He could see the sky-thing, slim nose pointed at the deep blue of the heavens. The low, earth-colored dome blended well with the tones of dirt, grass, and rock. He nodded. It was as it should be.

He pressed his heels against the gelding's ribs and

felt the animal move forward obediently. He'd taken a great deal of pride in the training of his horse. An amusing notion, pride. A selfish braggadocio—meaningless—as he'd been brought to see.

They were watching him now. They'd known of him for some time; he was certain of that. The vision assured him they would know of his presence. The gelding stumbled slightly, tired from the long ride. He was sorry for that, but it didn't matter. This was his last ride.

He could see them. They were walking out from the dome, maybe six star people. As he drew closer, he could see gadgets, instruments, and ordinary binoculars in their hands. Ah! There was the straw-haired woman! She would be so important!

Less than a hundred meters now. Chester pulled up on the reins; the gelding watched the star people with pricked ears, no doubt wondering if they would provide him with grass and a cool drink. Horses were that way.

Armijo Garcia swung off the gelding and dropped lightly to his feet. He raised his hands in the sign of friendship to show that he carried no weapon. He knew they wouldn't shoot, but it was mannerly—even for a Prophet.

Leading the horse, he walked toward the two women who stepped out. The rest hung back. "Welcome to World!" He shouted a greeting. One of the women, the dark-haired one, studied a box in her hands.

"Greetings." The box surprised him with its toneless voice.

Chester shrugged. "I am here. I follow the vision." The box spoke to the women in what must have been their language. With a flash of insight, he realized they did not speak the language of men! The vision had not shown him that. What else had the vision forgotten? The last shreds of the man he had once been urged him to leave.

No matter, he was committed now. He stripped off the saddle and let it drop to the ground. The box was speaking to him, but he ignored the words. They didn't matter.

"Home!" he said softly into the gelding's ear, hugging the muscular neck, feeling his love for the animal. "I shall miss you, my dear friend. We must each do as we were fated. Go! Home!" He slapped the animal on the rump and watched the gelding trot, then canter, out into the grass. The horse stopped a few hundred meters away, threw a look over his shoulder, and began to crop the dry grass, unconcerned.

Aching with sadness, Chester turned, picked up his rifle and threw the saddle over his shoulder. He nodded seriously as he walked past the surprised women and headed for the camp.

"Wait!" the box hollered at him. "Where are you going?"

Chester pointed with his chin. "To your camp. There are wires you wish to stick to my body. There are machines which will draw my insides and read the tracks in my blood. I have come as the vision foretold. Did not your Prophets tell you of this?" He could see the consternation as he walked past them.

The fire-haired woman's uneasy eyes were on his rifle. They might not speak the tongue of man, but he could read her concern. Without a word, he pulled the rifle from the scabbard and handed it, butt first, to the woman. Her mouth was open as she took the heavy weapon.

They were tagging along behind, the box still squawking questions at him. He ignored it; he knew where he was going. Inside his head, he could see the way the dome was arranged. The big, black-haired man was all curiosity as he came close. Armijo Garcia could feel the fellow's eyes trying to see into his very body.

He threw the black-haired man a big smile. "At last we meet, man-who-plays-with-bones. I am here. You may begin to learn me now. The women with questions may ask with their box while you see my body with your machines. It will take a while to teach them to talk like a human being. Now I will listen." So saying, he dropped the saddle and packs to the side of the door and strode through the entranceway. The bone man's eyes widened.

Chester was inside before they knew what he was doing. Guards, caught by surprise, were quick to follow him. Pandemonium raged as he looked around and stepped in front of the machine he had seen in the vision. With no more explanation, Chester sat in the seat and began to take his clothes off.

Chattering star people poured through the door in a frantic rush. The blonde woman was talking and gesturing at him in her own language. Guards fingered things at their belts that had to be weapons and looked uneasily from him to the red-haired woman he'd given his rifle to. The big, black-haired man saw where he'd seated himself and his eyes lit up—damping only when he shot a quick glance at the blonde woman. Surreptitiously, the black-haired man began doing things with the machine, sliding cautious looks at the blonde woman.

"Enough!" Chester ordered imperiously, raising a hand and bringing the tumult to a stop. The dark-haired woman listened to her box and muttered to the blonde woman.

The blonde woman took a deep breath and shook her head as she spoke. "Who are you?" the box translated.

"I am Chester Armijo Garcia, Prophet of the People. I have come. You wish to know me and my People. I have come to go with you to the big ship that floats in space. I have come to go to the place far away in the stars. It is the way. I have seen this in the vision. So have the Four Old Men. I do not know why I was chosen—but I am honored to serve my People."

"How you know we *** here?" The blonde woman insisted. "No one saw us *** here! Our *** showed the *** empty! Do you have a *** of ***?"

"Your machine does not speak well," Chester said politely.

"It takes time to learn. We have only had the radio transmissions." The blonde's eyes were puzzled. "Did you see us come here with a seeing radio?"

Chester smiled at them. "Our radio only talks. It does not see. I saw where you would come in the vision. I have traveled many days to find you here."

"Impossible!" he heard through the translator. They were talking to each other and had forgotten the box would translate.

"They had to have had some sort of *** that followed our ****!"

"Can't be!" The redhead was shaking her head negatively. She'd been whispering into a little box at her waist. "Ship reports no *** of our arrival. Further, they have tracked this man's progress. He was headed here—straight line from the mountains—for two days before our arrival."

All eyes shifted to Chester's face. The blonde still looked puzzled—unable to believe. "You say you knew we would come here, this very spot?"

Chester yawned and nodded agreement. Why were these people so concerned? To see the future was such a simple matter.

Most of the words they used to speak to each other didn't translate well into the words the machine used.

The black-haired man was ignoring them, running his machine while he looked excitedly at the picture box before him. It was time for him to put the wire on Chester's wrist. As in the vision, he reached out his left hand as the black-haired man pasted the wire thing to his skin. Only after the man was done, did he look uncertainly at Chester and swallow hard.

"How you know to do that?" he asked, frowning as he studied the readout from his machine.

"It was in the vision." Chester smiled. "Just like when the wind blows the metal pole over tomorrow. Just like when the three white ships fight in the sky. I will see the man with the big head, too. This I will do for the sake of my People."

"Babble!" The blonde said, mouth tight.

"Who are you?" Chester asked, raising his finger to point at the blonde woman. "I would know you. You are very important."

"I am Leeta Dobra," she introduced herself. "We have all come a long way through the stars to study your People. We hadn't quite thought to study you so soon, though. I must say you have surprised us very much."

"Yes. There was no reason to waste the time. Tell the red-haired warrior woman that I will not attempt to run away and she does not need to worry about me stealing her fighting rifle. Also, I will not try and get

114

into the ship without her permission." Chester nodded seriously at the shocked, red-haired woman.

Such interesting people! They had *women* warriors. "Warrior woman, have you many coups?"

"I'm Lieutenant Sarsa, Chester. You are free to go any time you please. What makes you think I have a fighting rifle? Further, how did you know I was worried about the ***?"

"He didn't get ***," the black-haired woman with the box told her. "Try ship instead."

Sarsa's wary eyes flicked back and forth from the black-haired woman to Chester. "I'm not sure I like this." Her eyes bored into Chester's. "Do you read tracks of minds?" the box asked in close translation.

"No. I see things that come in the future. I can see important things in the past." He looked at Dobra. "Like the man who killed himself when you left him. He was not worth the pain you suffer. It is pulling your life apart like bear does a young calf. The weak are meant to die. Ask this one." Chester ignored the ashen shock in Leeta's face and pointed at the black-haired, bearded man who was staring at Dobra.

The black-haired man was swallowing nervously; at the same time his eyes glowed with interest. Chester could see he wished to say something—but feared Leeta's reaction. The man nodded slightly in agreement.

"How could you. . . ?" Leeta Dobra's voice was strangling. Her hand clutched at the base of her throat, eyes bright with fear as she began to shake. "My God!" she cried, distraught, and ran from the dome.

Chester shook his head sadly. "I am sorry," he whispered. "I have not been a Prophet long. I still have much to learn. I did not wish to bring her pain. There is so much that comes and so little time to see through it all."

Wide, shocked eyes stared at him. The black-haired man wasn't even watching the picture box on his machine. Chester could see the pulses racing at the bases of their necks. He'd frightened them all. Odd, the vision hadn't shown him this. Indeed! What else hadn't he foreseen? The thought was sobering!

* * *

"They've got to have subspace transduction!" Leeta spat as she paced the conference room. Worry-lined faces peered up at her. "That's the *only* way they could have known about . . . Jeffray!" She still hesitated to mention his name.

"He knew exactly what I was thinking about security," Rita muttered wearily.

Leeta took a deep breath. "Lucky guess!" She sat on the corner of the table. "Look! If you were in another man's space port, what would you do? Put yourself in his place! It's just a logical deduction to keep us off balance!"

"Then who's studying who?" Bella Vola asked, running her fingers through her dark hair and glancing at Leeta.

"Brain function's different," Marty Bruk added. "He was sitting right in front of the REMCAT. The holos of the guy's brain are *different*. The entire brain images. The corpus callosum is four times larger than in a normal brain. The Fissure of Rolando, the Fissure of Silvius, the Parieto-occipital Fissure and the others are shaped differently, giving the lobes a unique morphology. The right brain in particular almost overwhelms the left when he's thinking about his visions.

"The readouts on the energy utilizations in IR and wave production are phenomenal. I repeat, the entire brain images on the monitor. It's like every nerve is sending and receiving at the same time. Oughtta be hopelessly schizophrenic—hebephrenic at best. He should lock up physically and emotionally—but he doesn't. He sits there calm as can be. You *saw* that!" Bruk was half out of his chair with excitement.

"But *prescience?*" Leeta Dobra shook her head vehemently.

"Nostradamus," Netta Solare whispered. "According to the literature, the Arapahos claimed their shamans could see the future. They claim to have foreseen air travel, peace with the whites, all kinds of things. Maybe the Prophets didn't die before they went to the reservation? Maybe we're seeing their shaman here, live, before us?"

"They never proved Nostradamus!" Lieutenant Sarsa scowled.

116

"Awful lot of coincidence," Solare lifted an eyebrow.

"So," Leeta held up a hand, "what do we tell Damen Ree and Emmanuel Chem? Do we get on the comm and say, 'Hey, guess what? These guys see the future in their heads. They know what we're going to do before we think of it!' Give the ramifications some thought. Consider all we know about reality, physics, and human psychology. If Romanans see the future . . . the whole damn apple cart is upset."

They were silent.

Rita Sarsa looked up, face pale. Her usually cynical voice subdued, she said, "I was thinking about what would happen if he got a hold of my rifle just when he said that."

"Oh! Come on!" Leeta gasped and lifted her hands.

"How did he know about Jeffray?" Marty Bruk asked, eyes down. "If they had a receiver for subspace transduction, why didn't they build a transmitter?"

"It's not that easy." Leeta shook her head. "They'd have to have a big power source. Takes a lot of energy to separate iota particles and bounce them to rega shift. Then they'd have to funnel the rega particle mass signal 'outside.' They'd need to direct it, too. No telling what it would do to global tectonics if they shot mass waves randomly about. We'd see the antennas somewhere. You can bet Ree didn't miss them."

"Then you just defeated your own arguments, Doctor." He was watching her coldly, professionally.

"They had to have received some sort of signal from Veld. They had to. *There is no other explanation!*" Leeta almost pleaded.

"Maybe they do read minds." Bruk shrugged. "That's at least physiologically possible. With enhancement, brain waves can be transmitted. Maybe these guys have an adaptation that makes them sensitive?"

"If I have to accept psychic phenomena, I like that better than prescience," Leeta agreed with a sigh. She walked to the dispenser and poured a cup of coffee.

"Doc," Rita caught her eye. "We're overdue to report to *Bullet*. Military requirements demand some kind of statement."

Leeta nodded, more to herself than anyone else. "I know. Send the physical information Marty picked up. We also have the analysis from the gun and the saddle. That's something. There ought to be enough data to keep Emmanuel busy for the time being. At the same time, ask Colonel Ree for a thorough scan of the entire globe. There just might be a power source somewhere."

"Got it, Doc." Rita stood and followed Leeta out, as the others exploded in a sudden babble of conversation. She gave Dobra a serious look. "He hit you pretty hard didn't he?" she asked softly.

Leeta clenched a fist. *"How in God's name did he know?"* Her voice hissed passionately.

Rita's cool green eyes narrowed. "In there," she shrugged a shoulder at the conference room, "I heard an allegation that we might not be the only ones doing the studying. I'm not much of a scientist, Doc. But from a military perspective, it always helps to keep your opponent off balance." With that she brushed past, throwing a quick glance at the guards around Chester Garcia's quarters.

Leeta felt her heart racing in her chest. An urge to cry built deep inside. She felt her lip start to tremble and bit it until the pain overshadowed her emotions.

How had something so grand suddenly gone so wrong? What else could she have done? Why was it all falling apart? What more could she do? Wait for the damn observation tower to blow over in the wind? Garcia had predicted that. Rita had had her men check the tower. It was fine. There was a guard on it to make sure no one fooled with it.

Rubbing her eyes, Leeta allowed herself to file the report and proceeded to bed. The sleep synch put her out like a light. Even with the computer stimulation, nightmares writhed just beneath her dreams.

Bella Vola worked up tests the following morning. By noon there was no doubt. Chester Armijo Garcia was running 100% accuracy on double blind, triple blind, and random comm generated tests. He did so with no anxiety and no fuss. At the same time, Bella Vola was picking up his vocabulary with little difficulty and making her notes. Marty Bruk had Garcia completely measured, probed, typed and indexed.

A little after noon, a dust devil tore through camp and blew the tower down. As objectively as possible, Leeta composed her report . . . and hesitated. The sun was slanting into the west. Feeling like a trapped animal, she locked the first one away and filed a noncommittal report. When she went to sleep, she took the Romanan language course the computer had milked Garcia for.

"Lieutenant!" Leeta called across the compound the next morning. "Let's take a scout. I'm about to go mad and I need some space. I want to get away and think about this. Too much is happening too fast."

Rita nodded soberly. "Think we ought to ask Garcia first?" Her tone was dry.

Leeta closed her eyes and took a deep breath. "No. If this is going to be a disaster—I don't want to know!"

They were in the air before Rita turned and asked, "You still haven't told Ree or Chem, Doc. I've stored a report on everything—just in case."

Leeta was seated, eyes closed, enjoying the momentary rush of air through her hair. An entirely new vocabulary ran through her brain. She opened her eyes and named the six-legged green thing that was vacuuming up the grass. Harvester it was called.

She gazed out over the western horizon. Out there was a settlement of the People. A place that was strange, sinister now, while at the same time so tantalizing. They'd barely scratched the surface with Garcia. They didn't know anything about the People. According to Garcia, only a very few were ever gifted with Prophet powers.

"These Prophets change everything," she admitted. "I still can't believe it, Rita. I mean, it seems to be so, but I can't accept it way down inside."

As they skimmed over one of the bears, Leeta gave it only passing glance, preoccupied with her thoughts.

The lieutenant shrugged. "You know, I'm not even sure I ought to keep a guard on him. If he can see the future, how can you keep him prisoner? Worse, what's the point of doing anything anymore? How can you gamble if someone knows the outcome? Think of the ramifications! We're got to tell the Colonel soon. This is a lot bigger than you or I, Doc.''

Leeta nodded, staring out over the vast golden brown plains. She could smell the dust, the dry grass, the very odor of the planet. In the distance, brown turned to deep purple as the overthrust plain dipped toward the far eastern sea.

Her whole project would be gone then. They'd send in others. Government types, psychologists, the military, physicists. The entire academic community. They might even interdict the planet! Colonel Ree could yank her clear out of the game. Pack up, pull the entire expedition, and space for Arcturus P.D.Q.

Then where would Leeta Dobra be? Under the psych machine in the Health Department? And Rita? Running for her life in a stolen space ship? Could she stand to watch the entire project fold because of one prescient shaman? There was too much here! She felt tears of rage building. The whole culture must be fascinating! Think of social evolution under the guidance of all-knowing mystics! What wondrous twists did the People take?

''I think we ought to send Garcia up to the ship,'' Leeta said at last. It was a chance. It would take Ree time to assure himself that Garcia could do all they claimed. Further, she could pawn the whole problem off on Chem. The old buzzard would get wrapped up in Garcia and forget Leeta's crew existed. In the meantime, her team could get on with the investigation of the overall culture. Brilliant!

''What about security?'' Sarsa asked.

''Doesn't a ship with *Bullet's* resources have a super jail facility?''

''You mean a brig. Yes.'' Rita Sarsa nodded.

''I'm not one to run from a problem, but why don't we let Ree decide. He's your superior. Chem is technically mine. I think you're right. This has gotten too big for us.''

Leeta saw Sarsa grin wickedly in agreement. ''I think that's the safest bet for all concerned. It covers us, *Bullet,* university, the Romanans, everyone.'' Sarsa nodded. ''And we're free for a while, Doc.''

Leeta grinned to herself as she enjoyed the color of

the landscape flashing past beneath them while Rita made the long circle back to camp.

"I know it sounds crazy, sir." Leeta remained steadfast as she stared into the disbelieving eyes of Colonel Ree and Emmanuel Chem. That's why we're sending him up to *Bullet*. We want our observations confirmed by a second party. We didn't believe it. Emotionally, we still don't. This is big; we think it's out of our hands. Given the stakes, we feel justified in dumping it in your laps."

Ree began to chuckle. "I like your style, Doctor. Very well, send him up."

"Doctor Dobra," Chem growled to clear his throat. "I have placed a lot of trust in you. This is a very serious project. I would be severely disappointed if this . . . *prescience,* turns out to be a lark of yours." She could feel his stare burning into her. Just as it had when she was an undergraduate, her mouth turned dry.

"I assure you, Doctor," Lieutenant Sarsa interrupted in a whipcord voice, "we're as serious as you are. I may not be trained in anthropology, but I am capable as an observer, strategist, and tactician. From a military point of view, we *might* have been duped by some clever tricks we don't understand. Nevertheless, we can't find out how he's doing it. You have better resources at your disposal, Doctor. We're *not* engaged in a *lark!"*

Leeta appreciated the stiff, insulted look Sarsa gave the professor. It made him back down quickly. He just nodded, saying no more.

"Send him up," Ree repeated. "We'll run him through his paces and see—"

"I'm sending the data along, too," Leeta added. "I suggest that you keep it a closed file until such time as you draw your own conclusions. After you have exhausted your means, a thorough inspection can be given to our material. That will provide two entirely autonomous bodies of data for review." It buys me more time, too! Leeta crowed to herself.

Chester Armijo Garcia showed no change of expression as he walked up to the grav lift.

"It will lift you like magic," Leeta said softly. "Do not fear, you won't fall. You can't. Once you're in the field, you can't get out. Don't be afraid! You'll be fine.''

"I know." He nodded. "This part I have not seen, but I know I make it to the big place in the stars. I have seen the future. I am not afraid." So saying, he set foot inside, almost fell over, and pulled himself into the grav chute.

Leeta hid her amusement as she watched Garcia's face contort as he was lifted from the ground. Turning, she ran for the shelter of the dome.

The roaring whistle of the shuttle drowned out everything as it lifted for *Bullet*. As the high pitch dwindled, Bruk put an arm around Bella Vola. "You know, in spite of the problems that boy gave us, I'm going to miss him. It's dull already."

"He was a very pleasant sort," Netta said with a wispy smile. "He was so mannerly. I never had a subject so ready and willing to be helpful."

Leeta flicked on a holo of the terrain to the north. "We'll see him again. In the meantime, there's a party of men here, 90k to the northwest. They have a small village. I suggest we contact them first and see if we can't gain some sort of idea as to the native attitudes before we hit the main village where the wreckage of the *Nicholai Romanan* is."

Leeta could see a flicker of changing expression on Rita Sarsa's face; the imp grin was growing.

As they flew north the following morning, Rita's eyes twinkled. "So? Rebellion's catching, huh, Doc?"

Leeta met the grin with one of her own. "Let's just say I think the time has come to take destiny into my own hands."

"Nice trick with Chester," Rita added under her breath so Solare wouldn't hear. "You bought us time."

Leeta spotted a small boy herding horses. Sarsa set her passengers down on the opposite side of the ridge. Netta had been abnormally silent during the flight. Now, without a word, she followed Leeta to the top of the ridge. Leeta waved at the boy. He saw them, turned his horse, and rode over, pulling up and watching them silently from fifteen meters.

Thin-faced, mahogany-skinned, his long hair hung over his shoulders to be teased by the wind. Crosses in blue and red adorned the hem of his tuniclike shirt while soft, calfskin footgear went up to his knees. The obsidian eyes looked reserved and no change of expression touched those dark lips.

"Greetings," Leeta called out in Romanan, throwing him a huge smile. "What can you tell me about your village? Who is headman? Do you have a Prophet? We are stangers from far away. We would trade with your people."

The youth—no more than thirteen, Leeta guessed—scowled. "What is your clan?" he asked, now obviously nervous.

"A faraway clan," Leeta smiled. "I told you, we are new to this country. We would talk to your headman about trade."

"You have horses?" he asked, hand resting on his knife as he looked at the surrounding hills as if searching for Leeta's companions.

"Where are your men?" he demanded suddenly. "I don't see any ***."

Despite his growing suspicion, Leeta continued to smile. Her linguistic training hadn't included the word the boy used.

"What is the name of your People?" Netta Solare asked.

"We are called Santos." The boy pulled himself upright, proud. "Our name for God is Haysoos. He is a man, not a spider."

"Christians!" Solare shot a whisper to Leeta.

"Wait!" the boy decided suddenly, a curious, dancing light in his eyes. "I will bring . . . traders." He kicked the horse in the ribs and pounded off over the hill that led to the village.

Rita Sarsa topped the ridge in the aircar. "Doc," she called. "Transmission from Colonel Ree. He says you might want to return to the base camp."

"What?" Leeta asked sourly. "Not now! We're about to make contact."

"The Colonel thinks he might have a clue to one of the words we've been wondering about. He also has some new information from Chester Garcia. He requests that we get everyone together for a conference."

Leeta took a deep breath, pulled out her belt comm, and pushed the send button. "Colonel Ree?"

"Here come the Santos," Netta called excitedly.

"Doctor Dobra?" Ree's voice asked.

"Give me fifteen minutes and I'll call back, sir," Leeta said quickly and shut the comm off. She turned to meet the oncoming riders.

"They've all got rifles," Sarsa noted. "I'm not sure I like this."

"No man ever shot at unarmed women." Leeta was laughing. She could feel her pulse pounding. At last, these were men, warriors who rode half wild horses, untainted by civilization, different from a prescient shaman. Here were real barbarians. She admired the way they sat the prancing horses as they pulled up in front of her. Others rode around behind the ridge as if to prove they were alone. Some eyed the aircar suspiciously.

"Wish I'd had the sense to wear my combat armor." Leeta heard Rita's growl.

"Greetings!" Leeta called out to the huge man who rode in the lead. He had several tufts of hair tied under his neck and along the seams of his coat and pants. He was a giant. In fact, he could have been the horseman in Ree's favorite holo.

"You come to trade with the Santos, eh?" the big man asked. "Where are your men?"

"Back at camp. We can bring them later," Leeta said politely. "We would like to talk first. There are goods we will bring in return for information. May we come to your village?"

The big man smiled a wide, satisfied smile. "We are always interested in trade with beautiful women!" There was a laugh from the men gathered behind. "Come, I will ride you into camp!" He held down a hand.

"What do we do?" Netta asked. She sounded shaken.

"We sure as hell don't turn them down," Leeta hissed sharply. "That might be a terrible breach of etiquette." With that, she grabbed the arm and felt herself lifted into the saddle behind the giant.

She could smell woodsmoke, horse, leather, and a

male odor. *He'd pulled her up like a leaf!* She stared at the broad shoulders before her, gauging the amount of muscle in them. The feel of the horse between her legs was strange. She'd never been on an animal before.

Netta Solare squealed as she was lifted up behind a stocky rider. Only Sarsa remained on the ground, staring uncomfortably at the laughing, swirling circle of riders.

"Come on, Lieutenant!" Leeta called. "This is a very unusual feeling! Why, I think you could get used to it!"

"I'm not sure about this," Rita said, turning back toward the aircar. Before she could take a step, a man had grabbed her, pulling her up. As Leeta watched, Sarsa gracefully flipped in midair, breaking the man's grip and landing unevenly on her feet.

"No!" Leeta almost screamed. "You'll ruin the contact!"

As Rita recovered her balance, her hand snaked for the pistol at her belt. At the same time another of the men rode up behind her. Wheeling, she was too late. Leeta almost vomited as she heard the hollow thunk of the rifle barrel on Sarsa's red head. The lieutenant crumpled into a limp heap.

"Oh, my God!" Netta Solare shrilled, and Leeta, clinging to the back of the big rider as his horse raced off, only caught a glimpse of the two men stooped over Rita Sarsa and stripping her of her uniform.

Leeta fought to control her building fright. She could try to jump, but the horse was moving too fast and it looked like a long way to the uneven ground.

Maybe it would work out all right. Maybe Rita had simply offended the Santos. She tried to believe that.

CHAPTER IX

Damen Ree said nothing as he leaned impassively against the bulkhead and watched the monitor. The explosive wasn't large enough to cause any injury. No one in the room knew it was there. Ree had the anthropologists working in combat armor under the pretext that Chester might do them harm. Only he and the Chief Armorer knew of the trap. The armorer was in sleep synch. Ree was brain shielded.

If Chester really did see the future, he would know. The explosion would be a traumatic thing to undergo. For the record, it would be an equipment malfunction.

"You say that the Prophets must go and seek a vision?" one of the graduate students was asking.

"That is only proper. It is as Spider has willed." Chester was nodding passively, fingers laced over his stomach.

"Spider is God?" The student continued. "Why Spider? Why not something else?"

Chester smiled and shrugged. "God is! I do not question God. But spider is the trickster, the way, the bringer of light."

"But a trickster is generally considered evil," Chem said from the side of the room. "The bringer of light is considered good. How can God be both good and evil?"

Chester didn't even turn his head. "Is there light without darkness? Is there pain without ecstasy? If God is the universe, is not the universe God? Good and evil are one, Doctor Chem. Everything is nothing. Need there be more?"

"Yes!" one of the students growled. "What about physics? There are laws which function all through the

126

universe. There are sixteen measurable dimensions in space! Hot things burn! Cold things freeze!''

Chester nodded his head in agreement. ''We are falling over each other's words.'' He looked at the silent faces. ''If there is law in the universe and God is the universe, then there is law in God.''

Chem was shaking his head. ''Then everything in the universe is God. At least according to your way of thinking.''

''A very good way to put a complex truth into mere words, Doctor Chem. It is the way of the People. I cannot tell you what God is.'' Chester's expression was pained. ''It is within you to find out for yourself. Know your heart. Climb the mountain. Fast, sing, pray, *SEE!*

''Can you explain light if I have always lived in darkness? Words are very poor things for such a subject. At the same time, see how powerful they are for other things.'' Chester's smile—serene, knowing and kind—was rapidly becoming familiar to them all.

''Spider was the Arapaho symbol for God.'' Chem looked thoughtful. ''Do all your People see God as Spider? Are there any who know *Wakantanka?* Perhaps among the descendants of the Sioux?''

Chester's expression didn't change. ''Wakantanka is another name for Spider. That name is known only among the Prophets. It surprises me that you know such a word. It must be from the records I have seen in my visions.''

Chester raised a stubby, tanned finger. ''Among the Santos, they do not know Spider. They say God took the form of a man. Like Spider, he was nailed to the cross so men could live free. They call this man Haysoos. He is a very nasty man-God who burns men in fire instead of recalling their souls like Spider does. Such a concept of God is very limited, I would think. The Santos do not let their minds go free. They do not climb the mountains for a vision. Instead, they hide in their huts in the dark and kneel on the floor asking to talk to God.''

''Mexican influence,'' one of the students muttered.

''You trade with the Santos?'' Chem asked. ''Do you share ceremonies with them?''

"There are . . ." Chester frowned. "Perhaps ceremonies is the right word. We get horses and women from them, through what you would call ritual behavior, but before I go into that, I should tell you now. It is time for us to leave. The noise will not physically harm anyone. But you, Doctor Chem, would have to be taken to the place you call surgery to have your heart started again." Chester slowly got to his feet.

"What are you talking about?" Chem cried. *"What noise?"*

Ree had pulled himself straight, a frown incising his craggy features. *It couldn't be! Impossible!*

Chester was pointing at the monitor behind which the explosive had been secreted. "That will make much noise and sparks. It was designed by Colonel Ree to test my ability to see the future. We have several minutes left. We could wait and see, Doctor Chem, but like I say, it would necessitate having your heart started again."

There was a mumbling of voices as Ree punched the vitals up on Emmanuel Chem. "Damn!" he heard himself curse out loud. He hadn't thought of the old man having heart trouble! There it was. Coronary condition, aggravated by excitement.

Chester was waiting by the door. "Please. Let us step outside for a moment. The thing you call a heart attack would not kill you, Doctor Chem. Still, it would be very unpleasant . . . and hurt. There is no need. Colonel Ree has the information he needs. He can wake up his bomb man now. There is time to save the piece of equipment from being ruined."

Slowly, they filed out the door. Ree picked them up in the hallway. How could Garcia know when? He himself didn't know. The damn timer was set on automatic so no one would know when it went off!

Ree mentally triggered the comm unit to the hall speaker where Chester was reassuring Chem and his people. "How soon until the explosion, Chester?"

Chester didn't look up. "I do not know your units of time, Colonel Ree, but long enough for me to walk half a kilometer. There is still time if you want to save your—"

Perhaps five minutes then? "I don't even know when

128

the explosion is set to go off, Chester. If you've seen this thing happen, what makes you so sure I can stop it? How do I know your timing is right?'' Ree found himself unsettled for the first time since academy.

"There is free will in the universe, Colonel. Things do not *have* to happen. Otherwise, existence would be meaningless—machinelike. We would not learn. Spider would not grow from our experiences and knowledge.

"Nevertheless, you will not stop the bang. You yourself still need to know that I am right about the timing. I can never *prove* free will exists. There is always an alternate explanation, is that not so?''

Ree thought it through while Chester waited, his arms crossed over his chest, a beatific smile on his face.

Ree found the loop in logic and took a deep breath. "If I stop the bomb, I can say that it really wasn't about to go off and you only read my thoughts, not the computer in the detonator.'' Ree nodded to himself, feeling a cold sensation growing in his gut. "What about Chem's heart attack? How do you prove that?''

Chester's face was placid. "I do not. You yourself like and respect the good professor. It is part of your training to protect from harm, Colonel. You did not know of his heart problems. You will risk the computer. You do not perceive of a computer suffering. However, Doctor Chem's pain would harm you with thoughts of guilt. Though I cannot prove it, your free will has changed what would be and made something else.''

"My God,'' Damen Ree whispered to himself. The little fool was right. He couldn't risk Chem. He was right about the damn explosive, too. To hell with the monitor. It was the last variable.

Ree didn't realize he'd settled into the command chair until later. His thoughts raced. Paradox after paradox presented itself to his befuddled mind. Where did it end? Why didn't Chester Armijo Garcia go mad from all the sights in his head? Free will? There was no end to the possibilities!

"How?'' Ree croaked, voice suddenly dry. "How do . . . do you think? If every move changes things,

129

options become exponential. It should drive you completely . . . completely . . ."

"Mad?" Chester gave him that slightly elusive smile. "It would. You see, I do not think of my actions, Colonel. I follow what I see in my head, knowing I could change things. The madness you imagine is always just over the mind's horizon. That is why my cousin, Philip, failed. The idea appalled him, tried to suck him into an eternal future following the forever branching paths of the future.

"Me, I am a simple man. I accept life and the harmony of existence. I will follow the path of least resistance through the future, Colonel. I know my ultimate destiny. I could change it, take destiny into my own hands. I will not do so although I will suffer in the end. It is to be. That is all."

"Think of the power!" Absently, eyes going blank, Ree croaked in a hollow whisper, "A man could control the universe."

"It is not so." Shaking his head slightly, Chester beamed benevolently. "I understand your worry. Only, as you realized just now, to do so brings madness. The human brain is not strong enough. A man would fall into the pit of options—self-absorbed—until he died. It has happened many times among the People. Only for several days do men change the future. Then they cease seeing the world. They only see inside their heads. They no longer eat, drink, or sleep. They can no longer make decisions. Obsessed, they—"

"Overload?" Ree wondered. "Complete mental overload?"

"I think you understand," Chester agreed, staring off into nothingness. "The explosion is next."

There was silence, Ree's mind blank from shock.

Whump! The muffled charge seemed anticlimatic. An alarm went off as the damage control crew was alerted. Automatically, Ree checked their response time. Chem stared, wide-mouthed, at Chester and then looked up at the speaker from which Ree's voice came.

"I'm sorry, Doctor Chem." Ree's voice was hoarse. "I hadn't thought of your heart."

He'd gone to his quarters then, leaving everything behind, seeking to create order from the chaos that had broken out in his normally meticulous mind. He accessed the antique ethnographies on the Arapaho. Chem had mentioned them and the Sioux. It was apparent that whoever these people were, they had come from those long gone groups.

Desperately needing escape, Damen Ree lost himself in a world long past. At first, he had to force himself to concentrate, but the words fascinated him. As he read, he became totally absorbed in the writings of Kroeber, Trenholm, Hyde, Grinnell, and Fitzpatrick.

Always a quick learner, he pushed himself as the headset shot information into his head. Images of warriors from the past fixed themselves in his eager brain. Anthropological papers, government reports, the Soviet Occupation Commission findings, all went into the keen mind of Damen Ree.

He slept then, dreaming of fierce raiders riding across grasslands like those on the planet below. He saw thin men wrapped in cloth, sneaking through the middle of a blizzard to set explosives next to a Soviet guardhouse. Image after image cycled through his dreams.

The sleep synch woke him. Feeling refreshed in spite of his mental activity, Ree sat up, ready to face whatever this new day would bring. He stepped into the shower and quickly completed his ablutions. On a whim, he called up the holo of the Romanan horsemen.

The lean, hawk-faced rider looked over at him. Raider! The word came unbidden to his thoughts. Frowning, he dressed and headed for the bridge.

"We have a report, sir," Captain Iverson's voice called as Damen prodded the coffee machine. Turning, Ree scanned the findings, knowing he had to make some sort of decision regarding Chester Armijo Garcia. "No trace of anything like a transductor or radar anywhere. Search completed as Lieutenant Sarsa requested, sir."

"Thanks, Neal." Ree sipped his coffee. Radar? That had been a major stumbling block for them. Raider? Radar? Was there a phonetic similarity in the Romanan language?

Comm, get me Chester Garcia, he ordered mentally. Turning to the screen he caught the image of the Romanan sitting on his bunk, looking at the speaker as if he knew it would speak at that moment.

"Good morning, Chester," Ree greeted. The fellow had taken to ship hours quickly.

"Colonel," Garcia's expression didn't change.

"I have a question. Know the answer?" He couldn't resist.

Garcia nodded. "Your assumption is correct. You have mistranslated Raider for the device you call radar."

Ree's mouth was open. He fought down a quick swallow. Fear shivered along his spine. God! Wouldn't this man leave him some peace!

"I will allow you to ask in the future," Chester said. "I'm sorry. I knew how much it would disturb you."

Ree just nodded numbly and flicked off the comm. He was shaking; coffee had slopped out of the cup. Taking deep breaths, Damen Ree fought to calm himself. A quick check showed the ship to be functioning perfectly. Hell, maybe he should have just asked Garcia when the bridge would require his presence and what he ought to do!

Instead, he called a meeting of all the scientific personnel onboard. The meeting room was filled with haggard people lined up on either side of the table. None of them looked like they'd slept.

"I think . . . I think we have a major problem, ladies and gentlemen," Ree began in a soft voice. "Comm, please patch me through to Doctor Dobra and her staff on the surface."

His eyes ranged over the anthropologists and a somewhat amused S. Montaldo. "We are going to have to make a report on this. I guess we all know how the planetside contingent felt."

There were muffled, nervous chuckles. Chem was looking into nothingness, oblivious to those around him.

"Lieutenant Sarsa here," came a voice through Comm.

"Colonel Ree here. Have Leeta patch through. I think we'd better do some talking."

"We're in the field, sir."

"Might want to get back to the base camp."

"Doctor Dobra's over the hill trying to establish a contact."

"Get her," Ree ordered. "I think you might like to know about a translation difficulty we've found. Also, my apologies, you were right about Garcia. We've got to get the whole brain corps together for a confab. This thing is getting out of hand."

"Yes, sir. Just a moment." Comm went dead.

The voices at the table were getting louder when Dobra's voice came through. "Colonel Ree?" He could hear something about Santos in the background.

"Doctor Dobra?" he asked.

"Give me fifteen minutes and I'll call back, sir." There was silence.

"Must be important," one of the graduate students shrugged and went back to the conversation. Ree brought the bunch to order, waiting for Leeta's response. Each of the groups gave their report as Ree asked himself, *What do I do about Garcia? How do I come to grips with this little brown man and his miserable planet.* He fought a sudden urge to recall his ground crew and blow the whole thing to atoms like a plague hole.

"Colonel!" Comm came through his mental channel. "Lieutenant Sarsa's comm is dead. She's no longer in her equipment belt, sir."

Get me status quick, Ree ordered. Aloud to the scientists: "Excuse me, please." He ran for the bridge, uncertain fear in his gut. *What would Garcia have to say to this?*

Leeta looked up in fear as the big man left the room. He'd run his fingers longingly over her breast, then—to her horror—lower down. They were all stripped now. Bound, hand and foot, they lay hacking from smoke in the damp, stinking squalor of a dark hut.

Rita Sarsa groaned and lifted her head in the dim glow of coals from a smoldering fire. Netta Solare was blubbering to herself where she lay, face averted.

133

"God," Leeta groaned as she saw Rita trying to focus on her in the dim light.

"They rape me yet? I mean while I was out?" Sarsa's voice was muzzy.

"No," Leeta whispered, aware Rita had voiced the worry she'd kept hidden. "I'm so sorry. I never dreamed they'd. . . ." Her voice trailed off.

"Don't worry about it, Doc." Rita sounded brave, at least. "My mistake for letting them catch me off guard. Where did we go wrong? God! *What a headache!*"

Leeta heard the "we" and her heart rushed. Sarsa wasn't blaming her—at least not in public. "Netta?" Leeta called. "Netta! Get up, we've got to plan."

The huddled lump stayed on her side in the dirt, refusing even to respond. Only Solare's trembling shoulders and muffled sobs indicated she lived.

"See if you can find anything sharp in here," Rita gasped, her bound fingers searching in the dirt.

"You going to try and knife them?" Leeta asked incredulously.

"To cut the ropes," Sarsa came back in a markedly sarcastic tone.

Stupid question, Leeta mentally agreed and began scrounging through the loose, damp soil. She found a small bone fragment and some moldy leather. She physically pushed Solare out of the way and searched under her body. Sweat ran from the unaccustomed use of her muscles.

"Nothing," she gasped at last. Sarsa was silent, eyes darting about the room while she thought.

"God!" Leeta moaned softly. "I'm so sorry."

"Cut it out, Doc!" Sarsa's iron voice warned. "First rule of warfare: never be sorry. Second rule—when things fall apart—fix them! What can you tell me about these guys? *Think, damn it!*"

Leeta struggled to make her mind work. A face shoved past the flap over the doorway and glittering eyes checked them. "Don't move so much. Makes the *** tight," he called as he ducked back out.

"Nice guy," Rita sneered.

Leeta tried to dredge up everything she could remember about the camp. Nothing but the peering eyes

134

of leering men came back to her. She remembered her shame as the big man had tossed her into waiting arms and they'd ripped the clothing from her body. In shock, it had been all she could do to keep from screaming. Fearing the worst—gang rape—she refused to allow the thought.

"Nothing but men," she whispered out loud, blinking back her tears.

"All right, I take your word. I was out, remember? Why's that important?" Sarsa prodded her, green eyes narrowed.

"Huh?" Leeta caught herself. Why was it? "Hunting camp maybe," she said suddenly, "or maybe a raiding party."

"*Raiders!*" Rita barked a short, sarcastic laugh. "We were worried about *radar!*"

Leeta felt her throat constrict. The words rolled off her stumbling tongue, "Like their ancestors were six hundred years ago." She raised her eyes helplessly. "God! How I fooled myself—all of us!"

"We've got a soft society, Doc." Rita shrugged despite her awkward position. "Don't let it get to you. The only ones who think war anymore are us deviants in the military. The only reason we do is 'cause of the tapes and synch training. Real people don't worry about it. Guess you'd better dig into those books of yours and start thinking that way. What do we expect? Any chance these guys will come in laughing, throw us our clothes, and say 'Great joke on you!'?"

Leeta ran her mind over the culture histories. "Santos. God called Haysoos. Christian. Maybe these folks don't have the Indian ethic? Maybe they are truly Christian? Still, I'd guess they won't kill us. Even the Mexicans bought and traded slaves once. There has to be some diffusion of traits. I'd say they are figuring out who's to be whose wife."

"*Wife?*" Rita's voice echoed her disbelief.

"Wife!" Leeta said firmly. "Remember. They came in one ship. Must be closed bloodlines. Bet on exogamy to keep the gene flow moving between groups. Raiding is a way of getting outside women as well as horses and goods. Wives must be real important to them."

135

"You mean like . . . *property!*" Rita was incredulous. "Like a damn horse! Sort of a pet! Huh-uh! Not this gal!" She was shaking her head. "They try that and I'm gonna kick some ass!"

Leeta chuckled in spite of herself, finding courage from her ability to at least think. "Look at the bright side. None of that foolish courtship! No more deciding if you really want to go out with the dumb nerd."

Leeta felt better as she realized her spirit was coming back.

It dropped again when men pushed through the door and hard hands grabbed her by the feet, waist, and shoulders. They carried her into the evening light, hard hands seeming to find her private parts. Closing her eyes, she somehow kept her mental grip and endured.

"Keep your guts, Doc." Rita growled as they were dumped in an area flooded by light from a huge fire.

Netta dropped in a limp pile, sobbing hysterically.

"We do have one advantage, they don't speak our language." Leeta tried to think of something positive.

"Yep. If they cut us loose, I'll take on a couple and you run for it, hear?" Rita's voice was harsh.

"What about you? What about Netta?" Leeta demanded, throwing a quick glance at her companions. The men were seating themselves in a circle around the fire, staring at them appraisingly. She could see the aircar, instruments smashed. They'd dragged it to camp.

"Don't worry about me, Doc." Rita sounded so confident. "This is the sort of thing I've been training for for years. As to Netta, she can hear us. Either she pulls herself together—or she stays here. Hear that, kid?"

Netta swallowed quickly and nodded, eyes fear-bright as she stared at the wolfish grins of the men around the fire. Flickers of shadowy light gleamed on their faces.

"You don't even have a weapon!" Leeta insisted.

"Don't need one." Sarsa hesitated and shot her a quick look. "Let's just say they don't give me a chance. You think you can handle what they'll do? It'll be worse than what's happened so far. You might even have an audience."

Leeta met that iron look, took a breath, and nodded. "I guess I'll have to, huh?"

The giant, Big Man he was called, walked up and raised his hands to the dark skies. "We thank Haysoos for such a wealth of new wives. We are strong to find such reward without bloodshed or death. Haysoos sees his People. He smiles upon us. We will be strong when we fight the Sobyets from the sky, *for here are their women!*"

Big Man grabbed up a fistful of Rita's hair. "See this! Hair like the sun at dawn! Never have we seen hair of such a color! This one!" He grabbed Leeta's hair and twisted, she fought to keep from crying out. "Rare is the hair of grass in the fall! There will be more in our families from now on!"

The men hooted and yelled, slapping their dirt-greasy legs with approbation.

"The Sobyets are here! We have taken their women! We are strong and powerful! Grace be to the Prophet of the Santos! He has sent us here to raid the Spiders! He has sent us here to claim the Sobyet women!"

They had jumped to their feet now, screaming, dancing in short, hopping steps, waving their rifles at the sky. "You get all that?" Leeta asked.

"Yep," Sarsa said shortly.

Netta let out a yelp as Big Man grabbed her and held her up. "Look at this one! Who wants this woman? She is strong—if a little too fat. Her hips are wide and will give you many sons! She is soft," he pinched her, bringing a yelp from Netta, "and will make your nights warm!"

"Hang tough, kid!" Rita hissed at Solare. "Ree'll be here soon. Don't worry. They know where the air-car was. We got a rescue coming."

Leeta nodded in sudden agreement. How long? An hour since they were captured? Maybe two? How long would Ree have waited?

"Martin Luis!" Big Man shouted. "This one is yours!" He tossed Netta bodily to the man who had hauled her up behind his saddle. There were shouts as

Martin Luis pulled his knife and cut the thongs. Netta collapsed into a whimpering bundle.

"I keep this one!" Big Man pointed to Leeta and threw her a nasty leer. "I pulled this one onto my saddle."

The man who had hit Rita with the rifle, came forward. "That one with the fire hair, I hit! I claim her!"

"Ah!" Big Man grinned. "But wait, Ramon, my friend. I, too, would like this woman. What would she be worth to you?"

"Selfish bastard!" Sarsa spat behind her. "Think he's enough for both of us?"

"You studied how big he is?" Leeta asked softly. "That's not fat in those trees he calls legs."

"Just so long as he cuts us free!" Sarsa growled in a calculating tone.

"One hundred horses!" Ramon called. There were oohs and ahs from the crowd.

"Ten," the big man shot back.

"You're worth a lot, Lieutenant," She could see Netta being carried away in the crowd. "Makes me feel second class."

Rita, it turned out, was worth fifty-two horses, a price that left the men wide-eyed and wondering. Big Man leered.

"Guess this is it," Rita stood forward and turned, presenting her wrists. Leeta swallowed her fear, and did the same.

"We follow, quiet-like, to his hut," Rita ordered. "Got a better chance there. I'll tell you what to do."

Big Man snorted. "You understand. Very well."

Leeta felt her heart pounding. Her bladder was full, her guts in an uproar of fear. Instead of the knife, she felt his hands and she was thrown over his shoulder to immense laughter from the men. Rita, too, ended in a like position.

The bouncing trip was short. Leeta dropped like a sack of wheat. Rita bounced off the sleeping pad next to her.

"We give better pleasure untied." Leeta couldn't believe it was her voice—so firm and steady—that said that. She looked up as he grinned down at her.

"Good!" He laughed. So quickly she couldn't follow, the long, narrow knife flicked out of the sheath and darted at her legs; the thongs severed before she could jump. Another motion of the man's hand and Rita, too, was free.

"Turn," the man ordered. The hardest thing she'd ever done was to turn her back on that wicked grin and the shining knife. Her hands fell free at her side.

"Almost there," Rita grinned. "Be ready."

A fire flickered in the center of the room, casting eerie shadows on their naked bodies and the big, leather-clad man. It would be dark outside now.

Rita smiled saucily at the big man and reached a hand up to caress his beard. Leeta watched in fascination as he leaned down to kiss the lieutenant. Later, she couldn't reconstruct it. Rita seemed to jerk spasmodically and the big man fell with a resounding, hollow thump.

"C'mon!" Rita grabbed up the knife and tossed it to Leeta. Sarsa grabbed the big rifle, and slung his cartridge-studded belt over her shoulders.

"What about Netta?" Leeta demanded.

"We'll get her later," Rita hissed. "We don't know where she is. Ree will come for us. We've got to get out of here. It's called minimizing loss, Doc!" Then she was out in the dark.

"What about our clothes?" Leeta was frantic, feeling the cool night air.

"Be tough." Then: "Shut up and follow!" Leeta gritted her teeth and tried to keep pace with the ghostly white body ahead of her.

Headed for the dark, Leeta could see the ring of men laughing behind her. They were drinking from skins and talking. Some sang. She ran faster—aware of sharp pains in her feet. Instead of crying out, she bit her lip until she tasted blood and sprinted after Rita Sarsa.

The rifle shots rang out just as they started up the steep, rocky ridge. Gasping, panting, and stumbling on pain-seared feet, Leeta pulled up next to Rita.

Shots in a ragged staccato filled the little valley. Men yelled, cursing and jumping around the fire. A thunder of horses' hoofs rumbled hollowly in the dark as fleeting forms raced through the camp. Leeta watched in fascination as flashes of light were followed a half second later by rifle reports.

"Come on!" Rita ordered, steering Leeta away from the bizarre scene.

"You kill him?" Leeta yipped as she stepped on something sharp. A lancing pain shot up her leg as she limped after Sarsa.

"I tried, Doc," Rita sounded disappointed. "I really did. Damn, he was big. There was so much muscle I think I just stunned him. Maybe the unknowns back there will finish the job we started, huh?"

Leeta considered the idea and hobbled along in Sarsa's wake.

Pain, searing pain, dogged each step, making her gasp. Wretchedness shut off something in her mind. In all the universe, pain spread. To Leeta's tear-blurred eyes, even the stars wheeled in pain. It ebbed and flowed between the planets as her reeling brain forced her after Rita Sarsa.

"Got to stop." Leeta couldn't bite back the words any longer. "God, my feet are shredded." She sniffed at her tears.

"Mine, too," Rita agreed, voice trembling.

"How did you keep going?" Leeta asked.

"Soldier trick. Special training." Sarsa let herself down on a rock.

"Where in hell is Ree?" Leeta almost cried. "What happened?" Another couple of shots sputtered back at the Santos camp. "Suppose that was them?"

"Never knew a spacer who rode a horse. Let's go. Come morning, we'll see an aircar. God alone knows how I'll feel when the troops see me like this!"

"Anything's better than Mister Big back there," Leeta shivered. "After them, I'll take anyone, anything—"

"Tired of anthropology?" Rita giggled. "And this your first time to do field—"

"I . . . shhhh! What's that?" Leeta hissed.

Rita crouched, the big rifle pointed out into the dark. Leeta stuck the knife out into the night—ready, she hoped, for anything. The hard arm that slid around her throat throttled her cry. Rita fell beneath a heavy body. She labored to draw air into her fevered lungs.

Leeta lost herself to hazy drifting in a world of darker and darker gray. And she sank into merciful . . . blackness. . . .

The sensation of motion—swaying back and forth—became endless. How unpleasant to move so! Why couldn't she stop it? On top of the swaying, her head ached in flashes of pain. The cry of oxygen-starved cells came unbidden. All right, she knew that academically, but it didn't lessen the agony.

Leeta sought to swallow, but something was stuck in her mouth. She struggled to pull an eyelid up and could barely make out the ground and the foot of something she thought might be a horse. Her bladder was empty. With some concern she wondered when that had happened.

"We camp here," a soft voice called.

"Philip. Help me." The voice was male. And it wasn't Big Man of the Santos. This was a new voice. Softer, it had a timbre that touched her, offering a momentary feeling of security. She heard a thump and hands—gentle this time—took her by the waist. She realized her wrists and feet were bound again and the fleeting sense of security fragmented into a shiver of fear. They lowered her to the ground.

She tried to sit up, seeing movement in the dark. A second form was dropped at her side. Rita?

There was a scratching sounded as sparks arced. A dark form bent down and began blowing softly at a red ember. Flames shot up quickly. The second man was tying up the horses. The fire builder looked around and pulled the gag from her mouth.

"Greetings, star woman. I am Philip," the bulky shadow before her stated simply.

Rita spat as the cloth was pulled from her mouth. "Frying pan to the fire, Doc?" Rita asked.

Leeta looked at her bloody feet. "Whatever, Rita. I don't think we're running anymore."

"Here come the flames, kid," Rita's voice was cool. They looked up at the lean man who bent down, rifle in his arms, thick muscles rippling under the soft leather he wore.

"At least he's handsome," Leeta heard herself say as she stared into those deep, pain-haunted eyes.

CHAPTER X

John Smith Iron Eyes filled his lungs and let the air out slowly as he watched the Santos ride wildly down into the camp with their captives. Warriors sang, thrusting rifles toward the sky, hooting and yelling as they darted back and forth with their horses in feats of horsemanship. Ululating cries of victory grated on Iron Eyes' ears.

Then the blood in his veins became ice; he recognized the big Santos. *Him!* This man had raped, tortured and murdered his Jenny. A yellow-haired woman clung to him in fear—obviously a captive. *John Smith Iron Eyes would take that woman!*

"We do it," he hissed at Philip. His cousin just nodded, eyes wavering anxiously. Philip raised a hand to signal the rest of the Spiders who held their horses down in the draw.

"Cousin," Philip said softly, hesitantly. "There is . . . a decision you must make now."

John Smith slid down from the rocky crest of the hill and cocked his head, irritated at the delay. "What decision?" His heart burned to be at the Santos, to feel blood on his fighting knife.

Philip took a deep breath. "You know I have been frightened. Today I must lose or you must lose. I am not important, cousin. But if I lose, the People lose. The choice is yours."

John Smith Iron Eyes suffocated on stifled rage. Yet a cool tendril of restraint wended through his heated thoughts. The People lose? *Philip had seen like the Prophets.* Striving to quench the embers of frustrated rage, his voice was forced. "What choice, cousin?"

Philip winced, hurt by the tone. "The Santos warrior.'' It came out as a whisper. "You must let him live—or you will kill the People, me, and yourself.''

"I do not understand you, cousin." John Smith Iron Eyes shot a dagger look at his cousin.

"Spider offers you the Santos warrior for your revenge." Philip's eyes dropped. "He will be in his hut, unconscious. He is yours if you want him. There will be many to help you carry him away for revenge.''

John Smith's hungry smile twisted his lips.

Philip's eyes grew more distant at the sight. "The choice is, the warrior . . . or the star women. They will be running to escape the Santos. If they get away, the People will die. It will . . . hurt me." He looked up. "It will hurt you, cousin."

"It will hurt *me* to let the Santos go!" Rage burned freely again. "What . . . what if I kill the Santos? Then we find the women! What then . . . eh? You saw like a Prophet, *tell me!*" He gripped Philip's shoulder, fingers digging into the supple hide and bruising the flesh below as his eyes bored into Philip's.

"I didn't see very far," Philip glared back hotly. "Don't you understand? *I was not meant to see.* I am not a Prophet. It is not in my mind. I fall to temptation too easily, cousin. I only know the decision is yours.''

Silence stretched between them.

Iron Eyes slowly let his cousin loose. "Then how good is your vision, eh, cousin?" He snorted in mockery.

Philip's head dropped and he took a ragged breath. "I do not know," the answer tore from a reluctant throat. "To see is to lose yourself in paths . . . that make more paths . . . that make yet *more* paths. I was falling into a hole from which I could not return. It is always there to lead me on. I am tricked by Spider. I am—''

"My choice!" John Smith Iron Eyes spat into the patch of bayonet grass to his left.

"The old Prophet told you of this." Philip shrugged, resigned. "It is in your hands now, John. The Four Old Men have gone to pray. They will not interfere. It is up to you, warrior of the People. Your cusp. Spider chose you to decide. How strong is your medicine? How powerful is your anger?''

"Why do they not tell me what I must do?" John Smith cried.

"They will not go mad for you! Fool!" Philip hissed. "It will be dark soon. What do we do, John Smith? Do we attack the Santos warrior and drag him off? Do we save the women? What is your choice?"

"What do you say, cousin?" John's voice was mild as pain raked him with the thought he could not kill Jenny's slayer. Memory of the vision returned. He could see the Santos glaring into his eyes, daring, mocking, laughing at him in his weakness. Fresh anger blasted along his nerves, muscles clenched in heat.

Philip had his eyes clamped shut. A shaking began in his legs, spreading through his body in a spasm before he crumpled limply to the ground.

Philip was falling into his mind—into myriad futures only he could see. In a sudden cold sweat, John Smith Iron Eyes grabbed his arms and threw him down the slope, breaking the spell.

Scrambling down next to his cousin, Iron Eyes looked into haunted eyes. "I can't," Philip whimpered. "I can't tell you. I would be sucked in. I would be mad. I can't tell you, cousin. I just. . . . I just. . . . I. . . ." He started to shake again.

John Smith Iron Eyes sighed. "We are tools of powers beyond us, cousin. Forgive me. I had no right to ask. Tell me no more. I have vowed on Jenny's grave to spread the Santos' blood. Now, you say I must choose between her and two women I do not know? The People's future rests with the women . . . but not with a warrior's blood challenge? Where is the sense in that?" He patted Philip's shoulder reassuringly.

"The sense is Spider's," Philip whispered. "What will you do?"

John Smith Iron Eyes pulled his cousin to his feet. "I will . . . I don't know yet," he mumbled, turning away.

By the horses, John Smith pulled the rifle from its scabbard. He checked the cartridge and levered the block shut. Around him, he could see the warriors staring at him curiously. He knew each one. How many raids had he ridden on with these men? How many

144

times had he danced with them? Some he'd played with as children.

There were others—the missing faces like Reuben O'Neal Andojar's and others. Men dead by Santos bullets. Dead of disease. Some eaten by bears—all of the People. All did what they had to for the People. Each had kept his word to the dead, to God, to himself.

And I must break my word? John Smith Iron Eyes wondered as he led the line of horsemen down into the canyon. It would be dark soon. What should he do? He looked up into the lavender sky and caught the image of Jenny's face in the clouds that rolled in from the west. The sting of guilt festered.

A half hour later, he had his warriors in position. Philip's eyes were on him as the war and prayer songs rose softly on the evening breeze to Spider.

Friday Garcia Yellow Legs slid down the slope. "They are giving away the women. All are at the fire. Many are drinking."

John Smith Iron Eyes shot a quick glance at his cousin and shrugged. "Let's go." Philip's eyes couldn't be made out in the dark. John kneed the black mare and set off at a trot.

The pounding cadence of hoofs spread out behind him. Some of the warriors still sang their songs of war, victory, and hope. John Smith gritted his teeth as the black mare—caught up in the fury of the charge— leaped ahead, struggling to be first into the Santos war camp.

A shot was fired to their right. A half second later came another shot. Sentries. A slight rise was topped and they were in the middle of the huts. Men ran, frantic to escape the firing, shouting, throwing knives, panicked before the assault of the Spider warriors.

John Smith Iron Eyes leveled the rifle and triggered the gun as he pounded toward a man who stood before him with a raised gun. As the Santos pitched forward into the dirt, John spun his horse. There were riders everywhere, clubbing down fleeing figures, shooting, singing victory songs.

As the mare pranced, Iron Eyes jacked another shell into the chamber. Complete surprise had routed the Santos. His men would take all the horses—and many

145

coups from this fight. Iron Eyes jumped from the mare and—with his knife—took coup on the man he'd shot. A figure limped away, fleeing from the fight.

Hefting the rifle, Iron Eyes shot the man between the shoulders. Blood lust possessed him as he knelt to take his second coup. The bloody hair swung at his belt as he charged for a hut. Several were blazing now as warriors fired them. He saw Philip struggling with a hysterical woman. he was pointing at the hills and slapping the woman across her bare buttocks with the flat of his bloody fighting knife to get her to run.

Iron Eyes glanced inside the hut and froze. As if in a dream, he entered and looked down at the Santos warrior. He reached carefully for his knife, aware of a presence at his shoulder.

He spared a quick glance to see Philip, perspiration beading on his forehead and lip as his frightened eyes darted from John to the big warrior. Philip's throat bobbed; his eyes were like pools of dark, bottomless water.

An image of Jenny's mutilation, the disgust and fear etched into her dying face . . . Iron Eyes trembled, looking into the slack features of Big Man. *Are you worthy?* the voice of Bear asked in his ear. *How do you use my blood?* Another voice, ancient, withered asked, *Do you use your anger against the People?* Images of faces, laughter, scenes from the Settlement, the dying eyes of Patan Reesh Yellow Legs, flashed through him as his fingers gripped the leather handle of his fighting knife.

"You . . . or the People?" Iron Eyes whispered to the unconscious man.

His soul turned in agony, ripped by burning anger. "For the People, I left Jenny to her death. For the People. . . . For Spider, I . . ." A trembling overpowered his muscles. Eyes pinched shut, Iron Eyes fought with himself for control.

"If I just take coup?" John whispered numbly. "That will make a difference?" His hands itched to cut just the hair from the warrior.

"I don't know." Philip's voice was hoarse.

"Spider would trick me." John Smith Iron Eyes knotted his fingers into a fist and shook it at the Santos. An cry of rage escaped from his throat as he ran—tortured by his decision—from the hut into the macabre atmosphere of the camp. Huts flared, men shouted. Occasional shots echoed around the valley.

He found the black mare where he'd left her. "Which way, Philip?" John called as his cousin walked from the hut. "I know not which way!"

Philip's head darted from side to side. Finally, he pointed at the nearest slope. "There! I think they would have gone there. That is right, I think. The vision was not very good from here on, brother." Philip caught up his war-horse and followed John as he walked his animal up the slope.

Brother? Indeed, they were brothers from this moment on.

"They are armed?" John squinted into the darkness where his cousin rode.

"We must not take chances." Relief seemed to drip from Philip's voice.

John nodded. At the crest of the ridge, he dismounted. "We go on foot. They will hear the horses."

Spreading out, John Smith Iron Eyes and Philip worked their way through the inky blackness. The clouds hid all three of the moons. A faint tapping in the night told John Smith Iron Eyes that his cousin had found the trail. On cat feet he moved over, bending and sniffing at the ground. Blood!

Fifteen minutes later, they heard the women. John tapped out instructions as he worked behind them.

Step by step he moved closer, crouching in the darkness. One woman stood before him. He could see the white of her skin. The second crouched off to her side, talking in a low voice. Had they no ears? Could they not hear the bending of the bayonet grass?

John tapped a ready on his scabbard and heard one of the women stop talking. At that, he leaped. She hardly struggled. He heard the knife drop from her senseless fingers. A sound of intense struggling, a hollow grunt of pain, and John could see wiggling where Philip had jumped the other woman.

"This one is ready," he called dryly. "Must I wait all night for you to subdue one skinny woman?"

It was still some time before Philip, panting, stood

up. "Next time—you get this one. I think she broke my ribs!" He drew a ragged breath.

"Watch them, I will bring the horses." At that he sprinted off in the dark.

Tying and gagging their quarry, John followed Philip's lead into the darkness. "The star men will come looking for these. We must go where they cannot see us from the air."

John Smith Iron Eyes stared upward at the inky clouds. "Who was that woman you sent from the Santos? The one you paddled with your knife."

"A star woman. Not one we want. They will find her in the morning." Philip's voice was unconcerned, relieved, alive.

"You don't sound very much like a Prophet anymore . . . brother." He couldn't keep the irony from his voice.

His cousin's voice was light—as it hadn't been since before the bear fight. "That honor and pain is left for Chester. I am happy with my lot now. I am alive with a beautiful woman tied onto my horse." A pause. "The People have a chance to live. Perhaps I will see many more years. Perhaps not. I don't care to know."

"You would have died?" John was incredulous.

"I would have. The life of an Old One is not easy. To be a warrior and ride the world in ignorance is a blessing, cousin." Philip laughed and whooped. "I saw my death there in the village of the Santos. Had you killed the warrior, I, too, would have died. It was the way it would have been."

"So when will you die now?" John Smith asked.

"I do not know . . . *and I do not care!*" Philip laughed again.

"And these women?" John Smith Iron Eyes looked at the limp form over his saddle.

"We must be nice to them. We must try and win their love. Outside of that, I know little more." He could see the faint form of Philip shrug only to wince. "Truly," his strained voice came back. "I think she broke my ribs . . . and with only her *fingers!*"

Love? John Smith Iron Eyes looked down at the head that swayed with each step of the horse. Love a star woman? He had no interest in love. Only Jenny could bring such to him—and she was dead. Big Man lived—a debt unpaid.

Guilt at his failure rushed from the back of his mind. Not until they laid his cold, lifeless body on the scaffold of the dead would he forget the sight of his enemy. There lay revenge. There lay Jenny's honor—and his. *Why had he turned away?* A tear burned at the edge of his eye as he remembered how she'd smiled at him, warm with life—and her mangled corpse.

He led them down through twists and turns of the canyon. They crossed the divide on a narrow harvester trail and cut cross country. Feeling numb with hurt, John pushed the black mare harder.

As faint gray tinged the cloudy skies, he found the rock overhang.

"We camp here," Philip called.

What to do about the woman—let her drop? Simply because he hurt was no reason to be rude. "Philip, help me," John called. Together they got the women to the ground and John led the horses to the bottom of the drainage for water, staking them under the broad canopy of sandstone.

Philip had the fire going as Iron Eyes squatted down to look at the star women. They were muttering in a senseless tongue. Could it be that they didn't speak?

Philip gasped as he straightened, hand on his ribs. John laid his rifle to one side. "Let me see. We may need to bind those ribs. I still do not believe such a small woman could hurt you so." Thoughts of Jenny subsided into a dull ache.

"I do not know how either." Philip muttered miserably. "It is a good thing she had only the rifle. The way she twisted, she could have killed me five times with a knife."

"Perhaps that was the other half of your vision," John half joked. "They do not speak like the People," he added, seeing Philip was in no mood for humor about that subject.

John grimaced at the bruise on Philip's side. It was already dark and ugly. Trying to be gentle, he felt the grating and he heard Philip gasp. "How did you ride so far without collapsing?"

"I am so happy to be alive, cousin." Philip's eyes

149

were animated even through his pain. "My life is changed. Not even Friday Garcia Yellow Legs will laugh more than me."

Shaking his head, John Smith Iron Eyes looked at the women, still bound, and pulled his knife. Sudden fear tightened in the yellow-haired one while the red-head glared wickedly. Smiling, he cut the bonds. "Do not hurt him more." He pointed the knife at Philip. "He does poorly fighting women!"

Chuckling, John got to his feet as lightning streaked across black skies. Seconds later a hollow boom rumbled through the hills.

Pulling blankets from the saddles, he took out his other set of clothes and returned to the fire. The women had the strips of binding off their wrists and were rubbing them. They still watched Philip with half wild eyes.

"I don't know if these will fit. The rains are coming. It will be cold." He squatted and looked at their stained feet. In the growing daylight, he could see that they were clotted with blood and dirt.

Philip was cooking dried steaks of harvester meat. Harvester wasn't very good to the taste, but it kept a man half fed. It took beef to keep a man alive. The women were wriggling into the clothing as best they could and pulling the blanket around them as they talked to each other in the strange tongue.

"They will not walk for some days, cousin," John Smith Iron Eyes looked up. "The bayonet grass and the knife bush have done them no good."

Philip was cutting what remained of his shirt apart after John had ripped it for his bandage. "Next time we rescue women, we must bring more clothes, eh? Still, they are both very beautiful—even in your poor scraps of clothing that not even a Santos corpse would wear." Philip was happy, joking, as he had never done before.

Iron Eyes' face went stiff at the words. "Jenny made those." He waved a limp hand at the clothing the yellow-haired woman was wearing.

Philip's eyes dropped suddenly. "I . . . I . . . Forgive this fool, Iron Eyes. I eat my words." Carefully, Philip tended the meat.

The hurt renewed and smoldering, John Smith motioned the women to extend their feet and carefully began to wash the dirt, blood, and grass stems from the wounds. They winced at the sting.

The red-haired woman drew a deep breath as he finished and lay back, letting her eyes close. Philip offered food, only to find the redhead was asleep. Rain started to pelt the ground beyond the rocks. John Smith Iron Eyes ran for more pole tree wood.

Finally, tired, he made it back to the shelter—breath condensing in the chill air—and dropped the last of the gnarled wood he could find. Both women slept. Philip, too, was snoring lightly. Checking the horses one last time, John lay down to sleep, his last thoughts of Jenny and the big Santos warrior he had chosen to leave free.

The drainage below their shelter rushed in a muddy torrent as rain ripped down in streamers. Leeta swallowed hard. She shot another glance at the sleeping men. With Rita following, she stepped out from under the drip line and into the cold water.

The narrow trail was ankle-deep in runoff. The pain that shot up from her wounded feet was excruciating—the sensation that of walking on raw nerve endings. But escape lay ahead. Ree would find them . . . somehow. Mere seconds away from the shelter she was soaked to the bone in spite of the thick leather clothing.

"Up or down?" Rita whispered into her ear.

"Up is closer to Ree," Leeta guessed. So saying, she forced herself to hobble up the rivulet the trail had become. Perhaps a hundred yards later they stared, disbelieving, at a roaring cauldron of water that blasted past narrow rock ledges, completely cutting off any chance of escape.

Leeta shivered violently as she looked to Rita for advice. "What next?"

"I don't know," Rita was shaking her wet head, and shivering. "We can't pass *that!*" Her eyes scanned the sheer rock walls. "Too slippery to climb. I guess we go down."

Miserable, defeated, soaked, cold, hurting, and

151

lost—hell of a fix, Leeta thought. "Maybe anthropology isn't so much fun," she announced.

The trip down the trail was worse than the one up. The overhang looked delightfully dry, warm, and cozy as they splashed past, trying to keep quiet. The horses were watching with mild interest, no doubt thinking in their equine minds how crazy humans were.

They had almost passed when a voice hollered out from the camp. "When you get cold enough and wet enough, we will have dinner ready for you. Do not try to cross the stream, you will drown!"

"You think they know something we don't?" Rita asked with an attempt at humor.

In Romanan, Leeta shouted, "We're trying to escape!"

She heard the laughter from the dry sanctuary of the rock shelter. "There will be time for that when conditions are better. Go ahead, help yourself to this glorious opportunity! John and I will stay here where it is warm. When your feet hurt too much and your stomachs are empty, come back. We will not hurt you. We are Spider People. We are men of honor!" There was pride in that last.

"Oh, hell!" Rita spat. "My feet hurt. I'm frozen. They've got horses, fire, and food." With that she trudged back toward the shelter, leaving Leeta to follow in the rain.

It rained for three days. In spite of their fears, the two men did nothing untoward. Making the most of a chance for field work, Leeta quizzed both Philip and the quiet John Smith Iron Eyes about the People.

"You say the Santos are always getting stronger? Why? Why is their population expanding while yours shrinks?" Rita asked during a lull.

Philip shrugged. "Once we constantly expanded, pushing into the plains beyond the Bear Mountains. That was in the time of my father. Since then, they have taken to raiding constantly. Only the radio keeps us from being wiped out. That and the strength of our warriors." Philip shot a quick glance of praise at John.

Leeta snorted derisively. "And I blithely thought we'd find a nice, peaceful group of herders. It's still

152

hard for me to get used to the idea of human beings killing each other. It's like we walked into the past."

"Thought that's what anthropology was all about." Rita commented.

"Why don't you make peace with the Santos?" Leeta insisted.

Unexpectedly, John Smith spoke. "It is not a matter for peace, star woman. Blood and death and ancient wrongs are at the heart of our hatred. Spider made the People and the Santos that way. Were it right to make peace, the Prophets would tell us so. Now, the Raiders keep us strong. They keep us quick, powerful, and victorious. Without war, we would die." At that he got up and walked to the far edge of the shelter, looking out over the rain-drenched gully.

"Why is he so bitter? What makes him so sad?" Leeta asked.

"The Santos killed his sister." Philip spoke in hushed tones. "The big Santos who captured you—he did it. He took her and raped her to death. Jenny Garcia Smith and John Smith Iron Eyes were taboo. It could not be—but they loved each other. He is a man who has been blessed by Spider. He had to choose between revenge and your lives. He had to choose between the Santos warrior and me and the People."

"You mean he knew about us?" Rita asked suspiciously.

Philip nodded uneasily. "I saw it in a vision."

"You're a Prophet?" Leeta wondered.

"No!" Philip shook his head vehemently. "I am not strong enough. Spider chose Chester. Not me."

"So John avoided a fight with the Santos?" Rita pursued.

"Not at all!" Philip looked shocked. "He killed two of them! Did you not see the new coup at his belt?"

"Coup?" Leeta frowned. "I've heard that word many times. All I see on his belt are his weapons and those hair things."

Philip pointed proudly at the lengths of hair that hung from his own jacket and belt. "These are my coups!" His grin spread. "I took this one when I was fifteen. I shot a Raider who was trying to steal my uncle's horse. This one I took when I was but six months older. It was on my first raid. I shot the Raider from ambush and cut this from . . .''

"You mean that's human hair!" Leeta gasped.

"Do not your star folk do the same? How do you keep track of coups?'' Philip was genuinely confused, looking back and forth. Then his eyes lit. "Of course! You are women! Perhaps your men do not show their coups for fear you would contaminate them.'' He nodded sagaciously.

Leeta found herself slowly shifting away from the man, her wide eyes pasted on the scalp locks, her shocked mind numb.

"Not quite, Philip,'' Rita had a carnivorous grin. "I'm a warrior among the star folk. I've never taken a coup. I don't think our war leaders would approve. Our People wouldn't either. They already think we're too savage.''

"You? A warrior?'' Philip's eyes showed disbelief. "A woman?''

"I hurt you pretty bad,' Rita was bragging. Philip's hand strayed unconsciously to his sore ribs.

"He seems too vulnerable to have killed someone,'' Leeta mused, her eyes on Iron Eyes.

Philip turned toward her. "When a Raider kills your family and steals your food and rapes your daughters, how do you deal with them?''

"Why, it doesn't happen!'' Leeta's face betrayed horror and incomprehension.

Philip shook his head. "I know your People are very different—but you cannot tell me that men do not raid. I do not believe that. That is how Spider made men!''

"She's right,'' Rita said sourly.

Philip looked smug. "And if men do not raid among the stars, why do they have warriors? Eh?''

"It's complicated,'' Leeta allowed, her eyes still on John Smith Iron Eyes' hairy belt. And she'd thought him a handsome man! With human blood on his hands? But what of the concern in his eyes as he had bathed their ripped and torn feet? A killer? Worse, a murderer? She shot a look at Philip. *He bragged of having shot a man from ambush!*

"Too bad you and John didn't kill that big warrior,''

Rita was shaking her head. "I tried. Should have knifed him while I had the chance."

Leeta turned her surprised eyes on Rita. "You sound like you would have enjoyed it." The lieutenant seemed to be in her element among these bloodthirsty animals.

"That's what they trained me for, Doc. Not only that, but I'm having the time of my life! I'm alive here!" Rita's eyes glowed. "From the time those Santos bastards grabbed us, I've been doing something for myself. I'm *capable* for this one brief, shining instant." She laughed. "And you can bet I'm gonna enjoy every last second of it!

"Just like you, here doing what you always hoped for. Tell me, how do the rest of the scholars at university treat anthropology? They look down their noses at you and tell you how useless your discipline is, don't they? Well, you're here now—and Health Department, with its *humane* psych machines is back there!"

Leeta snorted a laugh. "Yeah." She remembered the way Jeffray had smiled in amusement at her. She remembered how her parents had reacted. No one had ever imagined anthropology would do anything for her. And the psych machine. . . .

"Maybe the reason we're here is because for once we can prove something to those white-assed, thin-armed bastards," Rita continued. "Maybe this is our chance to get one up on them."

"How's that?" Leeta asked. "By murder?"

Rita's eyes narrowed and she dropped her chin on braced palms. "You ever thought about how the Directorate is going to react to all this? Think about how the report coming out of this barbaric little world is going to look. You're shying away from Philip here because he's killed a couple of men who fight with his people. You're something, Doc! I've seen the curiosity in your eyes when you look at John over there. Now you find he's got human hair trophies on his belt and you've got cold feet!"

"That's not fair!" Leeta cried indignantly while Philip watched uncomprehendingly. They'd shifted back to Standard.

"It isn't?" Rita's words were heavy with sarcasm.

"I guess you've forgotten how scared you were with Big Warrior. Back on the ship I thought you were all right, a little stupid about the world maybe, but all right.

"Now let me tell you about the bravest man I ever knew." Rita's eyes bored like hot irons. "Remember my husband? He was . . . I didn't tell you that they warned him. Do you think psych profiles aren't accurate? He knew the risks, but it was a dream of his! He took it and he never regretted it . . . and neither do I!

"What about you? Afraid to see what the other side is like? Afraid to question what you really believe, Doc? Maybe there's more to being a hotshot than you've learned in books? Maybe this world will break you and send you packing back to a university with guarded halls, no threats, and sweet, stinking security! Maybe it will—"

"Shut up, lieutenant!"

"Hell, no!" Rita exploded. "What do you think you owe the Directorate? Where's your damn noble society? The Gi-net? The balloon-heads? Where's our damn holier than thou superiority when Jeffray turns you in to be psyched? These people know who their friends and enemies are—do you? Think of that psych machine burning synapses closed, Doc. That's your moral—"

"Shut up!" Leeta cried, jaw clenched.

"And you can't go back, Doc," Rita's voice lowered. "You already made that decision. Leeta Dobra is lost . . . Jeffray condemned you."

In the sudden silence, Leeta looked at Philip with guilt in her eyes. How right was Rita Sarsa? How right was Leeta Dobra? How right were any of them? Wasn't that the lesson anthropology tried to teach? There were other ways to truth—weren't there? But human hair?

Shaken, she got to her feet and walked to the other side of the shelter to watch rain falling from the gray sky. Cold, she shivered and leaned against the mossy rock of the wall. She closed her eyes and reviewed her life. Jeffray, Veld, Chem, all of them. They came back to haunt her. As she thought of each, the lean, dangerous image of John Smith Iron Eyes kept forcing itself into her mind.

"*Star woman, do not move!*" The urgent voice said softly, almost in her ear.

She opened her eyes carefully, knowing John's voice. "Why?" she asked, unconcerned.

"I am going to shoot." came the calm return. "Do not move! It will kill you if you do!"

"I . . ." The concussion of the big gun was deafening in the rock enclosure. Spatters of rock and dirt stung her legs. In spite of the warning, Leeta jumped, horrified.

She spun, scared, heart pounding, ears still echoing with a high-pitched ring.

"Damn you! *You could have killed me!*" she shrieked at the Romanan as he lowered his big rifle. He wasn't listening. He was watching the ground at her feet.

Slowly, she dropped her gaze and stared at the thing that looked like slimy, black-brown mottled gelatin. It twisted slowly, brown fluid leaking from its body.

"W . . . what?" she whispered.

"Rock leech," Iron Eyes told her. "They come out in the rain. Had it caught your foot, we could have done nothing. Some are saved if the leg is cut off in time. It would depend on how strong you are, star woman. Out here, with only knives for cutting and fire to cauterize, it would have been very painful." He turned and slowly walked back to the fire.

Swallowing hard, fighting an urge to scream, Leeta forced herself to step around the still twisting thing and followed him—unable to stop her sudden shaking—back to the fire.

Philip seemed unconcerned while Rita looked oddly triumphant. "Worlds are all different, Doc." She went back to talking in low tones with Philip.

The next day, the rain let up. "Two days' travel," John guessed looking at the ragged skies.

"We can make Gessali Camp?" Philip asked.

"I think so. It will be hard on the horses. The women ride since they have no shoes. We run in the mud, cousin." John laughed.

Staggered by events, it was exhilarating to ride the

horse out of the canyon. Leeta felt her blood racing with excitement as the big black animal stumbled and slid on the slick path. John led the mare, walking surely. The constant drizzle fell on her unprotected head but, thrilled, she ignored it.

They climbed out of the canyon and headed across the open expanse of now verdant grass. As the men trotted before them, Leeta shot a glance at Sarsa. The lieutenant looked wild, savage in her skin clothing, the rifle she'd stolen from the Santos resting across the saddle.

In the long dim past, Leeta realized, her ancestors had lived like this, no safety anywhere but in their wits and weapons. The long roll call of humanity stirred her. She remembered the veneration with which she'd touched those ancient skeletons hanging in Chem's office. The had known this kind of life!

Hours passed. Reveling in the experience, Leeta wasn't even fazed when John and Philip stopped as one, looking carefully at the grass before them. Rita, better atuned, pulled up her rifle, scanning the wet grass.

"Santos warriors," Iron Eyes said softly. "Not more than two hours since they passed this way."

Philip looked up, a wary scowl on his face. "Perhaps sixty of them."

"Twenty apiece, eh, my good warriors?" Rita chuckled, checking the round in the rifle.

Leeta felt her heart skip. Once more she knew fear as her frightened eyes swept the empty grass.

CHAPTER XI

Colonel Ree turned his attention to the smoking remains of the Santos village. The other aircars flew support as skirmish lines of marines advanced, sweeping a few fugitives before them. Lieutenant Sarsa's disabled aircar lay on its side, dented, obviously looted.

Ree pulled his night goggles off and leaned back in the dim red light cast by his craft's instruments. "Still no sign, Neal?" he queried Iverson.

"No, sir. Got their equipment belts is all. Sarsa's blaster is still missing." He paused. "Sir? These bodies down here. I think maybe you'd better see. We've got the camp secured. Perimeter's in. Even if they could mount a counterattack, they don't have anything we can't handle half asleep."

Within a minute, Ree was bending over the body of a young man. A huge hole had been blown through the fellow's chest. Captain Iverson pointed to the bloody skull that glistened in the brilliant glow from the spotlights focused on the bodies.

"He's not the only one. All the dead have been treated similarly." Neal looked up at him, puzzled.

"I'll be damned!" Ree breathed as he realized what he was seeing "You know what this is? It's scalping!" He shook his head in amazement.

"Huh?" Iverson gave him a blank look.

"Proof of a kill. See the hair on this guy's jacket. Five'll get you ten that's human hair." Ree studied the corpse with interest. "I want this whole place documented. Pack up the bodies and send them to the ship. Let's get some answers out of the prisoners." Ree turned on his heel and strode over to where Lieutenant Moshe Rashid had established his interrogation center.

Half an hour later, Damen Ree was no closer to finding the missing women. "Send out sweeps. Stop any Romanans you find. Figure that for each hour since the attack, the search area has doubled. It's been four hours since the Spider strike. With horses, they could be anywhere within a fifty mile radius. Damn!" Ree pounded his fist into his hand. "Relay to *Bullet*. I want to know where each of the parties went. Patch through to comm. Follow out each lead."

"Colonel," Iverson looked up. "Comm advises a pretty good storm is coming in. High wind warnings, better than 120 kph at peak gust. The aircars can't handle that, sir.''

"How long till the front hits?'' Ree asked, feeling a building frustration. If anything happened to Dobra. . . .

"About dawn, sir. We've got four hours—if we push it.'' Iverson looked worried.

"Get moving. I want every human picked up. If they run, burn down the horses. If they continue to resist, stun them into submission.'' Ree muttered a curse under his breath and glared up into the black heavens. "Should have brought a complete assault crew. *Hell, horsemen can't do this to me!*''

Time became Ree's enemy and he chafed as it began to drag. The stock of prisoners grew. Bella Vola was patched in to do the interrogation, Ree distrusting the translating machine alone. The story was the same from both Santos and Spider warriors. The Santos had only seen the women until they were married. *Married? For God's sake!* The Spiders had seen no women, but their war chief was missing along with his sacred cousin. *What the hell did* that *mean?*

The wind ripped through the canyon in a sudden fury, scattering founts of dust and bits of dry vegetation as the sky lightened. Ree watched helplessly as one of the marines barely avoided wrecking an aircar in the bucking gusts.

"Colonel? It's a good half hour to the base camp. Wind'll get worse!'' Iverson really looked worried. "What do you want to do with the prisoners?''

"Bring 'em!'' Ree ordered.

"But sir, the weight! Flying will be bad enough as it is!'' Iverson protested.

"You heard me. Let's go. How long'll this thing last?'' Ree bit off a curse.

"Comm says three days, sir—then a second storm will follow this one.'' Iverson looked as if he'd swallowed something rotten.

"Comm!'' Ree growled as his suddenly unstable craft lurched into the air. "I want full assault teams dirtside. Move! He looked at a wide-eyed private beside him. "That way if the wind gets too bad they can pick us up. ATs can fly in anything.''

The only small victory was the recovery of Netta Solare. The last aircar spotted her as she crawled up a hillside, naked, muttering in broken phrases. Rashid reported that she was completely incoherent and recommended psych. He said it was obvious she had been raped. Ree's guts turned to ice as he glared into the swirling gray clouds.

Director Skor Robinson floated above the huge console. The Sirian economic crisis was deteriorating. Robinson's agile mind anticipated the riots and dispatched two GCIs full of comestibles from Range. He alerted the Patrol to be in the vicinity within twenty days, realizing that food might not be the only problem in the Sirian Sector. Had it been a mistake to allow Van Chow loose? There were always political machinations by the Independence Party. Van Chow was moving up in those ranks. No, one man couldn't possibly have that much statistical impact.

Satisfied, he allowed his mind to split into different modes, each handling a lesser problem. Almost at once, excitement in one mode caught him. It spread. Alarm. Intrigue. Skor dropped the other problems and turned his full mind to the report from the scientific expedition at Atlantis.

As a matter of routine, Skor routed any reports of new Stations, or, as in this case, a lost colony, through his boards before any knowledge became public. One never knew how a new station might affect a stable economy. People did not need to know about exotics—that led to social turbulence. Scanning the texts, Skor moved immediately to block information access to the Gi-Net.

Prescience? Warriors? Prophets? Religion based on seeing the future? A part of Skor's mind accessed biographical information on Emmanuel Chem, the author of the report. Ph.D., numerous academic citations, stable profile, considered aging but brilliant, not given to hyperbole or excess. Exaggeration didn't seem to fit the man.

Truth then? Could these men, Romanans they'd taken to calling them, really be prescient? Impossible. Outside of the realm of physical law. But should the information become known. . . . Skor devoted perhaps a half second to consideration of the implications to the economy, sociology, religious groups, and so forth.

Notice. The planet known as Atlantis is ordered interdicted. The Patrol ships of the line, Brotherhood *and* Victory *are ordered to change vectors from Sirius to Atlantis.*

Did leaving Sirius unguarded demonstrate prudence?

Skor's pale face strained below his helmet. For the first time in twenty years, atrophied muscles attempted to frown, bringing pain to his face. At first, the Director's mind had trouble identifying the sensation. Simultaneously, he attempted to block the transmissions of vital signs but was too late.

Frantic, he filed an explanation. Nevertheless, Navtov, Roque, and the rest would have noted. They would be very curious to know what had caused distress in the Director.

Perhaps it would be best to order Ree to sterilize the planet? Too hasty. Skor needed more data. Using a top military clearance, he sent his orders for further information to *Bullet*. Keeping control of his vital signs on the computer, he let his heart race as an odd sensation distracted him. What?

He realized in amazement the feeling was fear. Indeed! What a stimulant to the system! Skor struggled to bring his body under control as his mental excitement pricked little used neural passages to his thin limbs and torso. Skor silenced mental modes, letting quiet seep into his huge brain.

Fear was still there. He had *never* been so far out of hand! That fact gave him pause. Such a situation must never be allowed again. If Atlantis and the Romanans could bring such fright to him, think of the consequences should the public ever find out! Think of the danger of such knowledge in the hands of his enemies!

Skor moved his tongue about his mouth. He'd almost forgotten the tongue. How unsteadily it moved. Nourishment came from intravenous feeding. Excrement was removed automatically by catheter. Skor reprimanded himself and, by dint of mental effort, re-

162

gained control of himself and began to establish procedures should the Atlantis thing get out of hand. At the same time, his curiosity was piqued.

Skor canceled the routing of the food-laden GCIs to Sirius. He channeled Patrol priorities to Gulag Sector and credited the Independence Party with a half billion anonymous credits. Smokescreen.

In the meantime, he composed special orders and, with highest secrecy, dispatched them to Colonel Ree. Failsafe. Nice, clean, objective, a good way to deal with a potential threat to the Directorate!

Leeta shivered in the cold air. Lying on wet, cold, hard ground, she had never been so miserable in all her life! Chomping, grinding horse molars competed with the chattering of her own teeth. She shivered violently and huddled into the tightest ball she could, the chill continuing to creep up her legs from her clay-cold feet.

She heard a whispered sound and clenched her teeth to still the chattering. Sudden fear tempered her physical misery. The bump, bump of her heart loud in her ears, she prayed no Santos bent over her soggy blanket.

A soft giggle in the night and whispering were barely audible. The noises—definitely not Santos—continued as Leeta wondered, shivered, and wished for warmth, fire, a bed, and something hot to drink. Wretched, she looked over at Rita's blanket and saw it move. More noises. Dream?

She started to sit up, thinking to wake her companion. Then the blanket rose. A garment was raised and folded in the shadows. A male voice murmured. A female sigh answered. The sounds continued in a slow rhythm.

Leeta lay back and hugged herself closer, the language of sounds all too clear. On the hillock above, Iron Eyes sat watching for the Santos. Rita, at least, wasn't cold.

Loneliness spread with the cold. Why am I here? Anger flickered to life in her breast. She shivered again. Cold, miserable . . . and now lonely. Would this eternal night ever end?

The thought of snuggling next to Jeffray's comforting body haunted her thoughts. He'd been warm. Until she came here, she'd never been cold in all her life! Now look at her, soaked like a drowned rat! How long until hypothermia set in? How many calories did she have left to burn?

The slight sounds from the other blanket picked up in intensity. Leeta bit her lip and clenched her jaws. She sat up quietly, grimacing at the shrieking protest of her muscles. Horses did that to a human. The insides of her thighs and calves burned raw red. Her gluteus muscles shared attributes with pureed liver.

She forced herself up, wrapping the dripping blanket over her shoulders. A sharp intake of breath sounded from Rita's blanket. Then another.

Harlot!

Carefully, Leeta picked her way toward the top of the rise.

"It's me," she whispered as she neared the place where she'd seen Iron Eyes settle down to watch.

She staggered to the top of the knoll, finding only bayonet grass under her bare feet. Where was Iron Eyes? The breeze pulled any remaining heat from her body. Slowly, Leeta slumped into the wet grass, eyes searching the heavens for any sign of stars or moon in the blackness.

The tears came unbidden. She stifled a sob and bit it back, not willing to succumb. God! Why am I so miserable? What am I doing here? I'm a damn fool! Would it have been so bad to have been an engineer's wife? She and Jeffray would be moving to Range now. She'd have a house there. Open space. She'd be warm! Warm! Oh, God, to be warm!

And she'd be psyched! A nice, mellow human, perfect in every social way—and not an original thought in her mind.

She bowed her head and wiped a cold finger across her runny nose. The shivering was constant now. When she moved her toes, they rubbed like soggy wood. Reality was cold, wetness, misery, and suffering. That was life. Why the hell did anyone even want to live? Jeffray knew that truth. He'd done a sensible thing—gotten out! Her fault, brat that she was. He'd gotten out without her. She choked on another sob and shivered.

"Would another shirt help?" a calm voice spoke behind her.

She gasped and turned, searching the darkness for his form. "I c-can't t-take your sh-shirt," she said unevenly through her clicking teeth.

She heard him come close. Hide clothing rustled as he bent down. A warm finger touched her cheek briefly. *A warm finger!* "You are very cold. It is not good."

She heard him as he took his shirt off. His fingers pulled the blanket from her shoulders and felt of her damp leather shirt.

"Take that off," he ordered.

"But . . ." she started to protest.

"It will be warmer." His voice was friendly, caring.

Not quite believing she was doing it, she pulled the heavy, wet shirt over her shoulders. She felt shamed, as if he hadn't already seen her naked . . . and in the light, too! Still, he promised warmth. She helped pull his warshirt over her shoulders and . . . *thank God, it was warm!*

"I never knew something so trivial as a warm shirt could mean so much," she sputtered in delight.

"You should be sleeping," he reminded.

"I was so cold. But what are you going to do? You will turn to a block of ice!" She felt a sense of panic. It wasn't right that he suffer to make her warm.

"It is not cold. I cannot turn to a block of ice when water does not freeze around me." His voice was light, amused.

"I feel bad about taking your shirt," she muttered.

"I have my other shirt back," his rich voice assured her. "It is already on. You should get some sleep. It will be a long day tomorrow."

"I guess you might say that camp is busy," she hesitated. "Philip and Rita are, well . . ."

His chuckle startled her. "I am glad. Philip has never been close to a woman."

"But he seems so kind," she answered, her brow furrowing.

"Philip hasn't always been this way. The visions burdened him for years—even before the coming of the star people. He lived very much inside himself. Haunted by what would be."

"And you?" she asked. "Were you always the way you are now?" Haunted, Iron Eyes? That sadness behind your eyes?

"How am I?" he asked.

"Hurt," she said simply.

"I am a warrior." There was pride in that. "Warriors do not feel pain."

"She must have been a very wonderful woman," Leeta guessed. There was silence. "Tell me about her," she added, her voice betraying her interest.

Time dragged. She thought he would ignore her.

Then: "She was of my clan—of my family. My father's sister's daughter. She was Smith. We couldn't marry. Then she was killed. That is all."

"There was more, Iron Eyes," she added softly. "You told me more than you know."

"Is that so, star woman?" his voice mocked.

"It is so." She need add nothing.

They were silent for a time; Leeta shivered again. "The Santos will find us?" she asked.

"Spider will decide." His voice was noncommittal.

"There are a lot of them," Leeta reminded. "What happens if they do catch us?"

"We fight," he said without emotion.

"You can't beat that many of them, Iron Eyes. I don't care how good a warrior you are."

She heard him laugh at the seriousness in her voice.

"Do you expect to live forever, star woman?" He was amused.

"No, but to fight when you can't win? Why?" It puzzled her.

"Philip and I will fight." She could picture his shrug. "Perhaps the star warrior woman will stay and fight, too. While we fight you will escape. There is honor in that."

"Honor? Where? What good is honor when you're dead?" Leeta almost cried.

His voice was still calm. "If the Santos take us, they will kill Philip and me if we fight or not. There is

166

nothing else for them to do. Is it not better that we die as men than women?''

"I'm a woman, I don't feel whipped!" she snapped, suddenly remembering her earlier thoughts. Thank God this man couldn't see inside her head.

"Maybe your star women are different than Spider women," he agreed.

"It's only because you make your women that way. I'd bet they're never allowed to aspire to be warriors." She snorted her derision.

If he was offended, his voice didn't betray him. "It is the way Spider taught us. Do men among the stars fight?"

Leeta's mind touched hazily on Jeffray's image. "We really don't need warriors. Star people are peaceful. They trade among themselves. They don't raid."

"These people are not strong then?" He seemed to doubt her words. "What makes them brave? What provides them with challenge?"

"Other things," Leeta explained. "Challenges come in our heads. Can we find a better way to make something? Can we grow more food—or do things easier?"

"There is coup for those who do these things?" Iron Eyes voice reflected interest.

"Not exactly." She frowned. What was there? Academic recognition? She never heard about inventors. Come to think of it, she never heard of anyone outside of her own little community. Even the names of the actors, politicians, and authors were little known. The important thing—according to the Directorate—was the individual's contribution.

"Why do anything if there is no coup?" he asked, puzzled. "Is this what they would have the People become? The prophet said the star men would come and try and make us like them. If there is no coup—no challenge—I would not want to see my People's future."

"It's not like that, not really," she insisted. "There are things which make life easy. You can study what men have done in the past; you can see faraway worlds."

He laughed. "See the past? Make life easy? See things far away? What's good about that? How many

167

people see the future? How many people go to faraway places?''

"I came here," she said deliberately; but a seed of doubt had been sown.

"You came here,''he agreed. "Will they let me go see these other places? Can I take my People and go out among the stars without having to become like you?''

She couldn't answer that. How did a person get to travel? Join the military? Get assigned off planet? People didn't travel much. Even commerce was carried out with automated ships, GCIs. Only the stations moved—but men never left the stations. They lived inside these giant cans. It was a moving society, not a society of moving individuals. She finally whispered, "I don't know.''

"So if the Santos find us, I will fight while you go off to live. If I fight well, the Santos will remember my name. You will live long and tell my name among the stars. That way, even Spider will know me. I will be the greatest of the Spider warriors. Can there be more than that to life?''

The pride in his voice shocked her. To be known among the stars? Would the Directorate allow the transmission of such information? Would they allow the fame of a warrior to be broadcast like seeds into a fallow galaxy?

She shivered again. The cold—never having been totally vanquished—was returning. "I wish we had a fire,'' she whispered.

"And have the Santos see it? You would have me send my soul to Spider long before its time.'' He was laughing and she felt him sit down next to her. A warm arm snaked about her as the blanket was lifted from her and wrapped around them.

She thought for a brief instant to push back—away from this strange man. Then the warmth of his body began to seep into her leaden limbs.

"They'd never allow you or your kind free in space,'' she whispered, thinking of the psych sentence passed on her by Health. "You'd be an unsettling influence. They wouldn't know what to do with you, Iron Eyes. They can't predict your actions. They'd keep you for a laboratory specimen.'' She went on to explain a laboratory.

His voice was sad, resigned. ''Then perhaps we had better search out the Santos, star woman. John Smith Iron Eyes will not be a—as you say—*specimen*. If it means this for the People, we will fight the Santos and your star men to the death. We will be remembered that way. Only our souls are of Spider—our bodies we may use as we wish.'' He sounded so sure.

''You can't win.'' She looked up. ''That ship up there, *Bullet,* can blow this entire planet to dust, Iron Eyes. You can't fight. They are too powerful.''

''Then we will die with honor and send our souls to Spider proudly,'' he said simply.

That couldn't be argued. His God—this Spider—had told him how it was. It would take a while for her to change him and his People, that was all. She couldn't let them be destroyed, they were too noble. She didn't realize when she went to sleep.

Rita's eyes showed exhaustion when they climbed on the mounts in the gray light. Using Standard, Leeta gibed, ''Long night?''

Rita shot her a smile that reeked of satiation. ''I thought it passed rather quickly. Noticed you'd moved your blankets, too, Doc.''

''Iron Eyes and I had a long talk last night. I *sure* couldn't sleep in camp.'' She knew her voice sounded haughty and her chin had risen.

Rita was stifling laughter. ''If it makes you feel better, Doc. Sure, you and Iron Eyes—''

''Damn it! I tell you. . . . Oh, hell! You'd never believe me anyway. Think what you want.'' Her eyebrows went up. ''So, tell me, what do you see in Philip?''

Rita's body swayed with the gait of the horse as she looked over, eyes narrowed. ''Freedom, Doc. He's living for today. I like that.'' She was nodding positively to herself.

''What about tomorrow? You know Ree's out looking for us.'' Leeta looked up at the gray sky; she still shivered a little, but her stomach was full of meat now and she'd slept warm.

Rita looked about, wary eyes intent on the hills

around them. She let her gaze linger on the back of Philip's head and a slight smile crossed her lips. When she looked back, she shrugged. "I'm hoping tomorrow never comes." Her voice was wistful.

"It will." Leeta thought it sounded flat.

"I'm not sure I want to go back to being a squad leader on a star ship that never attacks anything." Rita took a deep breath. "You know, the first time I was ever in a fight for my life was with Big Man. The rest of my career was sleep synch, exercise and practice in an empty room, and boring duty.

"Just think, Doc. There's half a hundred men somewhere out there that will kill us if they get the chance!" Sarsa's eyes gleamed. "Makes each second count. Makes each breath something precious. Never know, in a couple of hours there might not be much breathing." She grinned. "And I'm a born rebel! Told you that clear back at university."

Leeta's brow furrowed. How did a person make sense of it? Where was the right? Sarsa wasn't a barbarian—not by training at least. The thought that a Santos would take pleasure in killing her scared Leeta down to the bottom of her guts! She *hated* fear. But anxiety seemed to be a stimulant for Rita.

A light drizzle began as the clouds bunched up on the horizon. The land was becoming more broken as they skirted the base of the Bear Mountains. Iron Eyes stopped and pointed. A streak of light moved on the horizon.

"AT!" Rita called sourly. "Ree's getting serious."

Leeta took a deep breath. Rescue!

"And there are the Santos!" Iron Eyes pointed.

Below them, at the point of a ridge the horsemen had pulled up, eyes on the AT. From the way the horses were milling, the Santos were baffled by the craft which had now swung toward them. "Well," Leeta began, "I can't say that it hasn't been informative. We owe you and Philip a lot, Iron Eyes, but a hot shower will—"

She never finished as the long white AT dove at the Santos, violet-white lines of light flickered into the horsemen to end in dust-spraying explosions of rock and sand and charred flesh.

170

"What the hell has happened?" Rita cried.

"They will come attack us?" Philip demanded, voice tight.

Rita's face paled as she chewed her lip. "Hell, yes! Philip, keep to low ground. Is there any place around here we can get under cover? They can detect the heat of our bodies. They can also see in the dark with those things."

He looked up at her and smiled conspiratorially.

Leeta, shocked, looked at the lieutenant. *"They just killed them!"*

"That's right, Doc," Rita gritted. "Looks like Ree's gone to war!"

John and Philip were running now, Leeta had to hang onto the knob on the front of the saddle. She'd become used to the movements of the horse but was still far from confident.

John Smith led them down a rough, rocky drainage. He jumped lithely from rock to rock, periodically casting an eye to the heavens. Leeta couldn't help but admire the agility of both man and horse even as she clung in fright, fearing a fall at any time.

She could hear the easy panting of Iron Eyes now. His bellows lungs didn't labor as he hurried them along. The black mare's ears were pointed as she picked a quick trail through the nasty footing.

Time stretched. The drizzle turned to light rain. "How long do the rains last?" Leeta wondered.

"Until spring!" Iron Eyes called back.

"That's not this afternoon, is it?" Leeta asked with at least an attempted enthusiasm, her mind still boggled by the AT's crazy actions.

He laughed. He actually laughed! "No, star woman. It is a long time yet. Fear not, we will have a dry camp tonight."

Not far off there was a loud crack followed by a piercing whistle.

Iron Eyes pulled up, listening.

"Damn!" Rita whispered. "AT just shot at something. That's a blaster. We've got to hide. Philip, will the horses stay nearby if we turn them loose?"

"They won't go far. I trained mine very well, but

171

the mare would take any opportunity to get away from John's ugly face.'' He grinned at John.

''The mare will not go,'' Iron Eyes snorted. ''Unless it is to drive that red gelding from her pasture.''

''Well, quit talking and let's get to it!'' Rita snapped, not even wincing as she jumped down on her tender feet. ''Iron Eyes! You and Doc under that rock! Philip, turn the horse loose and follow me into that crack in the rock. We won't stand a close shot with the scanners—but if they pass off to the side, we're safe.''

Leeta caught the concept and dragged a hesitant Iron Eyes under the overhang of the boulder. She began piling rocks around the outside of the little shelter. John was a quick study. Figuring she had her reasons, he pitched in to help.

Then they waited. ''How long?'' Leeta called across to the tumbled detritus where Rita had hidden. Hiding from the Patrol? She tried to swallow. First the psych, now the Directorate might actually shoot her down? In cold blood? Why? The questions echoed through her head.

''If they're searching, a couple of hours. Other than that, no telling. Depends on what they shot at! Shut up! They might hear us!''

''Hear us from how far?'' John whispered in Leeta's ear.

''I don't know,'' Leeta told him. ''Rita's the expert. We do what she says.'' She was acutely aware of his presence, smelling his odor, feeling his body warmth.

A faint whistling picked up in volume, and held steady. Checking the horses, Leeta decided. Then it shrilled off to the east.

Another hour passed as Leeta allowed herself to sleep in Iron Eyes' arms again.

''That's about it,'' Rita called soberly. ''They're long gone.'' The horses had strayed to the top of the ridge. Rita had that look in her eye—and Leeta knew what she and Philip had done while they waited out the AT.

Gessali Camp turned out to be closer than the men had thought. The big rock overhang lay along the bottom of a major drainage where the stream had truncated a ridge, then cut back into the old channel, leaving a perfectly protected camp.

Iron Eyes pulled up, studying the ground. "Horses, many of them."

"Santos" Philip spat. "Not more than half a day. They left at a run. See! The horses were panicked."

Iron Eyes was looking warily up at the rock walls of the valley. "I wish we had the heat seeing things of Rita's ATs."

"Better than your blind eyes," Philip agreed sincerely.

"Gessali Camp may not be such a good idea," Rita added.

"I suppose better cold again than dead," Leeta said glumly.

"You're learning, Doc." Rita chewed her lip as she studied the canyon walls, rifle up and ready.

They rounded a bend and found a gruesome sight. A burn on solid rock still steamed eerily in the cool air. Parts of three horses were scattered about. Leeta could see a human arm, a foot, and a blackened skull.

"What?" Iron Eyes looked up, feeling the heat off the glazed rock.

"AT blaster." Rita's voice was cold. "I guess we found what they shot at."

"Santos," Philip kicked the arm, making Leeta wince. "See the decoration? Santos color."

"It . . . it could have been us." Leeta felt her fear building. Her stomach lurched at the smell of burned man and horse. She fought to keep from vomiting.

Iron Eyes was saying, "They could be anywhere around here. That blaster bolt probably scattered them. I feel like a sitting duck out here."

Rounding another bend, they were into the band of Santos before they knew it. Fifteen men sprang to their feet.

"*Ayaaaaah!*" John Smith screamed, leveling his rifle and pulling the trigger as a man jumped up, trying frantically to bring his own rifle to bear. Then mad confusion possessed them all. Men were running, yelling, shooting.

Rita had pushed Philip's gelding forward as if she'd done it a thousand times. Leeta saw her shoot a man, the bullet hit the back of his skull and blew it open. Philip had shot and was wading into the fight, smashing with the heavy butt of his rifle.

The Santos screamed, running about madly, giving way before them. Fear and consternation reflected in their wide, demoralized eyes as they turned and sprinted for the few horses hitched beyond them. Then it was over, with a last few shots from the Santos, and Rita and Philip pursuing them, shooting, yelling like fiends.

Leeta barely caught her breath as the mad pack raced out of sight. She looked to where Iron Eyes stood, his feet braced. Why didn't he follow? she wondered, curiously upset at his lack of initiative.

He turned and looked at her, his face proud. "Did you see them run? The four of us, we have sent all of them running!" His face beamed as he fell face first into the muddy soil.

Leeta sat for a second, shocked. Then she leaped down to roll him over and stare at the spreading red stain that grew above Iron Eyes' stomach.

"My God," Leeta whispered as she pulled up the ragged leather shirt. Iron Eyes was staring at her as though she was very far away. "I fought . . . with honor . . . didn't I?" he asked absently.

"Yes," she agreed, sniffing at a sudden tear. "You fought very well." She wiped mud from his face.

"You are proud of me, star woman?" he asked.

"Yes, I am," she told him, realizing it was true. His head lolled to one side. Frantic, she checked his pulse. Alive! She pulled his long, wicked knife from his belt and began cutting strips from his shirt.

She struggled to get the strips under his muscular back. The wound gaped across his ribs, just under the pectorals. Suddenly, he ceased breathing.

Shock to the solar plexis? She began resuscitation until he was breathing again. Blood still welled through broken fragments of ribs. Pulling the strips of leather tight, Leeta bound his chest. She was gasping, sobbing, practically hysterical.

More shots echoed down the canyon. Iron Eyes lost consciousness as she smoothed his brow, weeping softly.

She didn't hear the man come up behind her. The

first she knew, he knotted strong fingers in her hair, jerking her head back. Crying out in pain and fear, she gazed into the smoldering eyes of a Santos warrior. She could see him slide his long rifle past her, centering the barrel over Iron Eyes' forehead.

"No!" she bleated in animal fear. Her hair ripped as she threw herself into his body. The rifle boomed—shattering her world—and she realized she still held the knife. A red haze hung before her as she howled, shrieked, and clawed at the man. She sank her teeth into his flesh as she kicked violently for his crotch. Pulling back the knife, she rammed it time and time again into his body while he battered her face with his fists.

They were on the ground, thrashing, when the knife was suddenly wrenched from her fingers. Gibbering with fear, anger, and desperation, she clawed his face, feeling her fingers gouging into his eyes. Adrenal fear lent her strength as she ripped the bloody orbs from his skull. She kept hooking her fingers into his flesh, feeling pain from her torn nails. How long did it take for her to realize he was dead?

Spent, she crawled to Iron Eyes—sight blinded by tears and blood. Laying her head on his, she collapsed into violent fits of hysteric sobbing. Totally exhausted, she lifted her head, wiped her eyes and stared at the bloody face that had belonged to Iron Eyes.

CHAPTER XII

The chosen captains sat stiffly at attention as Major Antonia Reary continued. "Damen Ree will not always retain command of *Bullet*, ladies and gentlemen. I selected each of you for your potential abilities—and your political aspirations. Do you understand?"

Several smiled grimly, one or two nodded, all wore

serious expressions. "Very well," Antonia continued, steepling her fingers. "You will look for the missing women. At the same time, Patrol policy is to respond in kind at the first sign of aggression. Others of your colleagues will follow Ree's orders to the letter. I, however, expect a certain *initiative* should the Romanans offer resistance. Questions?"

One by one, she met their steely eyes, seeing their resolve. Of course, there would be no questions.

Antonia wrapped her slender fingers around her coffee bulb. "Very good, I knew you would all realize that a debacle here will move each of you up the ladder of command when Ree and his favorites are replaced."

Captain Gen Tabson lifted a finger.

Antonia raised an eyebrow. "Yes?"

"What is the Major's policy if we should find the captive women in the company of hostile Romanans?"

Antonia granted him a thin smile. "Gen, resistance will not be tolerated. You must defend yourself and your AT—first and foremost." And the loss of an anthropologist and a potential competitor like Sarsa would embarrass Damen Ree most seriously.

"Very well, Captains," she concluded. "Dismissed!"

They filed out—faces thoughtful—and made their way to waiting ATs.

Wind rocked the aircar, threatening to tip it over. Ree snarled helplessly as the sky burst, hurling water in rushes. "Set down!" Ree ordered as he saw Rashid's car almost capsize when a gust drove it a good fifty meters off course.

Grounded, the wind still hammered them unmercifully. The plexidome rattled and shook under the gale. Ree took a deep breath and reported their condition. "We need those ATs, *pronto!*" he growled into the comm.

The aircars had landed in a ragged line. Ree looked at the five prisoners sharing his car: four Santos and a Spider. The Romanans never took their eyes from each other. Except for the marine standing guard with a blaster, they'd have been at each other's throats.

176

Ree—with nothing else to do—brought up the translator box. "So tell me," he began, the machine twisting out the Romanan translation, "what's the war all about?"

The Spider shot him a quick glance, but said nothing.

"We will destroy the Spider men and their four false Prophets," a Santos snorted. "They are weak—like women. We will leave their bones for the rock leeches. Their women will wail in our villages while they bear strong sons for the Santos."

"So you aren't fighting over any injury or insult. I take it this is a territorial blood feud," Ree pursued.

The Spider's tone was insolent. "They want the radio so they can call the Sobyets down to destroy us. Their false Prophet told them this was their only chance to enslave the People. The Sobyets will be destroyed if they ever come here. These," he sneered, pointing with his chin, "drink from their father's urine."

A Santos roared out his anger and leaped. The marine—ever vigilant—shot him down with a reduced charge. The Santos sprawled, his blackened skin already blistering and cracking as he writhed in excruciating pain.

Ree was on his feet. *"I'll not have that!"* he thundered at the captives. "You were told!" He glared at them, finger pointing from face to face. "You are prisoners of the Directorate. Your war is over as of right now!"

Not one of the Romanans even flickered an eyelash. They looked at him as if he were only a minor irritation—not to be taken seriously.

"Don't believe me, eh?" Ree asked quietly. "Let me tell you about it." He drew himself up to his full height and tried to stare them down. "As of the moment the Santos took citizens of the Directorate for the purpose of rape, and licentious behavior, you stepped beyond the pall of civilization! Now I've got one woman back and she was ravished! There're still two out there, hear? They're my responsibility!"

They still watched him impassively. "Let me put it this way." Ree settled himself on the console. "I'm like a great war chief, get that? I control more warriors than the Santos and the Spiders and all the other Raiders put together." That got their attention.

"From this moment forward, any raiding brings my soldiers down on whoever breaks the peace, you hear?" Ree glared at each Romanan in turn while the man on the floor groaned. "I burn villages to the ground from now on!" Ree's lips twitched with emotion. "No more war!"

The Spider looked up with an amused expression. "It is not for you to decide, star man. It is the decision of Spider."

Ree fought the urge to backhand him. Not since he was a junior grade officer had anyone spoken to him in that tone. "You tell me where to find this spider fella and I'll bust him into a thousand pieces!" Ree's eyes narrowed as the warrior's amusement turned into outright mirth. "What's so funny?" Ree hissed.

"Spider is God, star man. I want to see you bust God!" He laughed in open ridicule.

It drove Ree berserk. Suddenly he was standing over the Spider, his fists doing the work that even at his advanced age he trained himself for. The Spider tried to fight back, pushing up from the seat. Ree killed him quickly and neatly.

A wolfish satisfaction animated the Santos as the Spider slumped across the wounded man on the floor. Dead, the Spider's eyes still mirrored the fighting spirit snuffed within.

Ree took a deep breath, trying to calm himself. *He'd lost it!* Not since the Academy had he lost control of himself. Worse, he might have killed the Spider—but he hadn't defeated him.

The Santos—instead of being cowed—were now eying him like a piece of meat. As Ree shot them a quick look he could see the challenge in their eyes—and to hell with the guard and the blaster. Damn fools, didn't they care that he could kill them all! *Who are these people? What drives them?*

"See anything unusual?" Ree asked quietly, turning to the guard.

"No, sir," the guard answered evenly. "I do think one of the prisoners fell from his seat, sir. Perhaps we

178

should check the man for signs of heart failure? That or he might be needing air and we could leave him to revive later, sir."

Ree dug a water bottle from the supplies and took a swig. There might be an inquiry since he hadn't recovered the women. The killing had focused his attention on the problem.

And I lost control!

Accessing comm, he entered a report, noting that it had been at the insistence of Chem and Dobra that he'd neglected thorough security meaures. The scientists had been most adamant about maintaining a low profile among the Romanans. He'd accepted that they were the experts. When his fears were aroused, he'd tried to recall Dobra and her crew only to be turned down by Dobra. While attempting to perform a rescue within the parameters detailed by the anthropologists, weather had hampered the effort.

Ree smiled as he thought of his next steps and addressed comm. "Given the recalcitrant nature of the Romanans, I am taking precautions to ensure the safety of Directorate personnel on Atlantis. This is done to ensure that citizens and natives will be protected under the law.

"As a result, I hereby proclaim the cessation of hostilities. I order the return of all stolen property and the immediate repatriation of all hostage persons. Further, intercourse between the villages is banned as of this moment. The only Romanans passing between such points will be those duly authorized by the military authority.

"Those individuals and groups who ignore this proclamation will be subject to military discipline whenever merited. A military tribunal is hearby established under the direction of Captain Neal Iverson and seconded by Moshe Rashid. Any appeal to the above may be presented to Colonel Damen Ree, commanding."

He smiled wickedly to himself. "That is for immediate implementation." He threw a look of satisfaction over his shoulder to where the guards were heaving the body of the dead Spider out into the rain.

By the time the ATs dropped out of the sky, the air

179

in the cars had turned muggy. A happy Ree stepped out of the aircar and faced a saluting lieutenant. *Now I take over and handle it my way—like it should have been from the beginning!*

"Take us to the base camp," Ree ordered. "Establish a perimeter there for the detention of such subjects as authority deems necessary."

"Sir!" The man saluted and Ree made his way to the bridge. In less than a minute, they set down at the base camp.

Detention barriers had already risen around the installation. Ree could see the rain pattering off the distorted area. Marines herded the first Romanans into the square, where they stared in amazement at the rain bouncing off the seeming nothingness. One fellow bolted for the far side and almost broke his neck as the shield shot him back with equal velocity. *Let them work their hostility out on that!*

"Captain Iverson?" Ree accessed.

"Colonel?" Neal's voice came in.

"You will proceed to the wreck of the *Nicholai Romanan*. Once there, a military perimeter will be established and the proclamation read to the inhabitants.

"Rashid?"

"Here, sir!" came the familiar voice.

"You will proceed to the Santos main village and follow suit. As of this moment, there is peace on Atlantis.

"Further instructions. I want Doctor Leeta Dobra and Lieutenant Rita Sarsa located! I want it done now! I don't care if you have to move heaven and earth! Any unit which is not attending to pacification will join the search!" Ree sat back, trying to anticipate any problems.

"Neal, I want you to secure the *Nicholai Romanan*. Expect armed resistance. You shouldn't be facing anything more than primitive lead projectiles. Be sure you take that radio out. In the meantime, establish your own broadcasts of the proclamation and reassure the native populace that all is well. Their captured kinsmen will eventually be returned along with their property."

"Colonel?" Adam Chung asked.

"Yes?"

"Requesting guidance regarding resistance from Native personnel, sir. What are our options?"

"Anything which you feel is justified, Adam. We're here to pacify a planet—not play games." Ree smiled to himself. "Anything else?"

There wasn't.

Ree watched his ATs launch into the gray skies. Accessing a private channel, he added. "Avoid notifying the scientific community regarding the military proclamation. In particular, attempt to keep Dr. Chem from making too many waves. Inform him that his assistant, Doctor Dobra is being held hostage by the Romanans." That ought to keep the old duffer off his back.

"Priority, Colonel Ree. Your Eyes Only!" Comm spat.

Damen Ree's eyes narrowed. He accessed his identification and watched the message form on the screen. It was one of those rare opportunities in a commander's life when the eyes of the great and powerful were upon him. Ree swallowed hard at the sight of the Director's signature and acknowledged receipt.

He was a little shaken as he thought of the moves he had already put into effect. Thinking it over, he realized that the Director's instructions were pretty much in line with his own. The augmentation of his strength by two more ships of the line wasn't a bad break either. In the event of problems from the scientific bunch, he had all the aces up his sleeve.

Or did he? How often had he heard his people chafe at the eternal boredom of endless patrolling along unthreatened borders? *I am getting no younger. There is no other chance for me to make my mark in history.* How long before Reary replaced him? How long before they took *Bullet* away from him?

The Director had interdicted the entire planet. Ree triggered the comm and filed the Director's instructions. "Notice to bridge personnel. By direct order of the Director this planet is interdicted. Repeat. This planet is interdicted. Any approaching vessels not bearing Patrol clearance will be intercepted and ordered to avoid. Any vessel not heeding such instructions will be considered in violation of the law and seized.

"Further, no communication will be allowed between the planet, shipping, or other settlements, stations, or worlds, without the express permission of Colonel Damen Ree or his superiors. Any breach of such regulations will be considered treason to the Directorate and will be punishable as such." Ree grinned to himself.

"Colonel," Comm stuttered. "Mister Marty Bruk requests briefing on the situation. Will you respond?"

Ree fingered his chin for a moment before deciding. He accessed and saw the young physical anthropologist's face form. "Good day, Marty. May I help you?"

Marty Bruk and Bella Vola had watched the white Assault Transports settling around the base camp dome.

"Something went really wrong out there," Marty decided.

"You were there when they patched through the interrogation," Bella agreed. "They still don't have Leeta or the lieutenant. I think the whole game plan just got changed."

"What's that mean?" he asked. "I mean, how does that affect us?"

Bella bit her lip and dropped onto a crate, a cup of coffee in her hand. "You know how the military works things like this?" she asked. Marty shook his head. "They take over completely. That means we don't do anything without their approval."

"Yeah, but what about scientific inquiry? We have work to do here. Don't you see? There's a wealth of information out there. They can't just shut us off!" Marty was getting excited.

"Care to bet," Bella snorted. "You aren't using your head. I've studied this possibility and I think there's a way we can get by, but it will take brains— not emotional outbursts. The military will let us do whatever we want so long," she held up a finger, "as we don't get in their way, and what we're doing is perceived as harmless—or better yet—to their benefit."

182

So Marty called Ree.

"I'd like two things, sir." Marty gave Ree a concerned look. "First I'd like to know what's going on. Second, I'd give my right arm to get at the Romanans you're holding in that compound out there!" He put the emphasis on that last.

Ree smiled at him easily. "I'm afraid we ran into a snag with the Romanans. They are holding Doctor Dobra and one of my people hostage somewhere."

"You got Netta back?" Marty didn't fake the relief.

"She's not . . . Mr. Bruk, they raped her. We're sending her up to *Bullet* for psych evaluation. I'm afraid it was a pretty traumatic experience for her. You can see why we're worried about Doctor Dobra." Ree gave him a concerned look.

"Absolutely, Colonel!" Marty agreed, actually feeling relief. "Listen. Maybe we can help you? I don't want to step on your toes. You were very kind about keeping out of our way. Would we cause you any problems by continuing our studies? Perhaps we'd learn something to give you leverage with the Romanans. I'd like to know we could do something besides sit here feeling useless—but now you're the expert." Good twist, throw that back at him.

Ree seemed relieved. "By all means, Marty." First name, bingo! "I've taken steps that might be construed by some as extreme. I was afraid the scientific staff might be offended by necessary realities. Our first concern is Dr. Dobra, of course."

"I understand," Marty nodded with sincerity. "We're behind you one hundred percent. Do whatever you think necessary for Leeta's safety. Colonel, I'd still really like to do some studies on those prisoners you've got here. It's an unprecedented chance to gather data. Bella can continue to prod for information. Perhaps we can think of something you missed."

"Very good, Marty. Tell the corporal in charge you have my permission and approval." Ree was smiling.

"Thank you, sir. Also, if it wouldn't be too inconvenient, could you keep us informed? We'd like to be sure we don't cause you any grief. I think that's the least we can do, all things considered."

Ree nodded happily. "Will do, Marty, thanks for

your understanding. If you'll excuse me, there are some things I have to attend to."

"Thank you, Colonel!" The screen went dead. "Well?" Marty asked, turning to Bella.

"Good!" She nodded seriously. "Professional without offending. At the same time your sincerity was evident and there wasn't any hint of groveling in the tone of voice. You might make a politician yet."

"So where does that leave us?" Marty wondered. "I don't know what to believe. I'm not sure I trust Ree all the way. There's something suspicious about that prison camp he's building out there. On the other hand, what do we believe about Netta being raped? What do we believe about Leeta? You think she's being held hostage?"

Bella threw up her hands. "I . . . truly don't know. I do know that we've at least left ourselves in the position to find out. I'm not sure what Chem will do when he hears about all this, but we've established ourselves as allies in Ree's eyes. Now, let's see what we can find out. Grab that corporal and get some subjects in here."

Leeta pulled herself up, squeezing tears from her eyes. Rita and Philip should have been back by now. She dabbed at her stiff face, bruised where the warrior had beaten her. She looked down at the gore on Iron Eyes' head.

Her sore fingers rubbed the blood away, trying to find the bullet hole. Blood, grit, and dirt matted his hair. Speckles of powder had burned into his skin. Turning the head, Leeta saw the loose dirt and the crater where the bullet had missed by inches. *It was her blood on his face!*

She'd saved his life! Filled with joy, she stood and ran to the black mare, dragging the animal closer. From the canteen she wet the leather of the shirt and bathed his face. His chest rose and fell steadily now.

"Iron Eyes!" she called, patting his face with a numb hand. "John!" Eyelids flickered. "We've got to get up!"

He looked at her and swallowed. "What? Where?"

"I killed him, John!" she almost shouted. "Come

on, the Santos might come back! Get up! You call yourself a warrior! Help me, damn you. *I don't want to die here!*''

He trembled as he tried to sit up. Though he fought to stifle the cry, it slipped past his lips.

Leeta got behind, pushing, lifting, knowing the broken ribs had to be a killing agony. To her surprise, he lurched to his feel and grabbed the saddle, staggering.

"Use my hand, John. I've got to get you on that horse. You can't walk!" she pleaded with him.

He nodded slightly, pain creasing his face, glazing his eyes. As he heaved, she thought her back would snap like a twig. He hit the saddle on the flat of his stomach and cried out—an explosion of audible pain— but he swung a leg over.

"Rifle," he wheezed. "Knife and rifle."

She picked up the long gun and knocked the sand out of it. On impulse, she pulled a cartridge from his belt. She pulled down on the trigger guard the way she'd seen him do, and the empty brass flew out. She inserted the new charge.

"Coup!" he demanded through clenched teeth. "I want my coup!"

"Damn it, you're half dead! We could die here any minute! Our only chance to keep alive is by moving!" she hollered in spite of his obstinate expression.

"My coup!" he gasped. "Warrior coup. You said you killed. You take your coup, too!"

"No!" she cried, feeling hysteria growing.

"Do it!" he gritted. "Do it . . . or I do it myself!" Pain blasted across his face.

"Damn you, John Smith Iron Eyes!" She yanked the knife from the dead man's ribs and walked to the man she'd seen Iron Eyes shoot. Clumsily, her gut heaving, she carved the slippery skin loose. Handing it to him, she glared.

"Yours!" he grunted. "Your coup. Your honor. Make me proud." He winced with pain.

Fighting a whimper, she turned to the man she'd killed, forced to look at the havoc she'd wrought on his face. A sudden anger welled in her and she bent down, possessed by a need for vengeance, thinking of the way the Santos had tried to shoot Iron Eyes. She hacked the scalp off and held it up in the cold drizzle. Her coup!

She looked down again and stabbed the cold corpse viciously a couple of times before she stood and walked back to Iron Eyes. "My coup," she growled, feeling a repulsive pride. "See that you live for me now!" She grabbed up the reins as she'd seen him do and headed back for Gessali Camp.

Jagged rocks in the stream bottom hurt her barely healing feet as she stumbled along. *Now what? Iron Eyes has been shot! I killed a man. Knifed him. I scratched out his very eyes.*

She looked down to where the blood had dried on her arms, crinkling her skin.

Iron Eyes reeled in the saddle behind her, clinging to the horse by instinct alone. She bit her lips until she tasted blood. The rain had been holding off, but as she passed the blasted horses and men, big drops fell from the leaden skies.

Only a few hundred meters now. She could see the overhang that marked Gessali Camp. "Come on, John," she whispered under her breath, the rifle heavy on her arm as she struggled up the sloping fill under the shelter. "Hang on!" She pleaded as the mare buck-jumped up the steep incline.

Reaching the top, she realized she'd been scared to look back, afraid she might discover that his crumpled body had fallen dead on the slope. Instead, he clung there, lips moving as he spoke silently to himself.

Moving around the blowing mare, she took his arm. "It's all right. Lean on me. We're safe here. Come on, John. Help me."

He collapsed on top of her. She kept him from falling and gently eased him down, seeing the blood oozing around the leather binding on his chest. Terrified, she pulled the knots tight again.

The saddle finally came off the horse as she fought the intricate knot that tied on the cinch. She wrestled it over to where John lay on the dirt and set it beside him. Finally, blinking her eyes with exhaustion, she looked about the shelter.

There were lumps back in the darkness. Squinting in the poor light, she explored. The sight didn't even

aze her. They were all dead—six Santos warriors. The
ruesome burns could only have come from blaster
re.

The dead were piled around a fire pit that still smol-
ered. Left to keep them warm, no doubt. The Santos
nust have been shot up by an AT. They'd run here,
nly to be flushed, shot up, and chased down the can-
on. No wonder they'd bolted at the sight of her party.
'he Santos had already been so demoralized, any new
hock was too much.

Leeta thrust her fingers into the hot ashes, seeking
coal. There! Feeling the pain, she fished it out. Then
nother and another. ''God, help me remember,'' she
nuttered. She looked up at the blackened rock of the
helter. A spider—crudely drawn in the soot—caught
er eye. ''Spider, help me,'' she cried, hanging on the
dge of sanity. ''He's *your* warrior. I do it for him, for
he People. *Help me!*''

A fragment of her staggered mind saw Philip blow-
ng on twigs over a red ember. Her fingers hurt too
nuch to strip the wood from the thick branch so she
used her teeth—the bloody knife in her belt forgotten.
The strips she neatly stacked over the coals and then
he blew carefully. Smoke curled up from the tinder.
A little flame burst out and Leeta cried her triumph,
yes widening as she watched the smoke rise to the
Spider effigy.

''Spider is God,'' she whispered. ''Iron Eyes will
ive!'' She turned to the hideous corpses that lined the
helter. ''Hear that? You Santos bastards!'' She giggled madly as she looked at the stained clothing she
wore. The Santos scalp was in her belt next to the
bloodstained knife. Her blonde hair fell around her
bruised, filthy face in matted strands. Stick by stick,
she built up the fire.

''Spider is God,'' she whispered. ''He will make
Iron Eyes live!'' Where were Rita and Philip? Had the
Santos killed them? There had been a lot of shooting
down the canyon. What if the Santos came here again?
Her eyes suddenly darted out at the now steadily fall-
ing streamers of rain.

Foolish woman! She only had Iron Eyes' rifle. She'd
left two others beside the dead Santos at the fight

scene. She might need them. Frantically, she scurried
over to where Iron Eyes lay. "John! John! I have to
get the Santos' rifles. I'll be back, understand?" She
jabbered at him. His lips moved slightly and she nodded. "Spider will watch over you." Then she was
gone, running through the rain, heedless of the searing
pain in her feet.

Water was already running in the Gessali stream
bottom when she reached the bodies. She pulled the
first rifle from the mud and stripped the body of cartridges. She stared at the man she'd killed, seeing the
water pooling in the gaping orbits. The torn tissue had
been washed a light pink by the rain. He'd been a
handsome man—once.

She sloshed up the steep incline to the shelter in
darkness. A dim glow showed where her fire was.
Dumping the rifles next to the grinning corpses, she
added wood and blew the fire to life.

"Made it, haw!" she babbled at the dead Santos.
"Water was up to my knees on the way back. I'm
stronger now. I got Iron Eyes here."

She went to check on him, pulling the blanket under
his fevered body, then dragging him over to the fire
where it was warm.

The Santos warriors rested against packs. Pushing
the corpses out of the way, she dug into them and
found food, dried steaks. She sniffed them. They sure
weren't harvester meat.

Another pack held a small metal pot and crushed
leaves she suspected to be tea. Filling the pot from the
water cascading outside, Leeta made a soup of the
shredded, dried meat. She fought to get Iron Eyes conscious enough to drink it.

Famished, she made herself a full meal, stuffing her
stomach until it hurt. From time to time, her eyes
strayed to the darkness in fear. She kept Iron Eyes'
rifle on her lap while she looked at the new guns. Each
took a different sized bullet. Frowning, she took each
apart and using the rod she'd seen Iron Eyes use,
cleaned them of mud and grit.

Her eyes were growing heavy with the strain. She
threw an occasional chunk of wood on the fire, mind-
ful of the large supply someone had hauled in from

the surrounding pole tree-covered slopes. Stretching out, she allowed herself a deep sigh of relief. She glanced to where Iron Eyes was sleeping restlessly and then drank from the steaming cup of tea. Over her head was the Spider image.

Sleep brought a horrifying dream. Men chased her down a narrow hallway on a station. She was carrying Jeffray over her shoulder and Iron Eyes was wounded, running ahead of her, trailing blood on the floor. She turned to shoot, but she couldn't lift the heavy rifle in her hand in time. Screaming her fear, she got the muzzle up and pulled the trigger only to have nothing happen. Rough hands grabbed her, ripped Jeffray away, and held her as a psych machine was lowered over her head.

Then she was awake, staring up at the blackened ceiling as sweat trickled off her lip and forehead, tickling her skin. It was agony to pull herself up. She looked out to see gray light in the canyon. Rain still fell. She couldn't place the odd roaring sound.

She yawned, checked Iron Eyes, and saw he was sleeping, his chest rising and falling easily. Walking to the edge of the shelter, she dropped her pants and squatted to urinate. As she felt her bladder relax from the strain, she looked out, seeking the noise. Gessali Stream was a roaring torrent.

Fascinated, she stood and pulled up her britches, awestruck at the sight. The thundering brown water looked like a mighty, brown-skinned limb flexing anatomically impossible muscles where water surged over submerged rocks. The very ground trembled as water smashed against worn, resisting rock. Leeta shook her head, thinking of what would have become of Iron Eyes had she not brought him here.

She pried her gaze away with a physical effort. Closing her eyes, she could still feel the power of the mad river. Shaking her head, she looked back at the shelter. The fire burned brightly now. She could see the black mare cropping grass along the slope. Weary, she went back to fix breakfast for herself.

She ate, slept again, built up the fire, and studied the dead Santos. One had started to swell up. *Decomposition!* Fascinated, she took a closer look. The fel-

189

low had been badly burned through one side. He had probably been dead by the time they hauled him in here. She sniffed, noting the pronounced odor. She giggled to herself. There were no odors on stations. The hydroponics got corpses—like Jeffray—long before this. With resignation, she grabbed a stiff arm and dragged the body through the dust to the slope.

It wasn't such hard work tumbling him down the slippery mud. The limbs sticking out at odd angles did make it more difficult to roll him into the vortex of brown, foaming spray. She was soaked by the time she made it back to the shelter. Iron Eyes was mumbling to himself, moaning in a horrid dream he had locked himself into.

She found a piece of cloth in one of the packs and, boiling water, washed his face. The wound had caked to the leather and only after she accidentally spilled some water did she learn the material could be soaked loose.

A raw, red, ragged mess greeted her. A noxious stink came from the mottled flesh. Leeta felt her mouth begin to water. She threw up before she could stop herself. Gasping for breath, she leaned back and gulped air.

"He'll die," she whispered to herself. "If I don't clear that infection out, he'll die." She searched the packs, finding a needle and thread in one. In another, cloth of some sort. Then she found a skin of something liquid. Curious, she poured some out into her pan and sniffed it. Liquor. Whiskey!

Steeling herself, she doused the long knife blade in the fire, puckering her face at the sight of black smoke rolling off the blade. When the edge cooled, she bit her tongue and turned to Iron Eyes. With a glance at the Spider effigy, she began scraping out runny pus with the point of the knife.

Using the boiled cloth, she dabbed at the wound, making sure she didn't break it open. At the same time, she kept dripping whiskey onto the cleaned areas. With the knife, she picked out a clot of blood and pus to hear a hollow, rasping sound. Whimpering, she realized it was the suction and pressure from the diaphragm sucking through a hole in Iron Eyes' chest.

Swallowing hard, she took the needle and thread, soaked them in whiskey and tried to stitch the hole closed. At least it didn't wheeze and blow at her. Maybe an hour later, she finished. Shaking, exhausted again, she turned to look at her gruesome companions. "Bet you thought I couldn't do it." She sneered.

Her hands stank of pus. She washed them in a rivulet of water than ran down the cliff and splattered beyond the drip line. Next, she stripped and scrubbed the blood and filth from her arms, face, and body. What to do about her hair? Let the water run through it? It ran clean, leaving almost no mud or girt.

She was shivering when she rushed back to the fire with her armload of dirty clothing. She rubbed her pale flesh in the warmth of the fire, hearing her teeth chattering as she jumped and pounded circulation into her feet. Her nipples were hard brown knots, and gooseflesh stood out on her arms. The fire's heat felt warmly caressing on her thighs and stomach. Smoke whirled up along the curve of her breasts as she shook out her hair and fluffed it with her fingers to get it to dry.

Surprised, she realized how incredibly alive she felt. A surge of independence thrilled through her as she looked about her sanctuary. Her eyes played over the corpses. Really ought to dump them in the river, she decided. What was it Rita had said about living for the moment? She grinned at the remaining dead.

Who was she now? What was she now? Leeta Dobra, Ph.D. Who was that? Fleeting memories surfaced: white walls, Jeffray's condescending face, Veld Arstong's broad features, and her own nervousness when Chem cleared his throat and looked at her.

Another image suddenly obscured all of these—a desperate fight for life. She felt the slick length of steel as it grated on a warrior's rib cage, hot blood pouring over her hand. She felt a man's eyeball come loose in her fingers—heard the death cry in his throat.

She leaned her head back, clenched fists at her side, and drew deeply of the smoky air. She tensed her muscles, reveling in the feeling of life electrifying the entire length of her body. She flipped her blonde hair

191

over her shoulders and let the ringlets caress her back as she moved her head from side to side.

Life! *What a magnificent experience!* A low growl started in the base of her throat.

"Would that I were stronger," his weak voice didn't even startle her.

She opened her eyes to slits and looked down at him, the fire light flickering over her tense, vibrating body. "I suppose you'll have to live to find out about *this* coup, warrior," she mocked as she reached for her dirt-streaked clothing. A warm satisfaction kindled at the desire visible in his eyes. On the verge of death—his life hanging by a thread—and he could think of sex? Here, finally, was a man she could respect! He was asleep when she finished cinching her belt tight. Lightly, she kissed his forehead.

CHAPTER XIII

"For the first time in the history of humanity, we have the golden opportunity to bring a primitive people into the mainstream of civilized culture by careful syncretic acculturation!" Chem told them proudly, his knobby fist clenched to emphasize his point.

The faces around the table watched him speculatively. Netta Solare, hands clasped, shifted uneasily; they'd just let her out of psych. She seemed reserved, nervous, worried, as her eyes darted about, as if wondering what her peers thought of her.

"The past," Chem cleared his throat with a growl, "is full of examples wherein economic, religious, and military exploitation have destroyed the native cultures with great cruelty and suffering to the people. We read of the degradation of human nobility for the sordid motive of profit. Of what value—I ask you—are credits against the spectrum of suffering, disease, socio-cultural dysfunction, drug addiction, even suicide?

"Dearest colleagues, we sit at crossroads not reached since the twentieth century of Earth. We are on the brink of the greatest feat of applied anthropology in history. We've been sent a divine mission . . . a mission of morality allowed us by our own civilization! Indeed, a mission of the intelligent over the ignorant!" Chem's aged eyes gleamed as he let his glance shift from face to face.

S. Montaldo sat back in his chair, sipping at his coffee. His look of boredom was supplanted by an ironic smile, as he said, "And at the same time, they have Leeta Dobra."

Chem had taken a breath to continue, but bit off his next words, glaring, in irritation at Montaldo. "I don't think you've been listening."

"But I have, Doctor Chem. Just understand, I've completed the preliminary survey of the planet. There's one hell of a toron deposit around the north pole. I heard every word you've said and I wonder how important the Directorate is going to find some cattle herders who steal Directorate citizens versus a couple billion—"

"Doctor Montaldo," Chem's face reddened, "I didn't believe you could be so cavalier! We're talking about human beings who have feelings the same as you and I. Further, they have something else which is unique! I refer, of course, to a culture unduplicated anywhere in the universe! A single gem which must be studied, nurtured, and cherished for their future and our edification. I speak of their heredity—as valuable to them as Earth, the Soviet, the Confederacy, and the Directorate are to us!" Chem spread wide his hands, as if to encompass the entire audience. "We're talking of—"

"Nothing compared to the power of investors, Doctor." Montaldo shrugged expressively. "I don't think you see beyond your discipline. I'm sure the Directorate will take care to alleviate any adverse affects to the Romanans, but reality goes on around you. The toron alone will justify the opening of the planet. But consider," he indicated Garcia, "Chester here has a marvelous gift. You can't expect him to be your private little project."

"I would never—"

"Further, why are you so willing to condemn exploitation by others when you would bottle the planet up as your own little anthropological treasure? Are your rights greater than mine, or any other groups who might be interested in Atlantis. My God, man, there are whole continents here that the Romanans haven't set foot—"

"I will not have them destroyed for the sake of profit!" Chem thundered, smacking his bony fist on the table. "I refuse—"

"Refuse?" Montaldo cried, jumping to his feet. "You haven't even asked the Romanans what they want!" He thrust his hot face into Chem's. "There's more to it, Doctor! There are a lot of real problems in the universe outside of Atlantis and a bunch of feuding primitives. There's a very real shortage of toron! What do you think makes star ships function? Do you think toron lies around everywhere like the periodic elements? *Well, it doesn't!"*

Montaldo stepped back and looked at the men and women who watched. "Toron is a unique crystal. It forms inside novae. Speculation, based on the best mathematical models, indicates that neutron stars are filled with it. Phenomenal pressures are required to grow the crystal, literally billions of tons per square millimeter. The atoms formed are anomalous in that they are so phenomenally heavy. And, until now, it's never been found on an ordinary planet.

"The very qualities of the toron crystals allow them to handle stresses beyond anything men are capable of manufacturing." He turned back to Chem. "They are the only known structures capable of channeling matter-antimatter reactions—and that makes this world a unique treasure because there's a bunch of it down under the north pole!"

"But don't you see," Chem argued back. "If you open this planet for mining, you'll have support facilities, housing, entertainment, regular commerce, settlement. Eventually, someone will run into the

Romanans and when they do, someone will get hurt! We have to—''

''What's wrong with picking them all up and sending them to psych stations for training and integration with the rest of humanity? What's wrong with the way we live? Why should they be different?'' Montaldo demanded. ''At least we don't raid each other's stations and planets!''

''Because they are different!'' Chem gasped, stepping back, shaking his head in frustration. ''Because anthropologists think people matter in the end. We've seen what happens during the acculturation process!''

''How about it, Chester?'' Montaldo looked at the Romanan. ''Look about you. You've seen this ship. You've seen the hospital facilities, the shuttle, everything. You understand that we go among the stars. What do you think? Do you want this for your people?''

Chester folded his hands on the table before him. He looked uncomfortable in the chair. ''We would travel the stars,'' he said simply.

''There, see!'' Montaldo was smug in his triumph.

''My God!'' Netta Solare gasped wretchedly. She realized what she had said and clasped a hand to her mouth, eyes betraying shame and panic.

''Netta?'' Chem looked at her, suddenly worried.

''I'm sorry, Doctor.'' She kept her eyes down. ''I no longer have a quite unbiased view of the Romanans.''

''I don't understand.'' Chem studied her.

''You don't understand?'' she cried out. ''They're savages! Sure, a Spider rescued me! He sent me from the village after he killed that . . . that . . . that man who. . . .'' She sniffed and wiped her nose. ''But they are all foul beasts!'' Her eyes were accusing as she looked at Chester.

''You didn't see them cutting off men's hair! You didn't see them shooting . . . and screaming . . . and cutting with those knives. You weren't stripped, raped, degraded! Oh, no, not you, Doctor Chem! You sit up here safe! You study Chester here with his wonderful gift. But don't you dare let those *ANIMALS* loose on the galaxy or you'll have to hunt each one down like

195

the criminals they are and kill them!'' She lurched to her feet, her face a stream of tears and ran blindly from the now silent room.

"My word," Chem whispered. "I never knew she was so flighty. And she was such a good, solid student." He sounded sad.

"So," Montaldo's voice was soft. "Another point of view to consider, Doctor. Do you think Doctor Dobra and Lieutenant Sarsa are safe with these vulnerable studies of yours?" His eyebrows lifted. "Will the Directorate see it your—"

"Of course!" Chem waved impatiently. "Solare probably made some stupid mistake. Perhaps she unwittingly made some move that's considered an invitation among the Romanans. Perhaps like visiting Rykland. You never compliment a man's wife or you are expected to sleep with her," Chem mused.

"I'm not sure Netta was quite that naive," Montaldo snorted.

"What? Oh . . . one never knows," Chem had already forgotten the incident. "You see, there are a great many things which can go wrong. For that reason, we must establish a program whereby these people can remain masters of their own destiny, culture, and values, while at the same time, functioning as a part of the Directorate. It is essential that—"

"Have you ever thought of the press this will get?" Montaldo looked his amazement at Chem. "You refuse to accept that there is a whole wide universe out there, Doctor! You've been locked in your laboratory for too long! What do you think the Directorate is going to do with Chester, here? Everybody and his brother's going to want a piece of a man who can see the future! Think of the impact on politics, business, investment, medicine, military practices, manufacturing, professional gambling, or anything which entails risk!" Montaldo was shouting.

"You see," Chem was nodding, seeing it all in his head, "we can be of mutual benefit to each other, but it must be done with delicacy. There are well-established anthropological principles by which—"

Montaldo sighed vigorously. "You don't *have* time! You saw Netta's reaction. The bloody thing broke wide open the second Chester walked into your base camp and when I found the toron! There's already population pressure on Range—and this place grows cattle. Netta was raped! Raped, Chem! Dobra and Sarsa are prisoners. Their culture is completely antithetical to every value established by the Directorate. You're too late, Doctor! Face the—"

"It's *never* too late. This time we won't make mistakes. We have guidelines on how to avoid the tragedies of the past. Scholars have studied these things for centuries. Reservations, military occupation, revitalization, nativistic movements, suicide, these things result from improper contact, we call it negative acculturation. It must never happen—"

"It will," Montaldo fumed, seating himself to glare at Chem through slitted eyes.

Chem looked at Chester and added. "You understand?"

"We will go to the stars as soon as possible, Doctor. I am already here. It is for the good of the People to do this quickly. It is in the vision." Chester's voice didn't waver.

"Exactly," Montaldo chortled with a smile.

"You realize what this means?" Chem stooped to look into the Romanan's eyes. "The knowledge of Spider would soon be gone. The People would be spread among the Others. There would be pain . . . your planet ruined. There would be sickness. The People would not know themselves."

"Perhaps. Yet . . . it has already begun," Chester responded. "Soon I must go and see the man you call Director. He who floats in the air and changes the lives of your people."

"What do you mean? Already begun? There's been little contact, and Leeta is no doubt studying even if she's held captive." Chem's face was knotted with frown lines.

"You do not know?" Chester looked up, almost curiously. "The fighting men have seized the village of the People. Another of the smaller ships has landed in the main village of the Santos and the other Raiders have been occupied. My world, which you call Atlantis, has been shut off by your Director. There is no travel in or out without Colonel Rèe's agreement. Men have been killed, there is warfare.''

"Interdicted!" Montaldo snorted. "I guess it's all academic from here, Doctor." He met Chem's disbelieving eyes.

"No!" Chem whispered. "Ree wouldn't jeopardize the research! My God! He . . . he knows better!" Emmanuel Chem straightened suddenly, face pinching from pain, he gripped his left breast and winced. "I must talk to the Director immediately!" he cried.

"You had better call the medical team now," Chester told Montaldo easily. "He will die if we let him go too long."

"Die?" Montaldo quizzed.

"His heart. I shouldn't have told him like this, but it was better this way."

Montaldo was already accessing comm through his headset. Chem was sinking into a chair, his bevy of graduate students suddenly aware of the malady and rushing to his side. Confusion reigned as the med team flew in on antigrav and thrust the students out of the way.

It was over in ten minutes. Chem was bundled off to sick bay. Most of the students left, talking in excited chatter about Solare, Chem, and warfare. Montaldo reseated himself and scowled into his cold coffee.

Chester Armijo Garcia breathed a weary little sigh and settled in his place again.

"You saw that, didn't you?" Montaldo asked absently. "Why let the old boy suffer his heart attack? Why not stop it before he was hurt?"

"He would have been placed under arrest otherwise. That would have hurt him more in the end. He is a good man. I did not want to see him suffer," Chester said with regret.

"I've never had a heart attack. I hear they're painful." Montaldo's voice was dry.

"It hurts him, Dr. Montaldo. Yet, it is the lesser of the hurts which a man can suffer."

Montaldo looked up, skeptical, suspicious. "You don't seem terribly grieved by the whole thing."

Chester raised his arms helplessly. "It is nothing

compared to what is coming. It is difficult to be a Prophet.''

"What's coming?" Montaldo gave him a sour look. "What's your angle, Chester? If you really see the future, what's happening? What are you doing to prevent it?"

"Nothing. Ambition leads to change. Change leads to suffering. Suffering leads to conflict. Conflict leads to growth. Growth leads to knowledge. Knowledge leads to ambition," Chester replied.

"Perhaps," Montaldo was frowning. "What of it?"

"Is there ambition in your Directorate, Doctor Montaldo? You are a great skeptic. You see the world as a continually fermenting mess. Why are you so cynical? Your personality is out of balance with God and the universe."

Montaldo grunted sourly, "Perhaps. So?"

"Spider spun his web for men like you. Consider it an analog to constantly remind a man that everything must be in balance. A web is a thing of beauty, each strand must help support the whole. Webs are interwoven works of art, delicacy, and strength. Yet, with a poorly designed web—or without any web at all—Spider would forever fall. You see, Spider's web is like your life, Doctor. It must be engineered for art, delicacy, strength, and balance. Otherwise you will fall.

Chester's marine guards swallowed nervously and looked uneasily at each other.

Montaldo absently sipped his cold coffee and wondered why the Prophet's words bothered him.

As John Smith Iron Eyes yelled and shot, Rita's heart leaped. Synch training kicked in. Instinctively, she spurred the gelding into the midst of the surprised Santos warriors. She pointed the rifle and triggered the weapon. The recoil almost knocked her cold and she missed seeing the effect of her shot. When she looked, the man was on the ground, his head a mass of gore.

They were running! She heard the cry tear from her throat as she slashed down with the rifle barrel and clubbed with the butt. She thrilled as she heard a man's skull crack like an eggshell. They were around the bend now, racing after the Santos who had flung themselves on their horses and fled in terror.

She jacked open the breech and inserted a cartridge. Letting the horse run, she concentrated on the sights and shot. The recoil didn't seem as bad this time—but she thought she'd missed. The man kept riding, moving easily with his horse. Then, slowly, he slumped forward in the saddle before falling, one foot catching in the stirrup. The horse shied, kicking the limp, bouncing body.

Rita whooped again and slipped another round into the chamber. Racing close behind, she shot another of the fleeing men. This time the target threw up his arms and almost jumped from the saddle, smacking into the rock at the side of the trail with a sickening thunk.

As she cranked the action open once more, a man looked back to see only her in hot pursuit. Four of them were left now. She couldn't hear what the fellow hollered, but another looked behind and began to pull his horse up. Rita grabbed the reins and hauled the gelding down. The animal almost threw her over its neck as it slid to a stop.

The Santos were slowing, firing over their shoulders. Bullets shrieked past her ears. Standing still, she steadied the rifle. When the last man had slowed until she was sure of her aim, she calmly blew him out of the saddle and kicked the gelding into a run back up canyon. Three left.

How far had she come? A kilometer? Leaning over the horse's neck, she reloaded, noting there were only a dozen or so cartridges left in the belt. Philip had to be up ahead somewhere. He and Iron Eyes better be ready.

The gelding was a faster horse, she realized. The wiry steed had overrun the others in the mad chase down the canyon. Could he outrun them going up? The rush of adrenaline and fear ran like electricity in her veins. A bullet puffed rock dust and chips from the wall ahead of her.

She looked over her shoulder and in her frightened strength, held the rifle out with one hand and shot at the lead rider. It must have been close because he ducked, and slowed his horse.

Two hundred meters up the canyon, Philip stood over the body of a man. She screamed a warning as he grabbed up his rifle and sprinted toward her. With fumbling fingers, she dropped a cartridge in the effort to reload. Pulling another from the belt she got the job done as the gelding pounded past Philip.

She pulled the beast to a stop and threw herself from the saddle. Philip's rifle boomed and a horse screamed, pitching its rider face first into the mud. The next horse was following too closely and tripped over the kicking legs of the first, dumping that rider, too.

"Into the rocks!" Philip yelled as he reloaded on the run. Rita scrambled up the detritus as a bullet spattered her with molten lead, rock chips and dust, breaking the boulder under her hand.

She wormed into a hole and pulled the big rifle around in front of her. Oh, if she only had her blaster! With her pistol's wonderful IR sight, she could pick their eyes out at two hundred meters.

The second man was hunkered behind the dead horse, his rifle resting on the flank, seeking some sight of Philip. From where she sat, Rita could see his legs sticking out behind the animal. Settling the gun on rocks for a rest she edged as far forward as she could and squeezed off the shot.

To her dismay, the bullet landed short but skipped in a ricochet, clipping both the man's legs. Of course! The projectile dropped with gravity! How did they ever hit anything at range? Further, the bullet didn't travel at light speed so moving targets had to be led. And wouldn't wind would affect impact? She spat nervously. Primitive sort of thing!

She'd reloaded when she saw the wounded man trying to drag himself away by his elbows. She steadied and estimated the drop. This time, the bullet caught him in the middle of the back.

As she reloaded, she saw the fellow who'd been thrown head first start to move. Philip's rifle boomed and she saw the shot whack a rock on the other side of the canyon. Someone shot back. The thrown man moved again, groaned, and relaxed.

Rita kept an eye on him as she sought the last Santos. He and the man in the mud should be the only ones left. The rain started. Large cold drops pattered on the rocks around her. She carefully pulled the splinters of rock and lead from her skin. Little drops of blood welled with each yank.

The bullet was close. It clipped her hair and rattled off the rocks behind her. "Hey, watch that!" she hollered across the canyon. "You could put someone's eye out that way!"

"That is the purpose, Spider youth. You have come to die on your first war trail! The young women will weep for your name!" the Santos taunted.

"Wrong on all three counts, Santos!" she chirped. "One, I'm not Spider! Two, I ain't gonna die! Three, the young women wouldn't look twice at me *brother!*" She used the female form of address.

There was silence. "Who are you?"

"Rita Sarsa," she called back, grinning. "The star woman who just killed five of your warriors! Come to think of it, that's five coups in one fight. Not bad, huh? Almost ties John Smith Iron Eyes!" She felt a rush of excitement.

"You lie!" The voice held bored disbelief. "If you are from the stars, where is your burning weapon? You speak like a Spider. You are a young man with a dying imagination."

Rita steadied the rifle on the rocks, seeing a slight movement. A flat rock lay canted next to him. The shot that skipped into the warrior's legs had taught her something. Taking aim at the front of the rock, she fired. Dust puffed and she heard the sudden intake of breath. The man lurched suddenly as Philip's rifle boomed. He pitched over on his side, rifle clattering in the rocks.

"Any more?" Rita asked.

"No." Philip was on his feet, running nimbly toward the dying Santos, his rifle at the ready. Rita stayed put, keeping him covered, eyes searching the hillsides. Philip checked the Santos; she saw him speaking as he did something with his knife. Death stroke?

Rita stood and walked down to where the last Santos was beginning to stir. The water in the bottom of the stream was running as she pulled the man up by the scruff of the neck and took his knife. The fellow blinked at her and shook his head. She could see he was having trouble focusing.

Philip trotted over to the man he'd been standing over when she'd rounded the bend. He bent down with the knife and slid it around the skull. Rita understood.

"I told him that you hadn't lied before he died. He can take that knowledge to Haysoos. Half of this is yours." He held forth a bloody clump of hair.

Rita felt her mouth go dry. She couldn't force herself to reach for it. Philip watched her with his knowing eyes. "It is the most difficult thing you've faced yet, isn't it?" he asked, voice calm as the rain pounded them, running down their faces in little streams. "You can still go back," he added.

She took a deep breath, looking again at the grizzly trophy. "It's my choice, isn't it?" she asked hoarsely. "You know what you're asking?" She felt her fingers reach out and caress the long, wet hair. "It would be treason," she said simply. The water was running around her ankles now. The stunned Santos sat up, watching with wide eyes as he strove to understand.

Philip nodded slightly. "Perhaps they would see it so. We need you. You are in the vision—one of the cusps. You are the difference—one way or the other. You and John and Leeta and Chester and me. We are the major ones."

"Why no women of the People? Why no men from space?" She looked up suddenly.

"Balance," Philip's voice was sure. "Male and female, earth and sky. It is very old. Earth was mother, sky the father. We have reversed it. There must be a change in the old pattern. We will change in balance. We need you. I need you. I love you, warrior who has more coups than me." He was so earnest, eyes shining with the truth of his words.

Rita's fingers still stroked the hair, the water was climbing her calves. The Santos had crawled out and was sitting on the bank. She felt her fingers brush Philip's warm skin and easily took the coup from his hand. Her skin crawled at the touch of the cold, wet, bloody thing, feeling oddly of death and destiny.

"You need to take coup from the rest, Spider warrior," Philip said dispassionately. "It is your duty. It is the way. Kill this one and let us retrieve your coups.''

''No!'' she gave him a measuring look. ''The Santos lives. We'll need him.'' At that, she bent down and tried to figure out how to scalp a man.

''Like this,'' Philip showed her on the rider he'd shot.

She followed his example and grabbing a handful of hair, ran the knife around the skin as she pulled. She twisted and popped the hide loose, whirling it as Philip had, slinging off the gore. Philip tied the Santos in the saddle and carefully strapped the rifles to yet another of the captured horses.

The water was almost knee-deep as they rode down the canyon. Rita's corpses had washed down quite far. She found the last one wedged in a small tree. It didn't matter to her anymore. She was now practiced at the art of taking coup.

''We'd better hurry back and find out what's keeping John and Leeta,'' she shouted, feeling chilled and fatigued in the deepening darkness.

''That lazy Iron Eyes is probably resting in Gessali Shelter with a warm fire!'' Philip agreed. They turned the horses to head back upstream. The water rushed madly against the horses' legs, making the animals skittish.

''Better not try!'' Philip shouted suddenly. ''It's coming too fast! We could lose one of the horses.''

''But John and Leeta?'' Rita objected.

''They will be fine. They will come out when the rains stop. The canyons are unsafe during a rain. It is a lesson to remember. Follow me! It is a couple of hours to a dry camp. We may have to shoot the Santos out of it—but it's there. We call it Navel Camp.'' Philip turned, casting an uneasy glance at the Santos. The man had come to his senses enough to glare back.

''Why did you save him?'' Philip asked as they splashed down the broadening canyon. In spite of the widening canyon floor, the water stayed the same depth, merely running slower. One of the dead Santos floated past them.

''I'm on your side now, my love.'' She grinned at him as she shivered, wet leather clinging to her. ''You don't know how poor the odds are against us. I do. It's time the Santos, Spiders, and the rest quit shooting at each other.''

"I wish you luck!" Philip looked grim.

"I'm glad you do!" Rita nodded, water dripping off her chin. "We're gonna need a hell of a lot of luck!"

"When John gets out of the canyon, we'll go to the village. With the radio we can call a meeting," Philip decided.

"Won't do you any good," Rita disagreed. "You! Santos, what's your name?"

"I am José Grita White Eagle, woman," came the surly reply.

Rita didn't let the tone bother her. "All right, listen, White Eagle. The attack by the AT tells me something. Ree has gone all the way. He's taken the planet just like the book says and proclaimed martial law." She received blank stares.

"The Colonel will have an AT in each of the major villages. He'll have established a curfew. The radio is controlled by marines now. They watch from the skies. Any fighting between the Santos and the Spiders will bring instant retaliation." She had to explain terms like curfew to Philip and José.

"So they have not allied with the Spiders?" José asked suddenly, his interest stirred.

"Why should they?" Rita shivered. "The Spiders are small change. There's a rare, deep-space crystal on your planet. It's worth a lot—like horses to your people. Also, there's the Prophet, Garcia. They have definite interest in finding out how he gets his visions. We're all prisoners now.''

"This ship, *Bullet*, it really is powerful enough to destroy the planet?" Philip asked.

"Ree can literally turn this whole world into plasma. Uh—that's hot, glowing dust to the two of you. Don't worry about the physics. The ATs are small stuff, kind of like the way throwing pebbles would compare to those two cannons at the main village." She shivered again from the cold.

"Horses!" Philip muttered as he stared at yet another of the ever present caves that riddled the mountains. "That is the Navel. There are a dozen horses. I wonder whose? José, do you know any of those horses?''

The Santos shook his head. ''They are not of my village. We do not have a big brown like that.'' Lightning flickered in the sky.

''What matter?'' Rita asked. ''The time has come to make a finish to the shooting. Maybe we can talk them out of it. If I sit out here any longer, I'll . . . I'll *melt!*'' She walked her horse forward.

''Aha!'' Philip shouted as the horses shifted. ''I know that sorrel mare. It is the horse of Friday Garcia Yellow Legs!''

No sooner said than a man came striding out of the shelter, looking their way. ''Philip Smith Iron Eyes? It is you?''

''Aye, worthless friend of mine!'' Philip cried gleefully, spurring his captured Santos horse forward. Philip enjoyed a happy reunion with hugs and yells as Rita rode up, keeping an eye on the Santos. The huge shelter had them out of the rain. Spiders came running, slowing and fingering knives and rifles as they saw first her red hair and then the Santos warrior.

''A Santos!'' A strapping man with short-cut braids leered. ''My friends, tonight we will have great fun roasting his brain in his skull!''

Rita kept her seat on the gelding, rifle ready as the stares turned wolfish. Philip noted the silence and looked up.

''Who are these?'' Yellow Legs asked.

The man with short braids started for the Santos, pulling his knife from his belt.

''Drop it or you're dead!'' Rita hissed, her gun suddenly covering the man's belly.

''I do not hear women!'' he gritted through his teeth, disgust growing in his eyes. With a quick move, he turned and grabbed up his rifle.

''Here!'' Philip barked, slapping down the muzzle of the man's gun. ''Horsecapture! You will hear this woman. She is a warrior who has already taken five coups today and captured a Santos live!'' Philip met the man's stare and broke it.

''I do not believe it. No woman is a warrior!'' Horsecapture turned to rally the support of his fellows.

"You will believe it." Rita told him, dropping to the ground, handing her rifle to Philip. "If you can paddle my bottom with your knife, I'll keep my mouth shut, Horsecapture. Only you can't lay a finger—"

"I will not listen to this!" Horsecapture looked shocked. "I do not fight women—*I take them!*"

"Try it! Surely, there is no harm in trying?" she mocked. "If I'm wrong, what's a little friendly wrestling?" She handed the knife and scalps to Philip, enjoying their sudden, wide-eyed stares.

"No!" Horsecapture shook his head. Rita slapped him stingingly across the cheeks, bringing gasps of horror from the Spiders. Grita, seated stiffly on his horse, watched with growing fascination.

"Come on!" she growled. "I'm not going to be able to do anything with you until you learn to respect me."

The man blinked from the shock and stepping back, saw the derision growing among the others. He roared as he charged her.

Rita easily ducked the big, outstretched arms, pirouetted and kicked him in the stomach. Horsecapture bellowed in rage, and circled warily. Rita stood, arms crossed, giving him a look of disdain. He feinted, lunged, and she held out an arm. He grabbed her and jerked as she laughed.

When his fingers closed on her wrist, she deftly rolled into his body, twisted free, and slipped away, booting him lightly in the belly again. "Can't hold onto a woman? My, must be difficult for your love life," she quipped, standing several paces away. The guffaws of the men threw Horsecapture into a wild rage.

She let him come, grabbed his outstretched hand and dropping, threw him hard into the dust. He came at her again and again, panting, roaring, bellowing, seething with rage, no longer ready to shame her—but to kill. Each time, she easily threw him and stood waiting for more.

Dazed, he remembered his knife and drew the blade. Men rushed forward to seize his arms, but Philip stopped them with a rapid order. When he rushed, Rita rapped the knife from his fingers, and kicked him

207

hard in the belly. As Horsecapture doubled up, she smashed the side of his neck down low and kneed his chest hard. Horsecapture dropped in a ragged, gasping heap.

He looked up, agony in his eyes, struggling to get to his feet.

"Enough, Horsecapture. My point is made," she said, not even breathing hard. Her eyes shifted from face to face. Only Philip had a wry smile on his lips. In the silence, her voice rang with authority. "How many of you plan to surrender to the Patrol—the star men?"

Eyes slitted, mouths tightened as their expressions betrayed disgust at the thought.

"As I suspected," Rita's rebel grin bent her lips. "How many of you would fight to win?"

A flicker of interest began to grow on their faces, followed by understanding.

"That's right," Rita said seriously. "I can teach you—give you a chance at least against ATs and blasters." She pointed to where Horsecapture's dagger eyes pinned her with hatred.

"My purpose wasn't to humiliate Horsecapture!" she snapped. "I only demonstrated a combat skill. The star men know a lot of tricks you don't. They have a lot of weapons which are presently beyond your conception.

"Horsecapture!" She ordered, taking her coups back from Philip. She reached out a hand. She met the hatred in his eyes, refusing to yield until he reached out to her hand. Struggling for the first time, she grunted under his weight as she pulled him to his feet.

"Friday. Get the Santos down from that horse," Philip's voice carried in the cavern. "We have a lot of work to do!"

They stood in shock.

"You heard him!" Rita's whiplike voice sent them scurrying. "From here on out, you're with me—or against me. And, people, I'm your only hope!"

"Behold," Philip grinned at her, "the beginnings of our army of liberation!"

"Think we can do this? she asked soberly, studying

the hatred as the Santos was lifted—none too gently—from his horse. "Have you any idea of the odds stacked against us?"

He nodded. "I have seen only portions of it, my love." He shrugged. "I didn't see if we win or lose. Perhaps in the ways of Spider that is not important. I am satisfied to fight for today. If we die tomorrow, who knows? That is strength in itself."

"You know Philip Smith, I like your style." She took his arm, winked and grinned, feeling the warmth of love for this strange, strong man. It was desperate, she knew that. Still, what a way to go. Her fingers intertwined in his and her heart swelled as she watched the Spiders lead them to the camp they called Navel.

CHAPTER XIV

The rains were letting up. Leeta allowed herself a heavy sigh and looked back into the gloomy interior of Gessali Camp. From where she sat, she could hear Iron Eyes. His garbled voice muttered on, talking to Jenny, to Philip, to other people she didn't know. It would drive her crazy!

The fever had been worse yesterday and she'd stripped his body, bathing him with the cold water that ran down the cliff in an effort to keep his temperature down. At night he'd had the chills and she almost singed his hair off trying to warm him by the fire. Finally, knowing of only one other source of heat, she crawled under the blanket with him and held him, keeping him alive.

The food supply dwindled. The packs abandoned by the Santos hadn't held much. She'd eaten a lot and stuffed the rest into Iron Eyes every time he had a lucid moment. The black mare had just about cropped the curious vegetation from the camp slopes. Fortunately, it grew about as quickly as she ate.

Another hollow rumble of thunder boomed above her in the clouds. Bored—and a little chilled—she stood and walked into the shelter. She bent and placed a hand on Iron Eyes' brow. Was it her imagination—or was the man a little cooler?

Not much wood left either. The pile of scrubby brush had just about disappeared. She looked longingly to where the corpse she'd called George had sat. George—last of the dead Santos—had begun to stink too much the day before. She had had to drag him out and roll him into the river.

How lonely she was now! That shocked her. The twisted faces of the dead had been companions. George had been the best. He'd had a look of amazed interest to his features and his head had been cocked as if he was really listening to everything she said.

Iron Eyes—delirious—mumbled to himself, turning his head this way and that. When she talked to him, he'd interrupt and between the unintelligible mutterings, say things completely unrelated to her subject of conversation.

The wound had ceased to fester so badly. She no longer vomited at the smell. Several days of patient effort had been required, but she'd reconstructed most of the ribs. When she used the last of the thread to stitch the wound closed, the whiskey had gone with it. So much for fighting infection.

Leeta's eyes narrowed and she pinched her mouth, shaking her head as she remembered the first time he'd fouled himself. What else could she have expected? The memory of her shock made her laugh. Gessali Shelter wasn't a modern med unit where such things were taken care of by catheters!

How had she ever forced herself to care for him? She closed her eyes and shook her head, surprised she had managed. So much had changed. Her life would never be the same. "Oh, Jeffray," she laughed, "if you could see me now!" She ran her fingers over the coup Iron Eyes had insisted she keep.

Setting the last twigs of wood on the dying fire, she checked Iron Eyes. The crude diaper she'd rigged was full again. She could tell by the smell. She undid his pants and pulled the cloth out from under his buttocks.

After she'd washed it out in the falling water of Gessali Stream, she hiked back up the slick, muddy incline and into the darkness.

Drying the cloth to the best of her ability, she turned back to refasten the diaper. Iron Eyes was looking up at her. "Awake?" she asked—only half expecting an answer.

"Where am I?" He tried to frown. "Star woman? Is that who you are?"

She bent down, placing the diaper under him. "That's me," she said. "How do you feel?"

"What are you doing?" he cried out, suddenly aware of her hands. He tried to sit up—cried out at the sudden pain—and settled back, face stone-white.

Leeta leaned back on her haunches, studying him. "I'm putting a cloth under you. When you're fevered, you don't control your bodily functions. Now shut up and leave me alone!" she snapped, hastening to get the chore done and refasten his belt.

"Not right!" he protested. "It is the duty of a man's clan—not a stranger, or worse, a woman!" He groaned his shame.

Leeta let that sink in. Shaking her head in wry humor, she settled herself at his side. Dryly she offered, "I'm sorry. Would you rather that I let you die? I may only be a star woman, but I've saved your life more than once. Doesn't that earn me some rights?"

"I guess." Iron Eyes swallowed miserably. "Where are we?"

"Gessali Camp. It's rained for the last week in a steady downpour. Can't get in or out of the canyon—water's too high." She rubbed the back of her neck, realizing how matted and filthy her hair had again become.

"Where is Philip? I would talk to him." Iron Eyes looked up at her.

"I don't know." She looked into his suddenly worried eyes. "They kept on after the Santos when you got wounded. Remember that?"

He studied her. "They didn't come back? The star

211

woman and Philip, are they dead?'' he asked. She felt his fingers tighten on hers.

"I don't know," she repeated. "There was shooting down the canyon. The stream rose so rapidly I don't think they could get back to us if they tried."

He nodded. "You say the rains have stopped?"

"Mostly, it almost looks like the clouds are going to break soon. I hope so, we're almost out of food—and the wood's gone." She knew she didn't keep the worry from her voice.

"We must leave then. There will be no more food here. The melon nuts will not ripen for some weeks. When that happens, we could live here forever. Cork-bush bark can be eaten, but it lies bitter on the tongue." He was thinking now, his face showing his concentration. "I will have to ride."

"You can't!" She met his questioning eyes. "The bullet broke your ribs. They need time to heal. If you try to ride, you'll pass out within minutes and fall out of the saddle. I'm out of whiskey to keep your infection down. You can't ride, we'll have to do something different."

"Is there a wheel in the packs?" he asked.

"A wheel?" She raised an eyebrow.

"For a trailer to follow behind the horse," he told her, looking to see if she understood.

"Like a travois?" she asked. His eyes were blank. "No wheel, *but a travois!*" Leeta cried suddenly, jumping to her feet, a light in her eyes.

"What is this, woman?" He looked skeptically at her.

"It's from your own people's past, John." She was grinning in triumph. "I'll get you out of here! And they say anthropology is useless!" At that, she grabbed up his knife and ran for the hillside.

The plants that looked best—pole trees—weren't like trees exactly. They were more like half of a giant sea urchin, a starburst of woody rods that stuck out all over. The bark was like sharkskin, smooth in one direction, abrasive as diamond board in the other. Of course, the tallest of the poles was in the middle of the plant. Viciously, she attacked the first plant with the heavy fighting knife.

Skinned, bleeding, her fingers raw, she finally snaked the poles one at a time down the rocks to the shelter of the overhang. She promptly encountered another problem. The things bent when weight was placed on them; inside she explained her problem to Iron Eyes.

"Dry them on the fire," he told her. "They have had two weeks of rain. They are swelled with water. Dry, they are hard as rock."

She burned the Santos' packs to get the heat. There hadn't been much left worth keeping anyway. The poles sizzled and dripped in the smoky flames and she shared a victory smile with Iron Eyes.

It was cold when she woke the next morning. Her breath frosted and curled, easily visible beyond the blanket and she snuggled closer to John, wishing she didn't have to get up.

Roping the travois together gave her fits until Iron Eyes showed her how to tie a knot. Such a useful art . . . lost in the Directorate where everything had fasteners. She stood back and eyed her creation. The mare wasn't all that enthused either, but it fit the animal and at Iron Eyes' suggestion, she padded the rails that would have chafed the horse.

"You'll have to help me get you up on that thing," Leeta announced at last. The mare was stamping, trying to stand hip shot but unwilling with the new burden on her shoulders. Leeta noted less than a foot of water in Gessali Stream.

"Keep your back straight as you sit up," she whispered, fearing the pain he would have to endure. "I'll help you to your feet. It's only a couple of steps to the travois."

He nodded, took a shallow breath and winced as he pulled himself to his feet. Leeta did most of the work, seeing sweat popping out on his face as he fought the pain.

Iron Eyes tripped.

He screamed as she let him fall on her, keeping his body straight and breaking his fall. Little strained sounds were coming from his throat as he struggled up again.

"Are you all right?" Leeta asked, realizing she

213

wasn't breathing, her heart beating with fear, brutally aware of his pain.

"Hurts," he slurred. "Sorry, clumsy."

She scrambled from under him and got him to the travois. He jolted again as he sat on the poles that made up the seat. He was trying to breathe deeply without moving his chest as he lay back on the frame. She could see pain searing across his face. Mercifully, he lost consciousness.

Panting, Leeta took what line was left and did her best to tie on the rifles and supplies they'd need. She gathered up the reins and led the mare out, seeing Iron Eyes' head rock back and forth on the saddle she'd formed into a headrest.

The trip down the slope provided her the worst scare, but the mare—as if understanding—held the weight back. Reaching the stream bed, Leeta ran back to check. So far, so good. After she shouldered her rifle and snugged the knife at her belt, she led the black mare down the flood-scoured canyon.

Odd, there were no bodies—nothing at all left to indicate a bloody battle had been fought. It was like that all the way; not a trace remained to show that men had ever passed this way.

She hung to the left of the canyon, keeping close to the rocks, figuring they were less likely to be seen than if she were to ride out in the open.

What was that? She stopped the mare and shaded her eyes from the growing brightness. A man! A rider! Philip? Rita? Or a Santos? Should she yell?

In her indecision, she stood still, keeping the mare from moving, hoping the man wouldn't see her. Tracks! Had she left tracks? No, the travois had been dragged down the creek bed the whole way. Only at Gessali were there tracks and they just ran down the slope. She could have turned up or down.

The man rode over a rise and entered the canyon, headed upstream. Leeta took the reins and urged the mare onward, bending away from the direction the rider had come from. She checked the rifle, making sure a cartridge was chambered. She studied the sights, lifting the heavy gun.

She looked at her rifle with pride. It was a beautiful

thing. The wood was engraved with the forms of the dragons Romanans called bears. There were warriors, horses and women etched in the dark metal of the barrel.

Her rifle! The one she'd taken from a dead Santos. She let her fingers trace the smooth metal and wood of the stock. Pride flashed within. Not everyone won a weapon in battle. This power—the ability to kill— had been earned. She felt a sense of wonder and unrealistic superiority.

A weapon had elevated her ancestors above the rest of the Terran fauna. A weapon had made men safe, allowed them to protect their families, put food on the table and riches in their pockets. The Directorate was oblivious to such a reality. Sure, Ree understood. So did his warriors. But what of the rank and file living in secure peace? Hah!

Leeta lifted the rifle and sighted on the far hills, lining the blade in the narrow notch of the back sight. The gun didn't wobble as it had at first when her weak muscles fought to control the wavering muzzle. Strength had come to her.

She'd carried the rifle with her day in, day out. Wary of Santos warriors suddenly pouring into the shelter, her hands had grown used to it. They had beome one with the wood. If danger came, she would keep herself and Iron Eyes safe. She could do this thing. More, she would!

That night the stars were dancing as she secreted them in a patch of brush that hugged a canyon. The mare ripped low green plants from the ground as Leeta scouted around the camp. After she'd studied it, she put together a small fire. She'd practiced and learned at Gessali Camp.

The fire smoked from the damp stems she fed it, grubbing out the dead stuff from under the brush with her knife. The first time she tried to use her fingers, razor-sharp leaves cut her. Knife bush, she realized too late.

Iron Eyes had his eyes open, watching her. "Food?" she asked, offering him the pot full of steaming meat.

He ate carefully, and laid the empty pot aside. "We made it?" He nodded. "Your travois works well, star woman." He watched her with a strange light in his eyes. "Can the fire be spotted?"

"I checked," she told him, attempting to keep pride from her voice. "There was a rider earlier this afternoon. I didn't know who it was so I decided to stay hidden."

"Are they so wary among the stars?" he asked, his face reflecting a calm acceptance.

"No." She shook her head. "I was thinking of that earlier today. They are like your cattle. They keep their heads buried in the grass and munch contentedly. They aren't predators out there, John. They're . . ." She paused, thinking deeply. "They're domesticated." She looked up, meeting his keen eyes.

"Yet they would destroy us?" His lips twitched slightly.

"They have to." She realized it was true. It shocked her, started her heart pounding. "They can no longer understand you. The Romanans are free, John. The Directorate can't tolerate freedom. Such people upset the balance and predictability of society. The people no longer dare to challenge themselves." A cold shiver massaged her spine. "Or if they do, the psych teams are always there—waiting."

They were silent, lost in their thoughts.

"Where are you going?" he asked at last.

She looked at him blankly. "I don't know. We'd better get there quick though. There's only one more meal of dried meat."

"Where did we go today?" He was watching her.

"Down the canyon to where it widened out. I kept near the slope on the north side because I figured I could hide in the rocks and shoot if anyone saw us. We went all day until the sun went down and I hid us here. There's a great big pinnacle of rock that rises just up from this canyon. That help?"

He nodded. "Navel Camp is just over there to the south. That might be where that rider came from. We are bending away from the settlements. The Ship and my People are that way." He pointed.

"We'll try for them. I need to get you better medical help, John. You're not out of the woods yet. You could still die on me." She realized she was holding

216

his hand. The idea of his death disturbed her deeply. Love? she wondered.

"Watch out for bears," he was saying. "They are thick in here. Out there, beyond the ridges, are the herds of my people. The bears find occasional strays in here. If you see a cow, shoot it. It will give us food—things I need like liver and the brains. I will tell you how to butcher it."

"And if I see a bear? What do I do then, John? I heard Philip bragging that you'd killed one with your knife. Where do I stab this thing?" She felt her face smile though her thoughts were cold.

He was fighting a chuckle, aware it was going to hurt him. "Aim your rifle at the point where the two tentacles with the suction disks branch out of the body. The only place to kill a bear immediately is in the brain." He drew a sketch on the sand next to him. "Here," he pointed. Then he drew a side view.

"That's it?" She asked, studying the drawing.

He nodded soberly, eyes intent. "More, you must be close. The rifles are big because the bullet must penetrate so deeply into the bear. The only reason I killed one with a knife was because Spider willed it. Without the help of God, only a rifle will kill a bear."

"How close is close?" she asked, intent on his words.

"As close as you can get—and still keep your nerve." He watched her. "The farther away, the poorer the bullet penetrates. You may be safer, but it is harder to hit the brain. The closer you are, the better to kill—and be killed! You understand?"

She nodded, remembering his words, trying to imagine the situation, seeing in her mind how it would be, seeing the spot he pointed to in his drawing in the sights of her rifle.

"I have been a burden to you," he said at last. "I was thinking of the other day when I scolded you. I forget the coup at your side. You are not a woman, you are a warrior."

The words irritated her. Had he forgotten the night she'd stood before the fire?

"You have a man somewhere in the stars?" he asked, suddenly.

Uneasy, she lowered he eyes. "No. I don't."

His head shook. "I don't understand. You are a very beautiful woman. You have courage, strength, and at the same time, you are kind and gentle. You are very smart—very quick to learn. You talk well with men. Why has some man not taken you in his arms and run off with you? Among my people, a man who could not make you his by choice would steal you away!"

She laughed, thinking of Jeffray. "How different. The last man I had killed himself because I left him!" She felt the hurt, heard the sarcasm in her words. She was strangling suddenly, wondering why she'd told this violent, fierce man such a sensitive thing. With fear, she looked at him. Would he use it against her?

His voice was soft when he spoke. "I do not understand. You left him *and he killed himself?*"

So she told him about Jeffray and how he was psyched, what he had wanted from her and how she had cared for him. She told about how she'd never had time for men. One thing led to another as she spilled it all, alternately feeling fear and relief.

"So not all star women are like you and Rita?" He seemed somewhat relieved.

"Hardly!" She laughed. "We're oddballs, misfits. Most want to sit at home and have babies or pursue their careers. But they don't want to come someplace like this. They aren't strong enough; they won't take the risks." She shook her head.

"Like cattle, you say? Even the warriors like Rita?" He was thinking.

"Not the warriors!" Leeta told him in no uncertain terms. "Never underestimate them. They are perhaps the finest human fighters to have ever lived. They are trained constantly. Their only problem is a lack of wars to fight. The Directorate picks and chooses the soldiers, finding the best ones for the Patrol. They like their job—just like Rita does."

"But there are no wars?" Iron Eyes mused. "That might be their great weakness."

"I don't understand."

His eyes lit. "The People are tried constantly. All

218

young men go to fight the Raiders. Among our People and among the Raiders, there is great honor to give one's life for the tribe. Is this so among the star men?''

"Far from it!'' She frowned, kicking more brush into the fire with her Santos boots.

"Then they do not see defeat as the end of their people.'' He looked preoccupied.

"I'm not sure I understand.'' Leeta tried to figure out what he was thinking.

"The ATs shot up the Santos, right?'' His eyes glittered in the firelight. "That means the People are in great danger. This Ree will destroy us. You yourself said the Directorate will not leave us. You have told me of psych teams and how they work. The people will be destroyed. The Prophet said this and I see how it will be.'' He was nodding. "We must destroy the star men.''

Leeta felt her face pinch. "How can you say that so innocently? Don't you understand? They can cut your planet in half with that ship. The marines are invulnerable! Their combat armor will stop a blaster bolt! They won't even feel a bullet! You can't use a horse against an AT! My God, you can't even assemble an army without their electronic eyes knowing!''

Iron Eyes nodded. "Yes, that is the case. Except—''

"*So you're whipped!*'' she cried, wringing her hands. "There's too much to lose, John. So many will be killed and for what? Like those Santos—''

"You yourself said the People will be destroyed.'' he added evenly. "What good is life when what you believe to be right is broken and crushed before your eyes? I cannot become—as you say—domesticated. I am better off dead—than something I will not respect. You see, even if the war is already over, we have nothing to lose. If we must die one way in the star men's conquest—why not die the other in our defense?''

"But . . .''

He waved her down. "There are no buts. Many will die and the cost will be terrible, but if—of all the Spiders—one brings about victory, then the cost is worth it. The warriors would rather die than become like your Jeffray. Let them send their souls to Spider, doing

219

for their own and in honor. Besides, we have one thing the star men do not. The star—''

''Guts!'' Leeta snorted. ''Lot of good they do you fried by a blaster! Don't you remember the Santos in Gessali Camp?''

His eyes were warm as he smiled up at her. ''Yes, we have guts, too. The star men have ships that fly and the power to burn this whole planet, but we have something they can't counter. *We have Prophets!*''

She sat back, startled, remembering Chester Armijo Garcia. Did he really see the future? She shuddered as she remembered the way he'd predicted everything right down to the last.

''Bless you all,'' she whispered. ''You're lunatics, every last one.''

''The star men don't believe they can be defeated. This will help. Chester Armijo Garcia is on that ship, *Bullet*. That would frighten me very much if I were Ree. And then there are the Spiders, primitive men who know not of blasters and ATs.'' He shot her a shifty grin. *''But we can learn!*

''And there is the Directorate, which has never learned defeat. They can learn, too! And the marines? They do not have to fear destruction should they be defeated. That is an advantage for the Spiders!'' Iron Eyes was putting it all together.

''No matter, so much is tipped against you, just waiting to fall!'' Leeta visualized paths of fire lacing down from the sky. She imagined crisped corpses in burned out huts, glassy slag where men had lived. ''Will all the Spiders fight?'' she asked, picturing the women and little children.

''Yes, they will fight,'' his voice was soft, far away. ''Spider told them. Spider let himself be nailed to a cross of wood and died suffering that men would be free. If God did such for us—can we do less for ourselves?''

Leeta wondered. She remembered the Spider myth Garcia had told Netta Solare. The Spiders would do it. They would all die before they would submit.

''You'll need inside help,'' her voice was wooden. ''You can't do it alone.'' A dream shape, a huge psych machine, conjured itself in her thoughts. It was settling over her head. . . . She gritted her teeth and shook her head, vanquishing the vision.

What had Iron Eyes said? Nothing left to lose? A psych machine was her legacy anyway. Her keen mind—her ability to think for herself—already teetered in jeopardy.

He had his eyes on hers. "I had wished it would be that way," he said with a note of hope in his voice. "I owe you a lot—but I could not ask you to give up your people."

She sighed and took his hand. "Who are my people?" she asked, snuggling down next to him. "I can't go back. I didn't want to admit that, but it's true. I can't go back, Iron Eyes. They'd take my mind from me." She sniffed. "You know, death is easier to take than the horror of psych."

He ran his fingers over her hands as she continued. "What would I do? First time someone like Chem mouthed off, I'd want to kill him!" She bit her knuckle and looked up at the profile of his face in the firelight. "You know, the psych teams will put their equipment on my head and within a couple of days, I'll be who I was, thinking how silly this whole thing was and how terrible that I killed that Santos—*if I think at all.*"

"You will be at great risk," he reminded. "You could simply leave me and find an AT. Tell them you escaped—"

"No," she whispered. "John, I don't want to go back! I'm proud of myself. I did it all on my own . . . by myself! I kept you alive. I killed a man who was going to kill you! I beat the storm, built a travois, captured my own gun, threw the dead Santos into the stream. I did it on my own. You weren't there to help! The damn Directorate wasn't there to do it for me. I did it!" She clenched a fist and felt herself glow with emotion.

"So, you are ready to kill star men?" he asked, voice soft. "You could do that?"

Cold reality stopped her. "I—I don't know." She hadn't thought that far ahead. Could it come to that? "I . . . I suppose not," she whispered in defeat.

"Then do not do it," he shrugged and winced. "You said that we needed inside help. You can do that.

At the same time, you know the star men, how they react, what they will do. We must fight with more than rifles. We will need to fight with knowledge. You can direct that kind of fight?'' She felt his head turn so he could see the top of hers.

"I can," she said with sudden fury. That she could promise him.

"Then we will win!" Joy invaded his voice.

She shook her head. Didn't they realize they were dealing with a colossus? Prophets, guts, and her conspiring with them to boot—they just didn't understand. How could she explain holocaust to a child? An emptiness was forming under her heart.

"Iron Eyes," she whispered, pulling herself up on her elbows. "Kiss me. I need to be held." His arm pulled her close and his lips brushed her forehead. It wasn't quite what she'd had in mind.

As the sun turned a dazzling pink over the Bear Mountains, Leeta forced herself to trot along ahead of the mare.

She'd wanted him! Her body had *ached* for him! Her dreams had been wonderfully erotic all night long. She still longed to feel his arms around her, feel his hard chest against her breasts, feel him within her.

She took a deep breath and hefted the rifle in her arms. Reality stunk, she decided. Did he even think she was attractive? Sure, she'd cared for him—saved his life a couple of times—but did that mean he cared for her? That night in the shelter, he'd wanted her! Sure, and males could be aroused by visual stimuli no matter who the woman was, if the mood was right. Or had it been fever?

He still loved his damn Jenny! She fumed, feeling frustration as she tried to compete with a ghost. *"Hell!"* she spat, chopping viciously at an imaginary woman with the heavy rifle.

It could be worse, she decided. Jenny could be alive—and waiting for Iron Eyes in the Spider village. Her lips twisted. It wasn't fair!

Wasn't it? She had an even break. Either she could get his attention and hold it—or she couldn't. Jenny was dead. Gone. Buried! End of story . . . except the handsome, noble sap still loved Jenny.

At least Iron Eyes respected her. That was a start. So, to hell with it. Play the game around that. She could. . . . The mare snorted and stopped, quivering.

"Here, girl!" Leeta cooed, pulling on the reins to keep her from bucking. As she held grimly to the mare's head, she looked in the direction the animal was staring. Over the ridge came a huge bulk.

"*John!*" she screamed. "Over to the east! What is it?" But she knew. Only one creature on Atlantis grew so big. The bear moved remarkably quickly on its feet. She could already see the two suction disks on the waving tentacles.

The mare went crazy. In desperation, Leeta pounded the rifle barrel against the horse's nose and tied the shocked animal to one of the low bushes. Swallowing hard, she pulled three of the long brass cartridges from her belt and ran to meet the bear.

The creature suddenly stopped, seeing her running approach. Unusual behavior? The bear began shifting to her right. Leeta corrected her course, keeping between the predator and the mare. If the bear got around her, the black mare and John were easy prey. She wasn't fooled, the thing could move incredibly fast.

A quick look over her shoulder showed Iron Eyes, propped up on the travois, his rifle ready. He struggled to his feet as the bear moved, welding her attention. She sprinted to foil the bear's flanking maneuver.

"Go on!" she shouted. "Go away! I don't want to kill you!" She threatened with the loaded rifle, hoping the bear knew what the weapon was. The thing tried to slip past again and she knew she was being forced, pushed back against the mare. Why? So the horse would bolt and could be run down later!

Smart creature, Leeta nodded to herself. So it had to be done. She dropped quickly to her knee, steadying the rifle, and settled the sights on the bear. She could see one stalklike eye watching her as the gun belched fire and smashed her shoulder.

Feeling her heart beat, she frantically reloaded as the bear's attention switched back to her. Had she killed it? She held the rifle up again, seeing the barrel jumping as her arms shook with fear.

She settled the sights on the giant beast as it turned

and ran for her. The tentacles were out, wavering in the air, making circles and spirals. To draw her attention? Perhaps.

Leeta sobbed a breath, trying to slow her heart, fighting to maintain control of her lungs, nerves, and muscles. *God! How fast did the thing move?*

She heard a splatting sound and a half second later, the boom of the rifle. John shooting, hoping that he could make a difference from his angle.

It calmed her to know he was in it no matter what. He would at least be able to defend himself after the bear killed her. So this would be death. Killed by that huge monster and eaten? A wry thought occurred to her—it sure beat psych!

Suddenly it amused her. The whole situation was absurd! Humans didn't get eaten by anything in the universe! She was calm now. The bear filled her world. *"The closer the better!"* she whispered, remembering John's words. "Come and get it, damn you!" she gritted, feeling her jaw sliding along the stock of her rifle.

The tentacles parted wide and she shot. The rifle rocked her back and she struggled for balance, falling to one side as she clawed the breech open and inserted the last cartridge. As she slammed the action shut and tried to get up, something smashed into her side and sent her sprawling.

She kept the rifle in her hands somehow and collected herself, scooting around on her rear to face the bear. It tottered before her, weaving back and forth. The suction disk was swinging back her way. Desperately, she scuttled under it, feeling the wind of the huge disk as it passed.

She jerked up the rifle and took a quick breath, her aim was rock-steady even though she knew the other disk was striking for her. The front blade settled on target. She tightened on the trigger, not wanting to miss this time. She hardly heard the gun go off as she concentrated on keeping the rifle steady.

The bear shuddered violently and the suction disk shot past her, suddenly jerked off target. She was running, anything to get back out of reach! Over her shoulder, she saw the bear was still standing there, not pursuing yet.

She still had a cartridge! Whirling, she cranked the action open and inserted the brass. She dropped to a knee again. *Will I never kill the damn thing? Got to get it right eventually.* If she shot enough times, she'd hit the brain. It *had* to be in there somewhere. Of course, a drawing in the sand was one thing. The wall of mad flesh towering before her was another!

"Steady!" she ordered herself. "Take your time!" Her ragged breath was making it difficult to keep her hold. "Nice and easy!" The wavering front sight kept swaying past the target.

"Hold it!" she whispered, fighting to control her arms. "Easy! Breathe deep!" She kept trying to slow the waver of the gun. It jumped slightly each time her heart beat. Gasping deep breaths, she waited, wondering why the bear didn't attack.

She was calming down now, waiting on the bear, knowing she would relax soon enough. The gun didn't waver as badly, her heart was slowing, and she had a second before she needed to gasp a breath.

The front blade held steady and she let that shot go, wanting to be sure. Maybe a little lower this time? Maybe more to the right or left? Sudden indecision began to build. Where to put the shot? It clutched at her mind, as she worried. The last shot had stunned the bear. This one had to do it. She held a little lower on the midline and tightened on the trigger.

As she rocked back down from the recoil, the bear began to sink ponderously to the ground. The six huge legs folded slowly and the great wall of flesh quivered while the little stalk eyes kept her in sight. A great expulsion of breath whistled at her and the tentacles slapped the ground.

Suddenly shaking out of control, she turned and walked back to where Iron Eyes huddled on the ground, his rifle poking impotently into the damp soil before him. His eyes had glazed with pain as she walked up.

"Got him!" She giggled hysterically. "I did like you said and I killed him. Took four shots, had to hold lower on that last one. Oh, damn, was I scared!" The whistling in her ears must have come from the muzzle blast.

"I think I'm dying," he whispered.

She could see the red stain spreading. The recoil had broken the whole mess open.

"Whaa's that?" he asked, nodding his head foggily.

She looked where he indicated. A long, white craft was settling next to them. The mare was prancing nervously, eyes rolling.

"AT," she gritted as the hatch slid open and combat suited marines shot through the door. "At least you'll live, Iron Eyes," she added grimly.

CHAPTER XV

Leeta gave Iron Eyes a quick look. "I don't have time to explain, but you just became a specimen. If I act strange, you've got to believe in me, John. I'm going to have to play this smart. I don't know how it will come out, but I'll do my best. Remember, I'm still on your side!" She stood to meet them, rifle in her hands.

"Attention!" A loudspeaker announced in Romanan. "You are in violation of a military proclamation. Return to your village at once. Failure to do so immediately will end in arrest and confiscation of property. Drop your weapons immediately and explain the nature of your business to the guard!"

The marines were all around them, blasters leveled. "Drop your weapons! I repeat! Drop your weapons!" the speaker boomed.

Leeta shook her head slightly as she looked at the shining figures that surrounded her. "Or what, Corporal?" she hollered in Standard. "If I don't, you'll burn me down?"

"That's right!" came the stiff reply—in Standard if the Corporal had only thought about it.

"Look, fella!" Leeta snorted to cover her triphammer heartbeat. "I won this thing fair and square, so

226

you can go to Hell! Further, for your report to the Colonel, you can tell him you personally wasted Doctor Leeta Dobra! Now, what the hell took you goons so long?" By that time, she was almost walking right down the corporal's throat.

She stopped several paces in front of the man, seeing his shocked face behind the reflector on his helmet. "Shut that blast visor off and look at me, soldier," she growled. "I don't like talking to a mirror."

The visor flashed off, leaving her looking at a fair-skinned young man. He gulped, blue eyes wide with dismay.

"Wish you could have been here earlier. Had a time with that thing." She hooked a thumb at the dead bear. *"You!"* She pointed at two of the privates who'd flipped off their visors. "Get that man on board!" She indicated Iron Eyes. "If you hurt him, I'll personally have your asses served to me on a silver plate, got that!"

They nodded slightly and rushed over to where John lay, breaking out a portable antigrav in their hurry.

"D-Doctor Dobra?" the corporal stuttered. "I'm sorry ma'am. We . . . had no idea. I mean if we'd known, we'd a burned that dragon at the start!"

"At the start?" she demanded in a strained voice. "You mean you sat up there and let that thing almost. . ." She couldn't finish.

"But ma'am!" The corporal's eyes were wide.

Leeta's world narrowed. All she saw was the corporal's face. *"Get me Colonel Ree!"* she hissed viciously. "You get him right now! Patch through! I guess I'm a high priority item so hop to it or burn me down right here, 'cause sure as vacuum is empty, I'll get a report in somehow!"

"You get that, Lieutenant?" the corporal was shrilling into his helmet mike.

"Yeah, patch-through's coming," a faint voice could be heard through his helmet speakers.

The corporal wilted under Leeta's fiery glare. She could feel her mouth twitching with anger. "Ree, here," the tinny speaker voice said. Leeta leaned close. "What's your name, Corporal?" she thundered so the speaker could pick it up.

"Hans Yeagar, Corporal First Class, AT11, ma'am!" He snapped out a salute.

"What the hell's going on out there?" Ree's startled voice asked.

"You hear me, Colonel?" Leeta shouted.

"Yes, who is this?" His voice sounded perplexed.

"Doctor Leeta Dobra!" she said loudly. "I'm safe for the moment, no thanks to your shiny goons here. Thank God you assigned Rita Sarsa to me! She's competent! I'm coming in as fast as this AT can fly me, Colonel, and when I do, I want these guys! *I want them licking my feet!* Got that?" She turned and tromped to where they'd taken Iron Eyes into the hatch.

"See to the horse," she threw over her shoulder. "This thing ought to be able to transport an animal that size."

"Yes ma'am!" They saluted and broke for the horse at a run. The black mare—already nervous—saw their rush and spooked. She tore lose from the brush, cantering out onto the flats. Leeta enjoyed a mean smile.

It was definitely a ship she was in. Everything was white. A private saluted her at the door. "Which way did they take the native?" she asked.

"Follow me, ma'am. Captain's compliments, ma'am!" he said smartly as she returned his salute. When in Rome. . . . Wasn't there a saying about that which anthropologists should have learned by now? They thought her to be military? So, why not?

"Compliments in a rat's ass!" she snorted in her best Sarsa imitation, well aware they'd have monitors on her the whole way. That captain ought to be swallowing his lips by now. Ree had no doubt ordered everything recorded from the moment she'd dressed down that corporal.

Iron Eyes lay on a bed, looking his hostility at the med techs. Blood dripped thickly onto the white sheets. He threw her a quick look of relief. She didn't meet his eyes. "I want this man fixed," she ordered the techs. "I *don't* want to have to repeat myself. He's important for the pacification of this planet! Is that clear?"

The Chief Surgeon nodded.

"Good! There is severe trauma to the fixed ribs. The xiphoid and inferior sternal body are shattered. There is an excellent chance of peritonitis. Treatment has been worse than primitive—so I don't know how much of my damage you will need to undo."

She turned to John Smith Iron Eyes and bowed deeply. "I am sorry for this, Spider Warrior. Trust them. They will take good care of you. I expect to be able to return you to your people forthwith. If you have any questions, these men will call me immediately." She raised her eyes to the surgeon.

"I understand, star woman," Iron Eyes agreed with dignity. "I would thank you again for my life."

"And you for mine, War Chief." She turned to a private as Iron Eyes slid into an encompassing med unit. "Take me to the bridge."

The bridge was full of people suddenly busy with other things. One monitor showed a half dozen combat armored men chasing madly about the plain after the black mare.

"Doctor Dobra!" A tall man bowed without saluting. "Allow me to present myself. Captain Arf Helstead, at your service."

Leeta threw him a crisp salute. "So I noticed, Captain. Excellent timing. Of course, had I been eaten, the evidence would have been neatly missing, eh?" She pushed on, noting his half open mouth. "May I remind you that we're in the midst of a very serious situation, Captain. There is no time for idle dalliance. The planet is no doubt in complete revolt and you would sit in the sky and watch the two people who could stabilize this mess be eaten by a damn bear! Get me a line through to my people at base camp!"

He threw her a look of uncertainty and motioned. A tech was accessing through his headset. "Colonel Ree would like to talk with you first," he said.

Leeta took the proffered headset. "Colonel?" His image formed.

"Doctor Dobra, you have no idea how worried we've been over you." Ree looked jovial.

"Not half so worried as I've been, Colonel. We've got a lot to talk about, sir. If you don't mind, I would

229

rather do it elsewhere. It's not that I doubt the intentions here, but there are matters of policy which I think we might want to review, given the present situation regarding the Romanans.''

''I see,'' Ree's brows knit. ''Doctor, I want you to understand that I've been forced to take certain steps. . . .''

She waved him down. ''I more than understand, sir. I think a complete reevaluation of the Romanans is in order. I've learned a lot out here. I think I can be of substantial service to the Directorate and your efforts. I can fill you in later. What is the status of my people? Have they been cooperative?'' She narrowed her eyes, waiting. So much depended on his answer. God forbid Chem and Marty had screwed it up.

Ree nodded. ''Your base camp team has been extraordinarily helpful. We've had to detain certain natives—among them the Santos and Spiders who first took you prisoner.''

''Excellent. I'm happy to hear my people have not let themselves be misled by other considerations.'' Leeta gave Ree a real smile.

''Doctor Chem, however. . . .'' Ree hesitated.

''He's a great scholar, Colonel. I believe I understand. After having worked with him for so long. . . . Well, I'm sure this has been a stressful period for him.'' She gave Ree a confidential smile.

''You seem to be in excellent spirits, Doctor. I take it you have not been harmed. After finding Ms. Solare, we were very concerned. Do you know where we can find Lieutenant Sarsa?'' Ree's eyebrows went up.

''Last I saw, sir, she was shooting Santos warriors up the canyon. After the rains, who knows? If she's alive, she's fine. That's one hell of an officer, Colonel. If we get her back alive, I . . . I recommend a commendation!'' Leeta let her voice tremble.

''Very well,'' Ree seemed relieved. ''I imagine you'll want time to collect yourself. I'll see you back at your base camp sometime this evening.''

''One favor first, sir.'' She watched for his reaction.

Ree studied her carefully, eyes narrowing. ''Yes, Doctor?''

"If you don't mind, I want this crew at my disposal for the time being." She tilted her head slightly.

Ree's eyes glittered. "Retribution, Doctor?"

"Of a sort, sir." She grinned back.

"Very well. I'm sure Captain Helstead is present. He'll follow your commands so long as they are within the bounds of his general orders." Ree faded out.

Leeta turned to look at Helstead. "I suppose you have a holo copy of that fight with the bear?" she asked.

"Yes, ma'am." He looked like he'd swallowed a grenade.

"Good! I want it. One of these days I might want to show my grandchildren. Now how quickly can you get me to the base camp?"

"Less than three minutes, ma'am!" He saluted this time. "But we need to catch that horse first." The black was halfway across the plain now, the shiny marines trying unsuccessfully to box it as it ran past them yet again.

Marty Bruk watched over a hundred meters of white AT settle on the mudflat outside of the big dome. He'd gotten used to such things over the past couple of weeks. This had to be the one Leeta was on. He strolled out as Bella Vola caught up.

"Wonder what kind of a mess Leeta will be?" Bella asked, hooking his arm with her own.

"If we're real unlucky, she's going to be like Netta." Marty shrugged. "Can't tell. Natural selection. Some make it, others break it."

"I guess we did all right, though. She echoed our plan to keep on good terms with the military." Bella looked around at the marines guarding the area. "I guess they have everything pretty well under control." She could feel the long distance mikes trained on them.

"Sure is good to get Doc back. We'll be able to surprise her with some of our results." Marty was half allowing himself to blather on about the unique genetic findings he'd been making.

A hatch shot open and a native dropped to the ground, rifle in one hand, the other resting on a knife. A squad of marines followed her. At the same time, a

231

second hatch opened up and the Romanan walked over to lead out a black horse. The marines formed up to carry a wooden structure between them.

Marty stopped as the native led the horse up. "I don't believe it! Doctor Dobra? Is that you?"

She walked forward, eyes on him, giving him a careful scrutiny. "She's not the lady who left here," Bella whispered in spite of the mikes.

"Hi, Marty, Bella." She grinned at them. "Colonel Ree tells me you've been holding the fort quite well during my days in the field. *Corporal?*" she spit the word.

A combat armored man trotted up and saluted. "Ma'am!"

"Take care of my horse. See to her watering, feeding, and exercise. Oh, and Corporal?" she called as he took the reins with hesitation and obvious dislike.

"Ma'am," he muttered, looking at her fearfully.

"Don't muff it this time." Leeta's voice was cold.

The fellow nodded quickly and led the mare away.

There was humor in Leeta's eyes. She hugged Bella and whispered. "Talk loudly while I hug Marty."

"We were so worried about you, Doctor," Bella began.

Leeta flung her arms around Marty. "Is there a safe room where we can talk without bugs?"

"Don't know, Doc," he whispered back. "I can find out in about a half an hour."

"Good, you and Bella act natural. You're still together?"

Marty's eyes were gleaming which gave her her answer.

"Come on, I can't wait to show you what we've found!" Bruk let himself babble while his mind raced. He had it! "I want you to see the results on the DNA sequencing. We've got a valine substitution that's real important.

"By the way, did you know that while the plant community supplies all the necessary amino acids, the fauna are deficient. On a native meat diet, you'd starve to death in a couple of months."

He and Bella led Leeta to the desk next to the REM-CAT, pulling her down on one side, ignoring the fact

232

that she smelled of smoke. "Here," Marty began. "Look at the curves on the anthropometry!" At the same time, he accessed his personal screen while figures and holos flashed on the big monitor.

"What's up?" he typed.

"Need to talk. All is not as it seems," Leeta answered, covering by exclaiming over the stuff on the big screen.

"Figured," Bella typed.

"Ree's coming for conference this pm. Might have to make funny statements then. Keep the faith. This thing is real big. What's Chem's problem?" Leeta continued her small talk about the Romanan osteology.

"Don't know, communications no-go tween here and ship." Marty added.

"Blackout?" Leeta asked.

"Afmtiv," Bella typed. "Have set up info brokerage. What's your angle? We did right?"

"Did good!" Leeta typed in return.

"Thought something was fishy," Bruk entered. "We're in for anything that's fun, dangerous, and exciting. Don't like the way the military is handling this. Too many Romanans come in with blaster burns. Doesn't wash!"

"Tell you later," Leeta typed. "Good guy Romanan is being patched in AT. They'll send him in later. Give him A1 care. Important man. Can I count on you two? I'm looking for loyalty!" She muttered something about stature and looked at both of them.

"There's more, Doc," Marty said with a slight smile on his lips as he nodded. "I think we can deliver everything you hope we can."

"Amen," Bella added, eyes betraying her excitement.

"Good!" Leeta sighed. She typed. "For God's sake, *be careful!* The stakes are higher than you two can imagine. Men will die over this!!!" She squinted, wiping the memory of Marty's computer. "I'll tell you about my adventures later. It'll take a while and ought to be done over beers. Right now I want a shower."

* * *

Damen Ree read Leeta Dobra's report. It was preliminary, mostly detailing where she had been and what had happened to her. At the end was a series of recommendations he almost skipped. He studied them absently only to become engrossed.

As his AT set down next to the one Leeta Dobra had commandeered, Ree was locked in thought. Dobra's recommendations had an almost military ring to them. They were tailored to an occupation force seeking to avoid conflict. But how good where they? And why did she make them? Ree frowned as he strode down the hatchway into the sunlight.

There were lines of prisoners in the detention area. Too many too quickly. Spiders, Santos, and the little groups of Raiders who hung on the peripheries of the main tribes. These were the ones who'd fired first. On an average of every half hour an AT came in to deposit more.

Ree frowned. Figure that for every Romanan captured, there were two or more dead. The detention area held over three thousand, five hundred. Not good. If there were ever an investigation of this, who'd believe the Romanans, armed with rifles, hadn't surrendered to a superior force? Ree growled to himself. It was blowing up in his face.

He was led into the main dome by Marty Bruk. Ree returned his salute in a perfunctory manner. *What the hell are these scientists doing saluting?*

Nervous, uneasy, he followed Marty into the conference room. Leeta Dobra, dressed in her usual clothing, stood and saluted. "Come, Doctor!" Ree was taken aback. "You're not military! What is this?"

Leeta smiled. Were her eyes a little tighter than before? She'd lost weight, not that there'd been much to lose. She was leaner, somehow tougher looking. She had a strong, independent look.

"We're part of the system, Colonel," she replied. "I'm not sure where you want to put us, but I think—given the situation—we'd perform best as a functional cadre."

Why am I sure I'm being conned?

"Leeta, I'm not sure about this." Ree took his seat, noticing that the scientists sat after he did. "Now then, I read your report, Doctor. The recommendations you've made caught my eye. But before that, tell me about it—off the record."

Leeta related the entire affair, telling of the rescue by the Spiders. She told of Rita's bravery, Solare's insecurity, the escape into the hills, the rain and the cold and the nobility of the Spider warriors.

"When we ran into the Santos, there was nothing to do except keep the initiative. Rita and Philip pursued when they broke and ran. Iron Eyes was wounded and, to be sure, I'm not a soldier." She threw Ree a helpless look. "I stayed behind and cared for Iron Eyes, getting him under shelter.

"I think the meds in the AT can give you a complete report on his wound. After that, runoff closed the canyon, keeping Lieutenant Sarsa and Philip from making their way back—if they're alive.

"As to their fate, Colonel, I can't say. I saw no indication of bodies when I led the mare out yesterday, but given the power of that water, who knows? There wasn't even an indication humans had ever been up there."

Ree leaned back in his chair and fingered his chin. "I was afraid you might not understand the actions I took. Dr. Chem didn't. But you see, there was a threat to personnel. Further, given the, uh, proclivities of Chester Armijo Garcia, I was leery. I did what I thought was right." Ree raised his eyebrows as he looked at Dobra. A most evocative woman, dazzling with this new sense of presence.

"You are responsible for the safety of Directorate personnel and security, Colonel." Dobra was nodding her head. "In your shoes, I'd have done the same thing. I've been briefed by my staff regarding the fate of Netta Solare. I would have suffered the same except for Lieutenant Sarsa. The Spiders tried a rescue, but they were just a little late for Netta. Rita didn't wait for them.

"Regarding your proclamations," she looked up wryly, "I'd wager they're being ignored by the natives."

"That's an understatement," Ree answered dryly. "I noticed some reference to that in your recommendations. Would you care to elaborate on how you came

235

to those conclusions while waiting out the rains in a cave in the mountains?''

''You call it interrogation. We call it a subject interview. The man I brought out of the mountains—we need him. He's as close as you can come to a chief of the Spiders with the exception of the Prophets, and they don't bother that much with our world.'

''They don't?'' Ree suddenly felt relieved.

''No, their bailiwick is the future, Colonel. They don't like to mess with the everyday world. It makes them nervous. They see too much. Think about it. For example, little children they would like to know and grow fond of are seen dying of consumption a couple of months in advance—that sort of thing.''

''Makes sense,'' Ree agreed. ''But why will they not surrender in the face of overwhelming odds?'' He asked the question that had been plaguing him. ''It makes no sense from any military axiom I know! Answer me that, Doctor!''

''God told them,'' Dobra said calmly. ''And I've personally watched unprovoked AT attacks.''

''Huh? Like the old-time Moslems?'' Ree frowned, thinking of suicide attacks, bombings, and terrorism. Unprovoked attacks?

''Very similar.'' Dobra motioned for a cup of coffee and seemed to revel in the taste. ''That's why my first recommendation was to allow them any religious observances they desired. You see, according to them, God—his name is Spider—was nailed to a cross of wood so that men could be free to come and go as they wished. If you attempt to curtail their travels, who are they to disobey God? He showed them the way. If they don't follow, he will look away from them.''

Ree scowled. ''And if I don't allow them their religion and their travel?'' He watched Dobra, a suspicion building in his mind.

''You will have to kill each and every one of them.'' She gave him a level, measuring look.

That was too much. ''Come, Doctor! *Kill each one?* That's insane! No one would watch his people be destroyed one by one!'' Ree shook his head in disbelief. ''Doctor, you've been under stress.'' That explained it all. The poor woman had been too long with the savages. His suspicion was confirmed. She was undergoing a psych reaction. Best to get her up to the ship. Just like Solare, she needed . . .

"Colonel, what are your native casualty figures?" Dobra asked, never wavering.

He was stopped dead. "They have exceeded our predictions substantially." Unprovoked attacks? Was that where Rashid got off talking about entire parties blasted? Was some element of his command stirring the waters? Who?

Antonia Reary! She wants to discredit me—make me fail!

"Worse than that!" Leeta was pressuring him. "Your men haven't anything like an actual body count. I took the liberty of researching that Gessali Canyon fight. You have three prisoners reported taken, three horses and three men killed. On top of that I threw six bodies out of Gessali Camp myself. That's nine, Colonel."

He fingered his short beard. *Reary wants my ship!* Perhaps he needed a different ally?

Dobra continued. "From our best estimates, there are roughly three quarters of a million Romanans on the planet. You've captured maybe four thousand total. That works out to twelve thousand known casualties. A low estimate says perhaps twenty-five thousand men have been killed in the back country. Has there been any measure of cooperation?"

Ree leaned back. Damn her! She was sharp. What was there to do? He'd followed sound military occupation tactics. Reary was waiting for it to fall apart. No doubt already penning her report to Kimianjui—and Skor Robinson. Options? Ally with Dobra for the time being?

"And your recommendation, Doctor?"

"You've read most of them." She studied him. "Colonel, we're on the same side here. The situation has gone beyond the joy of doing a nice, quiet, scientific study. You and I both know that. It's a military operation now. If it blows up, it blows up in your face. It's your career, but it's also mine."

And I have my ally! But where does it lead me? Ree

smiled to himself. *And I do find her attractive. Where could we go in the future—she and I?*

Now she was offering compromise, not censure, not sanctuary, but compromise to help him salvage something out of what was becoming an intolerable situation. And after Atlantis?

"Perhaps we may come to a reasonable solution. I've read your recommendations. You want to leave the Romanans alone for the most part; allow limited travel between the bands; continued research by your team; punishment of violators of the peace; establishment of military bases in all the major villages, and a program of acculturation to Directorate values."

She said nothing, arms crossed, eyes on his.

"Further, you recommend modification of the socioeconomic system while at the same time introducing goods, livestock, and plants which can grow here. You recommend we ought to query the Directorate for foodstuffs which can be grown here and open the other continents for settlement immediately. I think this is reasonable."

How far can I push?

"Now, what about your colleague, Dr. Chem?" Ree leaned forward and let his interest show.

To his surprise, Dobra didn't hesitate. "Dr. Chem has his functions. I would recommend that we allow the major announcements regarding the Romanans to be issued under his name with individual credit going to the investigators such as Marty Bruk here. It gives us the professional standing we need in the academic community.

"Further, as part of the program, we, of course, continue to conduct our investigations and to accumulate data on the Romanans. In so doing, we can keep a finger on the pulse of the people and hopefully counter resistance before it becomes open violence. Perhaps with your muscle and our brains, this will turn out pretty well after all."

She seemed to have the answers all thought out. "You've been thinking this over, Doctor. I must admit, I'm impressed by your presentation. What of the wounded native? You say he's very important. Why?"

"He's the greatest warrior in the Spider tribe." She

didn't even hesitate. "Consider the culture, Colonel. These men listen to fighters who have taken coup—those are scalps by the way. This Iron Eyes has taken a couple of dozen. That's big stuff. Most men only get three or four in a lifetime. The People will listen to him and he's in tight with the Prophets. They've picked him as a means of salvation for the People."

"And for the Santos?" he asked. "You know of such a warrior among their men?"

"We can find him." Leera Dobra was self-assured. This was the woman who'd almost fallen apart when her lover killed himself? It didn't make sense. Then again, perhaps she needed that type of man. Ree accessed his comm. Curious, he scanned the med readout on Dobra. They'd done a quick physical. No traces of semen from her vaginal area. So, she hadn't been *that* close to any of the natives.

He leaned back. Bruk and Vola had been nodding in agreement with everything she'd said. If she wasn't in love with the natives, she was being coldly professional, aware that if Atlantis proved a disaster, she could write it off as military intervention and let him hold the bag.

"Could I see you alone, Doctor?" he asked, smiling at Bruk and Vola. Along with his staff officers, they got up and walked out. He accessed comm and had the bugs and monitors shut off.

"Why?" he asked as the door closed. "Why deal?"

She shook out her hair, leaning on the edge of the table. "Because I need this!" Her eyes burned into his. "There are a lot of people who said I'd never make anything of myself. 'Anthropology?' they cried. 'Where's the future in that?' " She laughed a bitter laugh. "Colonel, you did what a commander is trained to do. I lived with Rita in the field. You reacted the way she would have. Full bore, don't stop until you've won. That's good. I've seen that it's healthy from the standpoint of tactics and strategy."

Ree nodded. "So? Why not let me run off a cliff? My military tactics will give me this planet. What's the difference between your way and mine."

"Bad press, Colonel. The Directorate isn't forever. You ever hear of a General named Westmoreland? No?

He was a general who had every advantage you do—but he lost. You ever hear of a general named Hitler? He attempted to kill off an entire people. He lost, too.

"Me, I'm here because it's the only game in town. I don't get another chance. This is the first time in six hundred years there has been a group of primitives to study. I want the chance to put my name in the books as a classic—just like you want to be able to say you conquered a planet. That's the why in a nutshell."

Ree got to his feet and walked around the room, moving close to her "Together?" he asked softly, raising an eyebrow.

She smiled wistfully, "You're not my type, Colonel. I'm flattered. Under other circumstances, I might even be interested. Here—if it got out—it would damage both of us. My recommendations would be suspect—your command weakened. There would be too much talk. We're splitting up a planet. We can't afford mistakes on top of the ones we'll make anyway."

"I'd never be a Jeffray." He waited while she thought. *Too bad, she's cured of that little pain.* No lever there.

"So, you checked, huh?" She watched him with raptor eyes. "That'll cost you, Colonel. I'd have done the same thing—but I resent you for it. I want my cadre directly responsible to you. I don't report to anyone but you—and I'm not subject to boobs like Helstead. In fact, *I want him!*"

Caught! Damn! Ree forced himself to smile. "I'm sorry. I was curious about what could have hurt you so. Do not think me a total boor. You have your cadre. The orders will be issued."

Too many mistakes! Am I getting old? He walked to the other side of the room.

"I am a soldier, Doctor." He clasped his hands behind him and turned, facing her, reading curiosity in those blue eyes. "I can fight my ship through an entire squadron of ships of the line and never make a mistake." He waved an arm. "I can kill every living thing on this planet. I could do the same if it were as well defended as Arpeggio was in the days of the Confederacy. But here, I have to deal with men who ride horses, shoot primitive rifles, and will not surrender.

240

"I'm a commander who seeks glory, Leeta. I seek to be a Caesar, to return to the Directorate with conquered nations in tow. Instead I could return with dead barbarians by the thousands . . . and the name of a monster."

He hesitated and sighed, looking down at his combat boots. "Yes, we have a deal. You and I will split this world of ours." He hesitated. "If it rose with modern arms. If it thrust out into the Directorate, sacking, pillaging, and fighting like a civilized empire, I would break it like a glass globe."

He faced her again. "Why does no one fight like that anymore? These Romanans have spirit. They have guts, courage—and no way to meet me on equal footing. At last, I have found a worthy adversary who cannot rise to meet me in a contest that would try my mettle!"

She shrugged and there was silence.

"Now it's my turn." Her head cocked to one side. "Between the two of us . . . why did *you* deal? You really didn't have to," her smile taunted, "and I know it wasn't just to gain sexual favors. You're far more complex than that. You need me. Why?"

Ree narrowed his eyes. "Doctor Dobra. Something has changed you." He lifted a hand absently, dropping his next bombshell. "I know now why the Health Department wants to psych you. You're dangerous."

Her hard expression didn't change. "Your prerogative, Colonel. Do you need my brain impaired . . . or not?"

He chuckled dryly, happy with his ally—and wary. "Very well, my bluff is called." *Do I tell her?* "Doctor Dobra, I knew of the unprovoked attacks. They occurred in violation of my orders for the express purpose of embarrassing me and costing me my *Bullet*. And Doctor . . . *I will not lose my ship!*" he finished grimly, knotting fists in resolution.

Leeta bit her lip, dropping her head in thought. Finally, with lowered eyes, she asked, "And how far will you go to keep your ship, Colonel?"

He didn't hesitate. "As far as I need to!"

CHAPTER XVI

Rita Sarsa stared with admiration at the endless blackness. "The Navel! Of course! It's perfect, Philip. How far back does it go?"

"No one knows. Is it big enough?" he asked. "I would think you could hid the entire *Bullet* in here."

"*Bullet* wouldn't even come close," she told him. "An AT? Sure, it'll fit. The rest of the project will be difficult. We need to get trained techs to kill the sensors. I can't hide the thing electronically. That's way outside my specialty."

"So, how will we do it?" Philip asked, trying to see the cavern roof by torchlight.

"I don't know," Rita moaned. "That's the one thing I just can't figure. Patrol ships are made so that they can't be stolen." She tasted the bitter pill of defeat.

"We can still hide our warriors here." Philip sensed her dejection.

"That we can. There's more than enough room for training purposes. We'd better make that trip into the settlements and begin recruiting. I think after another couple of days, José will be ready to go, too. He's coming around just fine." She paused and shivered in the cool air that rose from the stygian depths.

"You really think it's desperate, don't you?" Philip pulled her down onto an irregular boulder. He ran his hands along her shoulders, massaging the stiffness from her muscles.

"We haven't got a rat's chances in hell, Philip," she said candidly. "You've seen the ATs. But you haven't seen what they can do when you turn one all the way loose. Ree's been playing nice. He doesn't want this to erupt into a blood bath. Sure wish Doc was here."

"They're alive." Philip repeated. "From the sign,

Iron Eyes was wounded. She cared for him through most of the storm. When the water dropped, they dragged something out behind the horse. John had to have been on whatever was dragged. I saw no other tracks. The fire still smoldered. I almost caught them.''

"Doc might see something I'm missing. She's kind of flaky. God help us if we ever need her to kill anyone.'' Rita worried over it.

"Tomorrow, we'll ride into the settlements. They wouldn't shoot us up if we were going to town, would they?'' Philip asked.

"Depends on the proclamation.'' She had relaxed under his fingers. "I'm going with you.''

"They'd know you!'' he objected. "If they capture you, what then?''

"I'm returning to report for duty.'' She shrugged. "Then later, I cut loose and make my way back here. Might be better in the long run. I can get a better feel for what Ree's planning and doing. Keep up on his security precautions.''

Philip dropped his eyes. "I'm not so sure I'd want that.''

She looked at him. "You'd miss me, huh?''

"I would miss you.'' He took a deep breath and let it out slowly, hearing the odd echoes of the Navel. "I never had time for women. There were always echoes in my head—like the ones here. Too odd, too quiet.

"I made my name on the war trail and took my coups as expected. The voices echoed. Then came the day when the Prophet said we would follow him into the mountains. No one turns down a Prophet.

"I heard the voices . . . saw a future I couldn't stand. So I ran. I just . . . I let John Smith Iron Eyes make the choice he had to. I lived when I could have died . . . and I found you.

"So much changed. My ribs will never be the same! But more than that. I remember fighting with you, wondering how any woman could be so strong. Then we made camp. I started the fire and looked at you . . . and something inside me changed forever. Warm where there had only been cold. Desire where there had been apathy. I was made whole.''

243

He kissed her soundly. "No, I don't want you to leave."

The torch sputtered, dancing the shadows over water-worn rock.

"I was married once." She waited for a reaction. None came. "He was a good man who had reality and wanted dreams. You had dreams and wanted reality. I want a reality of dreams. Make sense of that!"

"You had many men follow your path on the ship?" Philip asked. "As beautiful as you are, it must have been hard to keep the proposals apart!"

She shrugged. "Philip, you were a virgin before I came along. Things are different on ships. Maybe you'd better know that I wasn't exactly an unplucked flower." She studied his face to make sure he understood.

A slight frown furrowed his brow. "And if you went back to the ship, you would again be a flower for many hands?"

She looked at his honest concern. "No. I wouldn't." She hesitated and looked up into the darkness. "I was very much in love with my husband. Had a real nice relationship. I'd made the choice to have children—play the game of housewife and mother—maybe study on the side and pick up a part-time career.

"Things didn't work that way in the end. His dream broke him. I learned though; he taught me a very good lesson. So I joined the Patrol and I was damn good at what I did. I thought I had all the answers. Men came and went. Some I thought I might eventually love—others were for the enjoyment. But none of them had that vital spark. The didn't really know life, and tragedy, and how fragile existence is. They just weren't real. No depth, I suppose."

She laced her fingers in his. "Then Doc brought me to this little planet of yours. I found myself useful for once. I wasn't just good. You understand? I was. . . . I mean, you can be good without being useful. We got in trouble and all of a sudden Doc needed me. God damn! I got us out of trouble—well, almost. I guess I enjoyed your rescue."

Philip's teeth gleamed his amusement.

"And there you were, all smiles and laughter, and

it was all genuine! You didn't care about anything but savoring life. You were kind, brave, handsome, and intelligent. You touched something inside me, Philip. You've seen more of life than you want. A most unusual man.''

She kissed him passionately and cradled his head in her hands, feeling his warm flesh and the firmness of his skull. ''In answer to your question: no! I am yours until you find someone better. I'm madly and hopelessly in love with you. We're going to die in this maniac scheme of ours, but I'll die happy.''

''Do not be so flippant about seeing death,'' Philip chided. ''I've seen my death once. Not just an imagined death—but a real death, final and complete. Iron Eyes—in his limited wisdom—chose rightly so I didn't have to live the dream. If death comes, let it; but leave it the grace of its own good time, Rita.

''As to finding someone better?'' He shrugged. ''The women of the People are not warriors. You fascinate me. From what I hear, our women do not do the things to a man's staff you do. I experience the rush of coup when your legs are wrapped around me.

''You know of life, Rita. We are touched with the ways of Spider. He took us to the future and we are part of his web.''

Rita closed her eyes, running her fingers over Philip's body. ''You'll get your chance to prove your worth, love. Only a hero, a madman, or a moron would tackle the Patrol head on.''

''I do not have to prove myself.'' Philip's answer came easily. ''I have seen myself inside and out. I am no more than who I am. Spider must have meant it that way.''

He paused, frowning. ''Other warriors wouldn't like you, Rita. They would fear your powers and couldn't work with you in this mad venture. But you make my life into a light that shines even here in the blackness of the Navel. I shall never cast you out for another.''

He kissed her, letting his hands run down the length of her body, feeling the subtle female curves of her waist and hips. Running his fingers inside the hunting shirt and circling her breasts, he teased the nipples hard. Words were no longer necessary as they sank down off the rock in the fuller language of love.

Marty gave her a final nod as he closed the door. One of his monitors blinked where it hung on a belt clip. "All clear," he said.

There had been no time for a meeting until now. Leeta had worked with Ree's people for a solid week. At the same time, she was able to sound out Marty's feelings. Bella Vola had been working with Iron Eyes on increasing the Romanan vocabulary. Finally, Marty had managed to locate all the monitors and bugs. The fewest were in the shower. These he circuited to a computer loop to secure them privacy.

"I'm sorry we haven't had any time until now. We're still on a rushed schedule, so I have to gamble." She looked at Marty and Bella Vola. An amused Iron Eyes struggled with a new synch-taught Standard vocabulary where he sat by the door.

"Gamble how, Doc?" Marty asked, eyes skeptical. "We've pretty well got our research free and clear."

"It won't stay that way!" Leeta scowled at him. "Use your head, Marty! We've pasted a bandaid on a cracked hull. We're holding back a supernova with a flashlight. This whole planet's about to come unhinged."

Marty gave her a look of indulgence. Bella put a hand on Marty's arm and pushed him back. "Gotta beat him over the head with it, Doc. Marty's real sharp when it comes to his electrical gadgets for seeing inside people, but he's a little slow on motives. He's—"

"Aw!" Marty began to protest but Leeta waved him down.

Leeta gave Bella a halfhearted look of thanks and took a deep breath. "Before I go any further, I need to know how you feel about the Romanans. Give it to me straight. If you could save their culture, would you? To what lengths would you be willing to go? Have you . . . I mean . . . how much can I depend on you? Trust you?" She tried to see into the souls of her assistants.

Marty gulped loudly. Bella frowned. "It's pretty serious, isn't it?" she asked, voice subdued.

246

Leeta jerked a short nod. "It's very serious. I'm taking a critical risk with the two of you. If you're with me, you're in for the duration. I mean it. You won't be able to back out. You need to decide, right now. I can't give you time to think about it. Are you in or out?" Her gaze shifted from face to face.

"Doc?" Marty's face showed his unease. "You wouldn't be thinking of anything . . . uh . . . illegal, would you?" He swallowed.

"Beyond that, Marty," she assured him. "In a worst case scenario, I'm talking about professional ruin, probable imprisonment. Potentially you could die. Myself, I'm under a psych sentence by the Department of Health—I have nothing left to lose." She saw their shock and disbelief.

She assured them, "I'm committed. On the other hand, you need to make a choice on the basis of morality. I'll not use you as unwitting pawns. So you choose—now."

"What choice, Leeta?" Bella demanded, stress showing in the way her upper lip trembled. "Worse than a concentration camp and burned natives? We've seen some highly irregular things here."

Leeta lifted a shoulder. "I'm talking about the extinction of the Romanans. The Directorate can't allow them to be left free. Look at what you've seen here. You know how many critically wounded are being treated in the med units. You know how many ATs are on planet. You know how the Directorate would react to news of Romanan culture getting out." Leeta felt herself becoming emotional. She stopped, sucking a deep breath.

"Psych teams?" Marty asked.

Leeta gave him a cold stare. "Ree sent thirty prisoners up to *Bullet* for complete pyschological personality restructuring last week. It worked on seven individuals, eleven went violently insane and died most horribly . . . and twelve are unaffected so far as the psych teams can tell."

"I told you," Marty declared, "their brains are different. They exhibit a whole range from a slight variation from the human norm to a very different kind of brain. Chester Armijo Garcia, for example, is on the far end of the curve. I'd bet there's a one to one correlation between brain morphology and their ability to take psych!''

"Could be, Marty." Leeta agreed. "The fact is, the ones who are abnormal must be locked up or exterminated.''

"Isn't that getting a little extreme?" Bella frowned. "That's against Directorate policy!''

"So is burning down natives with blasters," Leeta reminded. "So is interdicting a planet, stopping the transmission of scientific data, concentration camps, and military law. We've seen all three here. What the Directorate claims differs from what it does. How much have we, as individuals, been duped?''

A lifetime of indoctrination needed to be discarded. Could they do it—see beyond?

"Look!" She gave them her most persuasive expression. "The Directorate has found a group of barbarians that it can't reprogram—can't subdue—and can't predict. *Garcia sees the future!* He's not the only one. What is the underlying principle of the Directorate? Security and predictability, isn't it? Well?''

They nodded.

"What happens to that security when men who believe in raiding are allowed their right to express themselves? What happens to security when a shaman can see the future? What happens to any venture of risk? When you think about it, the Directorate can't allow these people loose! They are a threat to everything the Directorate stands for! Not only that, but for my money, the damn Directorate is stagnant and needs shaking up!'' She smacked her fist into her palm.

Bella narrowed her eyes. Marty's face had lined in an expression of concern, eyes vacant as he considered the data.

"You see," Leeta said at last. "There is one ultimate way to deal with the Romanan problem. They must be destroyed—one way or another. I've led Ree to believe we can acculturate them over a period of time. But we can't. Psych won't work. They'd rather die than surrender. Chester has already made it out and the planet has been interdicted. The Romanans see the future! They know! They also know they have nothing left to lose—so they fight in order that their people might . . . just *might* survive.''

Marty shook his head. "They can't just exterminate an entire—''

"That's what's left when you boil it down," Leeta cut him off. "I see no other way to put it except in terms of the survival of a race. This is the first war in four hundred years—and we're in the middle of it. I'm asking you to take sides.''

"I take it you're with the Romanans?" Marty asked.

"I am," she said firmly. "I can't stand to see them go down. I think they have something the rest of humanity needs right now.''

"If it turns out the way you foresee, my data will probably be disseminated in the end. But what about Marty's?" Bella asked.

"It's already impounded when it comes off his press. You think the comm sends it up to *Bullet* and from there it's beamed to university. Only, it's not!''

"What?" Marty cried, his face stricken. "How do *you* know?" he demanded, the veins in his neck standing out.

Letta looked away. "Ree told me. He doesn't want you to give up your work. He thinks you might find a biological means to give him a victory over the Romanans. He doesn't want to use a virus—or other infectious disease—until the last, hoping to find some other way to provide the Directorate with a docile population to exploit. Further, there's always the chance it would delay colonization while they wait out decontamination.''

"Jesus!" Marty exploded. "You're really serious! *They're using me!"* He began pacing the small room and then stopped and pounded his fist against the wall.

"I told you," Leeta said, her voice firm. "We're fighting a war. Things are done dirty when the stakes get high. The destiny of a people and a planet are up for grabs. The Director wants Atlantis. He wants it with nice happy Romanans who don't see the future. He doesn't want it with Prophets, and scalp-cutting warriors! Ree is doing what he has been ordered to do, nothing more, nothing less. He's the Director's

249

puppet. The tune is called by Skor Robinson, Damen Ree just completes the footwork.''

"I'm in!" Marty cried passionately. "They can't jerk me around like this. I won't give them another piece of data!''

"Two things!" Leeta held up her hand, eyes hard on Bruk. "First and most important. There are plans of which you know nothing. I told you—the stakes are high. It's *war* Marty, and I'm the general. Will you swear to give me your undying obedience?" Her voice tightened, became forced. "If you don't . . . if you don't . . . I may . . . may have to kill you!''

Bruk's mouth dropped open with shock.

"Second, we'll give them all the data we can! We may leave out critical bits and pieces—but we do it! We're here on sufferance because we might give Ree the edge he needs to make a success out of chaos. Do you understand? That's our freedom to move! *We play the game!*

Marty sank down in the corner, looking up in disbelief. *"You'd kill me?"* He shook his head slowly. "I guess that's war. It's . . . *unreal*! I've never even seen anybody I knew die!" He looked at his hands, eyes stricken.

"I'm in, Doc," Bella Vola whispered. "I understand the situation. I guess I can take it, if you can. What about Netta?''

"She's out. I saw her in the village. Professionally, she's part of the team. You know, I'm counting on you both to act to the best of your ability. If we let it slip that we're not one hundred percent with Ree, we're out of play . . . and Ree wins." She kept her voice even.

"Marty and I were already playing that game," Bella said quickly. "We just didn't know how high the stakes were. What about the graduate students? We let them in?''

"No!" Leeta's reply was sharp. "No one! I repeat, *no one else!* You both have to be stable, hear me? Any psych probe could blow the whole thing and put us all in the brig!''

Marty had pulled himself to his feet. 'I'm in Doc. I

250

understand. Isn't there some sort of oath or something that people swear at times like this?''

Leeta grinned sourly. ''Maybe, but I'm new at this game.'' She looked down at Iron Eyes. ''You get all that?'' She asked in Standard.

''Most,'' he agreed.

''Well?'' Leeta asked. ''You like them? You accept them?''

Iron Eyes let himself study Bella Vola. He nodded quickly. He hesitated on Marty Bruk. ''You've never seen death?''

Marty raised his shoulders. ''I've dissected a pile of corpses. I've measured more human skulls than you've ever seen. I've seen a lot of the dead. I've just never watched a man die.''

Iron Eyes looked up. ''At least he's honest—but he's the weakest link.''

''Hey, I can do anything Leeta or Bella can!'' Marty flared.

''Then you can kill? The Doctor has. She killed a man with her bare hands. I watched as she took the coup. Can you do that, too?'' Iron Eyes never wavered once he pinned his flinty gaze on Bruk.

The anthropologist fought for breath, swallowed, and nodded hesitantly. ''If it's necessary, I guess I . . . I can make a specimen out of a . . . living man.''

''He might make it,'' Iron Eyes shot a glance at Leeta. ''He has told me about his natural selection these past days. Perhaps he will be selected to be a warrior, perhaps not, but he is honest.''

''Looks like you both live,'' Leeta said as she reached for the door.

''Huh?'' Marty's relief was evident.

Leeta nodded to Iron Eyes who lifted a pneumatic syringe. ''Doctor Dobra tells me that it would make you forget what happened. I wanted to use a knife.'' His voice was steady.

Marty looked in shock from one to the other.

''We have an appointment at the Spider main village in about a half hour. I'd suggest you take a tranq if you're nervous, Bruk. We're play acting within fifteen minutes.'' Leeta's hand was on the door.

''Nope,'' Marty muttered. ''If Bella can do it, I

251

can." He marched out steadily, already whistling to himself.

"I'm taking a hell of a risk with them," Leeta growled to herself as Iron Eyes grimaced with the effort of standing. He massaged his not quite healed chest.

"We need them" he said simply.

A half hour later, Leeta watched as Helstead set the AT down near the wreck of the *Nicholai Romanan*. She studied the monitor with mixed emotions. Over the ages, the alloys had corroded. The ship was a grayish brown and had partially sunk into the alluvial plain, its hull sticking out like some gargantuan turtle.

"That's where it all started," Leeta whispered.

People from the village gathered to watch. They did that every time a ship landed—or so she was told.

"Marty?" Leeta accessed the comm, looking out over the town Iron Eyes called the Settlements. There wasn't much to see. Huts, some fences for prized cattle, a couple of larger buildings that were used as storehouses, and the *Nicholai Romanan*.

"Here, Doctor!" Marty's voice chirped.

"Is John Smith Iron Eyes ready?" she asked.

"He's looking at the monitor. From the light in his eyes, I think he's ready to blow this joint."

"Let's go!" she called. Good, Bruk was holding up well.

"Keep her ready," she called to Helstead who saluted absently as he watched his scans, no doubt ready for any hostile move—wishing something would happen.

She found her crew in the hatch and let Iron Eyes lead them out. The Spiders stood back, recognizing Iron Eyes and whispering behind their hands. Leeta saw a lot of illegal rifles.

Ree had banned guns first thing. Then he found he had to personally disarm each of the Romanans. To do that, he'd had to kill them—or burn them so badly they couldn't resist. It might still be law, but like so many of Ree's laws, it was one which was only enforceable with blasters.

Iron Eyes didn't look left or right as he marched toward the *Nicholai Romanan*. He called it Ship—the center of the Spider world. Leeta could see the dark streaks left by blaster fire as she entered the main hold. Ree had killed the five warriors who had stood in his way. It was little enough resistance for the major Spider stronghold. The Prophets had kept the others away.

Leeta was surprised to note that the floors were dirt until she realized it was the mud of ages which had been tracked in and never shoveled out. Ancient Cyrillic writing could still be made out on the walls. The place was lit by torches.

The meeting hall, though, she found lit with electric lights powered by the remaining solar batteries. Dimly, light still burned in the ancient bulbs that had lasted for so many centuries. The four old men were seated at the far end of the room.

"The great thing about seeing the future," she heard Bruk whisper, "is that you never have trouble with late appointments."

John Smith Iron Eyes had walked up to within a couple of meters of the Prophets and lowered his eyes. Leeta stood beside him and looked at the wrinkled, parchmentlike skin of the old ones.

"We are here, Old Ones," Iron Eyes said in Romanan.

"There are electrical listening devices?" Leeta asked.

"There are," one of the old men stood. "They are in the hall of the elders where the children are now playing loudly. The star men did not come to this room. We hid it from them so that we could talk. Have you killed any bears lately, John Smith Iron Eyes?" he asked with a chuckle, shifting his eyes.

Iron eyes kept his gaze on the floor, where patches of metal could be seen through the dirt. "No, but this woman—this warrior—has killed a bear. She has taken coup. She has earned the honor to speak."

The Old One waved a hand. "The time for winning honors is past, John Smith Iron Eyes. We have seen your coming. We know what you wish and you shall have it."

Leeta studied the Old One with a slight frown. "Old One," she kept her voice low, "I am from the stars. May I know it is so? I do not see the future."

The ancient face crinkled into a thousand lines and he laughed toothlessly. "Yes, Leeta Dobra, we will grant our influence to keep the young men from raiding and shooting at the star ships and men. We will attempt to conform to as many of the star ways as we can learn in the time you are with us here.

"There will be many young men who will help you. There are already many at the Navel. Red Many Coups will talk to you of this later. I cannot tell you the outcome of your struggle. There are many choices, cusps, which need to be made. Chester Armijo Garcia has not yet been summoned to the Star Lord. Many cusps. Spider guards the free will of men well. The questions forming in your head do not have answers except that you must believe in God."

The Old One looked at Marty Bruk in silence before he said, "Translate this for me. Your young man does not have the tongue of the People." He indicated Bella Vola, who spoke softly to Marty. "Yes, there is much our two peoples have to offer each other. Look at Iron Eyes who would have been dead if the the star ship had not fixed his broken body. Your people have no spirit left in them. They waste their lives on fat and trivialities. They are no longer strong.

"My people are lean, young wolves—yours fat like old dogs. There is a lesson here. Which are smarter? The young wolves who rip each other's throats out over fancied insults—or the old dogs who would starve, letting the food rot in the bowl to avoid offending another by eating.

"You see!" The Old One nodded, smiling, his glittering eyes still on Marty. "It will cost. There will indeed be blood and death. That is the birthright of man, scholar. How painful to teach young wolves not to snap and old dogs to bite. Someone must muzzle the wolves and teach the old dogs the proper use of their teeth. The price of knowledge, scholar, is that no change is given freely."

The old man nodded happily at a speechless Leeta, then looked at Bella Vola. "The answer to your question, young woman, is that Truth has no beginning and no end. Truth exists, like love and war and life and death. It cannot be investigated with words. To try to

254

do so is as foolish as damming a river with a wish. To know Truth is to experience it. Nothing else will do.''

He paused only a moment, then his face beamed. ''Ah, I see! You are wrong. In the end, nothing makes any difference. The actions of men do not affect God. If all men were to die tomorrow, Spider would be a little poorer—but there are others in the universe to teach him. Yes, knowledge is the reason, it is the essence of Truth.''

Bella was swallowing rapidly as the Prophets smiled at her beneficently. Marty had his eyes closed, lost in thought. The entire atmosphere had changed. No one could speak. ''That is enough for now. Others come. We will do what we can.'

At that, a group of warriors ducked in from a side door. All but two dropped their eyes and nodded at the sight of the Prophets. Hostile eyes glared into Leeta's at the sight of her clothing.

''Philip!'' Iron Eyes called suddenly, reaching out to one of the men. Leeta echoed the cry and leaped forward to watch John and his cousin embrace.

A hand grabbed Leeta's shoulder and spun her around. ''Been missing you, Doc!'' Rita's caustic voice brought a lump to Leeta's throat.

''You're not dead! I'm so glad!'' Leeta crushed the lieutenant in a hug. ''I missed you, Sarsa. God! I'm so glad to have you back. You can help me fend off Ree! I'm lost at this game!''

''So you joined the revolution?'' Rita's eyes raised. She was adequately disguised. She looked just like any other warrior except for the belt of hair she wore. Only Iron Eyes had more coups in his belt.

''I've been fighting it,'' Leeta chuckled. ''Uh, look, remember so long ago in the bar back at university? Well, um, I guess being a rebel is catching. I got a good dose.''

Rita's eyes gleamed. ''Looks like I made a good call when I short-circuited those Heath Department files.'' She punched Leeta's shoulder. ''So what have you been up to?''

Leeta winced and rubbed her shoulder before grinning. ''I've been laying the groundwork for us while you were out lollygagging with Philip! Some aid! Leave me to do all the work!"

Rita's lips twisted. "Just who do you think's been training the troops, hiding in the rain, subverting the common folk, and planning ahead for this shindig? I don't have time to usher a bunch of scientists around the planet. I gotta figure out where in hell we can steal an AT! Then I have to figure out how to get the techs to hide it!" Rita looked frenzied.

"Jesus! And I told Ree you were competent?" Leeta mocked, shaking her head. "*I even recommended you for a commendation? What a fool I was!"*

"Huh?" Rita's jaw stuck out, hands braced on her hips. "You want your arm twisted out of its socket, Doc?"

"You do—and you don't get your AT," Leeta jeered, smug. She enjoyed the widening of the lieutenant's eyes.

"What AT?" Rita's voice was a whisper, her face had gone pale.

"The one Ree assigned me." Leeta let herself gloat in triumph. It wasn't for long. Rita punched her in the belly. Not hard—just enough to let the air out of her.

"You sleeping with Ree?" Rita cried. "That's the only way I know of getting around his military perfection!" Her voice cut like a whip.

Leeta gasped and glared up at the redhead. "One of these days, you'll pay for that!" Leeta straightened, eyes burning.

Rita backed up a step. "All right, Doc. I apologize." Her eyes were intent as she studied Leeta. "You've changed, Doc. I'm sorry. If looks could kill, you'd do it, right here. You're tougher. I approve. So how'd you get the AT?"

"Yeah, I changed," Leeta gruntly dryly. "Ree's in trouble." Leeta began to outline the conversations she'd had with Colonel Ree and the actions she'd taken. As she talked, she rubbed her stomach.

Sarsa let out a low whistle. "My heart is out to you, Doc. You've done one hell of a job!" Rita frowned. "There's no way I could have pulled the rug out from under him like that. So there's almost four thousand men at base camp?"

"Uh-huh," Leeta nodded. "John's been proselytizing with Bella's help. We're trying to overcome the tribal infeuding. So far we've made some progress, but can't spring any of them to get back to their people with the word. Too many tempers are cooped up there. Everything we do blows up."

Rita took her turn, grinning triumphantly. "We've almost got that licked. At least so long as Ree doesn't crack down on runners going between camps again. We're—"

"He won't," Leeta interrupted. "That's my policy."

"Good. The head Santos warriors are coming in." Rita hesitated. "It isn't all free, Doc. The man we've got to be chummy with is Big Man. John's sworn to kill him for raping his sweetheart. You understand a blood feud?"

"Damn!" Leeta cursed under her breath. "If John sets eyes on him—that'll be it." She sighed wearily. "I'll see what I can do."

Rita's grin was nasty. "Put your mind to it. You're the one with all the fancy trained brains. If he doesn't come around, kick his ass. Or didn't they teach that in anthropology?"

"Sarsa, I wonder about you sometimes," Leeta grumbled, looking to where John was talking animatedly with Philip.

"All right," Rita put up her hands. "Look, you do what you must with John. At the same time, we need a lot of supplies. You've got the AT, can you drop us a batch of rations at the Navel? That's sort of privileged information by the way. We've got to figure out how to feed a couple thousand warriors. The logistics are going to be incredible. Philip's warriors have a lot to learn."

"How can I do that? Helstead reports right to Ree. It may be my AT to fly around in, but I got it because they almost got me killed. I keep rubbing their noses in it, so I'm not exactly the star that shines for Helstead's crew!" Leeta locked her hands behind her back and paced.

"There ought to be a way we can make that work

in our favor.'' Sarsa's eyes came up. ''Colonel Ree suspect you at all?''

''I don't know,'' Leeta shook her head. ''Even if he doesn't believe I'm up to something, he'll keep a close eye on me just because that's his style.''

Rita was nodding her head. ''Yeah, he's not one to get caught with his britches down.'' She squinted, thinking hard. ''This is a political hot potato isn't it?'' She stared speculatively at Leeta.

''The Director's in it up to his eyebrows.'' Leeta agreed, motioning with one arm. ''There have been a lot of policy violations at the old bird's orders. Ree's scared stiff over it. Why?''

''Maybe we can cook up some sort of plan,'' Rita responded. ''Maybe con Ree into ordering some surgery on the monitoring equipment. We'd need a real good reason—something that had to be kept out of the records. Any ideas?''

''Not right offhand.'' Leeta frowned. ''Why are you so concerned with an AT anyway? How does having a tame one get us anywhere? We sure can't destroy the others with mine! That's even if we could get Helstead to agree!''

Rita grinned. ''To hell with the other ATs. I only need one—and I need it real bad. The shuttle still at base camp?''

''Yes,'' Leeta stuck a finger under Rita's chin and lifted it so she could look into the deep green eyes. ''What kind of insanity are you plotting?''

Rita shrugged, eyes devilish. ''Can't win the war without the hole card. I'm planning on capturing *Bullet.*''

Leeta felt her mouth fall open. Of all the . . . it was . . . How could Rita say it so . . . *casually?*

''You're out of your raving mind, Lieutenant!''

CHAPTER XVII

Rita spit into the mud as she watched the line of horses crossing the plain. "I want this done right. If it goes sour, remember what I told you. Each of you has a specific target." She turned back in time to see nodding heads where the men hid in the rocks.

José waved from where he rode beside the big warrior Rita knew she would never forget. She'd learned that his name was Gary Andojar Sena, but to his people he was known as Big Man. Apt name she decided, remembering his huge bulk.

Philip stepped out and lifted his hands to show they were empty. José had already dismounted, a smile on his face. "You see," he called, "I brought them." Rita stepped back into the shadows, thankful her hair was wrapped.

Philip placed his hands on José's shoulders. "Good work! Go on in and eat." He slapped him on the back as José trotted past.

Rita looked up at Big Man. The wind whipped his beard and clothing. His eyes didn't stop as they scanned the entrance to Navel Camp. He was wary, tight, like spring steel. His followers, too, kept their eyes moving, their hands on their rifles, fingers on the triggers.

"Come!" Philip called. "Eat with us. We have food prepared—a whole beef is roasting. We have a new drink called coffee, as well as tea."

"No whiskey?" Big Man asked, speaking for the first time. Rita bit back a snide outburst.

"This is not a time for whiskey. We need sharp minds and keen wits," Philip said smoothly. "After we have driven the star men from our skies and made our way to new worlds, then, in celebration, we will drink whiskey.''

Big Man didn't say anything. He gave the place one last look and slowly dismounted from the oversize horse he rode. Rita hadn't known horses that first time. Now she understood what a large animal he needed. The rest of the Santos were dropping lithely to the ground, rifles ready.

''Where are your men?'' Big Man asked. ''You are brave—or very foolish to meet us alone like this.'' His pig eyes tightened as he towered over Philip.

''Like you,'' Philip smiled, ''we do not take chances. There are many rifles covering you. Given the circumstances, why make you leery with fear of treachery? Our Peoples, our world, lie at stake here. You and I, we will make history.''

Philip turned and started for the entrance to the huge cave. Big Man made a motion with his hands and his men followed, some looking out to each direction, rifles in tense arms. Rita walked to one side. Her eyes caught the gleaming white at Big Man's belt. Her blaster!

Philip indicated a seat beside the roaring fire. Beef sizzled while drops of grease spattered, smoking, into the fire. The aroma of roasted meat hung in the air. Big Man and another man seated themselves while the rest of his guard peered into the half light of the shelter, looking nervously at the glow discernible deeper in the Navel.

''So you would ally the Spiders and the Santos?'' Big Man asked as Philip handed him a cup of coffee.

''It is necessary, Gary Andojar Sena.'' Philip gave him a quick, intent look. ''I do not say it will be easy— so much blood and death lies between our Peoples— but it is necessary.''

''Why?'' Big Man asked, looking nervously at his coffee. He handed the cup to Philip. ''Drink!''

Rita felt her muscles tensing. She could see the gleaming eyes of the Santos warriors watching as Philip held Big Man's eyes, took the cup, and drank. He had to have burned his tongue on the almost boiling liquid. Rita felt her lips curling in a snarl as she glared through slitted eyes.

Big Man never missed a beat. He, too, drank deeply of the coffee. "I would have more of this drink!" he rumbled.

Philip poured and looked up. "We cannot take the stars unless we work together. We need your cooperation. If we win, we will take you with us to the stars. If we lose, it makes no difference, our Peoples are dead."

Big Man cuddled the cup in his thick fingers and looked absently at the flames. "You know a way we can beat these star men?" he asked. "There were legends that the Sobyets would come again. How can we fight their fire and sky things with our horses and rifles? You tell me, eh?"

"We steal their sky things," Philip said evenly. "If we can capture the big ship, *Bullet,* which circles above the sky, we can force the star men to let us go."

Big Man sat there, looking thoughtful. "They have other worlds full of men. There are many wonderful things they have that would make the Santos rich. Their women have many colors of hair and I would taste of their pleasure." He looked up, eyes shining with anticipation.

Rita's gut churned as she saw the man's lips part and his tongue run over white teeth. She imagined the fate that would have been hers and Leeta's. She remembered Philip's description of Jenny's body after this man had finished with her. A coldness settled in her breast as she fingered her fighting knife.

Big Man continued. "So it might be a good idea. Our Prophet has told me to come. He has said that only through working with you, do our people go to the stars." Big Man leaned his head back. "From there, who knows?" He pointed a finger at Philip. "But tell me, Spider. How do we control the hatred between your warriors and mine? Blood has been sworn. Who will see that none spill it?"

Philip steepled his fingers over his coffee cup. "Gary Andojar Sena, together we take a war trail, do we not? What man, be he Santos or Spider, will break the oath of the war trail? If our Peoples take the trail, blood feud and knife feud must stop—"

Big Man laughed. "Stop? Blood feud? Santos do not forget the wrongs of the past, Spider man."

"Neither do my People," Philip agreed. "But such feuds must be stopped until we have beaten the star men from our skies. When we have won, the feuds may be finished until honor is satisfied on both sides."

"Very well, we will do this thing. Together. Spider and Santos shall ride to the stars, side by side, eh, Philip Iron Eyes?" He laughed heartily. "I speak for the Santos when I say this is war trail. As War Chief, I proclaim blood and knife feud is forbidden."

"Then we have a chance to win," Philip muttered, relieved. "You are one of the cusps, Big Man. Without you, it is even more desperate."

Big Man grinned at that—a big, toothy grin that swelled with his ego. "I will win it for you, Spider man." He chuckled. "But let us haggle price. When we have taken our coups off the star men, I want two women. One of them has red hair and the spirit of the bear in her. The other has hair of yellow, like the light of the sun on the grass of autumn. This one I want also. They were taken as my wives. They got away before I could drink of their beauty and sire my sons of them. I want them back!"

Philip kept his nerve. He didn't even flinch. "We shall . . . bring the women to you. It will be as you say—after we have taken the coups of the star men."

Rita faded back into the shadows, watched suspiciously by Big Man's guards. She found Friday Yellow Legs leaning on his rifle, watching as two men grunted and lifted the carcass from over the coals.

"Keep an eye on Big Man, Friday. If he makes trouble, you could probably see it before I would. I still have bad memories—and they just got worse." Rita stared at the silhouette of the big man and noted what a wonderful rifle shot he would make.

"All right," Friday whispered. "Where you gonna be if Philip needs you?"

"In back. I want to check on the rest of the troops. Holler if you need me." She turned, fuming, and left.

She awoke when Philip's cool skin slid in next to hers. She hadn't really been asleep, she decided. Her brain had still been working. "Looks pretty good," he said.

"Yeah," she grunted. "I can't wait to be handed over to that son of a bitch."

"What are those words? Son of a what?" She could hear the puzzlement in his voice.

"Bitch," she said. "It's a Standard word. Means female dog. It also has another meaning reserved for scum like him."

"Would you rather that I had turned him down right away? It would have looked bad to deny him two women for an alliance." Philip's voice reflected worry.

"Half of that bargain is *me!*" Her voice strained. "The other half is Leeta. If you'll remember, we're most of your strength, pal of mine!"

Philip leaned back and sighed easily, unaffected by the scorn in her tone. "I knew your feelings would be hurt."

"*Hurt?*" She fought to keep her voice down. "If I hadn't had my hair covered up, he'd a been trying to sleep with me tonight!"

"Relax, Red Many Coups!" Philip was laughing. "We have not won yet. Also, many things can happen. Our bargain was made pending his promise for alliance. If he breaks it—he loses you and Leeta. His pride and his honor are at stake."

"More like his life. I'll kill him, you know! If he lays one finger on my body—let alone raping me—I'll kill him!" Rita spat ferociously.

"Settle down!" Philip's tone was firm. "I'll not give you up! I'm bargaining for time. If you would look through your emotions, you would see I did what I had to do to gain Santos support! I'd no more let him have you than I would take coup off the Prophets! Use your brains for more than woman's spite!"

Rita balled a fist, held it, and relaxed. "You're right," she grudgingly admitted. "So what do we do if we win?"

"I kill Big Man," Philip said nonchalantly. "If he is dead, he can't take you or Leeta."

"That will split the Spiders and the Santos wide open again," Rita reminded.

"Then again, the Prophets have told us that many

263

men will die to free the People. Big Man, perhaps? You or Leeta? Maybe when it is all done, there will be so many star women for booty that he won't want you anymore? Who knows?" Philip shrugged, letting one hand glide over her body.

"The Prophets!" she growled, loosening up under his light touch.

"True!" He beamed. "Meanwhile, I am learning your star tricks so I can kill him if need be."

"I'm not sure you can." Rita paused, feeling her insides warming to his playful fingers. It was becoming difficult to concentrate. "What about my blaster? Can you get it back?"

"It would be of no use. He ran the charge out of it learning how it worked. When he found it would blow boulders apart on full charge—he didn't take long to drain it!" Philip choked on his laughter.

"Makes him a lot of status, I suppose." Rita's voice sounded far away as she began to move with his hand.

"It does." Philip began using his mouth. "I wonder how Leeta is doing with Colonel Ree?"

"Who cares?" Rita moaned as she bit his shoulder and reciprocated, feeling him stiffen under her fingers.

"Cares about . . . what?" he whispered, absently.

"Native police," Leeta said with a smile. "How much did you read in those old anthropology books? Do you remember reading about the Sioux Tribal Police? They were an extension of the Soldier Societies who enforced the orders of the chiefs; only they did it for the whites. Terribly effective. They were a powerful tool of acculturation."

Ree was walking along beside her, looking up into the dark sky. The lights of the base camp glowed behind them. The damp grass rustled under their feet.

"You say you have a group which would serve this purpose? What would be required of us?" Ree's voice betrayed interest.

She could feel his eyes on her. "We supply them with food, clothing, perhaps blasters and combat armor. We transport them on the ATs or provide them with aircars."

"why do all that?" he demanded. "Wouldn't they learn some of our secrets?"

"First, we give them status, Damen. If they're floating around in the air like we are, the common people see them as superior. At the same time, the people sit back and think. They say to themselves, 'Remember when Damen Ree Andojar was a little boy? He was so nice. Now he flies in the sky! Maybe these star ways are not so bad after all.' These are their neighbors and friends, Colonel.

"Second, sure, they learn some of our secrets. At the same time, they fly around. They get status. If anything happens to us, they lose that status. Worse, they become pariahs. So, you see, they get a stake in our success. Our goals become theirs.

"Third, and related to the second, they develop an understanding of our weapons' potentials which—you will admit—are astounding to a Romanan. While they do that, they directly interface with *Bullet* personnel. They make friends and, all of a sudden, we're people—humans just like them. Lo and behold, some of the Romanans actually like their new friends and want to be like them. Bingo, acculturation!" She smacked her hands together as if dusting them off.

"I like it." Ree sounded pleased. "Have you been working on this long?"

"About two weeks." She stretched her neck, fighting the slight headache she had. Thoughts nagged over what she still had to do—to learn.

"Uh-huh," he grunted. "Two weeks. Tell me, these Romanans wouldn't be out near where we found you?"

"Same bunch!" She turned as if surprised. "How did you know? They were the best bet. Since I'd had contact with them, I got in touch and felt them out. Planted the idea and left them a couple of bales of supplies as an inducement. I gave it a couple of days to ferment before I dropped in again. They're all for it. Star goods and the prospect for enhanced warrior status work wonders."

"And you thought I would say yes?" he mused.

"Of course. You don't have anything to lose. If it goes sour for some reason I can't foresee, we're back at square one. They're interested—and I admit I was worried they'd have none of it. The use of native troops is historically and anthropologically sound. If it fails here, I still learn something about the people. At worst, you just have another feud among thousands on your hands.'' She shrugged.

Reed chuckled. "You had me worried for a bit, Doctor.''

"Worried?'' Leeta turned back toward the base camp.

"I'd heard that you were supplying aid and comfort to the enemy.'' Ree's voice sounded amused.

"Helstead!'' Leeta laughed suddenly. "I'll bet that stiff-necked martinet had me shooting at *Bullet* in his reports. He'd like to get me real bad, wouldn't he?''

"You're not his favorite.'' Ree cocked his head. "You want a different AT assigned to you?''

"Not on your life, Colonel! I don't give a royal hoot what he reports.'' *Perfect!* Leeta enjoyed a glow of happiness which she hid behind a wistful look. "I'm going to make him suffer as long and hard as I can. Maybe I can get him to downright disobey. Then I can have the arrogant bastard broken in two!''

"You hate him that much?'' Ree's voice seemed honeyed. "I remind you, you don't really have military rank. You can't court-martial him.''

She nodded. "You've undoubtedly seen the bear tapes. It's one thing to watch from a safe height. It's another to face one of those things with a primitive rifle. I'll never forget he put me through that.'' Her voice turned venomous.

"I will confess, Helstead's reports barely stop short of accusing you of treason.'' Ree turned toward her. "I understand now. You and he are after each other. I don't want this little feud interfering with our work. Am I understood?''

"Perfectly, Colonel,'' Leeta said reasonably. "Am I to understand that it is your opinion that such interference has already resulted from my misunderstandings with Helstead?'' Leeta let her voice carry a note of dismay.

They were getting closer to the base camp. "Not exactly.'' He smiled. "I am here because of his report on your activities.''

Leeta stopped, staring at Ree. "You mean, you believed I was . . ." She looked stunned. "That *bastard!*" She ground her teeth.

Ree raised a hand, and gave her a winning smile. "Come, Doctor, would you respect my abilities as a commander if I didn't check these things out? Did I force you to tell me what you were doing with the natives? No, you almost bowled me over in your efforts to brag about your accomplishments and to sell me on your native police plans. You haven't tried to cover anything."

Or have you? What is your game, Doctor?

He put his hand on her shoulder. "Please! I can see the anger building in your eyes. It was simply a matter of routine investigation. Captain Helstead has filed some very severe charges. You would have done the same in my situation. I simply had no idea that you and he were so, shall we say, hostile?"

"I think hostile is a very good word for it," Leeta agreed resuming her steps toward the base camp. "Do you seriously think I've let a vendetta interfere with my work? Honest answer, Damen!"

He walked in silence for a while. "No, Doctor. Not in the slightest. I've reviewed the holos of your actions on the bridge. I've seen the results of your manipulations of the natives. While you have never been polite to Arf Helstead or his crew, you've never attempted to goad them into misbehaving either. I do think I should assign you to a different AT."

"No!" Leeta said firmly. "Damen, look at it like this. I think Helstead's incompetent. I'm looking to get him dismissed in the end. I'm not going out of my way to make him look bad. I don't need to. It's my opinion that he'll hang himself in the end." *And you won't believe a word of what he reports!*

They were in the lighted area now. "You know, Helstead's no different than any of my other captains. He was just following orders regarding the Romanans."

"I have a bottle of very good Zion wine. Would you care to join me, Damen?" she asked.

"Delighted, Doctor. I didn't think I was, shall we say, on your list of friends," Ree added thoughtfully.

Leeta took his arm and laughed lightly. "I'm sorry

267

I gave you that opinion. I value our 'professional' relationship very much. You've done things here that I disapprove of. I don't deny that. We just had two different means to what we hoped to be the same end. And we need each other. I need you for my study and to keep these people alive. You need me to keep this from boiling over so the Directorate doesn't replace you.''

He sighed. ''You never cease to amaze me, Doctor. Are you empathic? Do you have some psychic ability to read people's minds? Are you perhaps one of these Romanan shamans?''

''No, Damen, but if I were an empath, what would that tell you about Helstead?'' She raised an eyebrow.

''I really ought to separate the two of you,'' he repeated.

''Wouldn't do you any good in the long run. He's going to cause problems eventually. Under my eye, he can't burn down a party of Romanans for a fancied insult. Elsewhere, he could become overzealous and ignite a conflagration that would destroy all our work.''

''Speaking of which.'' Ree stopped at the edge of the compound. ''I have received numerous reports of discipline problems among my people.''

She cocked her head. ''Reary again?''

His smile was grim. ''I would hate to have you for an adversary. I am always impressed by your ability to assimilate isolated bits of data into a probability. But no, in this case, I have heard of fights between Romanans and my marines.''

''That doesn't sound like my area of—''

''But it might be, Doctor,'' he waved her down. ''They occur for the most silly of reasons—coup!''

Leeta frowned. ''Coup?''

''Indeed. The Romanans despise my men for not having taken coup. To the natives, it's a sign of weakness—since after all, any warrior worth his salt has taken coup. The obvious—''

''—result is that your marines feel inferior.'' Leeta finished, understanding. ''Warriors who've never met an enemy, never killed an armed foe, their courage and honor are held suspect by men they can burn on an instant's notice.''

Ree pinched his lips and lifted a shoulder. "I have ordered no less than five *officers* into detention for. . ." he hesitated, ". . . taking coup of their own."

Leeta laughed. "You've seen my own scalp, Colonel."

"And I never told you what I thought of it either."

"So, let your marines go." She paused. "Acculturation goes both ways, you know."

"I'll think about it," he said stiffly. "The Patrol is not made of a bunch of savages—"

"Do you need loyalty . . . or resentment among your people, Damen?"

He scowled, thinking.

She opened the door to her quarters and found the wine while Ree made himself comfortable in one of the chairs. Leeta turned and poured two glasses.

"To Atlantis," Ree toasted. "May she be brought into the Directorate with minimal trouble."

Leeta drank, watching Ree curiously. She caught a drip on the edge of the glass and seated herself on the bed, tucking her legs under her and leaning against the wall. "You know you have had a complete rundown on who I am. How about yourself? There are what, a dozen ships like *Bullet?* How does a man or women get to command such a ship?"

"There are eleven line class ships," he corrected with a smile and shrugged. "I was young. I wanted to go to space. I enlisted in the Patrol when I was admitted to university. You know, they have programs. If you make it academically, they keep you, if you don't, they set you free, your education partially paid for by—"

"It's not quite that simple, Damen. Remember I come from university. Maybe two percent make it through the first four years," she reminded.

His eyes twinkled. "So they sent me to the academy and I continued to impress them. I graduated number 63 out of 100." His lips curled with humor. "I suppose that made me work harder. I barely got a berth on *Bullet*.

"How did that make you feel?" Leeta asked. "I

269

mean, the first time you set foot on her decks, did you know she was yours forever?''

Ree had a dreamy look in his eyes. He twirled the glass in his fingers and studied the liquid. ''You know, I fell in love with her that day. I remember orientation, I suppose it was like the beginning of a marriage. I spent weeks learning her moods, her passions, her strengths and weaknesses. She became my life, my ambition, and my love. She still . . .'' He smacked his lips.

''Perhaps time has matured that?'' Leeta asked, seeing his euphoric look.

His laugh was easy. ''I suppose it's silly of me, but each morning, onboard, or even here on the planet, I call up comm to look at her. I've done that every morning since the day I stepped aboard. Does that make me odd, Doctor?'' He smiled at her.

''She's a dream, Damen. A dream should never be apologized for. You are one of the lucky ones—you've been dedicated enough to reach your dream.''

He looked sad as he met her eyes. ''I guess I gave up everything,'' he admitted. ''I never married. I never even saw my parents again before they died. I never had time for anything except my ship. Perhaps I sold my soul?''

''You made it. You got your dream. Do you feel like you sold your soul?'' Leeta sipped at the wine. Her headache was going away. She'd needed this time with Ree.

''My ship *is* my soul.'' He smiled guiltily. ''If anything ever happened to her, I'd have no more reason to live. I've invested my life in that tub of air up there. She's all I care about.''

''It must be difficult,'' Leeta mused. ''And the Director has the power to take her away?''

Ree swallowed, looking more nervous than Leeta had ever seen him. ''He does. And the Romanan situation hangs by a thread.''

''Which maybe we can weave into rope,'' Leeta added, gazing at the ceiling.

He studied her, his iron exterior softening. ''I have nightmares. I see myself down on the bridge. The blasters are making rubble of this damn planet. Then, the SD forms up a holo of Robinson and he tells me to turn *Bullet* over to Major Reary.

"My heart stops and I cry out in fear." He closed his eyes and leaned back. "I try to refuse and they pull their guns, forcing me from the bridge. I struggle and fight—but my arms don't move. My legs are paralyzed. I see my crew looking at me with disgust and they spit on me. Why? I've done so much for them!

"They pull me down to the lower pressure lock and throw me in. I scream at them, pounding my fists on the hatch. I'm mad as I engage the cycle controls, but they are deaf to pleas and threats alike. Then the outer hatch opens and I'm blown into the darkness, spiraling forever away from my *Bullet*. I scream and I scream because I hear the ship calling for me." He sat there, lost in his vision. After a long pause, he looked up. "Then I wake."

Leeta dropped her head. "All that time, all that dedication, and Skor Robinson could take away an entire life, just like that? Poof!" She blew over her palm.

Ree's quick nod was accompanied by a wry smile. "That's right. Just like that." He looked up, iron determination back in his expression. "That's why I can't lose here, Doctor. That's why I *won't* lose here!"

She refilled his glass again. "I'm in the same boat. I told you that when we made our deal. I can't lose either. I think I understand the stakes better now though. Does it make you resent the Director? I mean all that power? He's so far away, so impersonal!"

"I resent it, but what can I do, Doctor? I'm sworn to uphold the Directorate. That's a long-standing motto of the Patrol. It's a proud heritage to be a part of. Ever since the formation of the Confederacy—five hundred years ago—the Patrol has been the tool of civilization. Look at what we've built."

"We?" Leeta asked.

"We!" he asserted. "How far could the politicians have gone on their own? The blood and honor of the Patrol bought them time, Doctor. I'm part of that heritage. We've stood between the barbarians and civilization for centuries. We've paid with our sacrifices, our blood, our lives, and our ships—but we held it all together." His face shone. "Sure, I resent the Directorate, but it's kept us from warfare for four hundred years. Worlds or stations get mad. We show up and tempers cool. We're the final fail-safe.'' Ree nodded slowly.

"So long as you have your ships," Leeta reminded.

"That's right, Doctor."

"Damen, call me Leeta when we're alone." She refilled his glass.

"Leeta, such a smooth, lovely name." His eyes warmed "Perhaps you've reconsidered some of my earlier offers?''

Typical man! I give him an inch and he wants a mile. "No, Damen. It would do us more harm than good. I meant that. You know I'm right, too." She paused, frowning, knowing he was watching intently. "You know, we'd make horrible lovers."

"Are you sure?" His frank expression startled her until she realized it was the wine.

"Sure!" She sipped. "For one thing, I couldn't share you with your ship. For another, we're dominants. We'd end up trying to see who's stronger, smarter, tougher. That competition would make us bitter enemies in the end.

"For the next year or so, we need each other desperately. You need my expertise and I need your back up. We have to be an unbeatable team. This won't work without the two of us functioning like an oiled machine in zero g. It's delicate, Damen, so very, very delicate.''

"Things seem to be going very well so far." He sipped his wine and looked his question at her. "I thought we'd have it wrapped up within a month?"

She let herself laugh. "A month? Damen, we're changing a society. In a lot of ways, it's like changing an ecology. If you remove the predators, the herbivores go crazy and one thing affects another all through the system. Like the Romanans say, it's a Spiderweb. If you cut a strand, you may see no change in the strength of the web, but when Spider moves, the whole thing collapses. We're cutting a lot of strands at once. We have to be around to patch things when they fall apart."

"And if we do not have the time?" he asked, voice tense.

"You don't have dead warriors piling up to the rafters anymore," she told him. "The people aren't shooting at the marines. We're introducing space goods, building a dependency of trade. We've started schools on Directorate Policy. Surely, that is progress."

"There are other considerations. We can't have three warships tied up over this planet forever!" He waved in irritation.

"Three warships?" Leeta asked, taken aback.

"Three. Two more ships will arrive here within a month. Robinson is scared to death of Garcia's abilities. He's dispatched a supply ship to take Garcia to Arcturus for his personal examination. Damn pumpkin head!" Ree realized what he'd said and looked around, suddenly wary.

"Two more ships?" Leeta mused. "Line ships?"

"*Victory*, Colonel Maya ben Ahmad commanding—wicked old bat, she is—and *Brotherhood*, Colonel Sheila Rostostiev commanding. I never had any use for her either. I think she'd love to see me make a mess of this. She was my only competition for *Bullet*. Transferred after I was appointed Colonel." Damen allowed himself a sigh. "Nominally, they are under my command should the situation merit their intervention."

"I thought *Bullet* was more than capable of taking this planet apart!" Leeta worried. "Why two more ships?"

"Oh, rest assured, *Bullet* is more than enough protection for an entire sector of space. The other two ships are insurance. What if I sell out?" Ree asked. "What if something goes wrong? What if we've underestimated the Romanans? God knows how? But, what if?" He smiled. "You see, Robinson is scared."

Leeta poured more wine into Damen's glass and threw the empty away, pulling a new bottle from the cabinet. "It has to be the prescience," she decided. "He's afraid that will get let loose in the Directorate."

"Consider the consequences if it did." Ree studied the wine before he drank it. "Think! Everything would be turned upside down. Businesses would panic! Insurance? Who'd buy insurance? They'd hire a Romanan. It's mind-bending."

She shook her head. "The Prophets don't work that way. Didn't my report get through? I thought you said it had priority after you read it?"

"I sent it, Leeta." His look told her he had. "I think that Robinson won't believe anything that isn't worst case anymore."

"Playing safe," she agreed. "Just like the rest of society. Don't take a chance on anything. No risk, no danger, no responsibility! I think it damn well stinks!"

"Makes a fellow wish for the old days." He warmed to the topic. "We had heroes then. There was right to fight for and wrong to pursue. Men could believe in themselves." He looked up at the scalplock on Leeta's wall. "We could brag about our coups!" Ree's eyes glistened.

"To use Marty's words, ever think about blowing this joint?" she asked, watching speculatively. He'd had almost the entire first bottle.

"God!" He grinned. "Wouldn't that be something? Go out beyond Far Side just to see what's there!" His face fell. "That would stir up a lot of trouble. The Directorate is so perfectly balanced." He stopped, lost in what he was thinking.

"You mean stagnant," Leeta supplied.

"I couldn't do that," he decided. "*Bullet* is my responsibility. I took an oath to the Directorate. It's my heritage. I couldn't, Leeta. I just couldn't let the Patrol down like that. We're civilization! What happens if the Patrol pulls out? Who'd keep mankind safe?" He looked up, eyes pleading, as he said, "I couldn't ruin it for the rest. Too many count on me . . . on us . . . on *Bullet*."

She refilled his glass again. "Damen, I'm glad you're such a good officer. How in hell could I ever do all this without you? But let me pose a hypothetical question. What if you had to choose between *Bullet* and Skor Robinson?"

"Ship and honor?" he asked. "What is man without out honor? The Patrol has a proud tradition. *We are*

274

civilization!'' His head wobbled. ''I've had too much wine, Leeta.'' He blinked his eyes.

''I'll get coffee.'' She punched the dispenser, filling two cups. ''And the ship?''

''Oh, God,'' he whispered. ''I hope I never have to make that choice. I'd be damned one way or the other.''

She watched him get to his feet and make his way into the little toilet. ''So much at stake, my dear Colonel,'' she whispered. ''God knows, it may damn us all.'' And she wondered why she, too, felt so miserable.

Chester Armijo Garcia stopped and shook S. Montaldo's hand. ''It has been a pleasure talking to you, Doctor.'' He nodded. ''You are about to become a very important man. When events catch up to you, remember your humanity—and keep your faith in God. You are a cusp, Doctor. Spider will not let you down.''

Chester smiled and walked down the hatchway toward the supply ship. His ever-present marine guard escorted him with uneasy hands on blasters. Hell, they didn't need them, Montaldo growled to himself. Out loud, he said. ''What in hell does that mean? What's a cusp? Events? What events?'' He turned to leave. ''Damn you, Garcia!''

Montaldo was worried. He sat in the observation dome and watched as the supply ship nosed away from *Bullet's* hull. There were two escorts for the supply vessel. A bright streak of light marked acceleration as the supply ship turned toward far Arcturus.

Montaldo frowned. Chester had been such a gentle sort. What kind of a greeting would he face when he stepped off that ship and fell into Skor Robinson's clutches? Montaldo shivered slightly at the thought of the probes, monitors, tests, the poking and prodding that were all part of Chester Garcia's fate. He must have known.

''Brave little bastard,'' Montaldo muttered. ''Goodbye Chester. I'll miss you—even if I never could beat you at chess.'' Funny thing was, Garcia'd never seen a chessboard until he came to *Bullet* . . . and he'd beaten the computers. Montaldo pursed up his lips.

He wondered idly if Director Skor Robinson had ever played chess.

CHAPTER XVIII

John Smith Iron Eyes closed his eyes and took a deep breath. "Why?" he asked, trying to control his voice.

Sam Andojar Smith crossed his arms over his chest, eyes hard. "Honor," he said simply.

Iron Eyes chewed his lip, shooting a quick glance at the Old One who sat mummified in a grease-black blanket, his head bowed as if asleep. Iron Eyes reordered his mind.

"You know the People are on the war trail. We have a peace with the Santos until the star men are defeated. To have stolen Santos horses—"

"*You* have no authority, John Smith Iron Eyes!" Sam exploded, face darkening in anger. "*I* made no bargain with the Santos!" He spit the words, eyes shifting nervously to the Old One. In a lower voice, he mumbled, "There is no one man who determines what a warrior of the People can and cannot do."

Iron Eyes nodded, understanding the man's feelings. "That was before the star men came to destroy us. Today, we fight a different war than we fought against the Santos. We fight for everything. We fight for our whole world, for Spider, for all that we believe in. For the women—"

"We have always done that!" Sam protested. "I will not have you tell me I must return these horses that I took with so much skill and—"

"*We have not fought against sky weapons!*" Iron Eyes cried. He motioned toward the blue vault overhead. "Up there, Sam, they have a ship bigger than all the ATs put together! With their weapons, they can

276

kill the Settlements like we can kill a rock leech with a cannon!''

The old man's voice came soft and reedy from where he crouched in the dirty blanket. ''Sam Andojar Smith, you have reached a cusp. Here, now, you must make a decision and abide by it with all your honor as a warrior.''

Sam swallowed, gaze automatically dropping to the ground. Iron Eyes watched his bluster drain away like dust in the wind.

''Yes, Old One?''

Without moving, the old man asked, ''The choice is yours, Sam Andojar Smith. Do you choose to help the People—or maintain your concept of honor? Will you choose the ways of your fathers . . . or the ways of the future? Not all are mutually exclusive—but for now, what will you do?''

Sam shifted, shoulders slumped as he twisted his hands together, thinking hard. ''I . . . Old One, I look to you for guidance. Tell me. It shall be as you wish.''

The old man rocked slowly back and forth. ''I cannot see for you, my child. I look at you as I have known you all your life. I see the infant you were, naked, without manners, running and playing—and your joy. I see you with your first horse—and your pride. I see you when your father was killed raiding the Santos—and your pain. I see you shooting bravely at an AT—and your courage. I see you now, unsure, standing before me. I see two ways for you in the future. I do not choose. Spider guards free will. Which way do *you* chose to go, Sam?''

Andojar Smith shifted nervously on leather-clad feet, looking at Iron Eyes through lowered lids. ''I . . . I choose the People, Old One.''

The Prophet nodded his ancient head. ''Very well, Sam Andojar Smith. You have committed your honor. Obey Iron Eyes. Do as he says. He is the salvation of the People. Follow in his tracks. Spider watches your soul.''

Sam filled his lungs, face contorting in amazement. He started to lift a hand and stopped, letting his breath out. Iron Eyes watched the interplay of emotion. Distrust mingled with disbelief. Imperceptibly, the man shook his head.

"I seek no more than the way Spider has set before me," Iron Eyes added, friendship and understanding in his tone. "I have no love for this new way. I do only what I must."

Sam considered the words, his hostile eyes warming slightly. "Perhaps, John Smith Iron Eyes." He shrugged and sighed loudly. "I will take the horses back to the Santos. But then what? What does a warrior do? My women herd my cattle. Am I supposed to sit on my butt and watch the world turn? Where is the honor in that?"

Iron Eyes pointed to the east, to the ragged purple line of the Bear Mountains. "There. That way lies Navel Shelter. Go there. Red Many Coups and Philip will show you a way to serve the People. Honor is there, Sam. There lies the future."

Sam dropped his head again as he turned to the Prophet. "I go, Old One. Thank you." He turned and gave Iron Eyes a measuring look and left at a trot.

Iron Eyes settled down on a rolled bundle of salted hides. "Each day there are more and more who begin to chafe at this star peace. First they didn't believe we had peace. Now they think of ways to goad the Santos. Others have begun to think too long and hard on the wrongs of the past. Grandfather, how long can I hold my People back? Each time, I feel closer and closer to defeat. All my energy goes to keeping blood feud between us and the Santos stilled. Were it not for your good words . . ." He rubbed his hands nervously, eyes on the distant horizon.

"Spider has never made the path of the People easy, War Chief."

Iron Eyes stiffened. "War Chief, Old One?"

"You will be called that one day—if you can control your passions and are worthy. For now, think of what I said. There is a lesson in my words."

Iron Eyes looked out across the dusty plaza to where an AT rested, assault ramp down, Patrol marines standing idly at guard. Over 100 meters in length, its smooth lines were only broken by the matter-antimatter pods bulging at the back end. Heavy blasters nestled inside streamlined turrets. The reinforced nose ended in a needle point of alloyed graphite-steel—its purpose to puncture a star ship's side before disgorging the assault team within the other ship's guts.

"An easy path leads to weakness," Iron Eyes nodded. "A hard path to strength."

"How strong are you, Iron Eyes?" the Prophet asked, shifting, his rheumy eyes filled with curiosity. The old face looked like carved, weathered wood, wrinkled, bent, eternal. Gray hair in long braids shimmered silver in the sunlight.

John Smith Iron Eyes stared out at the lean shape of the AT. The blazing white was stark against the dusty hues of plaza and Romanan huts. It glared, a symbol of Directorate power in their very midst. A reminder of the threat hanging over them—just out of view beyond the blue sky.

"I don't know, Old One."

"Many things must change, Iron Eyes." A withered hand moved out from the blanket in an encompassing gesture. "Everything we know, believe, and think right will be challenged—if we live."

"And you cannot see our path?" Iron Eyes tried to keep the hope from his voice.

A dry chuckle caught him off guard. "No, Iron Eyes. I will not look that far forward. Too many cusps remain. When I look to the future, I see so many fates—each way decided by one person's free will."

A long silence followed while Iron Eyes let his mind prowl the trail the Old One's words showed him.

"But if we live, my son," the old voice cackled, "our People will be different. Our lives, our rules, our understanding of who we are will be changed, molded into something new, like wet rawhide over a saddle tree. We will never be what we are . . . or what we were. That is the way of Spider . . . to change . . . to learn."

"Is that good or bad, Grandfather?" Iron Eyes watched a dust devil that skipped across the plaza. Twisting, bending, whipping this way and that, it reminded Iron Eyes of his own tortured soul.

"That is up to the People—and Spider. Good is Spider and bad is Spider. Only the way we think makes good from bad.'' The Old One rattled a sigh into ancient lungs and dropped his gray head. "Now I will sleep, my son."

Iron Eyes smiled at the old man and got to his feet. Smoke rose in irregular shafts from smoke holes in the rounded hide roofs of houses. Women scraped hides, chopped plants to stew size, and chattered at the children running back and forth in their winter clothes. Horses stood hitched in ramshackle corrals and a circle of old men enjoyed the afternoon sun while they lied about coups taken, women captured, and spirited horses.

He let the life of the Settlement seep into his very bones, feeling his People move about him. A child cried as a sharp-voiced mother scolded. A clang came from the gunsmith's as he hammered yet another piece of the Ship into a fine rifle. Cattle lowed softly in the distance and laughter erupted from behind a closed door hanging.

"And what will the future bring?" Iron Eyes wondered as he nodded to a young woman. She smiled at him, dark eyes flashing, a load of firewood hacked from pole trees under an arm. Perhaps her hips swayed a little more as she passed. Perhaps there was an allure of invitation and hidden promise in her movements. Or perhaps it was simply his love of the People affecting his perceptions.

Iron Eyes pursed his lips. Something had changed. An alien wariness had woven itself into the fabric of his Settlement and People. Each of them waited—uneasy at the AT in their plaza—aware of the Prophets and the uncertain future beyond this day's sunset. True to the Old One's words, their lives had all changed. Each man, woman, and child went about usual chores, acting out the familiar in a rudely changed World. Here and there, mourning markers were up. The ominous platform alongside the square held one or two corpses, attended to by weeping relatives. Everyone knew at least a couple of warriors held captive—hostage—at the base camp.

Below the laughter and sameness, the People simmered, waiting—ready to lash into a fiery boil.

And Leeta put me in charge to see they don't. He

sniffed the air, happy at the old odors of manure, trash, tanning agents, smoke, and animals. The wind even carried a tinge of acridness from the gunpowder factory.

"Hey!" a voice called in Standard.

Iron Eyes turned. The marine was young, black-skinned with thick, inky black hair. "Yes?" he answered in Standard. Never would he get used to women warriors. There was an inherent wrongness to it.

The marine bit her lip, dropping her eyes. "Great! You speak Standard. Um, listen. You got a lot of them coups on your belt. Oh . . . well . . . what would it be worth to you? I mean, you know, like could I trade for one? Buy it?"

Iron Eyes barely got himself under control. Had he really come so close to lashing out at the marine? He took a deep, calming breath. "Woman, could I do you a favor?"

The marine nodded eagerly, her eyes lighting. "Yeah, sell me one of them coups!"

Iron Eyes shook his head; it wasn't the marine's fault. She didn't know. "Listen. My favor to you is this. Never, ever ask a Romanan to sell his coup." Iron Eyes forced himself to smile as he pointed to a young warrior riding a bay across the plaza. "If you'd asked him, for example, he'd have cut your throat for the insult."

The marine's eyes widened. "Uh, I didn't know. But, well, those things are worth three months' pay."

Iron Eyes fingered his chin. "To us they are worth a man's life." He paused. "But what makes them important to the Patrol?"

The marine's eyes lit. "Blast fire, man, it means you're a blooded warrior! You know, not just a—"

"I think I understand," Iron Eyes nodded, lacing his fingers behind his back, scuffing the dirt with his toe. *They think they can buy honor? What sort of people are these?* "Consider, Private. Would you sell your soul? Would you sell your body? How about your self-integrity? Your honor?"

"Uh . . . no. I mean, of course not! A person can't sell that, it—"

"Nor will a Romanan sell a coup—for just that same

281

reason. Do you see?'' Iron Eyes met the confused young woman's eyes.

The marine wet her lips and frowned. ''Uh, yeah, I think I do.'' She looked back at the AT. ''Uh, listen, we never realized you folks looked at it like that.''

Iron Eyes gave her a hard smile. ''We do.''

The marine looked at the ground, frown deepening. ''Well, uh, look, what would you sell your rifle for?''

Iron Eyes laughed. He pointed with a muscular arm. ''See that low building? The one with the smoke curling around the end. They make rifles.''

A sudden idea hit him. He studied the marine thoughtfully. ''But you'd better hurry.''

''How's that?'' The light in the marine's eyes intrigued him. She was a handsome woman, athletic, attractive.

Iron Eyes shrugged. ''Well, first off, you've got to be fast. The idea won't be yours alone for long so others will rush to place orders. You've got to barter with rations, equipment, holos, something the gunsmith can in turn trade to other Romanans. We don't take credits. They're meaningless. But that's not the hurry.''

The private was nodding, obviously a natural at bartering. ''So what's the rush?''

Iron Eyes made a futile motion with his hands. ''Well, you know the Directorate thinks we're a risk. The possibility exists that Skor Robinson could order *Bullet* to destroy the planet at any time. Your rifle might never be made. There will be no more Romanans, no more coup—nothing.''

The private's mouth fell open. ''Yeah, wow, that could happen, huh?'' Her eyes narrowed, bothered at the implications.

''And how do you and the rest of the marines feel about that? Without us, you're back to boring patrols among the stars, correct?'' Iron Eyes said sympathetically.

The young woman nodded. ''Guess so.'' She didn't sound really happy about it. ''You mean we'd just ride around and waste all you people?''

Iron Eyes shook his head. ''Not from what the Colonel tells me. He'll recall you and do it from space. He says the ship can destroy the whole planet from up there without as much wasted time."

"Yeah, *Bullet* can turn this whole planet into cinder." The marine was shaking her head. "No rifles or coup that way, is there?"

"No," Iron Eyes told her flatly. "These people," he pointed to the old men sitting in the sun, the woman scraping the hide and the romping children, "would die in your purple blaster lights." Iron Eyes cocked his head. "Does the Directorate fear our rifles so?"

The private started to laugh at that and then caught herself. "Uh, you know, I don't. . . . Hell, it wouldn't exactly be right, would it?" Her dark eyes searched Iron Eyes'.

Solemnly, Iron Eyes suggested, "That would be up to your honor as a warrior, wouldn't it? Is there coup in burning down women and little children?"

"No," she answered firmly.

Iron Eyes nodded. "Then I suggest you take your fellow warriors—you'll need a translating device—and go out among the People. Sit down and listen to them. Talk to them about honor and learn who they are before Skor Robinson orders them burned. You may be the only humans anywhere to ever know the Romanans. You will be our only legacy to the future of humanity. Listen to the stories about—"

"Uh, wait a minute," the private's face had lit with animation. "I mean, you don't think they'd just let us into their houses to sit around and talk?"

Iron Eyes nodded, a warm smile on his lips. "Of course they would. They will welcome you with open arms. Treat them with respect and a warrior's honor. Remember, we're humans, people who love and live and feel just like you do. Tell them you want to know them. But most of all, tell them Spider sent you."

"Damn it, yes! I approved the transfer." Ree pinched his lips and glared at Antonia Reary through slitted eyes. "Doctor Dobra wanted computers and supplies for the natives—I okayed it!"

"Equipment to the Romanans, Damen? Aid and comfort to the enemy? You've gone too far this time!"

She slapped the white dura-top table. Her brown eyes smoldered. "I've sent a report to Skor Robinson."

Damen Ree smiled wickedly. "I know you did, Major."

Her long face tightened, lines of anger forming around the too thin mouth. "Then, Damen, I suspect your days in command of *Bullet* are numbered. In my wildest dreams, I fail to see how providing supplies to an interdicted people whom the Director considers a threat to security will advance your position."

Damen shrugged and said, "I suppose you're right, Antonia. At the same time, I have already received the Director's personal approval of the distribution of materials to the Romanans. In fact, he—"

"You what?" She jerked to her feet, face reddening with anger.

Ree made a calming motion. "Sit down, Antonia. Come, sit. There, that's better." Ree reached for his coffee, giving her time to get control of herself. When her eyes narrowed, Damen smiled. "Of course he approved it. The Directorate wants to understand Romanan capabilities. We've an entire battery of experiments set up to see how quickly they learn, how fast they can pick up comm ability and—"

"All right, Colonel. What have you done?" Reary's voice shook with barely suppressed anger. "You've no right to censor my reports!"

"I didn't."

"But you've your spies to report what I send!" she hissed venomously.

"Antonia, you're quite good." Ree maintained his professional attitude. "At the same time, you still have a bit to learn about politics and command—which makes you unprepared to take over my position."

"Don't mince words, Damen," she added, voice acid.

His smile proved ephemeral. "I'm not, Antonia. I mean it all. You're not ready for command. You haven't learned a basic fact that's critical to holding this position."

She sniffed and raised her chin. "And that is?"

"Loyalty, Antonia." He turned the coffee bulb on the table, studying it absently. "You see, we've made a mess of the Patrol over the last couple hundred years. We're no longer a team. You know, us against them. We've turned the chain of command into us against us. And the results—"

"I don't want your moralizing, Damen!" Muscles rippled along her arms. "Reality exists, Colonel. You've been tainted by those blood-drenched savages down there! What place does any foggy idealism have for us? Power is the sum and total of Patrol rank. Come on, Damen. Live in the present!"

Ree laughed bitterly. "Tainted? By Romanans? Seriously, Major!" He shook his head. "No, I am living in the present. I'm thinking about the way you set your own people to burning Romanans down there. Poorly executed. You jumped too fast. Not only that, but it played into my hands when it came to pacifying the—"

"You still can't win in—"

"And you tipped your hand," he continued. "You see, I instituted countermeasures. That's how I caught your report before it got to Robinson's attention. From there, I've taken measures to circumvent your politics and undercut the loyalty of your people. Not that I didn't have better things to do, something's—"

"You . . . bastard!" She glared at him. "You haven't won yet!"

He lifted his fingers from the tabletop. "No, I haven't." His head cocked. "But my eyes are open now. Do you realize how vulnerable we are? I'd never thought about the consequences to the Patrol until now. Consider it, Antonia. If you aren't frightened, you're less capable than I thought you were."

She stared at him blankly. "Make your point, Damen."

His lips twitched. "Here we are, for the first time, faced by a people outside our control. Potential enemies. On that we're agreed. How does it strike you that at this first challenge in hundreds of years, we take this opportunity to divide ourselves? You, a major of the Patrol, pick this moment to weaken me. What does that say about our system? About our ability to defend—"

"Against half naked savages?" She chortled. "Oh, Damen, you *are* preposterous!"

He looked at her, seeing her mind working, not on what he said, but on what could be held against him.

What have we become? Are we all like Antonia? A sourness grew in his stomach. A memory of Iron Eyes, the Romanan, calm, self-possessed, always proud of who and what he was, crossed Ree's mind. At that moment, Iron Eyes was down there using his honor and reputation as a warrior to keep the Romanans from trying to tackle ATs with their bare fists—poor sap. While Antonia attempted to cut her own people's throats—and the hell with the consequences.

"Dismissed, Antonia. Leave me." He motioned with his hand, watching her get to her feet and walk stiffly out. The sourness had filled him, bringing a bitter taste to his mouth.

We are a nest of vipers striking at each other. Where once the Patrol was proud, capable, dedicated, we are rotten within—sucking our own blood. This cannot continue!

Floating in the eternal blue haze of the Gi-net console command, Director Skor Robinson turned his united mind to the Romanan question once again. The latest report from Damen Ree occupied him.

The Romanans appeared to be adapting well to Patrol control. He studied the acculturation program report compiled by Leeta Dobra, noting the substandard computer ability. All adult men? No wonder, true computer compatibility came from growing the brain and the comm unit together.

You have the latest Romanan data? Navtov queried.

I was just studying it. Is there any way we can bring these people into the fold? Perhaps eliminate this pre-science trait of theirs? Subvert their religion and their patterns of warfare?

Navtov's answer was precise. *I believe we should sterilize the planet immediately. There is too much dissent within the Directorate as it is. Disaffection, vandalism, and social crime are up by two statistical points. The situation on Sirius has reached a new high of twenty-two point six percent disenchantment with*

Directorate policies. The Independence Party has been substantially strengthened by an anonymous donation. We are still attempting to trace the donor for appropriate "adjustment." Director Robinson, this is not the time to embrace any risk. We all recommend sterilization for the planet Atlantis.

Skor Robinson cleared his mind of distractions. He could see prudence in what Navtov suggested. Robinson began composing a draft order to destroy the Romanans and sent a copy to Navtov.

I concur, came back along with the draft.

Robinson made several minor changes in text and hesitated before committing the missive to the Gi-net for execution by the Patrol. The hesitation, he realized, came from a sensation long unfamiliar to him: curiosity.

What did they really know about the Romanans? From the reports, Dobra was making progress at acculturation. The information acquired was fascinating for its implications for future social manipulation on other worlds. If the tools she was developing were so valuable for social control, was it right to stop the project before completion? Of course, the Romanans would have to die eventually—but had they sucked all the information possible out of them? To waste them before they had been drained of all usefulness was inefficient.

True, they were dangerous. Robinson considered the sterilization warrant again. All information regarding the existence of the Romanans channeled through him—and there it stopped. Only if it should become common knowledge would any danger arise.

A cold shiver passed up his spine. Darkness forbid that common citizens learn of these charismatic people, a people whose struggle might catch their imaginations and lead them from their carefully controlled paths! Imagination and dreams were the stuff of chaos.

And from the reports, the Patrol was in no position to interfere. Ree's people were at each other's throats over the succession of command. What a stroke of brilliance his predecessors had shown in defanging the Patrol that way! Neutralized by internal divisiveness, they posed no threat to Directorate policy.

Skor reread the sterilization order one last time. And what of this Prophet—this Chester Armijo Garcia? A final wild card? To what uses could a Director put such a man? No, before destroying the Romanans, prudence dictated at least an investigation of this alleged prescience. If true. . . . No, *impossible!*

Skor, his decision made, filed his order in the Ginet and turned to the problem of oversurplus in Ambrose Sector. Everything was still totally predictable. The Romanans posed no threat he could not control.

"That is a holo of one of my people," Ree told Leeta, rubbing his face and eyes wearily. He definitely looked like a good night's sleep was in order.

She took the cube and studied it. "Looks like a marine."

"Very good, Doctor. Your powers of observation astound me," Ree told her dryly. "Take a close look at his chest."

Leeta looked. The spider effigy was small, but it was there. "Is there a problem with that, Colonel?"

Ree's mouth was tight. Leeta noted the hollow look in his eyes. "Fraternization, violations of the uniform code, and possibly black marketeering."

"Damen, you don't look well." She handed him a cup of coffee and indicated a seat. As an afterthought, Leeta closed the door to her office cubicle. "Can I help?"

"What makes you say I'm not looking well?" he asked nervously. "Just because I'm sitting on the biggest political supernova in the galaxy, shouldn't I be concerned?"

"And Reary's burning more than her share of hydrogen?" Leeta supplied, cradling her chin on her palms.

"If I am relieved of command, Doctor, you're finished here, you know." Ree blinked, reaching for the coffee cup. "Just between us, you're up to something, aren't you? I keep seeing the lines between my Patrol personnel and the Romanans slowly blurring."

"That's acculturation," Leeta reminded. "If the lines blur so slowly and completely that no one knows the difference, we will have been totally successful."

Ree sipped the coffee, grimaced, and took a big swig. "Only I have a question, Doctor. Who's acculturating who?"

Leeta lifted her hands. "Well, traditionally, primitive societies are always absorbed by more technologically advanced ones. Oh, there have been a couple of aberrant examples of fundamentalist movements gaining control for a moment, but those are what we call nativistic or revitalization movements under negative acculturation. In our—"

Ree pointed a blunt finger. "You're hedging. Like a politician, you're talking around my question. My crew is divided, Doctor. Reary controls a faction—but I've got that bottled because that's my area of expertise. Another bunch is starting to like Romanans, wanting to take leave to go bear hunting and horse riding and to see Prophets. That sort of thing. You've got Romanans learning to use computers, talking Standard, studying technology. Now I've got Patrol people with spiders on their armor visiting Romanan villages, buying things locally with contraband Patrol supplies."

"And you've got a more basic problem than that, Damen." Leeta growled.

He snapped back, "I await your expertise on Patrol matters, Doctor!"

She slapped the table. *"Damn it, Damen!* Who the hell do you expect them to side with? Skor Robinson? Those plastic people like Jeffray or Emmanual Chem? They've met warriors! Real warriors! People who've actually lived what each of your people has trained for for years! They see their own kind of—"

"And discipline among my people is being compromised!" he roared. His eyes flared with anger as he locked stares with her. "And I've got another Patrol ship of the line on the way in. *Brotherhood* is four days from dropping inside. Rostostiev will get one look at the situation and have my head on a platter. Reary will be in command within a week." He sagged into the chair, turning the coffee cup nervously in his hands.

Leeta tensed. Four days? Blasted luck! "So we give

her a model planet to see. How long—by our reckoning of time—until Chester arrives at Arcturus?"

Ree thought. "Call it eight days." His hot eyes pinned her. "What are you up to, Doctor? I'm feeling pushed. I don't like being against the wall. All my life, I've controlled events. Now I get the feeling they're controlling me. If you're about to pull the rug out from under me . . . you tell me, because, Doctor, *I'm the only friend you've got!*"

Leeta forced herself to give him a reassuring grin, her mind racing. "Damen, you just be ready. I promise, we'll have this planet looking perfectly unified when *Brotherhood* shows up in orbit." She dropped her eyes. "Only one question."

"Yes?" He tossed off the rest of the coffee.

"How loyal are your men to you? You might think about the ones capable of betraying you—seek to neutralize them somehow." She waited, wondering if he'd explode.

Instead, his face went ashen. "How did it all go so bad? What if I'd just burned the planet at the start?"

Leeta shook her head. "You'd have hated yourself for the rest of your life. You're really an honorable man, Colonel. Atlantis, or World—as the Romanans call it—is simply a no-win situation under Directorate policies. We've—"

"Directorate policies?" Ree blinked, amazed. "What the hell sort of alternative do you see floating around out there? Remember, we live under Directorate policies! That's our system of civilization!"

"We've at least held our own given those policies and the reality of World. The future is in other hands than ours."

Ree shot her a ghastly grin. "I think a cusp—as Chester would have called it—is coming up, Doctor. Yes, I see through your interest in my crew's loyalty. Perhaps I will have to make them choose between Reary and me."

"And in the meantime," Leeta added, "I'll buy you as much time as I can down here. I can't control Directorate politics—but I can sure as hell pull strings to make Atlantis look textbook good."

He nodded. "I . . . I wish Sarsa hadn't been

drowned in that flood." He paused as he got to his feet, eyes narrowing. "No chance she's still around here somewhere? Part of your 'acculturation?' "

Leeta shook her head blankly. "Not a chance, Colonel."

He reached for the door handle and stopped. "Should she appear, Doctor, and should I be in serious trouble, tell her the security codes have been changed to Regga Green. She'll know what that means."

"Damen!" Leeta called, suddenly unsure. "Why are you telling me this?"

He smiled at her, his haggard features drawn. "Because, Doctor, I don't think you're against me. And, to be honest, I don't know what's right anymore." He lowered his gaze and rubbed the back of his neck. "And for the first time, I've been feeling my own mortality. If they take me, who knows, maybe you can do something to save a little piece of this."

CHAPTER XIX

Leeta walked out of the AT with John Smith Iron Eyes beside her. She could still see the furious look on Captain Arf Helstead's face. He'd made it obvious he had no use for the presence of a barbarian Romanan on his bridge.

"John?" Leeta asked. "Would you mind walking over this way. We must talk." She led him out of sight of the AT.

"This is the first time we've been alone since Gessali Camp."

"I need to talk to you of other things," she said softly.

"Very well." His mood changed as he read the distress in her eyes.

Leeta gripped his warm hand as they walked. "You know we've been trying to make an alliance between the Spiders and the Santos."

"With miserable results," he sighed, nodding, his pace matching hers. "So much blood, so many differences between Haysoos and Spider. So much war and raiding cannot be undone so quickly. Do not expect miracles. Romanans hate each other more than they hate star men. We will cut our own throats if Ree doesn't."

"Maybe not." Leeta stopped and swung around to hold him close and look up into his eyes. "Rita and Philip have established a line of communication with the Santos. Rita has been training Santos warriors alongside the Spiders for almost a month now."

"What? *Excellent!*" John hooted, lifting her off her feet. "Why haven't you told me before?"

"Granted, it's a tenuous alliance. Rita constantly has problems, but things . . ." She stopped, shaking her head, grimly studying his expression. "John, it's not that simple. I have to tell you. It was necessary. Damn it, there is something I . . ." She closed her eyes.

His hands were warm on her shoulders, reassuring. "You don't trust the Santos? Is that it? I don't blame you, but it's progress. We can't win without—"

"John," she held him closer, swallowing hard. "Philip and Rita . . . they had to make the alliance through the Santos warrior you've sworn to kill. You've given a blood oath . . . now it will have to wait. If you kill Big Man next time you see him, the whole alliance will blow up in our faces. Open warfare between the Spiders and Santos will result. Do you understand? I'm scared stiff!"

His eyes had grown cold. The muscles at the edges of his mouth twitched and jerked. She watched his soul turn to ice.

"John, there wasn't any other way!" she pleaded. "You think this was easy for Rita—or me—or Philip? Dealing with that bastard disgusts me! We had to do it! We just had to!" *And I will tell him of Big Man's other conditions later.*

Iron Eyes crooked his neck back and drew his lungs

full of air, body rigid, fists clenched, his face contorted. Leeta clung to him, feeling rippling muscles dance with anger under his skin.

Unable to think, his breath caught in his throat, ragged, suffocating. He blinked back tears of frustrated anger.

"Why?" his suddenly strained voice asked of the cloudy sky. *"Spider, you mock me!* You fling my counsel to others into my own face! Why can I never bring that pus-licking vileness to justice? Now I must call him friend? *NEVER!"* He thundered the last.

"If you don't, you will destroy the peace." Leeta's voice came from somewhere outside his anguish. Why did Spider play with him so? What of his honor—his debt? Jenny's ghost wailed piteously in his subconscious.

Defeated and empty, he looked down at her, marveling at the color of her eyes, so unlike those of the People. This star woman had saved his life. *And I owe her as much as I owe Jenny—more.* She had fought for him against an armed Santos. Now she fought for the People.

And now, I must choose again. For Leeta. For the People. For my own words told so fervently to others.

Against that, the bitter memory of Jenny's soft face rose in his thoughts. Could she have done so much for him? Could she have allowed herself to wash his wounds, care for his body, haul him from the canyon, fight a bear? The answer echoed a hollow *no* inside his mind.

Jenny would have frozen at the thought of being alone with a taboo male. She would rather have let him die than touch his profane body. She would have cowered behind him on the travois, expecting him to kill the bear as part of his male duty.

My People, what have we done to ourselves?

A growing mist of sorrow twisted with the outrage, blending into confused incomprehension. Nothing a man expected to be real existed anymore. A universe of familiar shapes softened and melted.

"For you, I can do this thing," Iron Eyes told her miserably. "For you, I can do anything." He gave her a smile of triumph in spite of the maze his emotions had become.

Her eyes twinkled in return. "I knew you would," she whispered. "I fear for you, Iron Eyes. You are so strong, I wonder that you can take so much without becoming brittle and snapping."

"I would be your strength. I never want to lose you." The words came suddenly, without warning, and his heart chilled. Oh, Jenny, have I betrayed you? he wondered.

Then Leeta was pulling his head down. Something inside him cried out with pleasure and his heart began to beat so loudly he feared she would hear it. They were out of sight of the AT that lay over the ridge. Still, he drew back, wanting her so badly, afraid of his reactions should he allow himself to touch her again.

Pinkish red tinged her skin, her breathing quickened. Excitement filled her eyes. "We wasted too much time on the trail, Iron Eyes," she said wistfully. "I didn't know I would come to love you so."

He'd resumed walking toward Navel Camp. "Why me, star woman? Colonel Ree is very enchanted with you. You could have your pick of the star men. Why a primitive warrior with the blood of so many on his hands? I am ignorant, knowing only of war, horses, and rifles. I cannot even read!" His eyes searched hers.

Her lips pursed. "Because you're strong, Iron Eyes. I've known too many men who didn't believe in themselves, in life, in honor, or in the future. You're unique in ways that thrill me. You've never been anywhere but here, yet you know the meaning of life." She cocked her head, peering sideways at him. "So you can't read. Learn."

He read the challenge in her expression. He'd already learned Standard. The sleep tapes made learning so easy. Could reading be so difficult? "I will learn to read," he told her, nodding affirmation.

She frowned. "My turn to teach, huh?"

He allowed his arm to sneak around her shoulders. "The Directorate can provide my People with many things. Your knowledge outstrips us."

"You'll see," she warned. "The Directorate is stagnant. Rot trickles down to touch every life—every thought or ambition. You've taught me life is uncertain at best and humans must try harder—come to know who and what they are. I know men who are maggots, soft, mushy, wallowing in the putrid flesh of a dead society. I was like that once.'' She smiled wistfully, fingering the scalp she'd fastened at her belt to Helstead's chagrin and his marines' envy.

"So you challenge your own People, star woman. Why?'' He'd wondered that enough these last few weeks. "If we are let loose, who will stop us?''

"For their own good!'' her voice rang out. "There are things here on Atlantis my People need. We've lost our way, our God, our purpose. Perhaps Spider will give it back!'' She looked at him, fire in her eyes.

"Yet they might destroy us before we get away,'' he reminded solemnly.

"They might,'' Leeta agreed. "We'll know better after our meeting. You've done an excellent job fooling Ree. As 'Director' of the Spiders, you've kept the lid on things. Ree thinks I'm the most precious thing to come along since free-fall coffee. We've bought time, soothed worried minds, and let the marines go to sleep. But now we're out of time.''

A guard hailed them and then jumped down the cliff. Iron Eyes didn't know him. He wore the colors of a Santos. The man saw Leeta's hair and promptly saluted. To John's surprise, he greeted them in Standard and waved them past.

"Standard?'' John asked, puzzled.

"Of course.'' Leeta's triumphant smile threw him. "One the first things we smuggled in here were tapes. We've been teaching all kinds of things. They'll need Standard badly. Most of them can read now. You've been too busy running Romanan society—instituting programs, keeping people calm, making sure no waves rock the boat. We needed your influence more there.'' She squeezed his hand. "You'll have time to catch up.''

They walked into a constant buzz of activity as they entered the shelter. Men were everywhere and Iron Eyes couldn't believe the transformation between the Navel of old and this new concentration of men and machines. He remarked to Leeta about it.

"This is nothing. The best is underground—back in the Navel. I let the marines inspect this area anytime they want."

John was surprised when they passed black curtains masking the electric lights illuminating the vast cavern. Here existed a whole different world. "Where did you get the computers?" he marveled.

"Talked Ree out of them," she said easily. "Told the old boy we'd have to see if Romanans could be trained to use them. After all, they'd need that if they were to be integrated into the Directorate. I must admit, the results are not as pleasing as I would like. But we make up some of the difference by organized competition between Santos and Spiders. So far, the Spiders are ahead, but the Santos are catching up."

Iron Eyes let himself look over the place. "What are they doing?" He indicated a group of bounding, kicking, striking, rolling figures.

"Hand to hand combat, John. They're learning the tricks of scientific fighting. Again, the marines are better at that sort of thing. This is just a quick survival course. Nevertheless, it might give us the edge."

Philip was making his way through a ramshackle collection of computers. He whooped and threw himself on Iron Eyes. "Cousin!" he shouted. "It has been how long? Months since I saw you last. Look at this! *We will fly to the stars!*"

Leeta took a turn hugging Philip, then whispered in his ear. Philip nodded soberly and left at a trot. "Come." Leeta took his hand and he could see that her triumph had again turned to worry.

She led him to a little room hacked out of the side of the cavern. A rough pole table and some benches proved the only furnishings. Leeta motioned him down beside her. "Well, what do you think?"

"I had no idea. The Prophets have just been nodding their heads at anything I suggest—remarkable in itself. All this is beyond me." His thoughts were jumbled, confused, as he tried to sort it all out.

A sweating Rita led Philip in, her belt of coups slung over her shoulder. Obviously, Iron Eyes decided, she was the instructor for hand to hand combat. Seconds later, a youth entered with a pot of coffee and thin slices of meat to be put on bread.

Rita flashed John a smile and gulped some of the coffee. Leeta took a deep breath and dove in, "How's it going?"

"Good," Rita said around a mouthful of food. She was ragged around the edges, tired from missed sleep. "We've got some of the lads to the point where I think they could pilot an AT if they needed to. Reading and writing are ahead of schedule. As to military tactics and strategy, they exceeded any of our expectations— they understand space war. They're very quick at hand to hand. Blaster training is about fifty-fifty—can't seem to learn there's no drop or windage.

"That's the good news." Rita swallowed and washed it down with a slurp of coffee. "The bad news is our free-fall training is miserable to say the least. All we've got is a water pool back in the cave and two suits to try and squeeze or shove everybody into. If anything happens to grav up there, we're in trouble."

"Discipline?" Leeta raised an eyebrow.

"About three fights a day," Rita mumbled. "Five murders from old blood feuds. We executed the violators of war honor in public like the code calls for. Things have settled down—but the hatred is still there. Tempers are on a slow boil."

Leeta sighed, patting Iron Eyes knee as he fought to keep the revulsion from his face.

"At the same time," Rita added before taking another bite, "we're slowly weaning the Santos to our side. We're perceived as pro-Spider—maybe true. But we get computers and offer the chance at coup. Makes a heap of difference. Big . . ." Her eyes went to Iron Eyes. "Uh, the Santos headman—"

"I told him," Leeta added softly.

Rita bobbed her head, chewing rapidly. "Big Man has been losing influence. He's been hanging out in his village mostly. All his women are there and we've been feeding him all the whiskey he can drink. His influence ebbs with each bottle. The other Santos aren't stupid. They take our orders, get treated right— and they learn about blasters and better ways to make war."

"We control access to goods. Must be making their Prophet nuts," Leeta was thoughtful.

Rita was saying, "Similarly, the computer training is worse than marginal for the older warriors—and mediocre for the young men. I think with more time—like three years—I could make them proficient. As a result, I've made splits on the basis of proficiency. Where I find aptitude, I let them specialize. In short, perhaps another six months and I'll start to feel we've half a chance." Rita's green eyes were thoughtful.

"We don't have another six months." Leeta calmly steepled her fingers. "Chester will be halfway to Skor Robinson by now; on the other hand, Rostostiev and *Brotherhood* will be here in three days." Leeta let the words sink in. "You know what that means?"

"I don't know how much that cuts the odds." Rita shrugged. "Might put us back to nothing."

Leeta nodded. "We've got to move now. Tomorrow. Can you do it?"

Rita's green eyes flickered uncertainly. "Do we have a choice?" John saw the lines around her mouth draw tight.

"How do we take *Bullet?* You've had a month to think about it. What do we do?"

Rita raised her eyes. "You find out anything about Ree? Where's his weak spot?"

"The ship." Leeta suffered a twinge of guilt as she said it.

Rita noticed immediately. "What is it, Doc?" she demanded.

Leeta shrugged nervously. "Seems like I'm taking advantage of his one human streak." She sighed. "To put it in perspective, it's like holding a man's family ransom."

"If we have to play that trump, Doc. . . ." Sarsa's words were cold. Iron Eyes felt his gut tighten as he listened to the two women plotting the destiny of World—of his People.

Leeta nodded. "War is hell, huh? About *Bullet*, any ideas?" She looked hopefully at Sarsa.

"I guess we have to storm the AT. Hope we can take it before they blow the whistle. Hope the number of casualties we take leaves us with enough to storm the lock, that is, if they don't blow us out of space for unauthorized ascent. Then we make a last-ditch attempt for the reactor.''

Leeta was smiling sourly. "I think I can improve on that.''

Rita's eyebrows rose. "I'm all ears, Doc.''

"You're all military, too, Lieutenant.'' Leeta laughed at the scowl she got from Sarsa. "How about I bring Ree here tomorrow?'' There was a look of shock. "Let's say I . . . want to show him riot control maneuvers. You know, the stuff we've been practicing with the AT. Ree's already been fed the information and the tapes by Helstead, of course, but I've developed the habit of following up Helstead's reports with Ree's personal involvement.''

Leeta frowned into the silence, thought etching her face.

She began to nod slowly. "And let's say that while the troops are loading, Ree falls over. Possible stroke.'' Leeta's eyes glowed. "And we . . . No. We . . . Uh, what happens if . . . if the med unit is out of whack? With the Colonel's life at stake, what's the best course of action?''

"Take him to the ship!'' Rita's wolfish expression showed her admiration. "Only one problem, Doc. Med units on ATs don't just quit.''

"Of course they do!'' Leeta looked surprised. "Especially when a man with Marty Bruk's understanding of bio-med equipment has just been in to . . . to evaluate the facilities!''

"Doc, I like you a whole lot better now than I did when I first met you!'' Rita whooped. Satisfaction appeared contagious, Philip's lips began to curl happily.

"What do you need me to do?'' John asked suddenly. It had bothered him deep inside that, so far, all he'd done was keep the Spiders in line.

Leeta shot him a warm smile of promise and hope. "You, John, are the new Director of World. It is only after we've done our part that you come into play. Neither Rita nor I can act as spokesman for Atlantis. You can. You've been Director of the Spiders—you will now be Director for the whole planet. You have what it will

299

take, John. The People will listen to you. They respect you. You're a hero."

"Why not Philip?" he asked. "He knows more than I do."

"I have not taken so many coups, cousin." Philip's eyes were soft. "I am not a hero—nor do I wish to be."

"I'll do what I can . . . for my People." John agreed, uncomfortable. What possible good could he do? He'd been out of so much of this. The plans were just words to him.

As though Leeta could read his expression, she elaborated. "John, the People know you. For all these months, you've been their leader. It's you they're used to listening to. You've become the symbol of hope for the Spiders. Big Man has been the hope of the Santos. We need the two of you. You represent a link to the People."

"Big Man?" John smiled sourly, feeling his hatred rise.

"Unfortunately." Philip looked uneasily at his brother. "He was their greatest warrior. He had to be the one."

"We will do what we have to," Iron Eyes told them, voice echoing resignation. He kept his face calm though his stomach turned into a twisted knot.

"Ree will recognize me," Rita said. "He'll want to review the troops on board. Also, Helstead will notify *Bullet* of the native troops on board. Security will be waiting on the docks."

Leeta added, "Wait—Ree said the codes had been changed to Regga Green. That mean anything—"

"Damn right it does. Means I better not be on the AT." Rita was thoughtful. "Is the shuttle still at base camp?" Leeta nodded. "Then I'll go up in the shuttle," Rita decided.

"I don't understand," Leeta frowned. "Surely, we could sneak you in while the troops are boarding."

"But you couldn't clear the security on *Bullet*," Rita reminded. "I was given certain clearances by Ree when I accompanied you scientific types to the planet. Regga Green gets me aboard *Bullet*, no questions asked. I know a man in comm who might be tempted to throw a switch when the message comes in, based on what he knows of me—and that clearance."

Leeta frowned. "I'm on Ree's good guy list. If I tag along when they get him to the ship, what will be said?"

"Nothing." Rita turned it over in her head. "Helstead will dock as close to the hospital as possible. That's real close to engineering. The reactor is practically next door. You had a brainstorm, Doc."

"Good. If I stick with him, I can be in a position to advise him through the crisis he's about to face." Leeta smiled. "Iron Eyes, you come with me. You're to be the chief bargainer. You might want to start thinking over what you want for your people."

"Do we know what we're doing?" Philip asked suddenly. "I mean, we won't get another chance, will we?"

Rita's lips were pressed tightly together, her face pale, freckles standing out. Leeta looked blankly at the stained wood before her. Philip carefully lifted his coffee tin and sipped.

"We tread the web of Spider," Iron Eyes whispered and, under the table, patted the hand of the woman he had come to love. Spider would take control of their destinies now.

Marty Bruk wished his heart would stay where it was supposed to. Doc had to be out of her mind! "How did mature, intelligent adults like us get into this fix?" he asked, looking at the women facing him.

Leeta's eyes were cool. "Because, Marty, we don't have any choice. Another ship of the line is due tomorrow. When Robinson has to deal with Chester, he's going to be scared just like we were—and he's going to order those ships up there to eliminate the Romanans—and probably us to boot. We know too much. It would add support to his case if he could claim we were killed by the natives, and he retaliated. I'm too young to be a martyr!"

Marty fought to swallow. When had the good doctor learned to think like a tarantula? He studied the cold-blooded look in her eyes and could almost believe it true. Still, all that enculturation he'd grown up with told him the Directorate couldn't do that to real people.

"Still don't believe me, Marty?" Leeta seemed to be reading his thoughts.

"Ah, Doc, it's just difficult to make this all real." He shook his head.

"Remember when you said you'd take my orders, no matter what?" She raised her eyebrows.

"Yeah," Marty agreed, remembering. "What the hell, it's only putting the do-dahs to a med unit. I won't be killing anybody. Use this." He reached for a flask. "This ought to have his nervous system doing flips for at least a couple of hours. It's a neat new protein I isolated from bear spit. Shouldn't do him any real harm and it won't pick up on portable field scans—they'll need a med unit to find it and neutralize it."

"How much?" Leeta asked, eyes on his, measuring.

"For his size, I'd say no more than five ccs." Marty measured out what he thought was a good dosage and sealed it in a capsule.

"Five minutes," Leeta told them. "We're on. I can see Ree's AT coming down through the window. Here, Marty, take this." She handed him a Romanan fighting knife. He took the long blade and let his eyes run down the gleaming steel. When the time came, *could he do it?*

His heart banged against his ribs, making it difficult to swallow. His mouth had gone dry and he thought sweat had to be beading and running down his face. Marty Bruk was as scared as he'd ever been in his life. He remembered the steady look of the Prophet. The uncertainty as John Smith Iron Eyes had stared at him. They all knew he was a coward at heart. Why go through all this?

Then they were walking out to the AT, and he felt the sun's warmth on his skin. He noticed Ree taking Leeta's arm. The idle chatter hardly fazed him.

If he tapped Colonel Ree on the shoulder and took him aside, he could explain Doc's odd behavior as mental aberration. He could bring an end to the whole damned thing! He felt relief cooling his hot heart. Yeah, Leeta just flipped out a little. Too much stress.

Neurosis. Imagination seeing more there than reality permitted.

He'd started to turn to Ree, when he remembered the Prophets. They'd known. They'd agreed with Leeta. Future truths? He hesitated, unsure, looking at Ree's broad back as the AT lifted from the ground. The Colonel still talked animatedly to Leeta.

Bella's eyes were on him now. If he did, he'd mess up the future. What would the reaction be? There were two more battleships coming in—one arriving tomorrow. Was that right?

Marty let his fingers run down the handle of the fighting knife. And truth? Right? He remembered the blaster burns on the Romanans. His mind flooded with the words of the Prophet, as he looked into those bright, knowing eyes. The unasked question was answered. He'd wanted to know if it was worth the potential cost in lives. If it couldn't be done for cheap.

Marty hardly thought about it as he swung the heavy blade against his forearm. It didn't hurt much at all. Almost casually, he said, "Damn! I cut myself! Doc, you oughtta learn never to give me anything sharp!"

"Get this man to med!" Ree ordered, seeing blood welling on Bruk's arm. Marty dropped the knife into the scabbard on his belt as a crew woman hustled him down the companionway toward the med unit.

They had him patched up within seconds. The med tech taped the wound and sprayed it. "Think I'll rest a bit, if you don't mind." Marty shuddered. "Hate to think what I'd a done if it had slipped the other way!" He giggled, his nerves making it real.

"Right!" The tech agreed. "Just lay down. I'm gonna watch the festivities. Patch into comm if you need me for anything."

Marty nodded and leaned back on the bunk, breathing deeply. The AT settled down with a slight scuffling jolt. Hatches clanged and feet shuffled; then it was quiet.

Bruk practically shook when he got to his feet. The fasteners came loose easily and he opened the med unit. So similar to the REMCAT! He allowed himself a grin, working swiftly, nervously. He found the board he wanted and slid it out. From the equipment pouch on his belt, he took a small capsule, then—with two wires—energized the board.

Balancing the board on his knees, he held the capsule over the place he'd located and carefully separated the two halves. A drip of salty water sizzled and was followed by the carcass of a drowned fly. With a fingertip, he wiggled the fly in place and turned up the juice. A wisp of smoke curled up, baking the fly in place, the damp salt shorting the whole board.

Sighing relief, Bruk unclipped his wires and dropped them in his pouch. He powered down the unit, slipped the board in place, and carefully closed the fasteners. Just to be on the safe side, he powered it up again and tried to take his blood pressure. Nothing! Victory!

Marty Bruk heaved himself onto the bunk and gasped out a sigh of genuine relief. He'd never stand up to psych. They could wiggle the whole thing out of him with a probe, but damn, at least he hadn't been caught in the act.

Leeta watched her crack native regiment standing at attention. They were literally vibrating with anticipation. Ree walked along smiling, nodding occasionally. He looked them up and down, noting the coups on their belts with distaste. At the end of the line, he gave the warriors a standard salute. Philip, speaking in Romanan, promptly ordered his men to return. The hands rose crisply and snapped down.

"Well, Colonel?" Leeta asked, her pride showing through.

"Excellent!" Ree grinned. "Though it has become a cliche, Doctor, I must say, your men have gone beyond my greatest expectations."

"We are all so pleased!" Leeta smiled. "Philip, please demonstrate our maneuver."

Philip sang out and the line formed. With precision, the Romanan warriors trotted for the open main hatch of the AT. Rifles were shouldered and the men marched like a machine, each in step. Within minutes, the entire four hundred men were aboard.

Leeta pulled a flask from her belt and took a swig, knowing Ree was aware of her action. As she handed it to the Colonel, she crushed the capsule on the rim, satisfied to feel the liquid run into the flask.

"Come, let me show you how well they've managed to strap in." Leeta pulled Ree by the arm. He smiled at her and handed the flask back. Following the Colonel up the ramp, Leeta dropped the flask into the thick grass. Two marine guards stood in the hatchway and saluted as Ree strode through.

How long till the stuff works? Leeta felt a sudden growling of panic in her stomach.

Ree proceeded, seeing that each man had himself correctly placed in an acceleration couch. On one man, he carefully straightened a strap. "Tell him that might have hurt," Ree muttered to Leeta and she translated.

The wolfish dark eyes of Friday Yellow Legs didn't even blink as he nodded his appreciation.

"You know, Doctor," Ree began, "even though they're working for us, it's like they'd all like to take me apart. Almost predatory, I'd say. . . ." Ree shuddered suddenly and grabbed at his stomach.

"Quick!" Leeta ordered. "Shut that hatch and help me! Something's wrong with Colonel Ree!" She beckoned to the two guards. One slapped a palm to the hatch as he came at a run.

The three of them hustled Ree up the companionway and into the med unit where Marty Bruk still lay on the bunk. His glance was knowing as Leeta stumbled in and he nodded ever so faintly.

"What's wrong?" he asked, knowing comm was now monitoring every move he made.

"I don't know," Leeta let her tenseness show. "He just collapsed out there."

The med tech pushed into the suddenly crowded unit. "Give me some room!" he growled, and ordered the guards out. They stood in the hallway, watching anxiously.

Leeta took a deep breath. Philip would be making ready. If they didn't lift in two hundred seconds, he'd try and take the AT by force. Leeta could visualize the hands of the warriors as they hovered over the quick release buttons. Pray to Spider they waited for orders.

305

"Unit's down!" the tech screamed. "Captain Helstead! *The unit's down!"*

"Fix it!" Helstead's hard voice came flatly over the comm.

"Snap to it!" Leeta ordered. She looked up at comm. "Captain, get us off at once. If this is serious, we need to get the Colonel to help. Signal *Bullet, get us there, now!* If the Colonel dies, so help me, God, I'll have each of you for breakfast!"

She heard the lift warning and the AT was off, grav fighting to compensate. Leeta settled herself in a bunk while the med tech struggled with the cover of the med unit. He checked board after board until he pulled one and stopped.

Bruk was leaning over his shoulder. "Christ almighty! A damn fly! That would have got me thrown out of Dr. Chem's lab in a second! How do you army guys get off so easy?"

"A fly?" Leeta gasped. "*Here?* Inside the med unit? I thought they were sealed?"

The med tech was turning a dull gray. "I . . . don't . . . understand!" Riveted to the spot, his eyes went glassy. He looked up at the comm, stricken. "Captain, I don't know how this happened! We take such good care, *just like the manual says!*"

"Fix it!" Helstead's voice, too, reflected panic. "Damn it, man, *'FIX IT!'*"

"The Colonel shall hear about this," Leeta was repeating under her breath, "God willing he lives." She looked up at the comm, trying to keep her voice calm, knowing the stress was evident. "How long until we reach *Bullet?* You have contacted them?"

"Five minutes, ma'am." Helstead's voice sounded defeated, as if, in his mind, he were envisioning his court-martial. "I'm sorry, ma'am. Nothing like this has ever happened on one of my commands." She could hear the pleading in his voice.

The urge to giggle hysterically was fighting with her ragged nerves as she looked up at the comm. "A little fly, Captain. I understand. I suppose it could happen to anyone. I'll do my best for you," she said, hoping the inflection sounded right. Helstead knew she held his future in her hands.

"Doctor, I'm grateful. Any assistance I can provide from now on, just feel free to call on me or the men." She could see his frantic expression. At this moment he'd sell his soul. Leeta whispered a silent prayer to Spider that they wouldn't need to shoot their way in. Lord knew how Rita was getting along.

The comm showed *Bullet*. They were out of atmosphere now. "They have everything ready?" Leeta asked, checking Ree who shivered spasmodically. A med tech was hooking up a portable unit. He read the instruments aloud, evidently on direct line to *Bullet* while the first tech frantically tried to patch into comm. It didn't work, since he needed to patch through the fried med unit.

"Two minutes to docking!" Helstead's voice came through.

Leeta watched, nerves getting ever tenser as the huge bulk of *Bullet* filled the screens. How different from the first time she'd seen the ship.

Ree's teeth chattered and Marty was bending down, his pocket monitors on Ree. It brought a quick chuckle from Leeta. Even here—in the middle of the greatest crisis in his life—Bruk couldn't help but collect data from a poison he'd concocted.

She glanced back at the screens. Helstead was counting down seconds. She turned and left the med unit, running for the bridge. Comm would be showing the warriors the awesome shape of *Bullet*. She wondered what passed through their minds.

On the bridge, she watched the AT slide into a docking berth. "We're close to the ship's hospital?" she asked.

"As close as we can get," Helstead breathed fervently. Grapples clanged metallically.

"You!" Leeta pointed to Corporal Hans Yeager. "Stay and keep your eyes glued to the comm. The rest of you, come with me. I'll need to explain this to the Romanans."

"Oh, hell!" Helstead cried. *"I forgot them!"* He was sprinting down the hall. Leeta and the others followed on the run. As she crowded in behind Helstead, she pulled the blaster from one man's belt. Flipping

off the safety as Rita had shown her, she leveled the gun, stepping off to one side.

"All right, Philip, tie them up. Let's just hope to God, Rita's out there waiting for us!"

Iron Eyes ran forward, his fighting smile on his face. Turning, Leeta palmed the hatchway as the med techs brought Ree out on antigrav.

"For Spider," she whispered as the hatch shot up.

CHAPTER XX

Rita Sarsa shivered in the icy predawn darkness. Carefully, she walked out from the shadow of the base camp dome and struck out for the shuttle. There would be no one aboard at this early hour.

Rita stepped into the antigrav lift and thumbed the button that powered it up. A faint glow indicated activation and she rose from the ground. At the hatch, she called out her name, rank, and identification along with the clearance codes Ree had given Leeta Dobra. Thankfully, the hatch slid open.

Inside, she powered down the lift and keyed up the comm. Fitting the headset to her brows, she began sifting through all the information the unit had stored up. Insofar as she could see, they were doing well. She found no hint of their mad escapade in the computer banks.

Rita stifled a yawn and leaned back in the comfortable seat. What a horribly wretched night. While Leeta had been able to transport her as far as the base camp—technically for some of Bruk's experiments—she'd had to be outside before the security perimeter kicked in. That meant a long cold night out in the grass.

She didn't realize she'd gone to sleep. Activity in the comm jerked her from fragmented dreams to wakefulness. Ree's AT was landing in the sunlit open space next to the dome. Rita yawned, stretched, and began to power the shuttle up.

This would be the tricky part. Obviously, if the shuttle just lifted, base camp would call Ree. He'd know something irregular was occurring. That would place him on his guard. She ate concentrates as she watched Dobra, her team, and Ree walking out to Leeta's AT. The Colonel's Attack Transport lifted into the sky and shot off to the north—no doubt to keep its now routine watch on the Romanans.

Rita keyed the comm. "Good morning, base camp. This is *Bullet* shuttle three, special clearance Alpha one one five. I am requesting takeoff on that security clearance. Confirm."

"Good morning! You surprised us! Request clearance code." The startled voice on comm formed into a private's face on the monitor.

"We're zero on the clearance," she told him, her face on visual. The code was a double check for agents in the event they had a blaster shoved into their backs. Supposedly it kept the shuttle from getting stolen by unwanted parties. I'm on special assignment. It is imperative that I get to *Bullet* under the Colonel's orders."

The private nodded. "I understand. This channel is sealed. You are cleared for take off. Anything we need to worry about?" he asked earnestly.

"Everything's fine. Carry on, Private." Rita began flicking the switches and felt the shuttle coming to life under her.

The lift-off was a little rougher than it should have been. *So, it's been a while since I practiced. What the hell?* Acceleration pushed her back in the control seat and she watched the sky changing color as she shot through thin clouds and into deeper and deeper blue.

"*Bullet* control, Shuttle three requests course correction for match up," she said crisply into the comm.

"Shuttle, we're feeding course correction," the voice came back. "Where you been, Rita?"

She flipped the automatic on and felt the attitude of the shuttle change with the new course. "Special assignment by the Colonel. It's a long story. He just turned me loose for a shower and hot meal. That you, Anthony?''

"Roger, shuttle. Buy you a drink when you get time. It's been boring here. Be glad to hear a long story." Anthony's voice seemed relieved.

"You are *on,* Tony. Shuttle three out." She cut the connection at his "Roger." On the screens, *Bullet* rose over the curve of the planet and slid into view. Rita felt the shuttle kick her into a higher orbit as the big ship grew behind her. She had always marveled at the sensation. *Bullet* seemed to be roaring down on her, closing the gap from behind.

The shuttle ceased accelerating and Rita reveled in zero g. The big ship filled the screens now. Attitude jets maneuvered her to one side and the shuttle slipped into its berth with hardly a tremor. Rita felt gravity return as she unbuckled, moving to collect the bag that held her rifle, coup belt, and knives.

As she stepped out into the shuttle bay, all eyes were on her—noting her hide clothing—and talk ceased. Security came at a trot.

She laughed and dropped lithely to the deck. Hands on hips, she shook her head. "What's the matter? You've never seen a barbarian fly a shuttle before?"

There were grins and a few chuckles as the crew went back to work. Good. The atmosphere here was still one of boredom. The shuttle deck crew figured that if she had flown in, her clearance must be in order.

The three security officers approached, only to salute when she punched her Regga Green code into the comm clearance.

She made her way to the lift, requested the deck on which her quarters were located, and waited as the lift carried her through the ship. From the lift, her quarters were only a few hundred meters—she passed no one. With regret, she shucked out of the hide clothing she had become so accustomed to and stepped into the shower. One thing about civilization—a shower was still the finest invention in ten centuries!

In uniform, she made her way to the armory and checked out a shoulder blaster—one that could do some real damage—and buckled on combat armor. So outfitted, she drew occasional glances as she made her way to comm. Anthony was sitting there—back to the wall—with another private she didn't know. He looked up, startled.

"Special clearance, Tony," she said seriously, leaning the blaster in the corner. She fed her clearance numbers into comm and Tony nodded as security certification came through.

"What do you need, Lieutenant?" He looked up at her with interest.

"Wait and see, Tony. Ree and I are working on a, uh, situation. You know. *Brotherhood* is coming in. Ree's worried about discipline. Time for a shake-up. Can you give me a delay before it goes into the system?"

"No problem." He indicated a seat and accessed a program through the headset. "I guess you know about Major Reary trying to twist the Colonel's tail? Never liked that broad. We give the Colonel all her transmissions for approval before we send 'em."

Rita nodded, sucking the information up. "Ree said you'd understand," she gave him a conspiratorial wink.

They didn't have long to wait.

"AT11 to *Bullet!*" A frantic voice called.

"Here it is." Rita kept her voice calm. "Throw the switch, Tony."

Arf Helstead's frantic report blared out the news of sickness and dead med units through the comm control room.

"That's straight?" Anthony looked up. "Colonel's down?"

Rita looked smug. "What do you think? There's nothing much happening dirtside. How does he know you guys up here are on your toes? How often does a med unit fail?"

Tony patched the hospital through to med on the AT. Rita waited. She could hear the strain in Helstead's voice and it amused her. Already at his wit's end over Leeta's machinations, now his med unit had failed. Grinning, she wished she could see the expression on his face. He'd always been a damned stuffed shirt anyway.

"Less than a minute to docking." Tony looked up, questioning. "Oughtta inform security."

"Nope. Colonel wants a panic situation." Rita checked the chronometer. "I'm on my way down to monitor reaction time. If anything comes in regarding security, cancel it out before it gets to comm. That's part of the plan. Colonel's playing this one close to his chest. If everything's on track, Helstead thinks the old man is really out of it. Remember, cancel any security alert." She went for the hatch, picking up the blaster.

"Got it, Rita. Have fun. We'll monitor up here. You're sure we're not involved? Canceling a security alert is pretty serious." He looked up, worried. "I want it on the record we reacted. I don't want the Colonel chewing on my—"

"Hey, trust me. We had fun cooking this one up!" she grinned. "Just let it all fall apart. Colonel wants to see how long it takes to pick up the pieces."

"We'll just sit here and do nothing," Tony agreed, still nervous.

Rita sprinted down the hall. She ducked into a lift and hollered for Dock 25. At the same time, she clipped a charge into her blaster. When the door slid open, she trotted out into an almost empty lock. The med team was already waiting.

Rita stepped up behind two security personnel and watched the AT sliding into the berth. She felt the slight thump of metal and heard the grapples drop. Stepping up behind one of the men, she stunned him with a careful punch.

Waiting until the second man turned, she zapped him too. The meds turned to stare, frozen at the sight of the blaster. How far would Tony let this thing go? Nervously, she ground her teeth, thinking about the route they'd have to take to reach engineering. Once there—if they could get in—they were safe.

The hatch began to open; Rita pulled up the big blaster. Med came rushing out with Ree on an antigrav. Rita shot a fast glance at the comm where she knew Tony and his pal were all eyes.

Leeta was hovering alongside, Iron Eyes and Philip following. "Quick!" Rita ordered, "Take the Colonel

312

to the hospital. Go!'' They went, Leeta shooting her the high sign, Iron Eyes and her team trotting after the Colonel.

"Philip! Let's go!'' she shouted, and imagined the surprise on Tony's face as the AT disgorged ranks and ranks of skin-clad warriors. Rita trotted into the main hatch and blasted the controls, locking it open. Smoke and sparks hissed out of the shattered box.

At a run, she sped down the hall. "How'd it go?'' she called behind her in Romanan.

"No trouble. Big Man is holding the AT and the dock with most of the warriors. Leeta and John are taking care of Ree.'' Philip was grinning, trying to see everything he was running past.

A startled man stepped into the corridor and Rita dropped him smartly. Gravity diminished and she felt light on her feet. "Easy!'' she shouted back. But it didn't take. The warriors were pushing on rapidly, running into walls, having trouble with momentum in general.

Her belt comm beeped and Rita fingered it. "Yeah?'' She demanded.

"Lieutenant, is everything all right?'' Anthony's voice sounded concerned.

"Are there any alarms yet?'' she asked, starting to pant a little.

"Only the blasted hatch,'' Tony's voice came back. "I've run ID, *those aren't marines.*''

"Native troops. Good work, Tony. You'll get credit in my report.'' She flipped off the comm and dashed around another bend to make the last run for the reactor. The comm was beeping again.

She flipped it on. "Tony, I'm busy!'' Rita shouted.

"Lieutenant Sarsa?'' The voice was female. "This is Major Reary. *What in hell is going on down there?*''

"Reaction drill, Major!'' Sarsa growled. "Testing reflexes on the Colonel's orders, ma'am.'' She snapped the comm off, they'd reached the end of it right there. And gone so much farther than she had thought possible already. It was true, everyone believed the ship invulnerable.

The last hundred meters. The big doors were before her. The standard two lazy guards were standing by

313

the open hatch. Reactor duty classed as drudge duty. Rita herself had stood it. Like everyone else, she hated it. "Lieutenant Sarsa!" she called on the run. "Special clearance Alpha one one five."

A guard turned and punched it in. He started a salute as Major Reary's voice sounded a counterorder over the comm. The Romanans were piling up behind her. There was no more time. Rita slammed the blaster into one man's stomach and kicked the other hard in the chest. Too late, the hatch started to shut. She punched the access button. The code had cleared. Slowly the door stopped its movement and slid back on its huge hinges. She slipped past and ran into the main reactor room. Techs looked up in surprise and she yipped out her victory cry.

Gasping, ragged warriors were right behind her. They piled up behind Philip, crowding close, wide-eyed, looking around in amazement with rifles pointing out in all directions. Rita ran forward, blaster leveled, catching Major Glick at his desk, staring, mouth coming open.

"Yellow Legs!" Rita called. "Any man touches that comm, shoot him and take coup!" She changed to Standard. "You men!" She pointed the blaster at the reactor crew. Keep the ship on normal. I want full reaction mass on the Colonel's orders!" She stepped forward. "Philip, see that gauge? If it drops below that red mark, kill a man. Major Glick, we're not fooling. We're desperate."

"Sarsa?" Glick was walking over, his face showing disbelief. "What *are* you doing?"

She pointed the blaster at his middle. He stopped. "Major. In the name of the Romanans, we have just seized this ship."

"*Lieutenant!* Seized. . . ." he gasped, thunderstruck. "Do you know what you're saying? You're—"

"Oh, quite, Major." Rita laughed. "Do you realize that for the first time in history, a Patrol ship of the line has fallen without a shot? I did that, Major. It is time for a new order."

"You're mad, Sarsa!" Glick shook his head.

"Philip!" she called. "See that big board there?

314

That's the main reactor control. If anything happens to me—or if I'm disabled—smash that panel!''

''No!'' Glick cried. ''You'll kill us all!'' His eyes betrayed his desperation a second before he dove at Rita. Before any of the warriors could react, she had reversed the blaster and laid him out cold. A Santos had pulled his knife and was bending to take coup.

''Not yet,'' Philip ordered and the man looked up, hesitated, and stepped back. ''I see. That controls the big fire, eh?''

''That's it.''

The face of Major Reary was watching from comm. Rita turned. ''You heard what I told Glick? We're desperate, Major. We've come this far. When the Colonel is ready to talk, we'll talk. In the meantime, no gas, no gravity tricks, no rushing the main door. If you do, I use this,'' she pointed to the blaster, ''on this!'' Her finger moved to the control panel for the matter/antimatter reactor.

''What do you want, Sarsa?'' Reary asked, her face wooden.

''Surrender of this ship to the Romanans, Major.'' She raised a hand at the shock in Reary's face. ''Please, the decision is not yours. The Colonel is aboard. He knows the situation dirtside. Too much hangs in the balance, Major. Don't do anything that runs us out of time.''

Glick was moaning and the techs were starting to recover. One tried to make a run for the hatch. A warrior shot him down on the spot. A horrified Patrol audience watched as the warrior leaned down and carefully took coup.

''Carry him outside,'' Rita ordered. She looked up at the comm. ''Get a med unit down to pick that man up. These are primitive weapons. You can save his life if you move quick.'' Philip was barking orders and the man was carried out.

Too many men. She had almost a hundred here. The rest were back in the AT, manning the controls, keeping watch. ''Send José White Eagle back down to the lift at the end of the hall. Have him take twenty men. They hold the hall until further notice. As to the rest, I guess we just sit.''

Philip went about making duty assignments. The tension began ebbing. They'd made it. The techs watched, horrified. Glick was bound and lifted into a seat.

The destiny of *Bullet*—and the Romanans—rested with others now. Rita slumped into a seat and ignored Major Antonia Reary and her demand for explanation.

Friday Yellow Legs stared defiance over his rifle. He cocked his head looking at Antonia Reary. "My friends. If that is how the other star women look, we were better off with bears!"

Laughter rippled through the room.

Damen Ree forced his eyes open and tried to blink. He saw only foggy visual images, as if someone had coated his corneas with gelatin. His tongue moved thickly and he had difficulty swallowing.

"What happened?" he croaked, voice scratchy. Rolling his head, he could make out the safe white of the ship. He felt gutted.

"Colonel?" A familiar voice reached his ears. Someone was shaking him now. Something pricked his arm and his eyes began to clear.

"That should do it. Given the nature of the protein, he should come out of it in a couple of minutes." A white clad figure stepped out of Ree's vision.

"Colonel?" The familiar voice finally made a place for itself in his mind.

"Reary?" He frowned. She ought to be up with the ship.

"Here, Colonel. Are you fit for command?" Something in Reary's voice pulled at his consciousness.

Every second Ree felt himself clearing more of the fog. A cup was pressed to his lips and he sipped a stimulant. Warm life rushed from his belly into his leaden arms and legs.

"What happened?" he asked.

"We drugged you." Leeta Dobra's voice told him.

"Drugged?" He turned his head and sought her face. She looked grim. Two marines stood behind her, blasters pointed at her middle. "Why?" he asked.

"We've taken *Bullet*." Dobra's voice was firm.

"Taken the ship?" Ree forced himself to sit up. The room swayed. Hospital! This was *Bullet!*

Slowly, Major Reary detailed the situation in the reactor room. Ree struggled against the cobwebs in his brain, trying to make sense of it.

"But why?" he demanded, feeling his mind growing clearer by the second.

"To save the planet, Damen." Leeta seemed at ease, ignoring the blasters at her back.

"I thought we were," he answered grimly. And Sarsa was alive?

"We've made progress, but Damen, Skor Robinson will order it destroyed." Leeta seemed so sure.

"How did you take the ship?" He scowled at her, rubbing the back of his head with a sweaty palm. Gods! Why did he feel so weak?

"Rita Sarsa and my Romanan troops are in the reactor room. They will turn us all into plasma if things go badly." Leeta still didn't seem nervous. The big Romanan she'd hauled out of the mountains was behind her, obviously backing her. Iron Eyes, that was his name.

Ree looked the question at Reary. She just nodded, glaring stifled hatred. Ree took a deep breath and tried to stand. He wobbled for a moment then his balance returned. "Medic, how long until I'm normal?" He blinked again, as his vision finally cleared.

"Perhaps five minutes, Colonel. You need to eat." The med stepped back. "The antibodies we gave you work fast. More than anything, you need food. You used up quite a bit of energy. Something solid will make a difference."

Ree nodded. He looked up at Dobra. "And if you get the ship? What then? How do you intend to outrun the Directorate? Where do you go? What do you do?"

Leeta shrugged. "Come on, Damen, let's get you down to the conference room. You need to eat. We don't have to solve the whole thing here and now."

He nodded. She appeared truly concerned. It didn't feel like an adversary relationship.

"Colonel Ree!" Antonia snapped. "You can't just let this situation—"

"Dismissed, Major!" he thundered. He needed time

317

to think. He could see the disapproval on Reary's hard face. "Oh, come, Major. We'll find a way to keep people from getting hurt." The thing was not to let this get out of hand. There still might be a way to save the situation.

"Comm," he ordered as he walked down the hall. "I want a psych profile on Lieutenant Rita Sarsa. See if she really would blow the ship up."

The lift was crowded. Leeta, Iron Eyes, Reary, and the guards all jammed in. Ree learned that the rest of the anthropological team was in the brig. "Why not you two?" he asked.

"Rita would have blown the antimatter." Dobra shrugged.

"So why's he here?" Ree crooked a thumb at Iron Eyes.

In heavily accented Standard, Iron Eyes replied. "I am here to speak for my people."

They walked down the companionway, Ree lost in thought. Seating himself at the conference table, he ordered a thick steak and wine. He scanned the psych profile on Sarsa. The final word? She'd do it. He recalled Bruk and Vola from the brig and assembled the rest of the scientists. He waited while the room filled. He could see Rita Sarsa watching on the comm. He nodded a civil acknowledgment of her presence.

His steak came and he suddenly realized that his stomach felt like a vacuum. He cut a piece and looked up. "All right, Leeta, tell me why you and Sarsa cooked this up."

"We had to do something!" Leeta's eyes blazed. "We can't let the Directorate just blast the Romanans out of existence!"

Ree chewed as he thought. "Why do you think they would?"

"Colonel, you think in terms of military tactics. Now, think in terms of socioeconomics. The Romanans are prescient. The Prophets see the future. Think of Chester Armijo Garcia. He's a threat to anything we think of as normal. Not only that, but there's a group of people here who shoot at each other and raid back and forth. Do you think Skor Robinson will allow them to be free among civilized people?"

"Damen, this is an outrage!" Reary exploded.

"That will be all, Major!" He glared at Antonia, motioning Leeta to continue.

"And in final proof, why does *Brotherhood* arrive tomorrow with *Victory* hot on her trail? Robinson is scared. He wouldn't be loading the dice like that if it weren't to make sure the Romanans hadn't any chance. He's so worried about the prescience, there's no telling what their orders are." Leeta raised her hands and let them fall. "What else could we do?"

True! Ree agreed mentally. And he'd not look twice if I burned them all to cinders. "And you're ready to die for these Romanans?" Ree asked pensively, chewing the steak.

Iron Eyes spoke, "I have learned a new term in your Standard language. It is sin. We—my Spider People and the Santos—know of only one sin. Sin to us is to give up or live without freedom. Our religion rests on that premise. We have no other heritage. In our belief, God allowed himself to suffer horribly that men would be free.

"We taught this lesson to Doctor Dobra and to Rita Sarsa. They learned and they saw a truth. Like me and all of my People, they are ready to die for this truth. Are you not the same? Did you not dedicate your life to what you believed to be a truth?" Iron Eyes sat, stiff-backed, his level look meeting Ree's.

"If I say my truth is the Directorate?" He cocked his head.

"Is it?" Iron Eyes seemed to see through him.

"I think not, Damen." Leeta interrupted his thoughts. "I remember a story you told me one night. I remember your love for this ship. But, Damen," Leeta's gaze was far away, "once a major debate raged among anthropologists that one of the definitions of humanity was the ability to symbolize. What does *Bullet* symbolize for you?" She cocked her head.

"Freedom," Ree heard himself say softly. He looked up and mused at the triumph in Leeta's eyes and the dismay in Reary's. He could see the Major accessing comm. Why? To prepare to usurp his command?

"And there is duty," Ree added. "I also told you

of the proud heritage of the Patrol. I have a duty to the people, Doctor. If the Romanans are a threat, perhaps the rest of humanity is better off without them."

"What if the greatest threat to the people is the Directorate itself?" Rita Sarsa demanded from the reactor room. "Colonel, when was the last time a major exploring expedition was mounted and sent out beyond the borders?

"We're told exploring is dangerous. Where is life without occasional risks? We've shared risk all through human history. Today there's no risk. There's no progress either! When was the last time we were stimulated? It's like the whole lot of humanity sits on their asses with their fingers in their ears. Look how applications for the Patrol have dropped!"

Ree studied the screen. "And you think the Romanans would turn the tide? What if they bring warfare back to civilized space? Suppose I grant them this ship? Suppose they begin raiding Arcturus, Frontier, Earth, the stations? What then would be our legacy? I ask you."

Rita was looking at him furiously. "It'd beat being a sheep!" she declared passionately.

Leeta Dobra was shaking her head. "Damen, it doesn't work that way. The Romanans would be just as changed—in fact, they would undergo the greatest acculturation. You see, we're the dominant group. We have more substantive things to offer than they do.

"What Rita, John, and I are betting is that the wonder of these atavistic warriors will infuse the rest of the Directorate with a desire to move beyond what they see as a normal life. At the same time, we will be bringing our culture to the Romanans. With the Prophets, they have a better chance at survival than other primitive groups ever had who faced a developed culture. In return, we get the ability to dream again."

Ree finished packing away the steak and leaned back, sipping the last of his wine. "Let's say I refuse. The lieutenant allows the reaction mass to become unstable and *Bullet* is gone. Where are the Romanans then? Sheila shows up tomorrow and finds wreckage, a couple of ATs on the surface, and scorches the entire continent of Star. End of problem.'' Ree raised his hands and shrugged.

S. Montaldo grunted. ''That might be the best thing, after all.''

Iron Eyes carefully interwove his fingers. ''No man lives forever, Colonel. I have listened during this last month. Marty Bruk has told me about humans. We all originated on Earth. First we were tool-using apes. Then we learned to hunt, collect, and protect ourselves by modifying the environment. Yet these early men are no more. I do not see such a man as the holos depicted here among us.

''Perhaps it is Spider's wish that the People, too, are no more. Perhaps what we have to offer is not meant to be. Perhaps Spider will watch our People depart and learn something more about the nature of man. This is our chance, Colonel. If we lose, we are no worse off. Your Director may kill us. At least we have hope. We take the risk. What would you do?''

''You could die so easily?'' Ree asked. ''You could watch your People burned and exploded out of existence?''

John Smith Iron Eyes shook his head. ''I will not need to. My soul will have gone to Spider long before your big blasters unleash fire and blood on the People. One way or another, Colonel, I am fighting for my People. If for some reason, Rita cannot explode this ship, I will die fighting with my hands, my honor, and my courage.''

The words touched something in Ree and he looked at Iron Eyes with a new-found respect. Here was a warrior. But then, weren't they all? His thoughts drifted back to the Spider whom he had killed that day in the aircar. He remembered the spirit in those dying eyes. This man would be the same.

''How long do I have, Rita?'' he asked, looking up at the monitor.

''Doc, what do you say?'' Sarsa shot a glance at Dobra.

''Five hours,'' Leeta decided. ''Damen, that ought to give you time enough to consider all the angles. Rita? Does that endanger your position?''

''Not at all.'' The lieutenant grinned. ''I'm just going to sit here and talk with Philip. If I lose consciousness, I won't be able to hold this here rubber band off the blaster trigger. If they mess with us, we all die."

"We'll leave you alone, Rita. I'm going to try and mediate a way out of this. Meeting dismissed," Ree said firmly and stood. He bowed punctiliously and walked out.

He'd barely reached his quarters when Major Reary wanted in. "Damen, what are you going to do?" she demanded. Worry was clearly etched in her hard face.

It was a shame, he decided absently. Antonia was one of those women who tried too hard to be professional. She never allowed herself to be feminine—and she could have without compromising her integrity. Somehow, that lack made her less than whole. A major flaw, Ree decided, thinking of Leeta Dobra.

"Iron Eyes is right, you know." Ree took a deep breath and dug one of his classic Terran cigars from his special humidor. He offered one to Antonia and she nodded, running the length of the cigar under her nose. Ree lit them and flopped in his chair, looking up at the Romanan rifles and knives he'd ordered hung on the wall. He studied them distractedly.

"Right? How?" Reary asked, drawing on the cigar.

"They won't be stopped short of death. We're stuck, Major. Either we eliminate them—or let them out." Ree frowned as he studied the delicate curls of smoke that rose toward the air vents.

"So we give them our word they can leave." Reary grimaced. "When we get Sarsa out of the reactor room, we cut loose with the blasters."

"Have they been in contact with the surface?" Ree asked mildly.

"Only that AT of Helstead's. We tried the lock a while back and they shot at the marines with those ridiculous rifles. We could take them anytime with a serious assault." Her eyes betrayed her disgust. "Or have you lost your nerve as well as your command, Damen?"

Ree pulled on the cigar and blew the smoke out in a cloud. "We won't be able to change our minds, Antonia. What we do, we must be committed to. That communication to the surface is to their damned

Prophets. Sarsa has a line through to the AT, doesn't she?''

"Yes."

"Then we're sunk if we try lying to them." Ree frowned trying to think of a way out. "The Prophets will call up to Sarsa and tell her we betrayed her. She'll blast the reactor panel."

"If they know the future, why haven't they already done so?" Mockery riddled Reary's brows.

Ree shot her a look of irritation. "Because of free will, Major. We're all what they call cusps. We have a certain range of decisions we can make which can change what they see."

"So they don't really know the future?" She scowled at him.

"Oh, they know right enough. They just can't predict which future we will experience. The ones who try and change the futures to meet their own goals, go mad. That's why the Prophets don't meddle with the people who are cusps." Ree closed his eyes and wished the whole thing would just go away.

"Damen, my decision is made." Antonia stood. "I'm going to fight them no matter what. It is a matter of Patrol honor. You have failed all of us. Your ship is in danger. Your decision may be anything you desire, but I swear, they will never have this ship. Either you're with me—or against me. Let me know, Colonel."

He opened his eyes and saw the blaster resting in her fist. "You are in mutiny of your commander, Major. Do you realize this is only the second instance of such behavior in over four hundred years of Patrol history. Worse, both instances are on my ship within a period of hours."

"Be that as it may. I'm sure the court-martial will clear me. I'm no longer sure you are capable of command, Damen." Her voice was level, in perfect control.

Damen Ree watched her through slitted eyes. "Very well, Antonia." He accessed comm. "Send in Dobra and John Smith Iron Eyes." *So I have reached my cusp. The decision was not as heartrending as I had feared.*

"I'm glad you bowed to reason." Reary smiled.

"Yes, it was reason," Ree mused absently. "Reason and experience." He looked up as the door opened and Leeta entered, followed by John Smith Iron Eyes. Leeta took in the situation and stopped. Iron Eyes let his lips curl slightly. He crouched like a big cat as he watched Reary.

Ree kept his eyes on the Romanan warrior. "The Major here has provided me with a very strong reason for the denial of your request, Iron Eyes." Ree smiled. "This situation severely limits my options. Do you understand?"

Reary's eyes narrowed and Ree could see the tendons in her arm tightening. *She was really going to kill him.* Had he been so transparent?

It happened too quickly for Ree to follow. Iron Eyes struck hard as Reary shot. The blaster bolt blew the stuffing out of Ree's chair as he dived to the side. The weapon clattered and spun crazily across the floor as Reary sprang for the Romanan.

It was instinct—not training—she relied on. Iron Eyes reached up, grabbed a knife from the wall, and neatly split Major Antonia Reary from pubis to sternum.

Ree scrambled for the blaster and rolled into position. Iron eyes was carefully wiping the knife on Reary's clothing. Then he gripped and handful of hair and ran the blade in a circle, popping off the scalp.

Ree felt his guts lurch as he looked at the spilled rolls of rosy blue-brown intestine and the red-streaked gleam of Reary's skull. Iron Eyes took pains to hang the knife on the wall exactly as it had been.

"Jesus," Ree whispered as he looked up at Iron Eyes, the blaster settling on the man's middle.

"Very well, Colonel," Iron Eyes said softly, crossing his arms over his massive chest. "I believe your options are once again open. May I be of further assistance?"

CHAPTER XXI

S. Montaldo walked down the wide companionway lost in thought. So Lieutenant Sarsa had taken the huge reactor? If she got an unexpected muscle twitch—she could blow the whole lot of them to plasma—he'd be no more than hot atomic particles.

His thoughts drifted to Chester Garcia and he turned off into one of the crew lounges and looked at the beautful ball of white cloud, brown continent, and blue water showing on the monitor. A wealth of toron lay there, the random accident of an exploded supernova. A fragment had landed here to disrupt the lives of men. How many millions of years had passed while those heavy crystals waited for human destiny?

What were the lives of men? How did a planetologist make any sense of the value that should be placed on such an amorphous concept as human life? Toron, uranium, metals, organics, they could all be estimated, weighed, priced, and decisions made as to how they should be profitably exploited.

He'd heard Leeta Dobra mention cultural values. Exactly what was a cultural value? Could you make money off of it? Did it put food on someone's table? Montaldo chewed his lip and tried to make sense of it. In his career, he'd mapped, evaluated, and passed judgment on over thirty planets. None had been occupied before his estimations of the planet's worth had been made. Why was this one different?

Chester had made that difference. The little man with the tranquil eyes had changed the scales of balance on this world—but Atlantis was still a plum. The plucking of it would make the Directorate a handy profit. The toron crystals here were large, unshattered, definitely of the quality required to run star ships. Only the Romanans stood in the way. Too bad, they must go—one way or another.

The tramp of boots in the companionway turned his attention from the monitor. As he requested a cup of coffee, he watched armed marines trotting by, their white combat armor gleaming. Curious, Montaldo grabbed up his coffee and hurried along in their wake.

The few words they'd uttered made him aware that action was anticipated. His pulse picked up. How exciting! He'd always wondered what sensations filled men when they marched off to death at the hands of other men. When he'd been young the thought had gripped his imagination. How must it feel to face your fellows over a blaster—knowing you must kill or be killed? Perhaps here, now, he would at least be able to touch the edge of such an experience.

Their destination didn't surprise him: Dock 25. He slipped up in time to see the marines take a position in the corridor. Beyond lay the heavy lock Sarsa had blasted open. S. Montaldo's heart pounded furiously. *If only he could ask them what they felt!*

He didn't hear the order given, but with a sudden crackle of blaster bolts, the marines dived through the hatchway. A rapid staccato of sound Montaldo guessed to be the Romanan rifles responded.

Something splatted off the wall next to his head and buzzed off behind him. Bullet? Here, around the corner? Ricochet, he remembered the word.

There were yells, screams, whoops and a crashing sound. Smoke was billowing his way. Unable to suppress his curiosity, Montaldo crept along. The first body he came across was blown almost in two. Montaldo's stomach tried to turn upside down. Despite the odor, he somehow kept himself from vomiting.

There were more. Romanan dead had fallen in a stack at one point. They must have charged straight into the blasters! Montaldo shook his head in amazement. Another bullet clattered down the hall to fall distorted and flattened after it bounced off the bulkhead. Almost with glee, he reached down and plucked it up. He yipped as he flipped it from his hand and sucked his seared fingers. Bullets got hot!

Another wave of crackling blaster fire erupted before him. Montaldo ran to see. The Marines were moving back now. The hindmost carried wounded comrades from the fray. Montaldo froze. One man's leg was crisped off. The Romanans had used blasters of their own! Where? The AT, of course!

An explosion thundered, the blast almost blowing Montaldo off his feet. He cowered back out of the way of the passing marines. What had happened? How could *they* have been forced back? Surely being so well armed and equipped, they couldn't have been beaten by mere savages?''

''What happened?'' Montaldo cried as one fellow ducked down next to him.

''Didn't think they could use the AT blasters that way!'' the man cried in shock. ''They dismounted one of the AT's big ones. Mounted it right in the lock. Damn them if they didn't try and run right over the top of us until they got the big one powered up.''

''You mean they outfought you?'' Montaldo couldn't believe it.

''Damn right!'' The marine shook his head. ''We got a recall order from up top. Didn't come a minute too soon! They'd a wiped us out in there. Hell! Major Reary ordered us in. She didn't tell us they'd have any gawddam AT blaster shooting back!''

Another tremendous explosion rocked the lock and Montaldo cringed. The marine took most of the force and spattering steel fragments on his battle armor.

''I'm pulling back!'' he shouted. ''I'll cover you!''

Montaldo nodded grimly and sprinted. Bullets were rattling off the walls around him and he remembered the hot piece of copper and lead he'd foolishly tired to pick up. The thought of such hot metal in his soft flesh became horror.

A hot blast pounded the air out of his lungs, tumbling him down on his hands and knees. Blood dripped from his nose. Through the sudden howling in his ears, he heard the marine cry out. Montaldo spared a look. The man was down, the whole of his back blown wide open in spite of the battle armor. Montaldo scuttled and ducked behind the bodies of the Romanan warriors which had held his attention earlier. Then he watched the marine die, fascinated.

Szchinzki Montaldo had never tasted death before. He'd never seen it so graphically displayed for his senses. A blaster bolt slammed into the metal over his head, showering him with searing sparks. Here the marines held. He could look out over the bodies and see them shooting around the corners. There would be no more retreat.

Sucking deep breaths of acrid air into his lungs, Montaldo waited. He was shivering now, scared—deeply scared—fighting nausea.

The voice spoke in a tongue he didn't know. Montaldo started and almost ran, but another rain of bullets rattled off the walls.

"Who's that?" he asked, peering fearfully over the pile of dead men.

A hand touched his leg and Montaldo cried out in terror, flinching. Slowly, he forced himself to look down at the fingers trying weakly to clutch at the fabric of his pants. Bending down, he traced the arm to a body—then to a face.

The eyes pleading with his glassed with pain. The lips moved, but the talk was garble to Montaldo. "You must speak Standard!" Montaldo shouted over another minor explosion.

"Water?" the voice croaked. "Please, I would have water?"

The pleading shook Montaldo out of his stupor and he stared at the cup of coffee, now mostly crushed in his grip. With shaking fingers, he pressed the cup back into the round and looked at the swallow left within. Cradling the man's head, he trickled the drops onto the man's tongue.

Horrendous screams echoed down the hall. Meds were stumbling out with marine casualties. "Here!" Montaldo shouted hoarsely, waving his hands. "I have a man alive here!"

A med ran in his direction, ducking as a blaster bolt took out another section of wall. "Hell! He's a savage!" The med looked his disgust and ran back the other way.

"A savage?" Montaldo sat back, forgetting the ungodly racket for the moment. He looked back at the fleeing man. *"He's a man like you or me, damn you!"* He shook his fist at the med.

"Water? More . . . water?" the man whispered dryly.

"None here!" Montaldo stooped down close to the face. "None here, understand. I've got to get you to the hospital." He looked at the pile of dead men. At least five of the burned corpses lay atop the man. How in hell's name had he avoided smothering?

Frantically, Montaldo pushed and pulled at the bodies, breaking down his last protection. A blaster bolt exploded one of the corpses next to him, beating him with heat and energy. He shouted his rage and saw a Romanan round the corner only to have one leg blown off. As the man crawled for cover, a marine took aim and blew his head off.

Only one corpse was left and he pushed at it. Something stung his arm and it flopped loosely at his side. Montaldo dropped, staring dumbly at the hand which wouldn't move. Blood was welling from his sleeve just above the elbow.

"It hurts," the wounded Romanan whispered, his glazed eyes on nothingness.

I'm shot! The thought came to Montaldo slowly. *No real pain, just a sting, like a bee might make.* And a numb feeling that tingled in his shoulder. Gritting his teeth, he pulled the Romanan out from under the bodies and stifled a whimper when he saw the man's other arm and leg—exploded, sizzled hamburger and bone. Cauterized by the heat, they didn't bleed. Even so, the nerve endings must be screaming.

Fighting with his one good hand, Montaldo got the Romanan over one shoulder, hearing the man's bone-grating screams. "Sorry," Montaldo whispered. "I'll save you. Hang on!" He raised his eyes to the blackened and ripped panels overhead. "Dear God. Help me. Let me save just this one! Let me save him if no others! *Just this one!"*

He struggled to his feet, dimly aware he wasn't as strong as he should be. With the bullets and blaster bolts whizzing and crackling around him, he made it to the last bend. Marines were sitting along each wall, eyes focused on the distance. Three or four dead ones lay unattended.

"Where's the hospital?" Montaldo demanded. A med pointed in the general direction where an antigrav was disappearing. Montaldo staggered after it. Passing the marines, he noted that some of them had fresh scalps hanging off their equipment belts.

"And Chester saw this?" Montaldo asked himself as he fought for breath and strength, his burden heavier with each step. "Hang on, pal!" he ordered the Romanan. "We'll make it—you and me." He vomited suddenly, almost falling in the stuff.

The hall started to sway and Montaldo had to stop. Leaning against the wall, his whole body felt hot. He gasped again and with his hazy vision, saw an antigrav coming his way. The two meds rushed to him, taking the Romanan off his shoulders.

"Save him!" Montaldo gritted. "Save him, or, by God, I'll make you pay!" The blurriness came from tears. Crying? Him?

The first med had already run the antigrav back toward the hospital with the Romanan aboard. "Lean on me," the second med said easily. "We'll fix that arm right up. Should have you out and about in a few hours. Bone's broken, you've lost a lot of blood. You'll be fine."

Montaldo nodded, staggering as the med almost carried him the last hundred meters to the hospital. As the med unit worked on his arm, Montaldo could see the Romanan submerged in some sort of yellow, fatty looking stuff.

"He going to make it?" Montaldo asked.

The med tech monitoring the machine didn't take his eyes off the screen. "Barely, sir. I think you just got him here in time."

Montaldo closed his eyes, feeling the med unit wiggling around under the skin in his arm. "I did it, God. I kept him alive!" Montaldo's relief was almost a physical ecstasy and he rejoiced in the hot tears that spilled down his cheeks.

"So what is the value of a human life?" he whispered. "How do you weigh it, measure it, or figure its intrinsic worth? Eh, Montaldo?"

330

"Do you have any idea how many reports I'll have to fill out, Iron Eyes?" Colonel Ree looked up, resignation in his eyes.

Leeta paused, her heart still pounding. "Damen, we're running out of time. The decision is yours. What do we do?"

He smiled grimly. "Do? Leeta, you put me in this position. How can I possibly argue that the Romanans are helpless when you've taken my ship, killed my number two officer and wreaked God knows what other havoc?"

"Be one with us, Colonel." Iron Eyes took a step forward, forgetting the blaster. "I see it in your eyes. You are a warrior. You are a man of passion. Is this not a time for passion? Why did you stay so long on the planet? Why do you have the collection of rifles and knives on your wall? What do they represent to you?" He searched the Colonel's eyes, seeking the answer.

Ree absently slipped the blaster into his belt, shifting his gaze from Iron Eyes. "I took an oath long ago. Besides, it may be out of my hands. Robinson gave me leave to destroy the Romanans if it appeared they might cause problems. Sheila will have those same orders. She may even opt to destroy my ship if she thinks things are out of control."

He stood up, the cigar still between his lips. "With Skor Robinson, who knows? Why did he send two ships? I'll tell you." Ree's eyes were hard on theirs. "Two ships have a chance to kill *Bullet*. Either of them, *Brotherhood* or *Victory* might not be able to pull it off. Together—if they hit by surprise—they could take us.

"Remember I bragged to you once that I was out of my league on Atlantis, Doctor. Against those two ships, I've got one hell of a chance." His hard eyes were shining as he envisioned it in his head.

"So why don't you do it?" Leeta asked, her face showing the strain. She turned and left the room, unnoticed by the men.

Ree suddenly slammed a fist into the wall, shaking the pictures and weapons that hung there. His eyes were frantic as he looked up. *"Because I've sworn an oath to the Directorate!* I've sworn to protect the people out there. How can you expect me to fire on my own people?"* His expression was anguished.

"Like a clan." Iron Eyes nodded. He reached out a hand and clenched Damen Ree's shoulder. He tried to impart a sense of empathy. "I understand, Colonel."

Ree turned under his grip and looked up, disbelief in his eyes as he read John's sympathy. He hesitated before admitting, "Yeah . . . I guess you do."

"Leeta's gone." Iron Eyes frowned.

Ree shrugged, his face a mask of conflicting emotions. Easily, he poured two glasses of brandy and offered one to Iron Eyes. "My heart is with you." He smiled slightly. "I killed one of your Spider warriors down there. I lost my temper . . . something I hadn't done in years. He wouldn't be defeated, so I killed him. I relearned a lesson I'd forgotten."

Iron Eyes listened carefully as Ree continued. "I remember when I was a child. I thought I would always be invincible. That's when I first thought of the Patrol. I lost that along the way somewhere. When I killed that man, it frightened me at first. Then I thought about it. I saw the way Leeta had been changed after she was out with you. I began to study your people. I learned a new strength there."

"Spider has much to teach, Colonel." Iron Eyes agreed. "He taught me not to fear for myself. He taught me the role I must play. I have acted this before. Only this time, the Directorate is the bear. My life for that of my People."

The comm sputtered in Ree's ear and the monitor flicked to life. Rita Sarsa glared out. "Call it off, Colonel!" She ordered, agitation in every fiber of her body.

"What?" Ree demanded. Iron Eyes could see he was truly baffled.

"The attack! Damn you, *call it off!* You've got five seconds or that control panel is junk!" Rita was almost trembling.

"What attack? I gave you five hours. I gave my word!" Ree was getting angry.

"Warrior!" Iron Eyes called in Romanan. "What attack? Tell me!"

"The marines have attacked the lock. They are trying to take the AT. After that, our link to the Prophets will be cut. We'll lose any chance to get out of here if need be—and a lot of men will die. They lied! I'm going to blow it." She turned toward the console and raised the blaster, determination in her eyes.

"As your War Chief, I order you to stop." Iron Eyes said it softly. "If you do not—you will bring dishonor."

Rita turned, her eyes amused. "My War Chief? Huh! What dishonor?"

"This man," Iron Eyes pointed to Ree, now ashen as he watched the blaster pointed at the panel, "has not ordered an attack."

"Reary!" Ree grimaced. *"Damn her!"* He pounded a fist into his hand. "She'd have set it up. She gave them a time and they went for it."

"Where is she?" Rita was still unconvinced.

Iron Eyes smiled. "I have taken coup, Red Many Coups. You have more to take to catch me."

Ree expanded the pickup so Rita could see the body on the floor. Slowly the blaster lowered. "Sorry, Colonel. Guess I'm a little jumpy." Her eyes were sober.

"I'm calling back the marines." Ree left the channel open as he accessed the marine commander and announced a recall. Rita watched wide-eyed as the man nodded, ducking in the middle of the fire fight.

Iron Eyes studied the monitor, fascinated as he observed the combat in the companionways around Dock 25. The marine captain ordered his men back and they executed it flawlessly. A blinding flash overloaded the screen . . . and there was nothingness.

"Patch me through!" Ree thundered at the monitor. He looked up at Rita. "You have comm to your AT? If you do, withdraw your men. We haven't lost atmosphere yet, but those maniacs could puncture the lock at any moment!"

Rita was facing another comm, rattling off orders via Philip. Iron Eyes translated for Ree as the Colonel supervised the withdrawal of his marines. It took a good fifteen minutes to untangle the eager combatants.

A man passed the monitor and Iron Eyes smiled at Ree. "It was a good fight. Your warriors have taken coup." He pointed at the scalp lock on the marine's belt.

Ree chuckled to himself. "It's been coming. So my folks have proved to yours that they're warriors." He sipped his brandy and gave Rita a sober look. "Let's talk, Lieutenant. Put your blaster down. I'm no longer the enemy. We've got to figure out how to handle two Patrol ships of the line." He flicked the comm off and toasted Iron Eyes.

"Why did you so decide, Colonel?" John asked. "When our peoples were killing each other and the end might have been one way or another, what made the difference?"

Ree raised his eyes. "It was the lock, Romanan. That's a fragile piece of equipment. I don't know what your people set off there, but it could have killed them all, Patrol and Romanan. Lord knows how many all told. You see, Leeta was right about me. I can't risk my ship over something this foolish."

"But you can against your Patrol and Directorate?" Iron Eyes asked.

"My heart won't be in it," Ree agreed. "I'd let Rita blow us all to hell if I didn't at least see an equal right on your side." He shrugged as his eyes read the damage control stats. "Right, or—as you say—Truth, is an interesting concept. If you believed your clan was wrong, what would you do, Iron Eyes? How would you handle it?"

John Smith set his glass down. "I don't know. I would attempt to show them their error, but there would always be the Prophets."

Ree frowned. "Yes, the Prophets. Too bad the Directorate doesn't have one." Ree's eyes brightened. "Would one of your Prophets be willing to come up? That might be an edge against *Brotherhood* when she arrives."

"You may request. The Old Ones will make up their minds based on what they see. It is their wisdom. You

334

understand?'' Iron Eyes searched the Colonel's face for comprehension.

"I'll have an AT set down near the *Nicholai Romanan.* I'll have the captain make a . . . request.'' Ree smiled at Iron Eyes.

"Colonel?'' Comm asked.

"Here!'' Ree watched intently. A white-faced Anthony appeared on the monitor. Leeta stood behind the man, one of Ree's Romanan rifles pressed against Tony's head.

"Damen. I've just sent a subspace transduction message to the Directorate. Included are the entire records of our operations here. All Marty's information, all the speculation, the observation, everything has been sent to university and anyone who has a receiver on at the moment the signal arrives.''

Leeta laughed wickedly. "Further, this man had nothing to do with it. As you can see, he was disposed to do my bidding.''

"That rifle isn't even loaded!'' Ree fought for control.

"But he didn't know that.'' Leeta grinned, letting the butt down to Tony's immense relief.

Ree had closed his eyes, taking a sorrowful breath. "I wish you hadn't done that,'' he whispered.

"Why?'' Leeta raised an eyebrow.

"Because while you were composing your message, Iron Eyes and I came to an agreement. Now, when *Brotherhood* arrives in system, odds are, she'll come in ready to destroy us.'' Ree frowned. "How did you get that man to send without alerting comm? All he had to do is push a single button!''

Leeta's look of triumph had cooled considerably. "Didn't I ever tell you? Jeffray taught me almost everything he knew about transduction. I did it myself.''

"Colonel?'' Comm requested.

"What now?'' Ree opened another channel.

The face of an AT captain looked out. "We're on our way up, Colonel.'' The man squinted. "Funny thing, sir. We set down and these two old men just walked out and were coming up the assault ramp the second it hit the dirt. I guess we got the right ones. They don't say anything. They just smile at the trans-

335

lation machine. We keep trying to tell them we need a Prophet. I guess. . . . Uh, can you make an ID. sir?'' The Captain looked confused.

Ree shook his head wearily. ''I don't think that's necessary, Captain. If they were waiting for you, that answers your question. Anything they want, give it to them!''

Ree snapped off all the screens except Rita's. ''You happy, Lieutenant?''

''I think so, sir.'' Rita had set the blaster butt down on the deck.

''Then if you don't mind, please turn Major Glick loose. I'm sure that given the circumstances, he'll understand about getting power up for combat conditions. I don't think the reactor crew can function at top capability with your weapons on them.''

''Coming out, sir!'' Rita snapped a salute as she grinned wolfishly at Philip. The screen went dead.

''I suppose I shall have to make an announcement to my crew.'' Ree said. ''They really should know that we're all on the same side now.''

''I'm sorry, Colonel. I cannot violate my oath to the Directorate.'' The young captain saluted sharply and walked stiffly to the AT hatch. The line wasn't as long now. Ree gravely took salute after salute.

Periodically, he would study a man or woman while his lip made a slight twitching motion. The haughty air to his posture belied pride and pain. Leeta saw the ragged division grow within the crew of *Bullet*. Hands were clasped uncertainly as old partners saluted and mumbled words of support and luck under their breaths. They glanced around—as if to see who was watching—wondering who was judging. A crew split by duty and belief, some stayed with their ship and Colonel; others remaining steadfast to their belief in the Directorate.

A string of privates walked past, saluting and keeping their eyes downcast. Ree gave his last salute and watched the final AT loading. The station-born would follow an intercept course to the incoming Patrol ships. The planet-born would be off-loaded among the Romanan settlements.

336

Damen Ree ran his palm over his tired face. "The death of a crew," he whispered.

"It was only to be expected, Damen." Leeta leaned back against Iron Eyes as the monitors showed the ATs departing.

"But so many?" Ree had a hurt look. "I always did my best for them. You know, I had fewer requests for transfer than any other Colonel in the fleet. I just assumed they would be behind me."

"They have to make their own road to right or wrong." Iron Eyes tightened his grip on Leeta. "An excellent piece of thinking on your part to set them down among the People. That action may save many lives."

Ree snorted bitterly. "I'm not a saint, Iron Eyes. I—I feel betrayed. I left them there to think. It's partly a nasty human response of mine. I'm not sure it will save any lives. They let me down—didn't back me up— and I've gone to the wall for a lot of them in the past. If they'd rather put their faith in the Directorate, so be it. Maybe *Brotherhood* won't cook them. Right about now, they're probably getting concerned about that very idea."

To Ree's amazement, Iron Eyes just nodded. "Every man must take responsibility for his actions and beliefs."

"We got two extra days." Leeta looked at the comm where Rita was providing an orientation for the Romanans who were filling in for Patrol personnel who had chosen to leave. Not much of a patch for missing skill, but they could handle damage control, med antigravs, run errands, and handle simple comm.

The two days came from a hesitation on the part of *Brotherhood*. After Leeta's subspace message went out, *Brotherhood* had veered off course and circled, giving time for *Victory* to jump in. The Prophets had said the Patrol would come in hostile. They said no more.

Ree rubbed his fist into his palm. Damn the old buzzards, they didn't give him any idea of the outcome. They just gave him those knowing smiles and calmly told him that there were still two major cusps yet to come.

Montaldo walked through, pushing a bandaged Romanan on antigrav. He waved and the warrior looked at them, eyes showing amazement at everything he saw. He turned and said something to Montaldo. The planetologist turned their way.

"This is the man you rescued?" Ree asked, touching fingers in greeting to the man's one remaining hand. There was a stub where the left arm should be. Wires proved electrostim was growing a new arm and leg. It would be a year yet before the man had to relearn to walk.

"Yes," Montaldo nodded. "This is Pepe Sanchez Grita. He may have something to tell you."

"I am all ears, warrior." Iron Eyes squatted to be on the same level as the antigrav.

"Blessed be to Haysoos, Spider War Chief," Grita nodded. "There is talk that Big Man thinks Spider is too powerful. He may or may not be trouble. I think you might want to keep an eye on him."

Iron Eyes frowned. "Blessed be to Haysoos." He crossed himself in the manner of the Santos. The warrior almost gasped at the sight. Never before in the knowledge of men had such a thing happened. "I thank you. Tell the Santos that Spider is one name for God. Haysoos is another. Spider would not want his People to be destroyed over the name by which men know God. Tell them that before the battle the Spiders will pray with the Santos if the Santos will pray with the Spiders. If we are to live, we must find tolerance now."

"I will tell the Santos." The man's head bobbed. "I am one man—but I will tell of this."

"What's that?" Ree asked. He'd had no time to learn the language.

"Big Man may be stirring up trouble. It's too early to tell." Iron Eyes shrugged. "I think I have it under control."

"Nominally, we still have him in control of Helstead's AT." Ree was thoughtful. "I doubt he can cause too much trouble there. I suppose though that he rails at the idea of a Spider War Chief. I had no idea it would be this complicated." Ree looked sour.

338

He stared up at the screens, seeing the dots that indicated the positions of *Victory* and *Brotherhood*.

"You're no longer a cynic, Montaldo. What happened?" Leeta asked, eyes on the planetologist.

He smiled wistfully at her. "I guess the meaning of life changed in that companionway. Perhaps Atlantis does that, Doctor."

"You could have gone down with the others," Ree said softly.

"Maybe my priorities have changed, Colonel. I may die with you. I may die down there. It's up to Haysoos." Montaldo shrugged.

"Huh?" Ree's brows knit.

"God, Colonel." Montaldo smiled. "Chester said I should remember my humanity and keep my faith in God. Who knows, if we get out of this alive, maybe I'll handle the rights to that toron for the Romanans. That'll keep them from getting skinned."

Comm activated. "Colonel Damen Ree!" A woman's face formed. Leeta could see that she had been beautiful once. Her bone structure was good, but her eyes had a pinched look.

"Here." Ree squinted at the sound of the voice.

"This is *Brotherhood*, Colonel Sheila Rostostiev commanding. By order of the Director. You are to turn over command of your vessel immediately. Do you understand, Colonel? Your commission is canceled and you will be placed in custody at first opportunity."

"And if I refuse, Sheila?" Ree sounded amused.

"I have orders to destroy your ship, Colonel." She smiled in anticipation.

Ree let a heavy sigh escape his lips. "You realize we're making history. This is the first time Patrol ships will fire at each other. Surely we have time to allow an exchange of views, to show what we found here."

"Unlike you," Sheila's voice was condescending. "I take orders seriously, Damen. Either you will consider yourself under arrest and allow your ship to be boarded—or we will destroy *Bullet*. Your choice, Damen." She gave him a gloating smile.

"You never were flexible, dear." Ree smiled lazily. "Not in bed, not in command, not in intelligence. I'm surprised you were elevated to command of *Brotherhood*. They must have had a poor lot to choose from.''

"Damen," she spat, "fawning like this does you no good. I take it I have your answer?''

He nodded slowly, eyes pained. "You do, Sheila. But tell me, do you really think this worth the price? You know me and my ship. We're good, darling. Will the numbers of dead and wounded meet the cost of a poor decision on the Director's part? Is blood spilled by the Patrol the way to cover the murder of a half million people? Are we not being played for patsies here?''

"You're transmitting this!" Sheila's eyes widened incredulously. "That's in violation of every regulation in the book, Damen! *Damn you!*''

"That's right, Sheila. I want the entire Directorate to know exactly why this is taking place. You see, dear one, I'm not a traitor to my oath. I swore to protect the people and the Directorate. I didn't swear to protect Skor Robinson or policies which are in direct opposition to the best interests of humanity.

The screen went blank. Ree turned to Leeta and Iron Eyes. "It looks like the die is cast. There goes the last of our chances to get out bloodlessly.''

They watched the screens with varying emotions. The two white dots represented death for some, pain for others, heartbreak or extinction for still others. Even the Romanans—trying to function in a completely alien environment—felt the rising tension.

"Two hours to maximum range," Comm called out.

Leeta reached up and whispered into Iron Eyes' ear. "Come on, we have at least an hour. Let's go to my cabin and use the time wisely." She led him off the bridge without anyone noticing.

Rita finished running through the tests on her fire control board. She gave one last look at the flashing green lights and looked up where Philip stood with a headset uncomfortably on his brow.

"Red Many Coups, you have led me a merry chase since the night I had to choke the very breath out of you." He grinned at her and rubbed his ribs.

"Philip," she pursed her lips. "If—by some miscalculation of Spider's—we live through this, have you

340

given any thought to what we ought to do with each other?''

He cocked his head. "No, Lieutenant, I haven't."

"What's the male side of your clan, Smith or Iron Eyes?" She rubbed a finger where her headset squashed her red curls.

"Smith." His eyes betrayed his distrust of her motives.

"Then maybe after this fight, we will start a new clan. The Smith Sarsas. Has a ring to it, don't you think?" She looked up curiously.

"A warrior can't marry a woman with more coups than he!" Philip cried in mock horror. "Of course, our children will be born with a rifle in one hand and a blaster in the other." He thought about it and nodded in resignation.

Marty Bruk ran his system through a check one more time to still his nerves. Bella let her cool fingers play over his hot neck. "Too bad about Netta. She really had a lot of potential."

"No good genes. Natural selection, you know. Atlantis broke her." He looked up, the comm set resting on his head at a jaunty angle. "Ree was crazy to entrust me with all this!"

"You're the only one who knows equipment well enough. I'm the best linguist we have. The only one—I might point out. Who better to handle comm?" Bella shot him a smile while Marty watched the computer monitor the entire ship.

"Funny," he said at last. "I'm about to die for sure and I'm not scared." He looked up at her, a faint smile on his lips.

"Good, Marty," she said heartily, "because, for once, I'm scared to death!" She shivered as he hugged her.

Big Man watched his Santos strapping into the acceleration couches on the AT. Things would happen soon now. His smile widened. There were women who would be his. That yellow-haired one who seemed so powerful and the Red Many Coups. Who would have guessed she was so great a warrior—but then, who else could have laid him out like that. *Only once, dear one.* He smiled. There was a cusp coming up. He nodded to the Santos Prophet who sat behind him. The time would be soon. Big Man studied the back of Helstead's head. Soon, indeed.

Damen Ree let his senses become one with *Bullet.* He felt every plate, rivet, power source, circuit, lead, and frame member. His life pulsed around him. For this moment—he truly lived. Perhaps here he would die. If that were his fate, it was a worthy one. He would die with her—with Bullet—and she had never failed him yet.

Her crew was a mongrel now. The fine temper was gone, but perhaps there was a different strength—one which was not so brittle. She would bring him through and to hell with Maya and Sheila. *Bullet* would shine on when they were just plasma.

At the heart of the ship, two old men looked at each other and nodded while Damen Ree watched the two dots of light that were destiny, death, and future.

CHAPTER XXII

Chester Armijo Garcia found the absence of any sort of gravity extremely upsetting. Fortunately the Patrol and Directorate people had recognized his disquiet. They'd provided him with a gravity device to make him feel heavy—even if it did bother his sense of balance and equilibrium.

Incessant demands on his time for tests, proofs of his abilities, and continual scans by machines totally beyond his comprehension had left him haggard. They'd poked him, prodded him, shocked him, scraped his skin, clipped his hair, milked his semen, swabbed his ears, subjected him to lights, weighed him, measured him, stuck probes up his anus and down his throat, and gleefully claimed every bit of his bodily excrement.

Through it all, Chester maintained a pleasant, almost ambivalent attitude. He smiled at them—even when their tests became totally ludicrous. He knew why the Prophets had rushed him. None of the Old Ones could have taken such physical abuse. Not that the scientists were deliberately cruel, they simply didn't see Chester as human.

This was the day. After the long wait, he was ready to perform his duty to the People. Life had become like a trance. Now, at last, the cusp was apparent. Today there would be excitement, change, uncertainty. Chester smiled at the honor guard of marines who came to fetch him. The marvel of it all had vanished long ago; he didn't even try to ease the fears of the master sergeant.

Instead of hooking him to his gravity system, they strapped him onto a sled of some sort and left in a rush along the brightly lit white corridors. He watched in fascination as the dream became first reality, then history. It gave a man a feeling of enlightenment to watch future, present, and past run together in an active sense.

He passed checkpoint after checkpoint while his body was monitored time and time again for weapons. They continually probed a metal splinter he'd run into his arm as a boy. Finally, one of the technicians used a device that pulled the callused fragment from his flesh. Chester smiled as the tech sprayed medical plastic on the small incision.

At last, the guards saluted and the final door opened. The sled took him into a room glowing with hazy blue light. Cerulean seemed to seep out of the floor, ceiling, and walls. Chester realized there was no up or down here, yet his ears told him he was falling again; and in tribute to his humanity, he clung to the sled, using it to create up.

The figure floating sideways before him was, at best, a poor caricature of the human form. Chester's vision hadn't betrayed him. The massive, skin-covered globe of skull was pinched oddly out of shape on one side by the morphology of a human face. The headset was shifted back to allow Skor Robinson to study Chester with his own eyes as well as those of the computer.

"Greetings, Director." Chester bowed insofar as his restraining straps would permit.

"I have studied the reports thoroughly. You and your kind have brought chaos." Skor's voice was impersonal, oddly ineffectual—as if he'd never grown accustomed to using the muscles or intonation; the speech uttered digitally.

"You might want to wait before you kill me," Chester said.

"Why?" Robinson's jaw seemed to pain him as he moved it.

"You are a cusp, Director. You have read the reports, you know what that means." Chester inclined his head slowly.

"My decision regarding your race is made. You would be a cancer in the body of humanity. You are disruption." Robinson's blue eyes seemed tiny, the nose but a pimple on the massive skull. An illusion, Chester knew. Still, the man was oddly inhuman.

"Director," Chester said earnestly, "you are wrong. We are no cancer. Like you, we are a form of balance."

Robinson's face quivered as if trying to form an expression. "Your kind would bring disorder. You are illogical. That makes your threat to humanity severe." The little blue eyes locked on his face.

"I am not illogical, Director. I am a Prophet." Chester's kind expression didn't change. "Prophets, Director, are teachers and I ask you now to learn. It was with pleasure that I learned to read from your teaching machines. In your vast systems there should be references to Arnold Toynbee's *A Study of History*. There are occasional flaws, but I think you will find the underlying truths pertinent to this discussion."

Robinson hesitated less than a second. "I find obsolete social theory. Challenge causing change is unacceptable behavior for humanity," the flat voice asserted.

Chester nodded. "You assume that growth must come painlessly. God does not let us off that easily, Director. I'm sure you will find two forces in constant opposition all through the history of the species; the quest for order—which your Directorate represents—

344

and the constant fermentation which brews curiosity, experimentation, and innovation.

"I repeat myself, but I must stress the balance of the two."

"Your race will be destroyed. I have no interest in ancient social theory." Robinson's milky blue eyes showed no emotion. "Why do you persist in trying to change facts I have established? It is futile behavior."

Chester shook his head. "I do not change. On the contrary, I am laying the groundwork for what is about to happen. You need certain bits of data in order to formulate your coming decisions."

"What decisions?" Skor Robinson's brow actually moved in a slight spasm of a frown.

Chester ignored the question. "As I understand the process explained by Dr. Chem, you and I are pieces of human evolution. The species has been let out of the bottle. Where adaptation was once keyed to the requirements of one limited planet with its specific atmosphere, gravity, elements, light, water and so forth, we are now being selected for in very divergent fashions. We are both attempts by the species to find balance. You exist to provide order, I to allay the inherent fear of the future. Each is a response to uncertainties in the universe around us. Perhaps each of us comes along at a critical time when the species is stumbling." Chester was lost in his thoughts.

"That is all, you are dismissed." Skor's helmet started to lower onto his head.

"Not that quickly, Director." Chester held up a hand as the sled began to move. Skor's helmet raised.

"No one has ever disagreed with me," the flat voice almost hinted at anger.

"It has stunted your humanity, Director." Chester felt pleased. "But that is not why I tarry. I want you to know that in the coming troubles, I can provide you with a means of establishing order. It will cost you complacency—but I believe that is a far cry from the complete disintegration of the economic system you have cherished. In your market society terms, Director, you will have a need and I can offer you a service."

"Your words are nonsense." The blue eyes didn't waver.

"As difficult as it is to believe, you are still human in your emotional construction, Skor." Chester chuckled. "You are about to be tumbled on your rear. I wonder how you'll choose? It is your cusp. Are you wiling to destroy yourself through your own vanity, or will you compromise for the sake of humanity?" Chester pursed his lips. "I have said all I need to. You might save yourself some crucial time if you don't send me all the way back to university."

Skor didn't. It took three hours after the crisis broke before frantic guards rushed Chester back into the hazy blue room. It seemed as if Skor Robinson hadn't even changed postion, but this time, his weird blue eyes showed fear.

"You will speak!" Robinson demanded.

"Of what?" Chester asked, listening to the words he would say as they sifted out of his future.

Skor's face showed a faint hint of shock. "There is revolution. The Sirians have detonated an explosive device in Planetary headquarters. They have seized ships and are arming them. There is war . . ."

Chester interrupted. "Before you waste a lot of words, Director, you have perhaps twenty minutes left before your Patrol fleet will be diminished by three ships. Colonel Ree is very determined. He will destroy all the Patrol ships in his last desperate gamble.

"You must choose now. It is the time of your cusp. You may bargain with the People whom you call Romanans, or you may bargain with the Sirian revolutionaries. Each provides a different future." Chester shrugged.

"You but bargain for your life," Skor tried to sneer.

"My life means nothing. I have seen my death many times, Director. I have seen it change through many fates in many different places. It matters not if I be poisoned tomorrow as you intend or—depending upon future cusps—die of a stopped heart forty years from now. God is. The soul is. Death is a simple matter of time for all of us. The result is truly the same today— or one thousand years from now. We are tools of God's purpose."

"What will happen if I choose your Romanans?" The skeletal limbs moved faintly in the zero g of the room as Skor waited impatiently for Chester's words.

"I told you, a Prophet is a teacher. You will learn a lesson from my service." Chester saw irritation but ignored it. "With the Romanans, the Directorate is doomed. It will deteriorate within the next sixty years.

"Should you choose the Sirians, the Directorate will be destroyed in all but name within six months. The lesson—as you see—is that nothing lasts forever. You must choose. In one way, your economic control evolves slowly into something else. In the other, change comes rapidly and violently. Either way, some will benefit, others will be harmed. Pain cannot be avoided.

"You yourself produced the problem when you sent the ships to kill the People and your own *Bullet*. You allowed others to be distracted by Sirius while you concentrated on what you believed to be a greater evil. You must now decide how you will live with your creation. For truly, your own humanity—as much as you deny it—has caused discord and disorder. I wonder, are you so much better than I or my People?"

"What of me?" Skor asked. "How should I choose?"

"No Prophet will tell you. You see, in spite of your fears, we will not try and influence the future. We will tell you the options and the potentials, but we will not take a hand. No man may play with free will, God guards that very well. There, you have learned."

"You are an abomination!" Skor's dead eyes were suddenly vacant. "I have always worked for mankind."

"Perhaps," Chester shrugged. "You must choose now. Or do nothing, which is a choice in itself."

Skor's eye's actually seemed to harden.

"Very well," Chester agreed, seeing blood, death, and warfare. There would be pain, some of it his.

Blaster bolts are strings of energy—highly charged particles that create blinding streaks of light across the black of space. Blaster bolts diffuse over distance. Particles react with each other, repulsing their neighbors, colliding, changing in the complicated physics of their existence.

Brotherhood shot from too far. Her bolts missed by a couple of hundred meters. Ree's gunners were on the vectors immediately, tracing the shots, studying red shift, and replying with better accuracy—if not effect.

"Let her come closer," Ree ordered. It had been a telling omen. Sheila had shot first and missed. *Bullet* had shot back and hit. Too bad the distance was so great. Nevertheless, that ought to cool her ambition a little.

"It is done," Iron Eyes said softly. The entire crew of Romanans had stood, praying to their respective interpretations of God. Aloud, Spiders had hallowed the name of Haysoos as Santos had whispered their hopes to Spider. Another plank had been laid upon a rickety bridge.

Big Man stared at Iron Eyes from across the crowded mess. This man—and his Spiders—had become the talk of the Romanan world. Who remembered Big Man? They talked of how Iron Eyes and Red Many Coups saved the People. No one talked of Big Man. His warriors had trickled away like grains of sand in the wind. Coup was needed.

Big Man turned to look at the shrunken man at his side. The Old One stared across the room, oblivious, eyes locked on the two Spider Prophets who stared back.

The Spiders weren't the only ones capable of dealing with the star men on their own terms. Big Man chewed his lip, eyes slitting as he studied Red Many Coups. Then he turned for his AT.

Victory waited another fifteen minutes to shoot. One of the bolts glared briefly on the shields and faded. "Maya has better control," Ree muttered to himself. "There must be a lot of doubt. I'll bet those folks aren't any too wild about shooting us up. That gives us better reaction. It's a black day when Patrol ships are killing each other."

348

"ATs are ready to go, Colonel," comm declared.

"Send them!" Ree's voice remained steady as the ATs broke loose to find their own part in the fray.

Iron Eyes watched as the ATs scattered in complex maneuvers planned to confuse enemy fire. They spread out, heading off to block attack paths, seeking to find any weak link in the defenses of the other ships.

Bullet changed course, weaving past a series of violet blaster bolts that leaped from *Brotherhood*.

"Like spiderwebs," Iron Eyes muttered. "They cast, hope to find the prey, and disappear."

Leeta shivered, uncomfortable in the battle armor. Feeling helpless to aid in the kind of battle they now faced, she was on the verge of panic. Grabbing a pen, she whispered in Iron Eyes' ear, and as he lifted her, she drew a diagram of a spider overhead like the one she'd seen in the sooty overhang of Gessali Camp.

"That's better," she crowed in triumph as she was let down.

Some of the runners who waited nearby smiled and two or three absconded with pens and snuck out. Iron Eyes nodded. *Bullet* was no longer just a Patrol ship, it was becoming a Spider ship.

Ree first noticed a Spider drawn on the front of a marine's battle armor. Then there were Santos crosses springing up on the white walls, the gleaming breastplates of the marines, the sides of the deadly blasters. The sight brought a smile to the Colonel's lips. Indeed, they were tempered, no longer brittle. Instead, his crew was something else, something new and powerful.

"Colonel!" Bruk's voice came over comm. "I just got this on *Brotherhood's* frequencies. It's supposed to be straight line, but I guess Big Man muffed it."

"What?" Ree leaned over the comm.

At the name, Iron Eyes pushed forward. He missed the beginning of the message. ". . . coming in. We have taken this AT and would join forces with you. With your help I may call on my warriors to destroy the Spider men and give you victory over this Colonel Ree." Big Man's perfidious voice went on.

Ree looked up coldly, "How do I fight that?" For

349

the first time, there was a hint of despair in Ree's voice. "There are Santos all over the ship."

Iron Eyes bit his lip. Jenny's dead eyes stared up from the visions in his mind. The blood oath rattled hollowly through his brain. He imagined the big warrior laughing his defiance. "Don't do anything yet. We need José Grita White Eagle."

It took less than five minutes to get Grita out of med and to the bridge. As José trotted in in his battle gear, he was followed by a Prophet. Grita threw a nervous glance over his shoulder at the smiling old man. The warrior had a cross superimposed on the carapace of a spider.

"Play the conversation," Iron Eyes ordered, eyes on White Eagle while he tried to ignore the Prophet.

"He would sell us out?" White Eagle demanded after hearing it. "He knows there is death for all—*and he would sell us out?*"

"Tell the crew," Leeta said softly. "If you believe in what we are dying for, tell them." Her sibilant voice betrayed her concern. "It *must* come from a Santos."

José Grita White Eagle looked at the comm as he'd seen the crew do and nodded at Ree. "My friends," he began, speaking in Romanan, "as the Patrol warriors had those of their people who would not fight for us, we ourselves have been betrayed by one of our own."

He went on to play the recording of Big Man's betrayal. Iron Eyes monitored the rising anger among the warriors as José talked passionately. The Santos showed disbelief and the Spiders looked nervously at their recent allies.

The Prophet motioned them aside as Grita spoke. "This is as it should be. The Santos have a Prophet of their own on the ship you call AT. This man waits to see which direction a cusp will work. The betrayal of Big Man could possibly save the Santos—at the expense of the Spiders—if the will of your Director is against us. There are many cusps which are being decided by José Grita White Eagle's speech. You have brought this about, Iron Eyes." After that the old man carefully walked out, leaving Ree frowning and Iron Eyes swallowing nervously.

"What is the fate of traitors?" White Eagle was shouting into the comm. "They have broken war oath!"

The Santos yelled as loudly as the Spiders "Death!" It thundered throughout the ship.

Iron Eyes stepped in next to José. "The Spiders and the Santos are a People. Our clans have mixed. I declare a knife feud with this Big Man who would sell out this new People. He has sold our new clan, the *Bullet* men. He has disgraced us all!"

Even without comm, Leeta could hear the roar of approval. One more hurdle crossed. "Permission to blast the AT, sir?" It was Rita Sarsa, eyes bitter.

"Shoot," Ree agreed. Blaster light laced the vicinity of the AT. Big Man's luck held. Then José Grita White Eagle broadcast the Santos sentiment to Big Man. At first, there was no answer. But a cusp had, indeed, been reached, and finally a return message indicated that Big Man had been overthrown, and locked in the brig.

The rebellion ended, Ree went back to studying the screen. His darting eyes watched the way *Brotherhood* and *Victory* were changing positions. Leeta could almost see the tension building. As *Bullet* shivered from attitude adjustments, the shields flared, deflecting the combined blasts from *Victory* and *Brotherhood*.

"Call from *Victory,*" Bruk's voice came through. A dark-skinned woman appeared on one of the screens.

"Colonel Ree? Will you yield and stop this madness? It is only a matter of time. Why sacrifice your ship and crew?" She looked genuinely concerned.

"Colonel ben Ahmad, this has gone too far," Ree smiled, his tension suddenly hidden. "Each of us is called upon at least once in our lives to make a decision. I will never again have a chance to fight my ship. My crew has sided with me. We have made a new alliance. We will face the test of our friendship and gamble for a better life in a changed Directorate. As one of my lieutenants put it, we have nothing left to lose."

Maya nodded. "Very well, Damen. I do not wish to do this thing, but I have my orders. I respect your decision. If you decide to save yourselves, call. In that event, I'll keep Sheila off your back.'' The screen went blank.

Ree went back to his comm, not a breath wasted, concentration intact. Finally, he straightened. ''I think I have it,'' he said with a flourish. ''There are two moons we're accelerating to pass between. From the Patrol vectors, we can dodge between one or the other depending on our situation and who is coming closest to roasting us at the time.''

''Like playing harvester and bear?'' Iron Eyes asked, seeing a plot of Ree's course where it wound through the moons.

''They aren't much protection, but they're better than nothing.'' Ree shrugged. The battle plan is in comm. We've done our best for this go around. If they don't finish us on this flyby, they'll have to kill delta V and come back. In that time, we make repairs and try and take them again.''

''I thought these things were just ten minutes of lights and explosions!'' Leeta objected.

Ree shook his head. ''This could go on for days. Think of the velocity they have. They hope to be able to concentrate their fire while their velocity makes them that much harder to hit. It's a trade off. We're going a great deal slower but we maneuver easier with less mass to shift. They're faster, but if we get a line, they can't dodge as easily. As they try and change V, we change. No matter what they do, we get to the moons at the right time. We can shift to keep in the shadows.''

It worked. Ree kept them alive while he scored at least one good solid hit on *Brotherhood* which brought cheers from the gun deck.

A day later, the two Patrol ships had slowed and were coming back. During all that time, Ree had lived with comm, plying the computers, thinking up scenarios, playing them out. Leeta watched his burning, red-rimmed eyes as he looked up.

''I know what they're doing.'' He snapped to his feet. ''We can't run. We have to protect the planet. They are going to try and shove us out of the way, blast Star until nothing is left alive down there, then kill us. They have ceased their fancy maneuvers.

Leeta, you get your short, sweet space battle. They want to move up and slug it out with us.''

"So what do we do?'' she asked.

"Our ATs are outnumbered two to one. So are we, for that matter. We'll try and sneak some of the ATs past their guns and board. At the same time, we'll see if we can't hold out long enough to get to one side.

"We'll take a beating, won't we?'' Leeta felt her heart skip a beat.

"Simple geometry says that between any two points is a straight line. If we can stay on that line, we can fight one ship at a time. That's our one chance, but it's tricky.''

The first hole was burned into *Bullet's* side three hours later. The Romanan damage control crew did well for their first space adventure. Leeta watched the shields and the return fire. She could plainly see that Ree was spending most of his fire on *Brotherhood*. *Vendetta*? A brilliant flash of light shot out from Rostostiev's ship. It veered suddenly closer to *Victory*.

"Damn!'' Ree shouted, his fist waving over his head. "Put one into her reaction control! She's getting too close to *Victory*. Change of course, come around! We hide behind *Brotherhood* now and we have a chance. *Victory* can't shoot through her!''

Rita Sarsa settled the sights of her battery as Ree's order to change course passed through the ship. She could see what the old boy was trying to do. She cleared with fire control and watched her battery send a narrow thread of blinding violet light into *Brotherhood's* shields.

Even from where she watched the monitors, she could see *Victory* appear for a quick shot before Ree jockeyed back out of sight. With a crackling bang, the deck shuddered and everything went dead. Sparks shot through the darkness like fireworks, the eerie light glowing in the smoke.

"What is this, Rita?'' Philip cried suddenly. "This is not right!''

"We've been hit, love!'' Rita announced, sending a few curses toward the unseen foe. Rita felt g fluctuating as the grav plates attempted to equalize.

"Quiet the troops, Philip.'' Rita waved toward a

cowering group of Romanans. She ran from comm unit to comm unit until she found one working.

"Colonel Ree!" she ordered. When his face appeared, she coughed some of the smoke from her lungs. "We've been hit pretty hard on port side, sir. All the batteries are out."

"Pressure?" he asked, face wooden.

She checked one of the monitors. "Dropping, sir. They must have breeched us through the main power leads. The only light in here is from the fires."

"Save as many as you can, Lieutenant." Ree's effort to hide his despair wasn't convincing.

Rita saluted and turned back to the hell her gun deck had become. "You men!" she shouted to a couple of marine privates who were wrestling with a fried generator. "Get those men past the hatches. Move them anywhere you can keep pressure!" She repeated the order in Romanan and with Philip's help got the men moving.

Another blast knocked them off their feet. The concussions continued, slapping the deck up and down, batting the remaining men into the air and scattering them like kernels on a piston. Rita threw herself vigorously at Philip and caught his foot.

A searing bright streak of light cut through the darkness. Blinking at the afterimages, Rita thumbed her visor and pulled Philip closer. She could feel him trembling.

"What is it?" he cried.

"I think we're about to die," she said soberly. "Put your helmet on! Hear that screeching sound. That's metal being blown out. We're about to decompress!"

"I don't have a helmet!" Another series of fireworks erupted as an electrical piece malfunctioned. She could see the wry humor in his eyes.

"Damn you!" she howled. "Where's your helmet? We've got to find it. Not much time left!"

"Gave it to a Santos. He didn't have one." Philip was laughing, half-hysterical.

Rita felt the change, her ears felt full as she automatically fought to pull Philip back. Perhaps she could get him into one of the pressure chambers before. . . . A popping noise was her only warning. A screech. A

354

whoosh, and ears screaming, lungs expanding, she activated her helmet and clamped a belt hook to a segment of conduit.

It took all of her strength to keep Philip. She heard herself scream with fear. White light lanced the blackness. The sun was shining through the rip. She could see the bodies, equipment, powdery ice crystals and debris, expanding outward from the breech.

She was whimpering as she looked into the bugged eyes that had been Philip's. He'd held his breath at the last minute. The blood was crystallizing as it leaked from his nose and mouth. She refused to believe the agonized shriek was really coming from her lungs.

Colonel Damen Ree's face went stony gray after Sarsa's report. Leeta guessed a major blow had been struck. She saw his eyes flicker to the screens where *Victory* was pulling out from behind *Brotherhood*. As *Bullet* rolled to bring her firing batteries to bear, Ree whispered an order and the ship nosed forward, heading for the two Patrol ships.

"What are you doing, Damen?" Leeta cried, seeing new determination on Ree's face.

"Destroying the enemy, Doctor." His lips were oddly twisted. "Buying time, I suppose."

"How?" Leeta asked, blood turning to ice in her veins. Was the damn fool going to ram?

"We will shoot our way between them before they have a chance to separate. When we are within two hundred kilometers, we will detonate the antimatter. We'll take them with us."

"Damen! *That's mad!*" she screamed. "What about the planet? Who protects it without us?"

His eyes narrowed craftily. "All this is being transmitted. We buy them time, Doctor. Someone in the Directorate will ask the inevitable question. Why did we sacrifice everything for one little group of men? It will take a long time, several months, for Skor Robinson to pull another battlewagon from someplace else to come and destroy this world. In that time, public opinion may well demand a fuller investigation. If we don't take those ships—we have lost everything."

Leeta shook her head. Her mouth dry, she said, "Damen, you know, you're a Romanan at heart.

355

You've got real style. I'm going back to see to my people. They need all the help they can get.

Ree shot a questioning glance to where Iron Eyes talked to his people.

"I'll be back before the end." She shrugged, feeling oddly composed now that death was so near.

He nodded soberly as Leeta left. "I just wish they could see our eyes. They would see that they killed us, but—by Spider—*they* never *defeated us!*" Ree mumbled a prayer to the soul of a dead Spider warrior and watched the thrust build as *Bullet* shot for her two tormentors.

Leeta hurried, she wouldn't be long. Ten minutes maybe? She could be back by then. She would have to tell her team. She had to do it in person. It was only fair.

So this was where it was all to end? She chuckled to herself. A child of peace and education, blown into dust by a hidden order from the Director. So what was her legacy? A planet? A people? An ideal?

The ship jolted beneath her. All her life she'd desired a different freedom. That desire had led her to books telling of long-gone men. Then to destiny—and now to a premature death. And when she reached whatever lay over that threshold? She could at least say she had learned what life was and who these humans really were in a way no books could ever teach!

As she had that day at Gessali Camp, Leeta Dobra felt truly, vividly alive! Every nerve tingled, her muscles were taut, her step proud, her heart full of love.

Smoke filled the companionway as she ducked around piled debris. She'd really made a difference. How many of the bloody fools could say that? She sniffed slightly as she thought of Jeffray . . . and Veld. She'd actually managed—

She barely had time to feel the heat.

A power lead severed somewhere, the shield buckled and plasma shot through the companionway. Metal became energy and explosion. As suddenly, a circuit kicked in and the shield reestablished. Just as rapidly, the atoms rushed into the black void of space, leaving an emptiness where deck and air had been. Only the shattered scorched body of Leeta Dobra remained, hanging in crackling cables.

Unaware, Damen Ree opened a channel to the other commanders. "Ree! What in *hell* are you doing?" Sheila demanded.

"We are all going to die. Unless, of course, you yield." Colonel Damen Ree was enjoying this moment. He had found destiny, glory—the path of a soldier.

"You would destroy your ship to kill us?" Maya ben Ahmad was shaking her head.

It will save the planet for a while. Perhaps saner men will have time to change the Director's order." He raised a cup of coffee to his lips. "But you see, I will keep you from destroying the Romanans. I will win this battle and all your lives will be for naught!" His hearty laugh was that of a victor and he could see the two women glancing at each other in disbelief. "You can't get away before I set off the reaction. You're too close together." He took a deep breath.

"Oh, God, no!" Sheila lost control, screaming insults and epithets at him. Comm didn't hide the two marines who suddenly appeared to drag Colonel Sheila Rostostiev from the bridge.

"I'll be damned," Maya ben Ahmad whispered. "The old gal broke."

"Five minutes, Colonel," Ree said, looking serenely at Maya. "Anything you want to add to our transduction message to the Directorate? We're sending on a channel open to all. We're being received all across human space—possibly even beyond."

"You old buzzard!" Maya was shaking her head. "We could have used more like you, Damen."

"Won't surrender? It's a chance, Maya." He cocked his head.

She bit her lip and shook her head. "Can't, Damen. On the odd chance that you're bluffing, I'd feel like a fool. Just as you've chosen what you think is right, I have to follow my orders. Just my quirk, you understand." She smiled in resignation.

"We're too glorious for that damn Robinson, you know that?" Ree saluted her, flipping the dead-man's box open, fingers finding the toggle that would drop the stasis separating matter from antimatter. Maya's eyes hardened, her color draining.

And then comm interrupted.

Obviously Maya was receiving the same thing. She looked up, eyes twinkling, and keyed an order through her ship. "Looks like the war's over, Damen. I guess you won. I have orders to break off and assist you in any way. Your broadcasts must have hit a nerve.

"Seems that Sirius is up in revolt. I suppose that Skor Robinson wouldn't take kindly to having the fleet cut short." She ended with a cynical laugh.

"Cease fire!" Ree ordered. "All batteries cease fire immediately. War's over, we've won for now!" He could hear cries throughout the ship.

"Colonel!" An officer called. *"Victory* and *Brotherhood* have ceased fire. They're dropping their shields."

"Tell me," Maya asked, eyes like flint. "I really want to know, Damen. Would you really have blown up *Bullet?"*

The little lines around Ree's mouth tightened. "Yes, Maya. I would have taken you—and the whole Directorate—with me if I could. *Bullet* has been my life. So, you tell me? What good is a life without a purpose? It would have been a glorious victory!"

Iron Eyes looked up at the commotion, stretching, pulling himself to his feet, piecing it all together. His beaming smile was one of triumph, gratification, and fulfillment. His eyes darted about the bridge, looking for the woman he loved.

Damen Ree grinned happily, looking at the effigy drawn on the paneling over his head. Yes sir, it was a damn fine life to live! Praise be to Spider!

CHAPTER XXIII

"And now, what have I wrought, Prophet?" Skor Robinson turned slightly in the haze of his control room.

Chester sat in a grav chair, expression bland. "I watch the future unfold, Director. A dam has broken, the future is rushing forward. So much—"

"And your barbarians are sacking stations and planets even as we speak?" The toneless voice had learned bitterness.

"No, Director, not in the way you would think."

Silence.

"And my concern, Prophet? You—who say you see the future—tell me my worst fears."

Chester lifted a shoulder. "It is not to be. Romanans are not loose, raiding and killing—stealing women, blasting a path of blood through the Directorate." Chester smiled and took a deep breath. "You see, Skor. We do not burst forth unaffected or unchanged. In saving ourselves, we are condemned."

Chester waited until Robinson's slight frown smoothed. "Condemned? By what, barbarian?"

"I offer you another lesson, Director. You—"

"I am tired of lessons! Tell me no more of—"

"A Prophet is a teacher," Chester reminded. "It is the calling of Spider. To learn is the purpose of the soul. We are driven—"

"I could order you removed from—"

"You will not."

"Why?"

"Because you have discovered curiosity. Your life has a new dimension. You have been exposed to risk—slight risk, true—but risk nonetheless. With risk comes fear—and you would know more of that emotion."

"Then . . . what would you teach me, Prophet?" Skor—in his most dramatic facial expression—blinked.

"That freedom is the ultimate condemnation, for we are free to learn from the universe. That is the price we pay—though none but the Prophets know it. Had you destroyed World, we would have died. But we are free to live—to learn and spread through the stars. For that freedom, my people will sacrifice everything they now value. You need us for our strength—but by using it, we will slowly but surely dilute that uniqueness which gives us power. New ways will come to World. New peoples will mingle their blood and ideals with ours. We are condemned to learn new ways, and many will be adopted. Already a young Romanan woman yearns for a warrior's—"

"What of the cusps?" Skor wondered. "There must be different fates for your people?"

"You know a Prophet sees myriad futures. In one, Spider will sweep the heavens, and Romanans will be disseminated, engulfed, adding their courage and philosophy to that which is human. In another, World lies blasted and sterile, its surface molten and cracked. Neither I nor Spider know which will come to pass."

"And that does not frighten you?" Skor demanded, uneasy.

Chester smiled and spread his hands. "No, Director. Spider's universe is an unsafe place. Only Romanan valor, the dedication of the Patrol, and a particular concept of God stand between humanity and total enslavement. A horrid prospect from your perspective, perhaps. From God's, a mere inconvenience—an experiment gone wrong."

"Why do I listen to you?" Skor turned back to the console, trailing his catheter tubes.

"Because you cannot help yourself. I have answered your questions. I have provided you something to consider. Sirius needs your immediate attention. Their threat dwarfs any potential my People might have to harm you. Ngen Van Chow solidifies his position. Daily, his power grows and consolidates."

"And what do you see of Ngen Van Chow, Prophet?"

Chester's face lined. "I see misery and death, Director. Along any of the futures, no matter who has yet to make their cusp, blood and pain and tragedy are his legacy.''

"What do I choose, Prophet?'' Skor asked, his warbly voice softening.

"That is up to you, Director. Your cusp. I will leave now.''

"Wait! Tell me about—''

"I am leaving.'' Chester turned his chair.

Robinson turned his head, changing his attitude in the room. "But I. . . . And what are you off to do?''

Unconcerned, Chester directed the grav chair toward the hatch. "I have learned to read. I found the most wonderful thing. It is called a book. Imagine, a story that lasts forever! Words . . . just as men wrote them four thousand years ago! I can share thoughts with Plato and Meister Eckhart and Nagarjuna and Sartre! I *knew* Spider sent me here for some reason!''

John Smith Iron Eyes let the black mare stretch her legs as she ran into the wind. The time had come when the spring sun began to bring new growth from the rain-soaked ground. The mare demonstrated her spirit and ran with all her heart, trying to beat the gray cloud that meant a spring shower as it raced in from the ocean.

Navel Shelter lay ahead. The mare would make it in plenty of time so Iron Eyes walked her down, feeling the unaccustomed weight of the blaster on his hip as he swung with the horse's stride.

He had talked to Chester the night before. The Prophet looked somehow serene, a condition his moody cousin had never exhibited. Chester seemed content but only smiled at the prospects on Sirius, his eyes sad and knowing.

The Sirians had taken complete control of their planet and were shouting defiance at the Directorate. Spies reported that the frantic refitting of merchant ships, for war was a twenty-four hour a day occupation. Citizen troops were drilling in the streets and the not inconsequential manufacturing capabilities of the planet were producing blasters and battle armor. Directorate estimates maintained Sirius would not be a viable threat for another six months.

In the meantime, a social softening propaganda was raining on Sirius. Maintaining a wartime economy took a lot of sacrifice—especially when no enemy showed in the sky, despite the reports by Ngen Van Chow's revolutionary government. There would be time to train before John Smith led his Romanans against the Sirians.

Romanan warriors had begun training with Patrol veterans. The transition was being made smoothly and the mostly unblooded Patrol marines were envious of the coups glistening on warrior belts. The newly arrived commanders derided the custom as barbaric—but Ree didn't do a thing about it, it gave his new crew better morale.

The men from *Bullet* all had combinations of Spider and Santos motifs on their combat armor. That would change in the other ships, too. Could less be expected when men and women who prided themselves on being warriors met other men who had spent their lives raiding?

In spite of the successes, the transition was marred by jealousies. Patrolmen had been awed by Ree's desperate ploy. They still shook their heads at the audacity that would have snatched victory through defeat. As a result, the men from *Bullet* swaggered and there were numerous fights. Two privates from *Bullet* had beaten up three men from *Brotherhood*—and taken coup. The *Bullet* men were in the brig while the *Brotherhood* bunch were in the med unit growing new scalps. There would be other growing pains.

Leeta had foreseen this. The thought turned his mind numb. Until the day he died he would see her burned features. The yellow hair had melted into a stinking, glassy dome that covered her skull. Her skin had charred black, cracked, and leaked the fluids of life. Explosive decompression had twisted her almost beyond recognition. The eyes which had once gazed softly blue at him had burst, seared. The last sight of Leeta Dobra's corpse left his soul tormented.

Purpose had fled the universe. What reason was there for him to continue? Life was pain. First Jenny had been torn from his future. Leeta had filled her place and outgrown the ghost which had let him free in his vision. Leeta had become the binding drive behind his goals.

She had loved him. The image of her standing against the firelight of Gessali Camp returned. He saw her lithe, tempting body in the flickering yellow light. He remembered the feel of her skin as he caressed her before the battle. She had hugged him close, passionate in an expression of love and life. Could she, too, be forever gone?

He turned pain-glazed eyes up and squinted into the gray sky. *Why do you mock me, Spider? Does my happiness mean so much to you? What is your purpose in my pain?* Anguished, he bit off a harsh cry and pulled up the mare. Easily he stepped down, gutted, without purpose.

Walking into the shadow of the rocks, he saw the men standing there. Good, things were as they should be. Everything so formal. The clans were united, the People strong. Law was to be maintained. This was knife feud. Through pain, vengeance would be his. Perhaps Spider would not take that from him.

Someone cut the bonds from Big Man's wrists and Iron Eyes handed his blaster to Rita Sarsa. She wore the star folk's black color for Philip. She met his eyes, sharing grief on a level only they could understand.

"You betrayed your People," Iron Eyes spoke formally as he faced the sneering Big Man. "You violated the war code, making your Santos—"

"They have become as water, Spider warrior. When I have killed you, I shall take this star woman as mine. Your coup shall ride my belt!" He laughed. "I shall urinate on your dead body."

Rita shook her head slightly, eyes narrowing on Big Man as she fingered the knife at her waist.

"You are a man without honor, Big Man. You disgust Haysoos." John Smith Iron Eyes settled himself on his toes, weight on the balls of his feet. The long fighting knife fit his grip like an old friend. Thirty centimeters long, the edge was sharpened like a razor. The false edge glistened in the subdued light, brass quillions polished to a sheen. The thick leather handle filled his hand.

Big Man rushed suddenly, his knife stabbing viciously. Iron Eyes backpedaled and threw himself to the side. The big Santos spun and thrust, the blade stinging Iron Eyes' shoulder. He ducked into a ball and rolled, coming out just in time to throw himself away from Big Man's swinging cut.

Once more the huge warrior growled his fury and threw himself at Iron Eyes. John ducked time and again. His war song rose to his lips as he sought that inner strength that had carried him in the past.

He saw Jenny's face and Leeta's. An empty hole in his soul cried out in fear and loneliness. He ducked another swing of the knife and went in low, thrusting as Big Man fought for balance. The blade bit a thigh muscle and was torn from his fingers as the Santos howled and kicked away.

Iron Eyes jumped, seeking to swing the knife up by its wrist thong. He didn't have time; twisting from the big man's dive, he felt the thong snap and the blade was gone.

Big Man was laughing now. Would death be so bad, he wondered? What was left to live for? Beyond the shelter, a drop of rain spattered into the damp soil. Iron Eyes avoided another rush.

In the distance, an AT whistled as it lifted for one of the Patrol ships. Iron Eyes began panting as he circled warily. Big Man crouched low, readying for another rush. Iron Eyes tried to duck to the side. His foot rolled on a pole tree log and he stumbled. He could hear cries from the crowd. Frantically, he grabbed a thick wrist and twisted, still falling.

The long knife thunked into the log beside his ear, driven by the huge bulk of the Santos. "For Jenny!" Iron Eyes screamed as he brought a knee up into the man's side. There was a slight gasp of breath as his other hand found the Santos' eyes and he jabbed, feeling soft flesh give under his fingers.

Howling, the warrior rolled off him, leaving the knife in the wood. Iron Eyes drove a kick at the side of his head and was satisfied at the woofing noise Big

Man made. Blinded and hurt, the huge warrior rolled into John's next kick and tripped him.

Iron Eyes felt those thick arms circling his body and the Santos began to squeeze. The very air in his lungs was being forced out past his lips, making gurgling, wheezing noises.

Desperate, Iron Eyes fought another finger into the man's eye and gouged. The crushing arms were gone and Iron Eyes scrambled across the dirt, gasping for breath. He blinked back the grayness, saw the knife, and dove for it as a heavy hand trapped his ankle and dragged him back into those monstrous arms.

Out there were the stars. Leeta had given so much for those stars. The Patrol wanted the People now, all of them, for warrior honors on Sirius. So many dead. Leeta's ghost beckoned.

Out in the grasslands, he could see a bear. Did it wait for him as in the vision? He had to see the stars. It would only be right. Leeta demanded that of him.

He spun, fighting to keep his wits as Big Man—still blinded—dove on the knife point John thrust up in a clenched fist. Blood gushed hot on his wrist and forearm as he twisted the blade and fought it through the intestines, the liver, the diaphragm, and into the lungs and heart. The huge man gasped, showering John Smith's face with blood-frothy breath. The Santos jerked spasmodically as Iron Eyes kicked free of the bulk.

He gasped as Rita Sarsa placed a water jug to his lips. "Quite a fight, Iron Eyes. I thought he had you a couple of times."

Iron Eyes fought air into his lungs. "It just took a while to learn to live again. Jenny's ghost had to be let free. I couldn't let Leeta down. The bear had to see I was worthy." He chuckled, looking over his shoulder. The animal was gone, vanished, as if it had never been.

The men from the various clans came to shake his hand and pat his back as Iron Eyes took his coup. He straightened, every muscle aching. Some of the warriors had mounted their horses, riding back toward their camps in the rain. Others had piled on aircars and pulled up the domes, scooting across the grass toward the villages. He saw several marines with spiders or crosses stenciled on their uniforms talking animatedly about the fight with men who must have come from the other ships.

Rita cocked her head, seated on a large boulder fallen from the roof eons ago. Her arms were crossed and the breeze was blowing strands of red hair across her shoulders and onto her breasts.

"We left so much here, Iron Eyes." She looked into the darkness. "It was a time of hope—a time of challenge. What fools we were to think we could pull it all off."

"Life is made for fools," he said, leaning on the rock next to her. With numb fingers he threaded the bloody coup through his belt, eyes blankly on the corpse. Big Man's relatives hadn't come for the body— a symbol of their shame at his betrayal. The man's blood was drying on his face like a tight mask.

"Damn, Doc!" she cried suddenly. *"Why her?* That was the last shot they fired! God, first Philip . . . then her." She shook her head, tears on her cheeks. "Why didn't he take time to see his future for once?"

"He'd seen one death," Iron Eyes replied, putting an arm around her shoulder. "Would you want to know the moment of your death?"

"No. I guess not." She shook her head. After several minutes, she looked up and rubbed away the tears. "I'm just tired of losing people I've come to love. Is it some divine justice? Is there some sin committed by loving someone?" She closed her eyes and took a deep breath.

His laugh was hot and vindictive. "I suppose so. Spider took Jenny from me. He took her before she was killed by that bastard." He kicked the Santos with a toe. "He took Leeta from me after I had again found love and life and meaning." His voice was soft. "What was I supposed to learn?"

"Maybe that the stars don't come cheap?" She looked at him, her eyes appraising. "Now what, John Smith Iron Eyes? You going out there with us? Should be hot fighting with the Sirians."

"I would see the stars." He nodded. "I have a couple of promises to keep. I will learn to read. I need to see the way I have helped build for my People. Philip would want that—as Leeta did." He felt the hurt building under his heart—black, empty and endless.

"I've never been too good at teaching," she said softly.

"I've never been a student." He shrugged.

Rita fingered her coups. "It won't be the same without Philip. I never knew a man like him."

"I've always been lonely. There has always been pain." His voice drifted off in his memories. "You seem tough, Red Many Coups. I don't see why you can't learn to live with it."

"But why?" she asked, cool green eyes on his.

"Spider's way." He shrugged. "Do you claim to know the workings of God?"

"No, but if I ever meet the bastard I want to kick his ass!" she growled. "Think sacrilege bothers Spider?"

Iron Eyes laughed. "Who knows? I always wondered about the Santos who grovel in the dirt before Haysoos. Why would God want me to walk before him like a subservient slave? I would have him see me full of pride and spirit. I would have him see me as a man. If you would truly challenge God—angry over what you believe to be injustice—with fire in your eye and demand an explanation, it would not be sacrilege. Being God—you would do Him honor!"

Out on the plain another of the ATs left a streak of light as it shot heavenward.

Rita's eyes followed it up. "I've never seen Sirius."

"Me either," he said, watching her wry smile grow. He walked over to the black mare then caught up the reins of Philip's gelding. He lifted her into the saddle and vaulted onto the back of the black. It was a long ride back to the new Romanan spaceport—and a longer one to Sirius.

Exciting Visions of the Future!

W. Michael Gear

☐ **THE ARTIFACT** UE2406—$5.99
In a galaxy on the brink of civil war, where the Brotherhood seeks to keep the peace, news comes of the discovery of a piece of alien tech]nology—the Artifact. It could be the greatest boon to science, or the instrument that would destroy the entire human race.

☐ **STARSTRIKE** UE2427—$5.99
They were Earth's finest soldiers, commandeered to fight together for an alien master in a war among distant stars. . . .

FORBIDDEN BORDERS
He was the most hated and feared power in human-controlled space— and only he could become the means of his own destruction. . . .

☐ **REQUIEM FOR THE CONQUEROR (#1)** UE2477—$6.99
☐ **RELIC OF EMPIRE (#2)** UE2492—$5.99
☐ **COUNTERMEASURES (#3)** UE2564—$5.99

THE SPIDER TRILOGY
For centuries, the Directorate had ruled over countless star systems— but now, as rebellion fueled by advanced technology and a madman's dream spread across the galaxy, the warriors of Spider, descendants of humans stranded centuries ago on an untamed world, could prove the vital key to the survival of human civilization. . . .

☐ **THE WARRIORS OF SPIDER (#1)** UE2287—$5.50
☐ **THE WAY OF SPIDER (#2) 01** UE2438—$5.50
☐ **THE WEB OF SPIDER (#3) 01** UE2356—$4.95
